ONE
MUST
WAIT

PENNY
MICKELBURY

St. Martin's Paperbacks

This book is a work of fiction. Names, characters, places, and incidents either are products of the author's imagination or are used fictitiously. Any resemblance to actual events or locales or persons, living or dead, is entirely coincidental.

Published by arrangement with Simon & Schuster

ONE MUST WAIT

Library of Congress Catalog Card Number: 97-29871

ISBN: 0-312-97186-9

Printed in the United States of America

Simon & Schuster hardcover edition published 1998
St. Martin's Paperbacks edition / November 1999

St. Martin's Paperbacks are published by St. Martin's Press, 175 Fifth Avenue, New York, N.Y. 10010.

10 9 8 7 6 5 4 3 2 1

FOR ARMENTHA JEAN

ACKNOWLEDGMENTS

I am grateful to Charlotte Sheedy, my agent, for making me proud to say those two words without flinching. You are, quite simply, the best.

I am grateful to Bob Mecoy, my editor, for being so good at his job that I don't have any editor horror stories to share with my friends.

I am grateful to Katherine Forrest, my friend, for being living, breathing, walking proof of the goodness of the human spirit.

I am grateful to the two people who inspired this story. You know who you are. I wish I could tell the world.

I am grateful to Archie Givens, Jr., and the Givens Foundation for African American Literature at the University of Minnesota for sponsoring the first Black Mystery Writers Symposium and, by doing so, honoring the work of the mystery writer as literature. Your generosity is forever remembered and appreciated.

And I thank my family—A.J., Cynthia, and Louise—for believing in me, and for reading whatever I write and liking it!

1

JUROR NUMBER SEVEN WASN'T BUYING IT. THE SET OF her head and shoulders and lips proclaimed loudly and clearly that Juror Number Seven flat out didn't want to hear that Tommy Griffin wasn't really a dirty cop. She didn't care that he was, instead, a self-effacing young man of twenty-five who always followed orders, even if those orders were stupid and illegal, not to mention a flagrant violation of the public trust. Juror Number Seven looked at Tommy Griffin and her flashing black eyes saw her hard-earned tax dollars follow her faith in government down the toilet and out into the Potomac to swim with the rest of the pollution.

Carole Ann Gibson looked at Juror Number Seven, aka Hazel Copeland, and knew instinctively, without doubt or question, that she and her ego had made an enormous, inexcusable, and unforgivable error. Hazel Copeland should never have been seated on this jury. Carole Ann knew this now, but now—with only closing arguments left—this was her jury for better or worse.

At the time of jury selection, little more than a month ago, Carole Ann had believed with unwavering certainty she could persuade this woman—could persuade all eight

women and four men—to see Tommy Griffin as she saw
him: a shy, vulnerable, determined—and misplaced—
product of the hard-luck streets and alleys of southeast
D.C. who had become a cop to escape certain destiny
rather than fulfill it. Not only grateful to be a cop, but
heartily committed to the belief that he could help tame
the forces of evil that ravaged his old neighborhood,
Tommy easily became the dupe for his drug-dealing sergeant, became the bagman left holding the bag.

Tommy Griffin had steadfastly and self-righteously
refused to accept anyone could believe him guilty of
such a heinous crime until he saw the videotape of him
following his sergeant's orders, dressed in the baggy,
butt-hugging britches and hooded sweatshirt of the contemporary gangster, climbing over a backyard fence,
exchanging drugs for money; until he saw his sergeant's
videotaped confession implicating him, Tommy, as an
eager and willing participant whose intimate knowledge
of the drug-infested community across the Anacostia
River from Washington's power center was crucial to the
illegal operation.

Tommy Griffin was green. A rookie. Fish, they called
him, then and now, in his old neighborhood—a guppy
who'd swallow anything that swam his way. Gullible,
perhaps, but Tommy was not stupid. His eyes and ears
absorbed every detail of every word and action around
him . . . every nuance of every word and action around
him. And when he'd dried his eyes and bandaged his
wounded pride, he ratted his sergeant out to a degree that
would have brought a smile to the tight lips of Eddie G.

Tommy had been a D.C. cop exactly eighteen months
when he was busted in the FBI-sponsored sting, not
nearly enough time to be any more than the peg he actually was in the well-run and well-established drug-
dealing business being operated by a coterie of vice cops

gone bad. Carole Ann had proved that. It had taken the better part of two weeks and had forced testimony so grueling that she herself was weary when it was over. But when it was over, she'd broken the three cops—two sergeants and a detective—who were the masterminds of the scheme, demonstrating along the way that Tommy's sergeant had been dirty since his Army days twenty years earlier, when as a supply clerk he'd stolen everything from eggs to nails for sale on the outside. But the dirty vice cops weren't on trial, Tommy Griffin was on trial, and making them look bad did not necessarily make Tommy look good. So, against all advice, solicited and otherwise, Carole Ann had put Tommy on the stand. And he'd been magnificent: humble and direct and open and polite and mightily embarrassed he'd been duped, and heartily sorry for it, even though it wasn't his fault. And that's when she'd won her jury. All except Juror Number Seven.

So dazzled was she by the brilliance of her own performance that she almost missed Juror Number Seven's message. She'd been watching the lead prosecution attorney struggle with and then abandon his fruitless cross-examination of Tommy, who had become so poised and confident she'd needed to remind him to be the inept innocent she'd said he was. Tommy was holding his own against the prosecutor, so Carole Ann was watching the jury. One by one she studied them: their posture, their degree of alertness, their level of concentration. One by one until she reached Juror Number Seven, and Carole Ann was snatched to attention by the unfamiliar. She'd seen jurors cross-eyed with boredom, had seen jurors yawn and fall asleep and snore. Had seen anger and antipathy, disgust, dismay, and disbelief. But this was the first time she recalled seeing outright, undisguised hatred emanating from a juror and it alarmed her. Carole Ann closed her eyes and conjured up the profile of Juror Number Seven.

Hazel Copeland was a forty-two-year-old Black woman born and bred in the public housing projects of Baltimore, the single mother of four children, whose entire working life had been spent cleaning up after other people. In defiance of every law of gravity, Hazel Copeland had worked her way up from maid to head of the housekeeping department of the swankiest hotel in Washington, D.C., and had never, as far as Carole Ann had been able to determine, pilfered so much as a pillowcase or a washcloth, a bottle of shampoo or a bar of soap; had never missed a day of work; had never been the subject of anything but the highest praise from her employer. Two of Hazel's four children were in college and the other two, both high school honor students, were on their way. And that's why Hazel Copeland, aka Juror Number Seven, didn't want to hear how the pitiful circumstances of Tommy Griffin's life had led him to betray his oath to serve and protect, no matter how unwittingly.

But that wasn't all of it. Carole Ann scrutinized the handsome woman—tall, erect, dark chocolate brown, with a full head of jet black hair just beginning to exhibit traces of silver at the temples—and Carole Ann knew Hazel Copeland was not the kind of woman to seek refuge from maturity in a bottle of hair dye. She sat ramrod straight in her chair and had not, in four and a half weeks, displayed a hint of fatigue or boredom. Hazel Copeland was the perfect juror. Except that she hated Carole Ann's client—the first innocent client she'd had in at least two years, and probably closer to three.

Carole Ann felt that realization shock her almost as much as the fact of Hazel Copeland's cold hatred of young Tommy Griffin, and then it frightened her. Frightened her to realize that for the first time in recent memory she held the fate of an innocent person within the limitations of her skill and ability; frightened her to realize that perhaps instead of hating him, Hazel Copeland merely believed him guilty as charged and, as a result, hated what he was accused of doing.

We're fucked, Carole Ann wrote on the yellow legal pad on the table before her, the emerald ink she used contrasting boldly with the fine, pale green lines in the paper. The attorney seated next to her, her second-in-command, frowned at the pad, looked over at her with a quizzical expression, and stared again at the bold green markings on the yellow pad.

Look at #7, Carole Ann wrote, and watched him as he did. The crease in his brow deepened as he studied Juror Number Seven's determined impassivity, searching for but not finding whatever Carole Ann had seen. Then, in that moment, Juror Number Seven turned her gaze toward the defense table and Carole Ann physically flinched. It was not Tommy Griffin Hazel Copeland hated, but Carole Ann herself, and Carole Ann knew why. She looked into the woman's eyes and saw into her soul: *Traitor,* Carole Ann saw Hazel's eyes say, *how dare you look like, be like me, present this boy who could be my son—our son—as criminal, and ask me to trust you and forgive him?*

Carole Ann broke eye contact first. The few seconds had been excruciating. Besides, communication with a juror was an ethical and legal violation, and they definitely had communicated, the lead defense attorney and Juror Number Seven. And they had understood each other perfectly. Carole Ann was, in truth, a traitor, though she hadn't known it until Hazel told her. True, she was a traitor only in the place where all the Hazels of America lived, but that was a very large and well-populated place, and therefore a very important place, and Carole Ann experienced a moment of debilitating guilt until she understood that Hazel was correct in her assessment only if Tommy Griffin were guilty and she, Carole Ann, wanted to help him get away with it. But Tommy Griffin was innocent, and therefore she wasn't a traitor . . .

These feelings and fears, revelations and recriminations Carole Ann had carried with her, within herself, for the last day and a half, becoming increasingly familiar with and even accepting of them, if no clearer about how to resolve them than she had been at the moment they first appeared. Now it was hang-tough time; do-or-die time; put-up-or-shut-up time; rock-and-roll time; shit-or-get-off-the-pot time; showtime-at-the-Apollo time. Whatever terminology a trial lawyer used to define or declare the moment when it was time to stand and face the jury on behalf of the client, it now was that time for Carole Ann.

"Miss Gibson, we're ready when you are," the judge intoned dryly, and Carole Ann realized she'd lost contact with reality for a moment, realized they were all waiting for her, that they had been waiting for . . . she didn't know how long. To the packed and expectant courtroom, the several moments of her mental lapse translated as a well-placed dramatic pause. She stood quickly, emptying her mind of her well-crafted and now totally useless closing argument, and crossed briskly to the jury box, where she immediately began her trademark pacing, effective and, she knew, impressive, because of her height—three inches shy of six feet—and her lean, sinewy elegance, clad today in verdant brushed silk with an almost daring neckline.

"Tommy Griffin is not guilty. He is not a drug dealer. He is not a dirty cop. But don't take my word for it. I know some of you don't think much of some of us lawyers . . . that you see us as the enemy. After all, we're the ones who, if we do our jobs properly, return the drug dealers and thieves and murderers and worse to your neighborhoods." She ceased pacing and stood directly before Juror Number Seven and looked into her eyes. "So, while we may deserve your lack of respect and confidence, Tommy Griffin does not. Do not make him pay for our errors."

She felt the stir in the courtroom, as if the hermetically sealed windows suddenly, miraculously, had opened, admitting the moist, warm late spring air to rush in and swirl about. The judge stirred. The reporters in the press section stirred. The two groups of lawyers before the rail stirred, as did those behind it. The spectators stirred. Only the court reporter remained motionless, his hands poised above the scrunched-up keyboard waiting for words—her words.

"So," she said, cruising down to the end of the jury box nearest the judge and leaning on the banister, leaning in toward the three jurors whom she knew for certain to be in her corner, "ignore me and everything I've said these past five weeks. I mean that. Pay me no mind. Just remember what everyone else has said during this trial and decide for yourselves who's telling the truth and who's lying. You heard from the three former vice squad officers who testified that Tommy Griffin was a willing participant in their drug-dealing scam, and you heard from the two assistant chiefs of police who said those vice cops were three of the biggest liars this side of the Chesapeake Bay. Who's telling the truth: the three fired cops or the two assistant chiefs?"

Carole Ann got the solicited reaction from the three jurors nearest her—two snorts and a chuckle—so she shifted position, sneaking a glance at the courtroom as she straightened. Every eye was on her and she liked it that way. She was in control of the courtroom, if not of her own thoughts and emotions. She strolled to the other end of the jury box and struck a similar pose, leaning on the banister and getting as close as allowed to the jury: some judges denied any proximity, while others permitted a nonthreatening, no-contact nearness.

"Who else did you hear from? Remember Mr. Lightfoot, the elementary school principal, and Mrs. Carpenter, the high school principal, and Reverend Ottwell and Captain Quarles and, of course, Rags, Moonshine, Heavy T, and Doctor Death, the dudes from the 'hood. All of them people who have known Tommy Griffin all of his life. People who said Tommy Griffin not only didn't, but couldn't do a wrong thing. Now I know that under different circumstances you might not trust the veracity of Rags and Moonshine and Heavy T and the Doctor; after all, they admitted to a certain . . . ah . . . familiarity, shall we say, with the illegal drug-dealing activities in certain sections of the southeast part of town . . ."

She paused to allow the humor to dissipate the built-up tension. There was a rustling of papers and a shifting of bodies and a clearing of throats that rode the wave of gentle laughter until it beached itself. Carole Ann used the moment to see where she was going with this instantly devised summation, and to resolve to get there soon, before exhausting its limited effectiveness.

"Just remember that it was Doctor Death who claimed the distinction of, and I quote, 'whipping Tommy's skinny ass every day,' because he wouldn't play hooky with the other boys." She held up the transcript from which she quoted. "'And why,' I asked Doctor Death, 'did you want Tommy to cut school and hang out with you?' And do you remember what he said?" She made a production of turning the transcript pages, of putting on her reading glasses, of positioning them on her nose so she could peer at the jury over the rims while still being able to read. " 'Because we liked him,' said Doctor Death. 'Tommy's a righteous dude. Always was. Still is.' 'What does that mean, "righteous dude," ' I asked. 'It means he's good. It means he wouldn't let something like a ass-kicking get in the way of friendship.' "

Carole Ann allowed herself to share the jury's amusement, to share its amazement, at the code of the street; to share its relief at having a different code. She stepped away from the jury box and returned the transcript to one of her assistant attorneys at the defense table without meeting the eyes she knew were filled with doubt or panic or questions or some other thing she didn't want to see or think about or deal with. They didn't matter anyway, not at this juncture. Only the jury mattered. Only Juror Number Seven.

"I ask you to remember Heavy T told you that not only did Tommy Griffin never skip school, but he refused to steal candy from the corner store; he positively would not drink a beer or smoke a cigarette, to say nothing of a joint; he refused to use neighborhood girls for easy sex. 'He was just one of those good kids. You know the kind I'm talking about.' That's what Heavy T said about Tommy Griffin, whom he's known since the two of them were three years old."

Carole Ann stopped her pacing before the middle of the jury box and locked eyes with Hazel. "There's always one good kid in the neighborhood. In some neighborhoods, there will be more than one; there will be an entire family of them: kids who would never do wrong, and everybody for blocks around knows it." Hazel blinked and Carole Ann, like a hawk with babies to feed, swooped in for the kill. "Tommy Griffin is that kind of kid. Everybody in the neighborhood said so. Tommy Griffin is a good boy. Tommy Griffin always has been a good boy. Never, from first grade through senior high school, missed a day of school or a Sunday at church. Never. Not once. Did four years in the Army and received every good-conduct medal Uncle Sam had to give."

Each of the four male jurors, middle-aged veterans, nodded, a succinct, uniform motion, and Carole Ann knew she could wrap it up. "You've heard it over and over, from schoolteachers and ministers, from police chiefs, and from Army captains, colonels, and a general, for crying out loud, who wanted to keep Tommy in the Army. Tommy wanted to go home and be a cop and help clean up his old neighborhood. They all said the same thing: Tommy Griffin is good. Is the general lying? Is the school principal lying? Is the minister lying? Are Doctor Death and Heavy T and the other boys from the 'hood lying? And if you think they could be, the boys from the 'hood, ask yourselves why they would. Why would people reviled by the criminal justice system, people who despised that same system, come into this courtroom and risk incriminating themselves to lie about Tommy Griffin's character? What kind of sense does that make?"

Carole Ann whipped around and crossed rapidly to the defense table, beginning the transformation for which she'd become known in courthouses in three circuits. As if she were the design of some cartoon animator, the gentle rationality and casual lounging on the jury box railing and steady pacing that had characterized her summation until this moment evaporated, to be replaced by molded, sculpted angles of brittle determination. She became a stranger. She'd long ago understood juries wanted to be treated as an equal foot of the justice tripod: the prosecution, the defense, and the verdict, much like the executive, legislative, and judicial branches of government. Sure, juries wanted lawyers to cozy up to them during the trial, to fight to let them see and hear things one side or the other might wish to keep hidden; to share complicated forensic and pathological and psychological information; to reveal the buried secrets of persons and institutions and governments. Juries wanted all this during a trial—and then they wanted the lawyers and the judges to get out of the way and let them feel their power.

She perched her butt on the edge of the defense table, distancing herself from the jury physically and psychically. She crossed her arms in front of her breasts, and crossed her feet at the ankles, long legs out in front of her. Her voice was clipped, almost cold.

"Let me repeat myself: Ignore me. I don't matter here. The judge and the U.S. Attorney don't matter. In fact, you and Tommy Griffin are the only people who matter here." Let the prosecution wiggle around that one! "And truth is the only concept that matters. Not justice, not fairness, not equality. Truth: who told the truth, who lied, and who you believe. You are not being asked to do Tommy Griffin a favor, or to give him a break." Carole Ann was still as death. Nothing moved but her eyes, which traveled from juror to juror—once again, for the last time, finding, meeting, holding Hazel Copeland's gaze.

"After all, why should you give Tommy Griffin a break when many of you have struggled and survived without so much as a howdy-do from another living soul? But Tommy doesn't need a break. Nor does he want one. He wants the truth. It's your job to give it to him." She stood up straight.

"Thank you, Your Honor. I'm finished." And without another word or another glance at the jury box, Carole Ann took her seat at the defense table and turned her outward attention to the prosecutor, though she later would remember nothing of his closing statement. She would remember little of her own, save that she was freezing cold throughout it, that her insides were shivering when she sat down, that her fingers and toes were as numb as if she'd jogged the entirety of Rock Creek Park in the middle of winter. She didn't remember the judge's instructions and charge to the jury—only that, because it was almost eleven-thirty, they'd eat lunch first and then begin their deliberations at two o'clock that afternoon. She didn't remember the ride from the courthouse through the snarled lunchtime traffic north on Pennsylvania Avenue to the sleek high-rise building that housed, on six floors, the law firm at which she was a full partner. She didn't remember returning to the enveloping comfort of her corner office with its panoramic views, or asking for or drinking the pot of tea now empty before her on the table. She was aware only of observing herself from a hazy distance and being surprised at the behavior that seemed to be hers—and of enjoying the distance from herself—until the senior partner for litigation charged into her office.

"What in Satan's hell do you think you were doing with that summation?" Bob Pritchard all but shouted at her, his wiry body twitching like that of a young terrier. Bob was sixty years old and as excitable about lawyering as a new inductee to the bar. "Of course, I heard it was masterful, as usual. But it wasn't what we rehearsed yesterday afternoon. And who the hell ever heard of a fifteen-minute summation?"

Carole Ann slowly filled her lungs with air and just as slowly released it, and stood up from the couch and put her shoes back on. She still was numb inside, frozen, and not only was Bob's friskiness annoying, but his very presence was intrusive. She didn't want to talk to him. She wanted to think about Hazel Copeland and traitors and innocence. But she was glad to learn how much time she'd actually spent with the jury—that was important to her—and she was about to tell Bob that fifteen minutes was sufficient for the innocent, when, puppylike, he bounded on to the next topic, and followed her from the couch across the plush claret carpet to her desk.

"I hope you're hungry, because Pat Delaney's on his way over with a catered lunch. A champagne lunch, I might add." And he actually licked his lips in anticipation.

Carole Ann had deleted Delaney from her mind's storage disc and needed several seconds to drag her memory back to someplace that not only recalled who he was but cared, since his embezzlement and corruption trial had been over for six months. He'd faced a thirteen-count indictment, and had been convicted on two of the least serious charges, resulting in a sentence of community service and a fine. Her closing argument in his defense had taken four and a half hours, proving, in her mind, that her new theory relating innocence and the brevity of the closing argument had merit.

"And?" she asked wearily. "What does he want?"

"Just to see you and to thank you for saving your ass." Bob tilted his head back, laughed, and rubbed his hands together. "He can't sing your praises loudly enough. If it weren't for you, he'd be in prison right now."

"Which is where he deserves to be," she said.

"Where he des—. What the hell kind of response is that?" Bob was not miscast as the overseer of litigation. He was a vigilant guardian of the firm's biggest revenue-producing department, and his mood changed from jocular to defensive in a heartbeat. "The man is our client and what he deserves is the best we have to offer!" he snapped at her.

"The man stole a million and a half dollars from his own construction company, causing the bankruptcy of his two partners, not to mention the failure of a half-finished senior citizens' home and the dissolution of his marriage," Carole Ann snapped back, aware but not caring that she was skating on very thin ice.

"Since when has that mattered a damn bit?"

"Since I almost lost Tommy Griffin, that's since when!" Carole Ann was so far out on thin ice that she couldn't have made it safely back before falling in and drowning even if she'd been trying, which she wasn't. She matched Pritchard's hostile glare, aware that he was looking more like a Rottweiler than a Jack Russell every second.

"And let's get back to that, why don't we. I don't take kindly to my lawyers changing summations without notice, especially when I hear that you blamed lawyers for putting murderers back on the street. I got five calls from outside the firm. What did you think you were doing?" He bristled and almost imperceptibly widened his stance.

"I just told you, Bob. Trying to save an innocent man. I know that's a rarity around here, so much so that I almost didn't recognize it when I saw it, and I almost lost it." Having the words leave her thoughts and come out of her mouth caused a return of the shivers.

"Griffin is a pro bono case, for crying out loud! Pat Delaney paid this firm a lot of money."

"Most of it stolen, no doubt."

"The man is our client!" he thundered, all the cute terrier traits now replaced completely by the big-headed mastiff that was his true, if well-concealed, self. "And I'll not have you refer to any client of this firm in any way but respectfully!"

"Tommy Griffin is our client, too, Bob. Our innocent client. Our innocent, pro bono client, I hasten to add . . ." She was watching the blood rise in his face like mercury in a thermometer when her secretary, Cleo, opened the door and stuck her dreadlocked head in. She gave Carole Ann the hooded-lid look that asked, *Is he being a pain in the ass again?* Then she smiled brilliantly at Bob, and said "Sorry to interrupt, but the Griffin jury is back. One hour and eleven minutes. It's a courthouse record. The car is waiting for you."

Carole Ann allowed her mind to fill to overflowing with trivia. How could the car be waiting? The driver had barely had sufficient time to garage it. Had Cleo called for the car before telling Carole Ann the verdict was in? Wouldn't the driver be at lunch? At least she wouldn't be forced to eat at the same table with Pat Delaney. She was halfway downtown, awash in useless thoughts, before she realized it was a different car and a different driver. How many cars and drivers did the firm have? she wondered. Three-hundred-dollar-an-hour lawyers didn't worry about such things; they worried only that the car and driver were available when needed. Still, she wondered. This driver was a woman, a young white woman. All the other drivers were male, and older. And Black. Was this a new trend? As the color and gender of the legal profession changed, would it follow that the color and gender of those who served them would change also? Certainly Cleo was the first executive-level secretary in the firm with dreadlocks, a fact upon which the most senior of the senior partners never failed to comment whenever faced with her presence. Just as they never failed to comment upon the novelty of Carole Ann's own presence as a partner, as an equal, among their ranks . . . .

CAROLE Ann slowly scanned the packed courtroom. It was a standing-room-only crowd, just as it had been a scant four hours earlier for her closing argument. She'd become accustomed to that; a good many of her clients were high-profile—like their crimes—and she was an expert performer. She knew that. She had worked hard over the years to perfect her technique. The spectator section was overflowing with people who appeared to be relatives and friends of Tommy and his family. The press section had filled to overflowing and was crowding the lawyers' section, which always produced tension. Carole Ann watched without particular interest as the members of the third and fourth estates challenged each other for the right to sit down. She realized she no longer cared about such matters, and turned her attention to what did concern her.

Tommy was nervous. He stole sideways glances at her, the first time he'd ever done that, and it reminded her again what a youngster he really was, despite his size and the size and weight of his problem. He slouched in his chair, again a behavioral departure, and he kept looking over his shoulder at his parents and grandparents and giving them so sickly a grin that the poor people must be weak with terror. She poked him in the ribs with her elbow and he straightened up and faced forward. Then, unable still to control his fidgets, he leaned over to her.

"Do quick verdicts mean guilty or innocent? I don't remember," he whispered.

"We'll know in a very few moments," she whispered back, and nodded toward the concealed door in the side wall of the jury box which had just opened to present two guards, followed by the jury. They looked so relaxed and casual that Carole Ann went numb again, and fought with herself to understand the feeling and the reason for it. She'd never before regretted the return of a jury. Of course, she'd never before had one return in an hour and eleven minutes. Still, she struggled to give identity to the new feelings inside her.

First and most certainly there was fear. She did not want this jury to find Tommy Griffin guilty. Which, she clearly understood, was different from not wanting to lose the case. No part of any feeling that she was experiencing had anything to do with winning and losing, which also was new and different for her: Carole Ann liked winning, and since she won more often than she lost, was accustomed to it. Then there was a sense of dread, which she understood to be connected directly to Hazel Copeland. If the jury decided Tommy was guilty, then she, Carole Ann, was a traitor, and this she did not want to be. She'd rather lose than be branded a traitor in Hazel Copeland's belief system. Then there was the fatigue. Whatever the outcome, she didn't want to be inside a courtroom again for a very long time. These realizations she identified and accepted—welcomed—as valid, their strangeness notwithstanding.

Instinctively Carole Ann stood, pulling Tommy up with her, when the judge entered, and just as instinctively, she sank back down when the judge sat, her legs suddenly unable to support her. Her eyes sought out Hazel Copeland. True to form, the woman sat tall and strong and impassive, her eyes focused on the judge, who was reaching for the folded paper upon which the few words of the verdict were inscribed. Again acting on instinct, Carole Ann rose and pulled Tommy up with her, aware he had become dead weight. For the first time, he was afraid. She looked up at him, at his little-boy face at odds with the muscle builder's body, and smiled, and all the unfamiliar emotions drained from her. She took his hand and held it in both of hers, tightly, and waited.

She never heard the words "Not guilty." She was watching Hazel Copeland's impassive mask of a face, and it wasn't until she heard Tommy's roar in her ear and felt the breath squeezed out of her as he lifted her and whirled her around that she understood what had happened.

"Tommy, please put me down," she said calmly.

"Yes, ma'am," he said with his little boy grin, returning her to her feet but keeping her hands locked in his. "Thank you, Miss Gibson. From the bottom of my heart," he whispered to her, his eyes boring into hers, the two of them ignoring the pandemonium around them. "You really came through for me."

"Thank you, Tommy, for being the best client I've had in a long time," she said, returning his grin, and adding, "But you came through for yourself. Don't ever forget that."

His eyes clouded and his grin faded. "I really am innocent, Miss Gibson. I really and truly did not do those things," he said to her with an intense, insistent ferocity.

"I know that, Tommy," she said, puzzlement and concern in her voice and face, the question unasked.

"I wasn't sure you did, not really, not until the end," he said, with the kind of little it-doesn't-matter shrug that carries tons of hurt and pain.

"Then I apologize for that. I believed in your innocence from the beginning and I wish you'd known that from the beginning, if you didn't." The guilt washed over her in waves that felt like nausea. She controlled the dizziness.

"Yes, ma'am. Thank you again," he said, and after a quick, self-conscious hug, turned to find his family.

"Tommy!" she called before he'd taken a full pace away from her, her outstretched arm grabbing for him before his name sounded. "We need to talk in a couple of days about your future plans . . ."

"I'm a police officer, Miss Gibson."

"They'll make your life a living, breathing hell if you go back there, Tommy," she hissed with a vehemence she hadn't intended to convey.

"Yes, ma'am, I know that. But I'm reporting for duty tomorrow morning." He straightened his already perfect posture and squared his Muhammad Ali–like shoulders and fixed a determined frown on his handsome young face and waited for her to try and talk him out of it.

"Do you want me to go with you?" she asked instead.

His grin was a thousand watts of pure joy. "Yes, ma'am! I'd really appreciate it," he answered.

"On one condition," she snapped in irritation.

"Yes, ma'am! What is it?" he responded, startled by the change in her.

"Stop calling me 'ma'am,' goddammit! I'm not that old!"

"Yes, ma'am! What should I call you, ma'am?" He was laughing at her, laughing full and hard and purging himself of the long year of anguish and humiliation and frustration during which she knew there hadn't been much room or reason for mirth.

"My friends call me C.A., Fish." They held each other in a brief but fierce embrace. Then she released him and told him to go and personally thank each of the jurors, especially Number Seven, and she described Hazel Copeland in detail, which made him frown at her, perplexed.

"How come you know Number Seven so well? You been jury tampering?"

"That's not cute, Fish. Or funny. And when you finish with the jurors, it'll be meet-the-media time."

"Oh, shit," he groaned. "I hate those bastards. They tried and convicted and sentenced me a year ago. Why do I need to talk to them?"

"To show them the error of their ways," Carole Ann responded with more calm than she felt, propelling him into the crush of well-wishers through which he'd have to travel to reach the jury box. Her dislike for reporters was legendary in legal circles. She had held fast to a policy of no interviews after being excoriated in a print article for having the dubious distinction of being "the black female who has become the attorney of choice for white-collar white male criminals."

The reporter had pointed out, explicitly, that few if any residents of predominantly Black D.C. could afford her

high-priced legal talents, ignoring totally that not only
had she been responsible for forcing her law firm to support a pro bono program, but that she shouldered a huge
percentage of that burden. Also ignored in the article was
the fact that her acquittal rate for her pro bono clients—
most of whom were Black and collarless—was higher
than for her white-collar white male clients. The reporter
had set out to nail her, and succeeded. Her retaliation was
never to speak—on or off the record—to another
reporter, which, if anybody was keeping score (and Carole Ann certainly was), had her far ahead in points. She'd
defended more than a dozen high-profile criminal cases
in the last several years and had achieved an almost total
press shutout, virtually unheard of in Washington, where
the press seemed to make the news instead of reporting it.
She deliberately orchestrated her cases so that any leaks
would have, of necessity, to come from the prosecution;
and once, having proved that very thing, had had a case
dismissed by a judge so furious that she'd sent a Maryland state's attorney to jail overnight for having leaked
information to the press.

Carole Ann followed Tommy, his parents, grandparents, other relatives, and friends out of the courthouse
and into the sunny spring afternoon, where they were met
by a swarming, buzzing hive of reporters, who took turns,
it seemed, trying to outshout each other, each question
more inane than the previous one: *How do you feel,
Tommy? Are you glad it's over, Tommy? What are your
plans, Tommy? Do you feel vindicated, Tommy? How
many wins is this for you, Carole Ann? How does it feel,
Carole Ann? What's your next case, Carole Ann?* She listened to their wails, amazed, as always, at the extent to
which a once honorable profession had deterio-
rated . . . knowing that untold numbers of citizens had the
same feeling about her own line of work.

Carole Ann allowed Tommy to push her forward to the cluster of microphones, and he leaned down to whisper that he would not speak. She stood and waited for the shouting to cease. Then, a slight smile lifting the corners of her mouth, she made her first press statement in more than three years: "Despite your best efforts and worst examples, the jury in this case listened and weighed all the evidence and concluded that Tommy Griffin is innocent, both of the charges legally brought against him and of the vile and slanderous innuendo printed and broadcast by you and your employers. We are grateful that the women and men of the jury possessed the dedicated citizenship required to give more than a month of their lives to vindicate an innocent man, and the good sense to ignore anything they've heard or read from you."

In the moment of stunned silence that followed, Carole Ann turned away from the crowd of reporters, shook Tommy's hand again, accepted hugs and kisses from his family and friends, and was looking for an opening in the crowd when, simultaneously, peals of laughter erupted from the spectators and howls of protest from the reporters. *What do you mean by that, Carole Ann? Are you questioning the integrity of the press, Carole Ann? Are you challenging our First Amendment rights, Carole Ann? Are you threatening a libel or slander suit, Carole Ann? You tell 'em, Miss Gibson. Way to go, sister. Naw, we don't listen to 'em 'cause we know they lie. That's right. Reporters are worse than the government for lying.*

Not only did the crowd part in Biblical fashion to permit her exit, but it closed behind her, preventing the reporters from following immediately. Her long-legged stride allowed her to cover the block and a half around the courthouse, from the front to the rear, where her car and driver waited, faster than the reporters could swim against the tide of the crowd and follow her, and she was more than slightly impressed by the dexterity with which the young woman driver effected their departure, at one point easily jumping a curb and speeding the wrong way down a one-way drive reserved for court officials and merging into the dense, late-afternoon traffic before the guard stationed at the private entrance could react to their unauthorized and illegal presence.

It seemed to Carole Ann these days that any time of day was rush hour in D.C. Traffic was always congested; the fact that it was now almost five o'clock did not alone explain the tortoiselike pace with which cars and trucks, bikes and cycles, buses, taxis, and vans followed Pennsylvania Avenue as it changed directional nomenclature from Southeast to Northwest, winding past such tourist favorites as the FBI building, the elaborately restored Hotel Washington, the White House, Blair House, the Old Executive Office Building, looping around the circle guarded by George Washington University and its massive hospital on one end and the entrance to Georgetown on the other. Carole Ann knew the time of day had minimal effect on Pennsylvania Avenue traffic because this was her neighborhood. Her home and office were on one end of the avenue—the northwest end, called Foggy Bottom—and several of the courts in which she practiced were on the southeast end and adjacent Constitution and Independence avenues. She shopped on Pennsylvania Avenue, and jogged on it, and went to the movies and the ice cream parlor and the dry cleaners and the liquor store and the restaurants on it. And no matter where she was going, no matter the time of day or night, traffic was a mess, and she never ceased wondering where all the cars and people were coming from and where they were going.

Joining the nosy wonderings in her imagination was the understanding that she deliberately was not thinking about the events of the day. She'd escaped the court-house, leaving the hungry young associate attorneys to handle the court's paperwork. Not that there was any-thing wrong with that—no senior litigator she knew or knew of fooled with the minutiae of lawyering. Which was precisely why she did. She always made it a point, especially at the conclusion of long, contentious trials, to personally acknowledge juries and clerks and bailiffs and court reporters, the judge, the judge's personal staff, and to personally attend to the clerical odds and ends, whether they entailed filing notice of appeal or accepting a verdict or decision. Today, she wanted none of that. Nor did she want to return to the office to bask in the false adulation that would be spread on much too thickly, because she knew that with the exception of Cleo, nobody in the firm had believed in Tommy Griffin's inno-cence. And there was a distinct chill in some quarters of the office, the residual fallout from her accurate predic-tion of acquittal in the O. J. Simpson case.

Carole Ann had taken her unpopular-to-the-point-of-dangerous stance not because she was a Simpson apolo-gist or because she'd paid particular attention to the abomination that had masqueraded as a trial, but because as a Black native of Los Angeles, she understood the dis-like and distrust Black residents of that city had for a police department that had brutalized and humiliated them with impunity for generations. She understood that Black Angelenos carried with them always the slap in the face that was the acquittal of Rodney King's attackers. So she understood that unless the police department pre-sented incontrovertible evidence against Simpson—and she suspected it would not because the LAPD rarely took Black citizens seriously enough to build airtight cases—no Black on the Simpson jury would vote to convict. That thesis she outlined in painstaking detail more than once, and was both surprised and dismayed when her colleagues reacted angrily to the correctness of her prediction. For the most part, they still were angry with her: angry because she hadn't wished for his conviction, angry because she hadn't shared their anger when it didn't come. So their congratulations would ring hollow and she wasn't in the mood to ignore or excuse or understand.

She opened the console, released the phone, called Cleo, and got an earful: not only was there awe and disbelief at the Griffin verdict, but collective outrage at her statement to the media. They were, Cleo imparted, gunning for her. She told Cleo to tell them what they could do with their weapons, and, gratified that she'd determined not to return to the office before learning of the hostile mood there, she turned off the phone.

"Miss?" She leaned forward to the driver. "I'm sorry I don't know your name."

"It's Wanda, Miss Gibson. What can I do for you?"

"I'm not going back to the office. Drop me at home, please," she said, knowing the firm's drivers could take her home, to her gym, to her doctor or dentist or hairstylist without once asking for an address or directions.

"Yes, ma'am," Wanda replied crisply, shifting from the right lane and executing a left turn so quickly and smoothly Carole Ann wasn't certain it had happened until she saw the outline of her apartment building directly ahead of her.

"You're a hell of a driver, Wanda," Carole Ann said dryly, though with true admiration. Wanda turned around and grinned her thanks, and Carole Ann marveled at the speed and agility with which she pulled up in front of her building, then got out and sped around to open the rear passenger door. Did people get training for this, or did Wanda watch lots of movies?

"Do you want your file cases inside, Miss Gibson?"

"No, Wanda, I don't. Take them to Cleo, please."

"Yes, ma'am," she responded briskly, closing the car door with the same energy and preceding Carole Ann to the building entrance just as the doorman appeared with a nod, a touch of his hand to his cap, and a mumbled "'Afternoon, Mrs. Crandall."

Tired now of the servitude that became an intrusion when she just wanted to be alone, Carole Ann turned her back on both of them and crossed the lobby, her heels a rapid staccato on the rose-colored marble. The elevator was open and waiting and she strode in, pushed the button to the penthouse, and rode home in swift silence, grateful it was early enough that her neighbors weren't flocking home. Enough of them knew who she was and what she did for a living that it could have taken half an hour to traverse the distance from front door to elevator door. She didn't think she'd ever seen the building lobby totally empty of residents, and she was quite certain she had never in her life come home from work at—she looked at her watch—five twenty-three.

She exited the elevator into a small, private foyer. She dropped her purse and briefcase in a heap and slipped off her shoes while she punched in the five-digit code that simultaneously opened the door, deactivated the alarm, and turned on the hall lights. Every time she came home she alternated between gratitude at not having to search for and fumble with keys and worry about what would happen should the advanced technology that made life so easy ever fail. Al, who believed in the superiority of technology, also was a lapsed Buddhist who adhered to the belief that every thought sent out to the Universe returned as one's reality, and constantly cautioned her against worrying about the impossible lest she make it real. She sighed in relieved gratitude when the door clicked open, and kicking her belongings in ahead of her, silently vowed for at least the millionth time to stop holding her breath waiting for the door mechanism to malfunction, just in case Al was right, as he very often was. About many things.

The apartment, bright and warm due to the sunlight as well as its decor and furnishings, welcomed her arrival. And though she needed more than anything to talk to Al, to tell him all the new thoughts and feelings and understandings that had become part of her interior landscape in the last three days, she relished the time alone. Once a staple of her existence, private time and space had become a rare commodity, one missed only occasionally since she'd learned from Al the value and virtue of sharing a life. But she'd spent the last three days exploring her interior terrain alone, roaming and searching and questioning and discovering; and while some moments had been frightening, she'd enjoyed the experience, and wasn't quite ready for it to end. She also didn't know what to do now that she was home at five o'clock on a Wednesday afternoon. She realized she didn't know what normal people did at home at this time of day: she and Al rarely got home before nine.

She walked the entire length and breadth of the apartment twice before returning to the front hallway and retrieving her purse, shoes, and briefcase. These she put away, and changing into shorts and a tee shirt, she went into the mirrored bathroom and cleansed her face, carefully removing the just as carefully applied makeup that she knew to be invisible to all but the most astute—meaning invisible to men, noticed with appreciation by most women. Feeling free and easy, she returned to the dining room and slid open the balcony doors, admitting a swirl of still-warm air that wrapped around her like a hug. In a couple of months, the humidity for which D.C. was infamous would feel more like a wet, woolen blanket than a hug, but right now it was delightful.

She contemplated briefly going for her daily run and quickly dismissed the notion, preferring to save that pleasure for after sundown, and crossed into the kitchen. She placed a bag of popcorn in the microwave, set the timer, and strolled out onto the balcony that wrapped around three sides of the building, providing views north, east, and west. She looked east toward the Potomac River and the bumper-to-bumper traffic snaking its way out of Washington and into Virginia. That slow procession would last until long after sundown, evidence, according to many, that sleepy, Southern D.C. was no longer a one-industry, nine-to-five government town. Carole Ann disagreed. Washington, D.C., was still essentially of, for, by, and about the Federal Government, which had merely grown beyond the wildest imaginings of its creators and, like some monster in a 1950s horror movie, needed constantly to feed, to gorge itself, never attaining satiation. So, more and more politicians and their lackeys, lawyers and lobbyists, associations and organizations flocked to town to feed and feed on the massive government; and, parasitically, there followed the smaller beasts that feed on the politicians and lobbyists and associations. Suburban Washington now extended as far north as Baltimore and as far south as Fredericksburg and still the beast was ravenous.

The breeze brought the scent of popcorn to her nostrils, and she crossed into the kitchen just as the rapid pop-pop-popping subsided. She got a beer from the refrigerator and the popcorn from the microwave and a fistful of napkins from the cabinet and padded down the hall to the den. She plopped down on the sofa and opened the popcorn, leaning away from the heat of the escaping steam while savoring the scent. She could eat popcorn for dinner every night—and did on those nights when Al worked even later than usual and therefore could not ridicule what he called her pedestrian eating habits. She switched on the television, curious to see how the news programs would handle Tommy's acquittal in light of their heavy-handed and opinionated coverage of his arrest and indictment. She was horrified to find herself the focus of the news instead of Tommy. She flipped from channel to channel, each time startled to find herself looking at herself: at the emerald silk and linen dress with the plunging neckline she'd just removed and hung in her closet; at the carefully made-up face she'd just cleansed; at the perfectly coiffed hair she'd run her fingers through and rumpled; at the tall, imperious icon that resembled herself but was not herself. They'd made her the story instead of Tommy. They'd made her words a threat to the free press instead of a repudiation of an irresponsible one.

She worked the remote control, switching back and forth between channels, watching the various news programs the way people watched the aftermath of disasters—earthquakes or fires or train or plane crashes: with a horrified fascination tinged with equal parts fear and excitement. She ate popcorn and drank beer and watched, ignoring the ringing of the phone, for she could easily imagine that the caller, whoever it was, was calling about what she was watching on the television. Looking at it was difficult enough; she certainly didn't want to talk about it. Finally, as if on an agreed-upon cue, the programs all switched from her to Tommy, rehashing the charges against him, complete with the innuendos of his guilt, until they grudgingly got around to reporting the not-guilty verdict—one of the news readers actually said "got off"—and she laughed out loud. At least, she thought to herself, the heat finally was off Tommy. Perhaps he could resume his job and his life . . .

Their private phone rang, the one only family and the closest of friends knew the number to, and Carole Ann muted the sound of the television and picked up the phone at the beginning of the second ring, expecting Al. It was Cleo.

"All hell is breaking loose over here. Pritchard is howling like a junkyard dog under a full moon and the old farts are hyperventilating. If one of 'em has a heart attack and dies, can you be charged as an accessory?"

"Only if he dies with my name on his lips," Carole Ann said, laughing, "and then it would almost be worth it to suffer the indignity of a trial. Do you think Bob would represent me?"

"Not in this life or the next," Cleo said with a snort of disgusted laughter. "And he is furious that you're not here to take the heat yourself."

"Well, I don't want you taking his abuse, so why don't you pack up and leave—"

"I already tried that, but Bonnie Sam informed me that the workday for support staff is nine a.m. until six p.m.—"

"You tell that little cretin you work for me, not his office pool, and that if he ever again . . . On second thought, what's his direct number? I'll call him myself—"

"Relax, C.A. It's almost six anyway, and by the time I catalog all the phone calls you've received in the last hour, it'll be quitting time and I can leave with Bonnie's blessing."

"Have there been that many?" Carole Ann still could not believe how completely the focus had shifted from Tommy to herself, and Cleo's snort in reply shocked her further. "How many, Cleo?" she asked almost plaintively.

"Let's put it this way: Don't be surprised if I'm overcome by a twenty-four-hour virus sometime in the next twelve hours. 'Bye, C.A. See you tomorrow," Cleo said with another snort that converted itself to a deep chuckle at midpoint.

"Perhaps not," Carole Ann said, with her own snort. "I'm feeling a little under the weather myself."

"Are you serious?" Cleo asked, a tinge of panic replacing the earlier irreverence. "You've never not come to work, not even when you had walking pneumonia!" Cleo gave in fully to the panic attack and Carole Ann reined her in.

"I'm quite serious, but I'll be there after I make an appearance with Tommy at his precinct. Don't worry, OK?"

"If you say so," Cleo replied, voice heavy with skepticism. Without further comment, she disconnected.

Carole Ann sank back into the sofa, knees pulled up in front of her and resting on her chest. She wrapped her arms around them and rested her chin there and thought about all the thoughts she'd had in recent days: new, challenging, questioning, bold, frightening thoughts. Thoughts that made it possible for her to contemplate not going into the office tomorrow because she truly questioned the value of what she did. For the first time in almost twenty years, since graduating from college, she challenged herself to justify her existence. The last time she'd engaged in such an exercise she'd ended up in the Peace Corps, digging ditches in West Africa to bring water to crops so that people who might have been her kin could eat. So moved was she by the feeling of actually doing something useful that she'd seriously contemplated staying there—perhaps would have stayed—had not a young man from South Carolina challenged her to return home and help her own people. She was not, after all, an African, he'd reminded her, any more than he himself was. And grateful as he was for the African experience, what he'd really learned was that he was needed in his home state where, despite the prevalence of technological advances, people who truly were his kin were living a West African–village existence.

Law school had been her response to that challenge. She'd fled the familiar idyllic ambiance of Los Angeles for New York—what could be more different?—and immersed herself with a vengeance in Columbia's law program. She'd graduated cum laude, law review, and married to Alain Langston Crandall who, true to his poetic namesakes, was the most romantic man she'd ever met and the only man who'd volunteered, without being asked, to return with her one day to West Africa and see how the crops were doing. Almost twenty years. And the only useful thing she'd done lately was save Tommy Griffin from jail and she'd almost botched that by believing she was, as she'd been told often enough, one of the best trial lawyers on the East Coast.

Where did it come from, that kind of arrogance? When and how had it begun? With the first big against-the-odds courtroom wins? With the advent of the really big money? With the invitations to the White House? With the recognition that Supreme Court justices and attorneys general and U.S. Attorneys were personal friends? She and Al didn't believe themselves to be status seekers, social climbers. In fact, they rarely, if ever, made appearances on Washington's high-level social scene, preferring small dinner parties with their closest and oldest friends. But to be a Black attorney and a full partner in a major law firm was still rare enough in D.C. to attract notice; for them both to have achieved such status kept them in the spotlight and under the microscope. So, with or without their acquiescence, they routinely were included at or near the top of all those "power couple" and "Washington insider" lists. And to the extent that those designations carried weight, they were Washington heavyweights.

Irritated with herself and her thoughts, Carole Ann jumped up from the sofa and hurried down the hall, through the living room, and out onto the balcony. She took deep breaths of the heavy, moist air. The time had "sprung forward" last Sunday, providing the extra hour of daylight, and the sun was bright and sunset still at least two hours away. She paced the length of the balcony, around the corner to the bedroom and back, down the combined lengths of the living and dining rooms. Was she actually considering quitting? That was the feeling inside her, the one that had taken root and would not go away. She didn't want to be a lawyer anymore. At least not the kind of lawyer she had become: the kind who placed winning above all else. Well, perhaps not *all* else, she wanted to believe. She had never compromised an ethic or a principle—unless almost costing an innocent man his freedom counted in that category. Which, of course, it did. She could not free herself of the guilt, the remorse, the pain, and the fear that welled up within her every time she envisioned Hazel Copeland's eyes calling her a traitor. Had it not been for Hazel, Tommy Griffin would be in jail now, and she would be guilty of the worst kind of client misrepresentation.

She thought of Patrick Delaney, who deserved to be in jail. The man was a thief. But she was a better lawyer than the U.S. Attorney. Or was she? Suppose Hazel had been on Delaney's jury? She was tying herself in knots until she unraveled the strings of her thoughts and returned to the salient point: she hadn't cared about Delaney or the U.S. Attorney. She'd cared about winning. And yes, had the prosecution been better or cared as much about winning, Pat Delaney perhaps would be wearing khaki and eating industrial-strength beef stew instead of delivering champagne lunch to her office. Who the hell did he think he was?! And again, she answered her own question: He was a man she'd convinced a jury not to send to jail and he was grateful and he wanted to display his gratitude. She directed her anger where it belonged—at herself—and let it dissipate.

Annoyed again with herself and her thoughts, Carole Ann turned her gaze to the Potomac shimmering in the near distance and tried to enjoy the scenery. She could not. But she could hear Al admonishing her against *trying* to enjoy a view . . . or anything else for that matter. He hated the word "try." He said it had no meaning. One either did or did not do a thing, based on one's level of desire. She either wanted to enjoy the view before her, or she didn't. She waited for herself to decide: she didn't. Enjoying a view didn't utilize nearly enough of her conscious mind. She needed something else. She turned, sliding the door half closed behind her, and headed back to the den. She'd finish watching *Shawshank Redemption*. She absolutely loved Morgan Freeman, the only man, she'd told Al on more than one occasion, who could steal her attentions. But Al was safe, she'd assured him, since there was precious little likelihood of her ever meeting an Academy Award–winning actor. Then there was the White House dinner where they'd met Morgan Freeman . . .

She giggled to herself, remembering Al's almost real alarm as she'd almost swooned in the actor's presence: he was fine as wine and cool as a cucumber and she was mesmerized. She started the VCR. They'd watched about half the film before falling asleep on Sunday night—it was, after all, their third viewing. She'd watch the remainder and eat more popcorn and wait for Al . . .

"C.A.? You here?"

She jumped up and scurried down the hall. "What are you doing home so early?" She flung herself into his embrace, aware he was juggling several bags that were emitting delicious odors. "What's in the bags?" she said into his mouth.

"What's more important: kissing me, your beloved spouse, or what's in the bags?" And they laughed together, knowing what her response would be.

"There are levels of priority, my good man," she said, laughing and taking the bags from him. He followed her down the hall to the kitchen. "And Beirut is Level One." Beirut was a Lebanese restaurant, one of their favorites, and the source of the food in the bags. "Tell me you've got hummus, stuffed grape leaves, and marinated chicken and I'll be yours forever."

"I did and you are anyway. You're also in hiding from the press, I take it?"

"Is that why you're home so early?" She bristled and backed away from him. "And how dare you accuse me of hiding from those scummy assholes!"

" 'Hide' may be a little strong; let's try 'avoid.' And the way they're after you? Yeah, I can believe you're avoiding." He took off his jacket and tie and tossed them over the counter and onto the couch in the living room. "Hell, one of 'em even showed up at my office looking for you. That's how I knew something was up," he said, releasing the top three buttons of his shirt.

"At *your* office?!" Carole Ann exploded. "Who the hell came to *your* office?! What idiot would look for *me* at *your* office? Probably one of those blow-dried Barbie-Kens TV news seems to buy in bulk from the toy department at Target—"

"That's too nasty even for you, C.A. Calm down and tell me what the hell is going on." He began unpacking the bags of food. "Of course I know you're not afraid of the press, but I also know you've got some good reason for coming home at this time of the day. And I figured if it was good enough for you, it was good enough for me—"

"Besides which, you haven't had lunch . . ."

"How did you know that?" He frowned at her and licked hummus from his fingers.

"Wasn't it dog-and-pony-show day with the P-P guys?"

"I don't want to talk about that," he snapped.

It was Carole Ann's turn to frown and she looked at him so long and so hard he relaxed his face into a grin.

"I'm concerned about you, OK?" He wrapped his arms around her.

"And I'm concerned about you, OK? So just give me a hint." She backed out of his embrace and held his gaze, noticing his eyes were so squinted the brows almost met in the middle of his forehead; that his shoulders were hunched almost to his ears; that his hands were fists stuffed into his pockets. That much tension compressed in her husband was so rare she was much more than merely concerned.

"I'd like for Parish Petroleum to sink quickly and permanently to the bottom of the sea," he said seriously, "and I'd like never again to have to devise a legal means for oil and gas multinationals to break the law and live not only to tell it but to profit from it. Now. Why are you home?"

She felt momentarily too conflicted to respond—her own turmoil combined with Al's to create a sensation of pure, dizzying confusion—so she busied herself transferring the food from the carry-out containers to serving bowls; and then, gathering knives, forks, and plates, she began setting the dining room table. He watched her for a moment before pitching in to help. They were seated at the table before she answered his question with her own.

"Suppose we didn't do this anymore?"

"Didn't do what anymore?"

"Practice law," she said.

"OK. I'm supposing. Now what?" He cocked his head to the side and looked at her in a way that, from the first time he'd done it to this minute, always made her feel warm and safe inside.

"How does it feel?" she asked.

"Considerably much better doing it with you than doing it alone. But then that's true of practically everything," he said with an easy grin, and just as easily, began serving the food. Easily, matter-of-factly, naturally, simply. The way he did everything. And in that, she saw herself and how it happened that she could have become—had become—someone and something she professed to dislike: She did nothing easily or naturally or simply. She did everything with an edge, an urgency, an intensity. Winning back some of what had been taken from her people had become winning at any cost, and guilt and innocence had become the same in that such concepts ceased to matter. Only winning mattered. Winning despite odds and obstacles. Winning in the courtroom and on the tennis court. Running four miles every day instead of three. Taking the black belt in two years of study instead of the usual three or four or five. And none of it easy or natural or simple. And yet he could—had and did—contemplate radically altering his life with the same grace and ease with which he applied shaving cream to his face or tied his tie.

"How long has this been going on?" She crooned the question to the melody of the popular song, using the tactic to both calm her nerves and quell her irritation with him. For she was growing irritated that he'd apparently had the thought, before today, of quitting and had not shared it with her.

"Don't quit your day job," he said grinning and popping a stuffed grape leaf into his mouth. "Shirley Horn you ain't."

His good humor diffused her irritation and they ate in silence for a few moments, giving in fully to the pure enjoyment of the food. He got up, went to the kitchen and got them beers, kissed the top of her head on the way back, then sat and studied her. She knew he was assessing her, taking her emotional pulse. He was good at gauging her, at understanding both the source and sense of her moods. She knew he knew that if she thought seriously enough about something to articulate it, action was close at hand. She watched him watch her, giving him the time and space he needed to formulate his response; for despite his natural ease, Al was not necessarily spontaneous. He merely had the ability to make everything look easy. He was deliberate and methodical. If either of them were ever to make a snap decision, she would be the culprit.

"Do you remember Tennessee?" he asked her, and then grinned sheepishly at the silliness of what he'd asked. He knew neither of them ever could forget the harrowing weeks he'd spent in the remote, desolate Tennessee mountain town where every living thing was dead or dying from the poisonous filth spilled into the river from the ancient, ugly, inefficient smelting plant that was the largest employer in three counties.

The company that owned the Tennessee plant and four others like it in the most rural corners of three Southern states was headquartered in Virginia, across the Potomac River from Washington. When the Environmental Protection Agency began questioning the company about its compliance with federal toxic waste disposal regulations, the company had hired Al and his firm to formulate a response—in essence, to negotiate a way around full compliance with the federal regulations. What began as a routine filing of responses to the government had turned quickly into a personal nightmare for Al.

He'd visited each of the plants—in Tennessee, Kentucky, and Arkansas—and had witnessed personally the ruin they'd caused over the years, both to the land and to the people. And he'd witnessed the people who both lived with the destruction to themselves and their environment and were resigned to it. He'd told her he'd known there were white people who were treated the way Blacks always had been treated, but he'd never before seen them. Their misery, he'd said, was palpable. Their acceptance total. Not only didn't they realize their governments—county, state, and federal—could and should help them, they didn't expect or want the help. It had ceased to matter. The people still alive were waiting to die, just as they waited for the remaining fish, deer, rabbits, and vegetation to die.

Because it was the Tennessee plant that originally had sparked the EPA's attention, that is where Al had spent the majority of his time. Every family in the region had at least one member who worked at the plant; and most had several, their years of service spanning two generations. And every family had at least one member—usually a woman who'd watched first husband, then sons, then grandchildren wither, waste, and die—who believed the plant was the cause of the sickness and death. Because these were mountain people, part of their natural existence was hunting and fishing. And because the natural existence of the deer and rabbit and quail and fish depended on the river and its tributaries, the inhabitants of the area—fish, fowl, and two-and four-legged mammal—not only breathed the noxious air emitted from the plant's smokestacks, but ingested its poisons. Also because they were mountain people, they accepted what they understood they could not change. And they inherently distrusted any outsider's view of their condition . . . especially if that outsider happened to be a Colored man in a suit and tie and shiny shoes talking educated.

Before the EPA could jump in and impose the heavy fines the plant deserved, Al negotiated a plan that resulted in the gradual closing of the Tennessee plant, a lump-sum payment of fifteen hundred dollars to each person employed by the plant, a signed release of liability, and a promise—never kept—by the plant owners to clean up the river. That agreement also bought a five-year margin of time for the company to clean up its act in Kentucky and Arkansas. Before that time elapsed, the company had closed all its plants and moved its operation to Central America, leaving behind not only blighted land and diseased people, but heavier poverty and deeper hopelessness. And the promise that more of the same would be visited upon some raw and unexposed place in the Central American interior . . . some place that resembled the raw, unexposed places in North America.

That had happened almost eight years ago. And Al was asking if she remembered . . .

"Since then. I've been thinking about quitting since then. I was never more ashamed of myself than when I negotiated that agreement. It made me a murderer—"

"That's absurd!" She jumped to his defense, slamming her hand hard on the table.

"Really?" He cocked his head at her again. "Then why do you want to quit? Surely not because of the embezzlers and drug dealers and murderers you've returned to the streets?" His words were questioning. There was not the slightest hint of mockery in his tone. Yet she felt as if he'd hit her. Tears sprang from a deep well and filled her eyes.

"Because I almost let an innocent man go to jail. Because I do my job like the only thing that matters is the law and how the law defines guilt or innocence. Because I'd forgotten there's such a thing as good and evil and those things have nothing to do with the law. Because Tommy Griffin is a *good* man and I didn't recognize him as that . . ."

She stopped because the tears overflowed and spilled. Al stood so quickly he knocked over his chair as he came to her, scooped her into his arms, and held her so tightly she had difficulty breathing. She willed the tears to stop and looked up at him. "Because I am a traitor, if not a murderer, and perhaps I am that, too. If you are, then I must be. We do the same thing. Don't we?"

He tightened his grip on her. "Yes. We do. Only I don't call myself a criminal lawyer, so that makes you a hundred times more honest. And at least the courts call your clients criminals. Mine are called CEOs and COOs. Businessmen. Giants and captains of industry." He released her and crossed over to the balcony doors and looked out toward the river, as she'd done earlier.

The sun was setting and reflecting copper off the river. Early stars blinked in the darkening sky, brighter, even in the vast distance, than the lights below: the lights that the earth needed in increasing numbers to create the false sense of security from the evil ugliness that was random crime. The streetlights glowed softly, not deterring a single rape, robbery, or drug deal. Just as softly, lights switched on in the spaces people called home—lights that would not prevent a burglary any more than their warm glow could spread love and warmth among those who shared the spaces. Oh! but how serene, how placid it looked. How far above it they'd thought themselves, safe in their penthouse, arrogant in their success.

"Parish Petroleum is worse," Al said so quietly she

wasn't certain she'd heard him; and after she convinced herself she'd heard the words, she fumbled for a moment to find their meaning. Parish Petroleum was worse than Tennessee? Could that really be true?

"How much worse?" she asked, afraid of the answer.

"Enough that I plan to quit tomorrow."

"Quit the case!" She struggled through her shock to understand what it would feel like to quit a case at midpoint. Long hours of emotional and intellectual investment bonded a lawyer to a case in such a way that severance often was debilitating to the lawyer, and certainly to the case. It would be extremely difficult for another attorney to pick it up at midpoint; and in criminal law, few judges would permit it anyway, especially in federal court. What in the name of God could be so awful Al would withdraw from a case, risking reprimand from the bar?

He turned to face her. "Quit the firm."

She laughed and knew he knew better than to think she thought anything was funny. Laughter often was how she dealt with the unbelievable, the unacceptable. Laughter was her cover when words failed. And she had no words for him. She looked at him, standing silent and still, silhouetted against the now full darkness, the world a dramatic backdrop for his pronouncement. She stopped laughing when her words were ready.

"Well, if you've been thinking about this for eight years, I don't have to ask if you're sure."

"I'm sure, C.A. And I'm also angry and disgusted. This Parish Petroleum business stinks. And it's not just the Louisiana swamps I'm smelling, but my esteemed bosses, the senior partners who only smell the big bucks. Especially that damned Larry Devereaux. What a nasty bastard he is! I've been trying to warn him for months that something about this case stinks and stinks bad, and you know what he said to me? The little prick actually told me my job was to solve problems, not create them. And all because nobody wants to risk cutting off the flow of dollars! Do you know I've already billed more than three hundred thousand?"

She tried to remember when he'd begun working on the Parish Petroleum case. They knew the general outlines of each other's cases, but not the particulars. And not for any professional or ethical reason: they just didn't want to bore each other. They had enough to talk about without discussing their cases in minute detail. There were sufficient interests and activities and concerns and pleasures in their lives that work could be, and often was, relegated to second or third place. So, when had he taken on Parish Petroleum? She recalled she'd accompanied him on his second trip to Louisiana just before Thanksgiving. And he'd been on the case perhaps a couple of months by then . . . so eight months? He'd billed more than three hundred thousand dollars in just eight months!

"What do you mean the case stinks, Al? What stinks?"

"That's why you're the best, C.A. You cut right through all the crap. Any other lawyer would be focused on the money."

"Remember the Philly bagman, Al? The bastard sidled into my office and whispered to me that his uncle told him a first-class defense of what he was charged with would cost half a million dollars. Then he opened his bag and dumped half a million dollars on my desk. That money actually stank, Al. You remember I told you how it smelled?" She wrinkled her nose at the recollection.

Al relaxed his face almost into a grin, crossed to the couch, and collapsed on it, long legs splayed out in front of him. "I can document five instances of flat-out bribery of government officials. State and federal. And the payments are part of their official records, C.A. These peo-

ple pay bribes and record the transactions, for Chris-
sakes! Are they that damn stupid or am I the one missing
something?"

"Well, you know, I've heard Louisiana is different.
Kinda in the same way that New York and New Jersey are
different . . ." She paused, aware of the potential absurd-
ity of what she'd just said, but finding no need to clarify.
It made perfect sense, she was thinking, until she realized
he hadn't heard, that he was far away in his own thoughts.

"Then people started vanishing. Every time I go back
to Louisiana, somebody I contacted the previous trip is
gone. Disappeared. Vanished. Nobody knows where or
why or even when. Except that it was after contact with
me, the most recent occurrence being in January. And if
you thought I had a hard time talking to Tennessee and
Kentucky hill people, you oughta see me trying to talk to
Louisiana swamp people! And these are my own people!
Black people. But I might as well be beamed down from
the starship *Enterprise.*"

"What do you mean by 'disappear' and 'vanish'? What
people? And what kind of people? Oil riggers or house-
wives?" She was both interested and concerned. Interested because unexplained behavior was the kind of thing
that interested her, and concerned because she heard
something almost like fear in Al's voice, and he was not
the kind of man who frightened. Easily or otherwise.

"You know what? I don't want to talk about this anymore. I—"

"The hell you don't!" Carole Ann strode over to him,
hands on hips, and angled her torso in his direction. "You
think you can give me half an explanation for quitting
your job and have that be OK?"

"Do I have to give you any explanation?" he asked
with his easy grin.

"Damn straight, buster!" she snapped at him, hands

still firmly planted on narrow hips. "I want the whole deep and skinny. Who vanished? Who got bribed? And what's frightening you?"

They held each other in a locked gaze for a long, tense moment. He bristled at her insight and the accusation it brought, and she tensed in anticipation of his reaction to her accusation. Then, as if taking a director's cue, they both released breath and tension. Carole Ann stepped back out of her attack posture, and Al unhunched his shoulders and relaxed his brow.

"I don't know who or what Parish Petroleum is. I can't unravel the pieces. And they—whoever *they* are—don't want me to find out, and I've been trying for more than seven months. As far as I can tell, C.A., there is no such entity as Parish Petroleum except on paper: on checks, on contracts, on stationery, on twenty-year-old legal documents. I meet with men who say they work for Parish Petroleum. I spent all day today with three of them, and if I'm honest, I have to say they're what frightened me. These guys are evil, C.A. And don't ask me how I know, OK? 'Cause the best I could do is tell you they have dead eyes. And then there are the lies. According to Larry Devereaux, our firm was hired to help bring Parish Petroleum into compliance with EPA regulations. But that's a lie! I *know* it's a lie just as sure as I know those three guys I was with today are evil. And if my clients are evil and my boss is a liar, where does that leave me? I'm tired of worrying about what to do, babe. So I decided I won't do it anymore. I just can't." These last words sprang from him as supplication: Could she understand, condone, forgive, accept?

She knelt down before him and rested her chin on his knees and looked into his eyes. Then a slow grin spread over her face, pulling her full lips up and causing her eyes to sparkle and dance. He sat up, puzzled.

"Your mother's gonna have a fit and fall in it when you tell her we're both unemployed!" Carole Ann began to giggle at the spectacle of her hoity-toity mother-in-law receiving the news that her high-powered lawyer of a son had quit his job. "What are we gonna tell her we do for a living now? I hear catfish farming is pretty lucrative. Or we could open a bed and breakfast down in the islands someplace. Oh! I know! A dude ranch! In Arizona, or maybe New Mexico . . ." She was laughing out loud now, enjoying the specter of her mother-in-law's discomfort as well as Al's own. Certainly he hadn't gotten as far in his mental processes as telling his mother of his decision. "Well, you can console her with the fact that we've got lots of money." She sat up straight. "We do have lots of money, don't we?" That was one thing she left completely and totally to his discretion. Discussions of money bored her, as did the people whose job it was to discuss money.

"Depends on what you mean by 'lots.' By Hollywood standards, no. But if we're careful, we don't ever have to work again. Not for someone else."

"Oh, I like the sound of that! Catfish, here we come!"

He leaned forward and grabbed her, pulling her off the floor and into his embrace. She sat half in his lap, half on the sofa, still laughing. He playfully bit the back of her neck.

"So when did you decide?"

"This afternoon," she replied, then hesitated. "Or maybe yesterday or the day before . . ." She paused, wanting to be precise. She took a deep breath, calming herself, clarifying her thoughts, and told him about Hazel Copeland from beginning to end. And when she was finished he held her tightly and kissed the top of her head.

"What time are you meeting Tommy in the morning?"

"Roll call," she groaned. "Six-fifteen."

"And then what?"

"Back to the office, to quit." She said the words, felt the feeling, searching for signs she was making a mistake. There were none. "I've never quit a job before. How do you do it?"

"I don't know," Al said, surprise raising his voice half an octave. "I hadn't thought that far. Write a letter?" They held the question between them, and they laughed. They weren't just quitting jobs; they both were partners in multimillion dollar corporations, with legal and fiduciary responsibilities. They could not just write letters of resignation, clean out their desks, and tell everybody goodbye. Besides, and Carole Ann was jolted by the thought, they had employees: she had Cleo and Al had Ernestine, women who worked for them, not for the law firms. They'd have to find jobs for them, but that, considering the dearth of expert legal secretaries, would not be difficult. Now C.A. was feeling what quitting would mean and so, she saw, was Al.

"Do you have depositions scheduled for tomorrow?"

"No," he said. "Not until Monday."

"OK. Let's meet for lunch and work out a strategy," she said. "We can review our contracts . . ." She started to laugh. "Here we are, hotshot lawyers, and we forgot we have contracts that tell us what we can and can't do. I don't even know where mine is!"

Al laughed with her. "With mine. In the safe-deposit box. Way in the bottom of the safe-deposit box," he said through the tears his laughter had brought.

"I've never read the thing," Carole Ann managed to stutter through peals of laughter. "I just signed it. Suppose we can't quit?" They collapsed in laughter, hugging each other, holding each other, holding on to each other, supporting each other.

2

CAROLE ANN INITIALLY WAS MYSTIFIED BY THE crowd that milled about on the lawn in front of the police precinct. The happy crowd. People standing around as if in attendance at a social function, half of them drinking coffee from their kitchen mugs, and talking and laughing in a quiet, friendly manner. Some were dressed casually, in shirtsleeves and jeans, while others clearly were dressed for the workday, in suits and summer silk dresses. A gentle familiarity prevailed. Nothing out of the ordinary, their behavior proclaimed. Except it was six o'clock in the morning and there were four television vans parked on the sidewalk.

Why the hell did they always think they were above and beyond the law, Carole Ann fumed to herself. If any ordinary citizen had the temerity to park on the sidewalk, in front of the police station no less . . . and then they, the crowd, were pointing at them, at Carole Ann and Tommy. Laughing and pointing and surging en masse toward them.

"What in the world . . ." Tommy began before the grin broke out and spread over his face as he heard them calling his name. They were here for him. These were residents of his neighborhood. They were here to welcome him back to work, back to his job of protecting and serving them. Back to offering them some small comfort from the harshness of the reality of their surroundings, for they lived in one of the worst neighborhoods in D.C. Nobody would dispute that, including the people surging toward him. They were Black. They were the working poor. They were captive to the tiny houses and housing projects they called home. He knew many of them, especially the older ones; but many of the younger ones, too, those still alive or not in jail.

"A hero's welcome," Carole Ann said, the lightness of her tone not quite covering the emotion welling up inside her. "You were right to return to work, Tommy. I'm glad you didn't listen to me."

"Just as long as you know it's the only time I didn't listen to you." He fixed her with his serious face and she laughed at him, grateful for the spontaneous outpouring of support and understanding fully how important such a display would be for the top brass in the department. Now police officials could claim Tommy's return was a mandate from the public and could, therefore, embrace him and distance themselves from him at the same time. Legally, the department had no choice but to permit his return: he was guilty of no crime, had done nothing to violate his oath of office. But department brass claimed to be concerned about any lingering effects the months of bad publicity could have on Tommy's effectiveness. The friendly gathering would suggest Tommy's image was untarnished.

Carole Ann was pleased with her ready grasp of the impact the crowd's presence would have on her client's status with his employer, but dismayed her mind so effortlessly found the deviousness, the political, the expedient in every situation and circumstance. Did she do that in every corner and facet of her life? With her family and friends did she assess the motive and meaning of their every word and action?

"Miss Gibson . . . C.A.?" Tommy tugged at her arm like an impatient five-year-old.

"What is it, Tommy?"

"The damn reporters again. Will you . . ."

She shook her head with a rueful grin. "Not today, pal. This is your show. You can talk to 'em or not, doesn't matter to me. But my lips are sealed." They walked in step toward the squat, ugly precinct house, tan with chocolate trim, a government building if ever there was one. Tommy smiled and waved, shook the hands offered to him, addressed several people by name, accepted the hugs of several women who most probably were friends of his mother and grandmother. Then there was a rustling in the crowd, and the mood shifted. Carole Ann tensed, then relaxed. Doctor Death and three of his companions approached them from across the street. Tommy stood and waited for them. She waited with him.

The four of them dressed as one, in clothes that were huge and hideous—dark, baggy, butt-hugging denim trousers and matching hooded jackets and white sneakers with soles that appeared to be three inches thick and vibrating colors of purple and turquoise. Carole Ann knew the attire was expensive, and had frequently wondered at the mentality of the garment manufacturers who produced clothes for hoodlums and for the poor youth who emulated them. The hoodlums sold drugs to be able to afford the clothes; the kids who emulated them robbed people like the ones surrounding her to be able to afford the clothes.

Doctor Death walked as if he were the Grim Reaper, with a deliberate slowness that intended the obvious insult. He swaggered. He grinned, showing gold to complement that in his ears and around his neck. Thick-rimmed, black-lensed glasses hid his eyes from the dawn. His pockets hid his hands and whatever they might hold. And Carole Ann did not doubt for a second that Doctor Death and his posse were armed.

She watched Tommy watch them, watched the crowd watch Tommy and the thugs. It was a fascinating dynamic. The crowd knew Doctor Death had stepped up to the plate for Tommy, and that his presence and testimony had carried weight in the courtroom. They also knew he was, in truth and actuality, certain death to their neighborhood. They wondered, Carole Ann knew, how much gratitude Tommy thought he owed. The answer was immediate.

"Fish," Doctor Death intoned. "What up, man?" He offered his hand and Tommy took it, firmly . . . briefly.

"I didn't know you got up this early, Charles. You turnin' over a new leaf?" Tommy's use of the gangster's given name startled him, then annoyed him.

"I ain't turnin' nothin' but dollars," he growled.

"And that won't be for much longer," Tommy said quietly but forcefully, and the two young men stood toe to toe, eye to eye for a long, breathless moment. Nobody, it seemed, breathed in the few seconds they held each other by the eyes.

Carole Ann was fascinated by their sameness: They were approximately the same height, weight, and build. Both were handsome young men, though Tommy's good looks were enhanced by the light in his eyes and the goodness of his spirit, while Doctor Death oozed mean-ness and hostility. But both were strong-willed, strong-spirited, and determined; and Carole Ann, as she watched them, saw who and what they were, understood, as they understood, that one of them would destroy the other and do so soon. And in that moment, Carole Ann knew her decision to change her life was the correct one. She knew she could never again defend a drug dealer or a rapist or a murderer, the defendant's right to counsel notwithstanding. She looked at the beleaguered citizens of this neighborhood, standing outside in the dawn warmth, their fear of and hatred for Doctor Death and all like him as palpable as the spring morning air, and knew there needed to be somebody standing up for their rights. She looked at them and saw a crowd of Hazel Copelands and vowed never again to put them at risk.

Tommy and Doctor Death broke their visual hold on each other and went their separate ways, the drug dealer sauntering back toward the housing project that was his refuge and his victim, the cop striding into the building from which he'd been banned a year ago, to reclaim his gun and his badge and the identity that separated him irrevocably from Doctor Death. She watched one, then the other. Tommy stopped, turned, waited for her to catch up to him, the puzzled look on his face testimony to the fact that he did not understand her holding back to watch him was a gesture of pride, of gratitude, of love. A woman in the crowd spoke her thoughts for her:

"You go on in there, son, and keep your head up high. We're with you all the way!" A spattering of spontaneous applause and a gentle murmuring of assent followed them into the building.

Carole Ann thought of Al, who at this moment probably was running his four miles around the track at George Washington University, unless he felt he had time to run down to the Ellipse. She would relish telling him of these moments this morning, of how the rightness of her decision—of their decisions—filled her with a joy she'd not felt in a very long time. As she thought of him, thought of who and how he was, she envisioned him running faster this morning, with a lightness brought on by more than spring. He would be at the bank promptly at nine and get their contracts from the safe-deposit box. They would meet for lunch at one, read the documents, and finalize a plan of action. Her most difficult task between now and then would be not quitting before she knew whether or not she could.

"**DIDN'T** you hear a word I said?" Bob Pritchard roared at her, eyes and neck veins bulging.

"I heard all of your words, Bob. I just didn't hear any that explained how or why you found my words to the media yesterday so upsetting. Perhaps we could take it from the top—"

"Don't you dare patronize me." This was a new Bob: icy cold and menacing. He clenched and unclenched his fists and looked at her as if having difficulty controlling the desire to strike.

"I wouldn't dream of it, Bob," she said, maintaining her airy tone. What she was controlling was the desire to tell him to go fuck himself. But she leaned back in her chair and fixed him with a completely mild and unthreatening gaze. Then she leaned forward. "But you really will have to help me out here. Are you saying you've changed your opinion of the press or of my personal preference for dealing with them?"

He opened and closed his mouth but no sound came out for several seconds, and when it did, it was through tightly clenched jaws. "We carefully devised a strategy for your media relationships—"

"No, Bob, *we* did not devise anything." She cut him off with a razor sharpness that so startled him he backed up a step. "*I* decided to stop talking to reporters. That was *my* policy. It was not a strategy or a game plan or any other sports-related thing. I decided to break that silence yesterday. It was a mistake—"

"You're damn right it was!" It was his turn to cut her off, but she held her ground, and simultaneously held his gaze so steadily that she perceived his growing discomfort.

"Well. I'm glad we agree. So I will return to my policy of across-the-board 'no comment' to the media," she said with a calm she did not feel, and stood up to signal she wished him to leave.

"We have reached no point of agreement, Miss Gibson. You will address the media at one-thirty this afternoon in the partners' law library to explain your comments made yesterday."

"I have a one o'clock appointment, so it won't be possible for me to be here at one-thirty. But even if I didn't, I wouldn't. I have said all I have to say to the media. And you, Mr. Pritchard, do not schedule time for me. Not now, not ever." Carole Ann wanted to remember if she'd ever been as angry as she was at that moment; the effort to remember was what prevented her loss of control.

"I will do whatever I think is in the best interests of this law firm. And right now, what is best for this firm is that there be some explanation of your comments. Jesus Fucking Christ, Carole Ann, you accused the people of slander!" What had begun as a barely audible, clenched-jaw pronouncement ended as a roaring tirade. Carole Ann closed her eyes and wanted to cover her ears.

"They *did* slander him, Bob," Carole Ann replied wearily, opening her eyes and focusing them on her boss. "They called him a drug dealer; they called him a dirty cop; they said he was Doctor Death's best friend—not that the two had been best friends in kindergarten and elementary school. The boy's grandfather had a heart attack as a result of the things the press said about

Tommy Griffin—whose name, by the way, is Thomas Lee Griffin the Third . . ."

"Do you not realize the firm absolutely *must* make a response to your comments?" It was his turn for weariness.

"Then as the chief of the litigation section, Bob, please feel free to make a response. After all, I work for you," Carole Ann replied so dryly that he quickly looked for the sarcasm that must have been intended.

"You have an obligation to this firm!" He pounded her desk with his fist so hard Carole Ann winced for him; it must have hurt.

"Just how much of one I intend to ascertain before the end of the day," Carole Ann responded softly, more to herself than to him. And understanding he'd been defeated, he turned and stalked out. Before the air could settle, Cleo's presence filled the space.

"Don't tell me Al has finally rubbed off on you," she said with mock disbelief.

"What do you mean? Rubbed off on me how?"

"I've never seen you so calm. I've never seen you not get furious when Bulldog Bob gets his hackles up. So, you meditating now or something?"

"No," Carole Ann laughed, "but I have found inner peace."

"Oh, where?!" Cleo screeched, "and is there any left?! I need some baaaaad!" The two of them giggled like schoolgirls, and Cleo quickly closed the office door. Both had been warned by the overseer of office protocol—the office administrator—that their behavior was not befitting the executive–support staff relationship. Carole Ann walked around her desk to the wall of windows and looked out on the activity down below. She tried—and failed—to feel some sense of loss at relinquishing these familiar surroundings.

"Maybe Al is responsible after all—" Carole Ann

began, but Cleo cut her off with a snort and a wave of her hand.

"If you say it's a function of good sex, I'll quit on the spot, I swear I will! Billy's still confined to that damn back brace, which not only makes sex, good or bad, impossible, but makes him meaner than a snake." Cleo's irritation was deeply felt, but Carole Ann laughed anyway. She really was full of a peace she'd never before experienced, and "good" didn't begin to describe last night's sex. If that's what being unemployed did for their lovemaking, they truly never would work again. Not for an employer, at any rate.

"OK. I won't say it. But tell me this: If you quit here, where would you want to work?"

Cleo looked at her as if she'd begun to sprout gills and fins and backed up a few steps. "What exactly are you trying to tell me? That I'm fired or that you're quitting?"

"I'm quitting," Carole Ann said quietly and waited for Cleo's response, which didn't come because Cleo was staring at her openmouthed, uncomprehending. So Carole Ann gave her the rest of it: "Al is, too. We're going to . . . we don't know what we're going to do, but it won't be this."

Cleo began shaking her head back and forth, in denial or disbelief or both, and Carole Ann put an arm around her shoulders. Cleo shrugged it off after a moment and crossed to the opposite side of the office.

"What happened?" Cleo folded her arms across her chest, as if arming herself against whatever Carole Ann would say.

"Tommy Griffin."

"You thought he was guilty, didn't you?" Cleo asked quietly, only the tiniest hint of accusation present in the question.

"Not really, Cleo. It's actually worse than that. The

problem was that I saw him only as a client, and not as a decent and innocent man, and because of that, I almost cost him his life and his freedom."

Cleo studied her and Carole Ann relaxed and allowed it. She and Cleo had worked together as boss and secretary for almost ten years, and while they weren't friends in the sense that they shopped together or went to movies together or shared secrets together, they were friends in the sense that they spent more waking hours with each other than with any other human except their spouses. They spent the kind of time that either binds people with the cement of respect and admiration and trust, or fosters complete distrust and dislike. Carole Ann and Cleo fit easily into the first category, and Carole Ann understood the nature of their relationship would dictate Cleo's ready, if not easy, acceptance of her decision.

"And what about Al?" Cleo asked. "What happened with him?" Cleo rubbed her hands back and forth against each other, as if attempting to warm them.

"He's got a case that frightens him." The truthful words were out before Carole Ann could censor them.

"You're the one who cozies up with murderers and rapists and drug dealers. What's Al got to be frightened of?"

Carole Ann laughed at Cleo's genuine consternation. "What's the difference between a commodities broker or a Wall Street raider and any of our pro bono clients?" she asked.

"The color of the collar," Cleo said with a wry laugh and stepped quickly up to Carole Ann with a warm embrace. "I envy you two. I wish Billy and I had the financial security to go out on our own . . ." She let the thought hang in the air with the unfinished words. "We talk about it but that's as far as it gets. It would take our entire savings for Billy to start his own company and he could do it only with me in the front office. But we'd also need my income from . . . from some . . ." The tears welled up and ran down Cleo's face. She hurriedly wiped them away even as Carole Ann pulled tissues from the box on the coffee table.

"You know that I will find you a job, Cleo."

"I know. I'm not worried about that, C.A. I am worried, though, that I won't be able to work for another lawyer. You're the best. I mean that. As a person, as a boss, as a lawyer. I know I'd forever be comparing whoever I work for to you."

"Thanks, Cleo. That means more to me than you know. So. Who do you want to work for?" Carole Ann already was thinking of the trial lawyers she knew who would jump at the chance to have Cleo.

"I don't care, as long as it's not here," she said with a grimace of distaste. "And as long as it's not with the Squid," she said, adding a shudder to the grimace. One of D.C.'s most notable litigants was also a notorious molester. Why no woman had filed a charge against him Carole Ann did not know. The man could not keep a secretary, and had once been beaten severely by the husband of a secretary whose breast he'd grabbed.

"You make a top-five list and I'll make one and we'll pare it down to the object of your desire."

Cleo nodded her acquiescence and then put on her serious face again. "So when are you leaving?"

"Al and I are meeting for lunch to decide that—"

"Jesus Christ! Can't you two quit a job like regular people instead of like lawyers? Do you have to have a meeting over lunch to get it done?"

Carole Ann laughed and explained the need to review the contracts neither of them recalled in detail, and it was Cleo's turn to laugh. After dryly stating that she always knew exactly how much money she earned, when it was paid, and how much notice she had to give to leave a job, Cleo extracted from Carole Ann the admission that she herself did not know exactly how much money she earned, when it was paid, and certainly not how long she'd have to wait until she could consider herself unemployed.

"**Technically,** you can leave now," Al told her. "You're not involved in a case. You don't owe the firm any money. You can't withdraw any money you've invested in the firm or any pension benefits for ninety days. But you can walk this afternoon."

Carole Ann sat grinning like the storybook Cheshire, the grin growing wider and wider, complementing the warmth spreading within. "I had no idea I would feel like this," she said in almost a whisper. "I wish I could describe for you how I feel."

"If your face is any indication, I think I'm getting the message," Al said, taking her hand across the table. "Will you wait for me, darling," he crooned in his best Nat Cole imitation.

"For how long?" she snarled, sounding more like Moms Mabley than Esther Phillips. "You've got a bear-claw contract?"

"No. I can give notice now, but I can't leave for a month because I'm in a case. But I can use the case as the reason," and he pointed out a clause in the five-page document that she read and reread. The words and their intent remained the same, so she grudgingly accepted the inevitable.

"Well, I can't walk out today anyway. I've got files to put in order and a job to find for Cleo . . . did you tell Ernestine?"

Al shook his head and looked up in anticipation as their food arrived. "Do you know when we last had lunch together?" he asked, eyeing their Greek salads appreciatively.

"Uh-huh," Carole Ann responded, chewing an olive she'd picked out of the salad with her fingers. "Your birthday. Three months ago."

"I propose we meet for lunch every day for the next month, whether we eat or not," and Al raised his glass of iced tea to meet her glass of sparkling water. They sealed the agreement and Carole Ann told him about the press briefing taking place at that moment and they took turns imagining how Bob Pritchard was explaining what Carole Ann had intended—and not intended—when she accused the reporters of slander.

WHAT Carole Ann could not have imagined was the reaction of the senior managing partner of the firm when she submitted her written resignation at six-fifteen that evening. Clarence Fox was a tall and massive man with a voice the size of his native Texas. He was red and florid because he drank too much, and he had a full head of wavy white hair that he ran his fingers through a million times a day. He was a damn good lawyer and a better politician. In fact, he'd studied the fine points of maneuvering and manipulating at the feet of Lyndon Johnson and had learned his lessons well. He didn't mind twisting arms or kicking butts or lying or whatever else occurred to him in order to get his way. He was one of the few partners in the firm that Carole Ann truly liked. And she liked him because he truly didn't care whether anybody liked him or not. He'd been brought in thirty years ago, straight from Capitol Hill and Johnson's tutelage, to bring several necessary components to the firm: he was a Southerner with ties to the then-new political order in town (the founding members of the firm had been and remained

Eisenhower and Nixon Republicans); he was young—
then in his late twenties; he was nakedly and openly
aggressive in an era still bound by the hypocritical stric-
tures of the 1950s.

After his initial and genuine surprise and shock at Carole Ann's letter of resignation, he tried reasoning with
her. Then he tried sweet-talking her, spreading it on so
thick and gooey that if it were any other issue, she'd
probably have capitulated. Then he ranted and raved and
cursed and chastised. Then he cried. Real tears. Then he
lied: big, bold, magnificent lies about what the firm
would give her if she stayed—even make her a managing
partner. Carole Ann, flattered and amused and entertained
and almost embarrassed, held her hand up to stop him.

"Clarence, please, don't make this more difficult than
it already is."

"Give me one goddamn reason to treat you nicely!"

"I'm asking you, Clarence. Please."

"What the hell are you gonna do, Carole Ann? You say
you're not goin' to another firm, and I believe you. You
say you're not hangin' out your own shingle, and I
believe you. So what the hell are you gonna do?" He was
plaintive, pleading.

"Nothing, Clarence. Not for a while." She stood up and
walked toward the door. He stopped her with another
question.

"How old are you?" he asked, his florid cheeks turning
an even deeper hue of red.

"Oh, no you don't, you crafty son of a bitch!" She
crossed quickly toward him but he was ignoring her,
punching the keys on his keyboard and watching the
computer screen as a grin lifted his mouth.

"Well, hell, Carole Ann," he drawled at her, grinning
almost lewdly. "Why didn't you say so? My wife left me

on her forty-first birthday. Stayed gone a whole year. Came back tan and fit and better than ever—"

"I'm quitting this shitty job, Clarence, not my marriage. And I am really, truly, irrevocably quitting. My contract says you're the official I'm supposed to notify. You're notified. If there's anything else I need to do, let me know." And with that, she hurried out of his office before he could comment. She ran the two flights of stairs down from the executive floor to her office rather than wait for the elevator, and she scooped up her waiting briefcase and purse and left the building by the freight elevator. She didn't slow down until she reached the subway station at Connecticut Avenue and K Street, and then she all but ran down the escalator instead of waiting for it to deliver her, with all deliberate speed, to the platform.

The after-work swarm of people and their pent-up energy swirled around her, a buzzing, humming mixture of sound and motion and energy that approximated what was happening inside her. She'd never before experienced so many intense emotions simultaneously and she had to will her internal organs to cease their pounding and churning. Willpower failed, so she played a mind game with herself: who among the throng on the platform were lawyers; who were lobbyists; who were Congressional aides. She realized she couldn't tell the difference at the same time as she felt the rush of air that signaled the arrival of the train, just seconds before she heard its whine. She merged into the press of bodies inching toward the train's open doors and, lemminglike, followed the crowd into the cramped compartment.

The calm achieved from her mind game on the platform was short-lived. The restless, charged energy returned, and by the time she exited the train a short two stops later and walked the three blocks to her apartment building, she was too wired for any peaceful activity. So Carole Ann quickly changed into running clothes and was back downstairs whizzing through the lobby door before the startled doorman could touch his cap and mumble a greeting. She preferred running under the moon and stars, when the world was still. But she couldn't wait for dark. This evening nothing could still her, so she ran. Beside the Potomac, past the Watergate and the Kennedy Center; around the Tidal Basin and the Lincoln and the Jefferson memorials; halfway across the Fourteenth Street Bridge. Oblivious to the steady stream of vehicular and pedestrian traffic and the boats on the river, unaware of the brilliance of the sunset, unaware of the pungent odor of the fish market at the Southwest Wharf, she ran. Finally, she caught up with herself and slowed to a walk.

It was done. The panic was gone, finally, and she felt it fully. It was done and she was happy and relieved. She imprinted the date on her memory: April 18. For the first time in days, she felt like herself on the long walk back home as she noticed every thing and person and sight she'd ignored earlier: flowers and birds and children and boats and blossoming trees and the rising moon. The air was warm and moist—not yet hot and humid—a sensuous caress. She felt light and easy. It was done. She would go home and wait for Al.

No, she wouldn't wait, she decided on the elevator ride up to the penthouse. She'd call and ask what time he was coming home. Then she'd go shopping for the ingredients for roasted potatoes and Western omelettes, pick up a bottle of champagne, and wait impatiently for his arrival. She smiled congratulations to herself when she punched in the front door code without an accompanying prayer, and debated whether to shower first or call Al. Al won. She kicked off her shoes and padded down the hall to the den. She reached for the phone and saw the blinking light on the answering machine. She pressed the button, the tape rewound itself, she heard Al's voice:

"Hey, babe. The cowboys have circled the wagons and I think I'm the native in the woodpile. I've been in meetings since I got back from lunch, and there's no end in sight. The head honchos are livid, accusing me of breach of contract, among other evils. Larry has been screaming—and I do mean screaming—for the past three hours that I'm wrong about Parish Petroleum. And to tell you the truth, he's making me a little nervous. I've never seen him this out of control. Anyway, we're having dinner with the boys from Louisiana at eight at Pierre's. I should be home before midnight if I eat fast and walk home even faster. Think you can stay awake? I'd be most grateful. Love you. 'Bye."

The machine beeped and Carole Ann cursed Parish Petroleum loud and long. Then she showered, slipped on clean shorts and a tee shirt, and prepared her solitary dinner of popcorn and beer. She settled herself on the couch and reached for the remote control. The second half of *Shawshank Redemption* awaited. And while she watched Morgan Freeman, she heard Al's lascivious chuckle on the "I'd be most grateful" part of his message. She'd see how grateful he could be . . .

CAROLE Ann woke to a blank television screen and the persistent chiming of the doorbell. She sat up with a start. What time . . . Jesus! Two in the morning! And Al! She jumped up and ran into the hallway, encountering a heavy darkness punctuated by the constant chiming of the doorbell. She switched on a light, sprinted down the hallway, and flung open the door. There were three men—the night doorman and two strangers she intuitively recognized as detectives. She knew they were detectives because all detectives looked alike. They couldn't help it. When police departments issued detective badges, they also issued a tacky suit requirement. Carole Ann recognized one of them but didn't remember his name. He spoke.

"I'm Detective Graham, Mrs. Crandall . . ."

The nausea rose in Carole Ann before she could control it. Both cops saw it and rushed her, caught her before she collapsed and bent her over, got her head down below her knees before she lost consciousness. Then they lifted her, one cop on either side, and carried her down the hallway to the living room and over to the couch, and gently sat her there, head still forced down between her knees.

"Mrs. Crandall—" Graham began again.

"No. Please no. Please no. Please no." Carole Ann could not hear what anybody calling her "Mrs. Crandall" at two o'clock in the morning had to say. Especially a detective. Especially a homicide detective, for that's what Graham was. She remembered him, where she knew him from—some case. He was homicide. Suddenly she straightened up, raised her head, and looked at them, at the detectives. First at Graham and then at the other one. She stood, swayed, steadied herself before they could touch her. She waved them away. "If this is about my husband, tell me. Quickly. Now."

"He's dead, ma'am. Shot and robbed. His wallet and watch are gone. His briefcase was open and papers scattered all over. I'm very sorry, Mrs. Crandall . . ."

"He didn't wear a watch," Carole Ann said. "But his ring . . . where's his ring? I want his ring. I want that ring, do you understand me? That was my father's ring. My mother gave it to him. And the Army gave it back to her in a bag. I want that ring!" And Detective Graham caught her before she fell.

3

CAROLE ANN STRUGGLED AGAINST THE NIGHTMARE
and it struggled back like it had a mind of its own, and on
it, a definite purpose. But she didn't want to see Al in the
dark box deep within the earth. Nothing about that image
reflected Al and the truth of him and she fought against it.
And it fought back. And it was winning. Until the scream
saved her. Loud and piercing and freeing. And the image
of Al in the box in the ground was replaced by . . . her
mother's face. Close to her own, tear-stained and full of
love, little more than a shadow in the soft glow cast by
the night-light. "Mybabymybabymybaby. Oh my sweet
little girl, I am so sorry, sosorrysosorry."

Carole Ann sat up in the darkness, the arms still tight
around her. Her mother's arms. Not Al's. Oh God, not
Al's. Not ever again. The dream that was the truth. No
place to hide. She held on to her mother and wept like a
child.

"What am I going to do, Mommy? What am I going to
do? How am I going to live without him? How did you do
it? Please tell me!" And she awaited the answer. Her
mother must know, her mother who had lost her husband

to a war in a place called Vietnam before it was called a war, when it was Indochina and a problem for France. Her father, a thirty-two-year-old soldier who'd left behind a wife and an eight-year-old son and a five-year-old daughter who now, every day, ran past a sliver of black marble where his name was carved. Thirty-four years ago. Her mother must have an answer.

Instead the mother held the daughter close and whispered her love and sorrow as the daughter again demanded an answer.

"I don't know, baby. I don't know," the mother replied.

"You must know, Mommy. You've had time . . ."

"I miss him every day. Every moment of every day. It doesn't hurt like it did but I still miss him . . ."

"When did it stop hurting?"

"Not for a very, very long time. I'm so sorry."

So sorry. That's what Carole Ann had said to Al's mother, asleep now in the guest bedroom down the hall, her grief that of a mother mourning an only child. So sorry. That's what Al's father had said to Carole Ann as he'd held her, awkwardly, gently. A man who had genetically programmed gentleness and humor and compassion into his only son. A man who'd mourned and grieved with her for a week and then taken his leave, returning to his second family and law practice in Atlanta with the promise that in thirty days he'd come back and "handle the business and legal end of things." A promise echoed by her brother, Mitch, who after two days of grief and mourning had also taken his leave, unable to share or shoulder any of the pain pervading the penthouse. Was that because he was an accountant? Or perhaps he, too, had been genetically programmed by a father dead for thirty-four years. Was it fair to think of her brother as cold and emotionless? Was it fair to think that of the father she didn't remember? Did it matter?

Not to the women, to the wives and mothers left with their grief and unable to comfort each other. For Carole Ann was not comforted by her mother. Grateful for her presence, yes. They loved each other fiercely, depended and relied on each other, trusted each other, Grayce and Carole Ann Gibson. But the daughter found no comfort in that love and trust. Not this time.

"You can't help me, Mommy? You can't say or do anything that will help?"

"No." Grayce shook her head many times. "No. I can't help. But I can warn you that the grief will kill you if you don't find some other thing to do with it. I had you and Mitch and you were so young. You needed so much from me. I had to be everything for you, do everything for you. Be both parents. Work two jobs. Love you enough so you'd trust I wouldn't leave you, too. You and Mitch are why the pain didn't kill me. You must find something to keep you alive. Something worth living for."

Something worth living for. Al was worth living for and Al was dead. Fourteen days dead.

"What is worth living for, Ma? Can you tell me that?" But this time Carole Ann didn't expect an answer. Knew there was no answer. She thought about the events of the past two weeks, about the people who had given themselves to her, beginning with Cleo. Detective Graham had refused to leave her until someone came to be with her, until she'd given him a name and number to call. She'd given him Cleo's name and number and she and Billy had been with her every moment until her mother and brother had arrived the following night. And Cleo had been a presence ever since, thinking of and handling everything, like making sure the daily infusion of food and flowers got delivered to hospitals and hospices and shelters.

And Cleo wasn't the only one: the apartment was full of people every day and night for more than a week. The

church had been full to overflowing for the funeral, and
the procession to the cemetery stretched literally for
miles. The newspapers printed thousands of words, the
broadcast media devoted many minutes of airtime, the
public howled loudly about street violence, and the police
responded with sweeps and busts that would clog the
courts for months. None of it was worth living for.

"Should we have had children, Mom? We should
have," Carole Ann answered herself, not waiting for her
mother's response. "Then I'd have something to live for
now." And she wept again until she returned to the sleep
that was no respite from the sorrow of her awakened
state.

With the new day came the welcome news that Adrienne, Al's mother, would return to her New York home.
Carole Ann was relieved, not only because she and Adrienne had never achieved a real closeness in the fourteen
years she had been married to Al, but because Adrienne's
grief was too heavy. Took up too much space. Adrienne
didn't share her grief like Dave, Al's father, who'd held
her and wept with her and shared memories of Al with
her. Adrienne kept her grief to herself, guarded it as if it
were something rare and precious, instead of something
foul and festering and dangerous. Even Carole Ann knew
enough not to try to hold everything within. She gave it to
her mother, to Dave, to Mitch, to Cleo. She'd tried with
Adrienne. But Adrienne didn't want to share. So Carole
Ann was relieved when she left. Was saddened when her
own mother departed the following week, though grateful
for the solitude. It was time to be alone. To feel life without Al.

Her aloneness was theoretical, for Cleo came every
day and remained with her for several hours each day,
compliments of the firm. She had given a month's notice

the day after Al's funeral and parceled her time between clearing up Carole Ann's job-related life and Carole Ann's personal life. It was Cleo who sorted the piles of mail and logged all the calls from both answering machines. It was Cleo who ordered and sent the thank you cards. It was Cleo who talked—or in this case, didn't talk—to the press and the idly curious. It was Cleo who blended nutritious fruity shakes and forced Carole Ann to drink them, using the promise of popcorn as an inducement. And it was Cleo who noted the paltry nature of the condolences from the hierarchy of Al's firm. Several of the associates had sent cards, but of the contingent of senior and managing partners, only Larry Devereaux, whom Al had neither liked nor trusted, had visited. And his visits hadn't been in the nature of condolence calls.

"Are they that pissed off that he was leaving?" Cleo had asked, her nose wrinkling in distaste. "I never thought I'd have the warm fuzzies for Bulldog Bob and the others from our former shop, but I've got to give credit where credit is due: they've been here for you, Carole Ann. The entire firm has."

And they had. Carole Ann had been more than surprised to find the three living founding partners of her firm and their wives in her living room, their sorrow real and palpable, their words of solace as genuine as their offers of assistance, as real as their willingness to welcome her back to the firm whenever she chose to return. And every lawyer and associate of the firm, every secretary and paralegal, every messenger, clerk, and driver had signed or sent a card, visited her home, attended the funeral; had, in some way, acknowledged her loss. Why not the same response from Al's firm since Al was the one who died? His firm had sent a floral arrangement to the funeral, but only Larry Devereaux had visited in person.

Twice. The memory still rankled. And caused a flutter of discomfort she could not define or explain, beyond acknowledging a sizable dislike for the man.

The first visit was the night after Al was killed. Carole Ann's mother had just arrived from Los Angeles. Al's mother had been alternating between hysteria and catatonia since her arrival earlier that morning. The apartment was filling with people, and Carole Ann had just come from an extensive interview with Detective Graham at police headquarters that had left her weak and trembling. Al had been dead less than twenty-four hours. And Larry Devereaux had arrived, asking to speak with her in private. His first words to her hadn't been "I'm sorry," or "How are you?" or "What can I do to help you?" He'd asked whether Al had left any work-related files or documents at home. He'd wanted to check and see. And he'd wanted to know if Al had talked about the case he was working on.

"You came here to talk to me about Parish Petroleum?" Carole Ann had asked, incredulous, and even grief and anger hadn't prevented her from noticing how he'd stiffened at those words.

"What did he tell you?" Larry had demanded.

"Get out of my house," Carole Ann had ordered, and had literally pushed him down the hallway and out of the door. She'd then succumbed to an attack of the shakes and had to be half carried to her bedroom by Mitch, who'd wanted to follow Larry Devereaux and kick his ass.

Devereaux had come the second time the day after the funeral, with the same request: to know whether Al had left any files, "any property of the firm," Larry had said. And to ask whether Al had discussed the particulars of the case he was working on.

"What exactly do you want to know, Mr. Devereaux?"

Carole Ann had asked, and watched the color rise in his already ruddy face.

"Al was working on a very sensitive matter, Mrs. Cr . . . ah, Miss Gibson . . ."

"What. Do. You. Want?" Carole Ann had cut him off and stared into the palest of pale blue eyes as they narrowed in anger at her response.

"What did Al tell you about Parish Petroleum?"

Carole Ann had looked at him long and hard before answering, noticing his tiny, pale eyes were not the worst feature in a face that seemed comprised of parts that didn't belong where they were. There seemed to be too much forehead and not enough chin and insufficient distance between nose and mouth. And the mouth seemed too full to be in such otherwise parsimonious company. "Everything Al said about you, Mr. Devereaux, is true. And he didn't quit soon enough. Now get out of my house, and do not ever return." And that day she'd called loudly for Cleo's Billy, and asked him to show Mr. Devereaux to the door.

"Are you all right?" Cleo touched her arm and brought her back to the present.

"I was pondering your question about Al's former colleagues, and the most charitable thought I can manage is it's their fault he's dead." Carole Ann did not need the answering machine to replay Al's final words in her head: ". . . *The head honchos are livid . . . Larry has been screaming . . . for the past three hours . . . making me a little nervous . . . having dinner with the boys from Louisiana . . .*" If they'd behaved in any manner approximating decency then, Al would have come home to her that night instead of . . .

"Of course, Ernestine has been here several times," Cleo added, once again returning Carole Ann to the present. "I told her you'd be in touch . . ." Cleo left it hanging, left it for Carole Ann to pick up and make the proper response.

"Thanks, Cleo. I will. Do you know what she wants to do? Where she wants to go?" Al had been as devoted to Ernestine as she herself was to Cleo, and she'd pursue a job as diligently for Ernestine as for Cleo.

"Back to school," Cleo replied with a wide grin that expanded at the look of surprise on Carole Ann's face. It was the first time in more than three weeks that anything had moved her sorrow aside. "She'd been wrestling with how to tell Al she wanted to quit. Now she's sorry she didn't tell him, because he's the one who convinced her it wasn't too late for her to become a social worker. She's only thirty-seven."

The sorrow returned to both of them, hung over them, draped across their shoulders like a shawl, not heavy, but present. There was nothing warm or comforting about it but it was familiar nonetheless.

"What does she want me to do?" Carole Ann asked.

"Write letters of recommendation and justification," Cleo answered, and explained: "Some colleges and universities now give credit for life experience, and Ernestine says her life has been an experience!"

And Carole Ann laughed again, grateful again for even a momentary lifting of the sorrow. She envisioned Ernestine, a combination of Whoopi Goldberg and Mother Teresa, and laughed harder. Ernestine was a longtime volunteer at homeless and battered women's shelters, where along with food and clothing and love and compassion, she dispensed a brand of humor that was both rare and raunchy, for Ernestine laughed at misfortune. Made a joke of it. She did not laugh at homeless people or at battered women or at their personal circumstances, but at the pitiful society that conspired to create the circumstances that made such evils commonplace. Ernestine could laugh because she'd walked the walk and talked the talk. Ernestine had spent two years on the street as a battered homeless woman and had told them she began laughing at herself the day she cried herself empty of tears. Carole Ann would recommend and justify the hell out of Ernestine! She was still smiling to herself when Cleo turned serious.

"You know I begin at BBG-and-R on Monday," Cleo said quietly, referring to the D.C. branch of the largest firm of litigators on the East Coast.

"So soon, Cleo?" But it wasn't soon at all, Carole Ann knew. May was more than half gone. It was time for Cleo to get on with her life. It had taken Carole Ann exactly one phone call, to a former Columbia Law School professor, and Cleo had been hired on the spot. Cleo had signed and returned her employment contract before she ever met her new boss, Gerald Larson, whom Carole Ann considered a friend, a mentor, and a thoroughly decent human being. She'd been more than a little surprised to learn he'd forsaken the classroom for the courtroom; less surprised when she learned the reason: his wife was fighting breast cancer and he needed more money to take care of her and their three children.

"I want you to know, Cleo, how much I appreciate your being here . . ."

Cleo waved away the thanks. The moment was getting too heavy for both of them, and both were grateful when the phone rang. Cleo looked at Carole Ann, who shrugged and turned away. She hadn't answered the phone in more than a month, and saw no reason to begin now. Cleo picked up the phone.

"Hello? Oh! Thanks, Ernesto. Send them up." Cleo hung up the phone and cocked her head in a quizzical look at Carole Ann. "Al's father and your brother are on

their way up?" She made it a question and Carole Ann
groaned.

"Jesus, Cleo, I forgot! I'm sorry. They're going to handle the business side of things . . . the things Al always
did. The insurance and banking and . . . and . . . all the
things I hate to do . . ." She blinked back the tears and
stood up to go let them in, amazed at the passage of time.
If they were back, a month had passed. Al had been dead
for a month. Longer: for thirty-six days. She suddenly
was aware how quiet it was. How empty. How much she
would welcome Dave and Mitch, their arrival nicely
timed to balance the void Cleo's leaving would create.

She blinked and took an involuntary step backward
when she opened the door. Had she never before noticed
how much alike Al and his father were? The older Crandall was grayer and fuller, but as tall as his son and, like
him, possessor of an easy, lanky elegance that immediately comforted. Dave hugged her, patted her back as if
she were a little girl, kissed the top of her head the way Al
used to do, and said he was glad to see her up and about,
that he'd worried about her.

Her brother's greeting was brotherly. "You're skin and
bone, Sis. When was the last time you ate?" But he
embraced her tightly and held her for a long moment
before letting go. "You holding up OK?" He searched her
face and she was moved by the concern in his eyes. How
could she have thought him cold? His love for her was
tangible and visible.

"Today, so far, yes. Yesterday, not at all. Tomorrow?
Who knows?" She gave him a crooked grin, which he
returned, their similarity striking in that moment. They
were not physically alike, brother and sister. He was
square and muscular, like their father, while she was long
and willowy, like their mother. But in their faces, the
genetic blend of features proclaimed their kinship. "How

did you two manage to arrive at the same time? And why didn't you call me? I'd have picked you up, you know."

She led them down the hallway into the living room, where they both greeted Cleo with familial warmth, and explained how Mitch had flown from his home in Denver to Atlanta so he and Dave could take the same flight to Washington. They made small talk, the four of them, for a while, and drank lemonade and ate cheese and fruit and crackers. Carole Ann wanted it to feel normal, natural. These were her friends and family, people she loved and trusted. People she needed. But they weren't Al. Did that mean they weren't worth living for? She didn't know.

She turned off the part of her mind that wouldn't be quiet and listened to the conversation as if she were an eavesdropper. Listened as Cleo told them about her new job, about Billy's bad back, about the surprising outpouring of support from Carole Ann's colleagues, about the lack of support from Al's. Listened as Dave explained how he had a copy of Al's will and a spare key to the safe-deposit box—things Carole Ann hadn't known. Why hadn't she? She hadn't wanted to know. Had never wanted to know about the business of their lives. Was surprised when Cleo told Dave and Mitch that the last five years' worth of tax returns were in a box on the floor of the closet in the den, along with bank statements and other papers. Had Carole Ann known this? Surely she must have. She used the den closet. But bank statements and tax returns would not have—had not—registered in her consciousness. Why? She knew it was not that such matters were "boy things." Cleo was the most detailed, business-oriented person she knew, more so than Al. That's why she would take notice of something like a box full of tax returns and bank statements. It's why she, Carole Ann, hadn't known about Al's will, didn't know about her own. Where was it? She knew she had one because Al had insisted. Did Dave have hers, too? Or her mother? Or Mitch? And who would handle these matters for her when the time came . . .

"I'm going for a run!" Her announcement startled them as much as it startled herself. She hadn't run since the day Al was murdered. Since the day she quit her job. Since the day her life changed forever. For more than a month she hadn't run. But running was something she could do that still made sense, something that required no part of her mind or spirit or emotion. Running was something she still needed that was available to her without emotional cost. She could still run, and practice karate. And cook. She derived sensual pleasure from manipulating the colors and textures and tastes of herbs and spices and food, and this she would do for Dave and Mitch while they were here. Since Al no longer was here to proclaim her culinary mastery, she would cook for Mitch and Dave every day, she decided while running. Running harder and longer than she ever had. For five hours she was out, running, walking, sitting, thinking, weeping, running again, until exhaustion brought her home to bathe and cook and eat and fall into an exhausted sleep that for the first time since Al's death was not shattered by nightmares.

When she awoke the following day, it was, to her surprise, almost noon, and she felt rested. And hungry. And something resembling her normal self. But she didn't get out of bed immediately. She lay there feeling small and alone; feeling the finality of the knowledge that she never again would share this space with another person. She scanned the room, its almost monastic austerity a testament to the man it reflected: the king-sized bed on its low platform of dark rosewood and an overstuffed chair were the only furniture. An antique brass swing-arm lamp stood guard at one side of the chair, and contrasting high-tech halogen lamps sat on the headboard. And everywhere—on the floor beside the chair, on top of the headboard—were stacks of books. Wardrobes and chests of drawers were built into the closets. The television was in the den, as was the telephone. For Al, the bedroom was a place of peace. In it he wanted to meditate, to read, to make love, to sleep. She allowed herself to feel the peace. Then she got up.

In the kitchen she found a note from Dave and Mitch outlining their schedule for the day: visits to the bank, to the insurance company, to the stockbrokers, to the investment counselor, to the accountants. People Carole Ann didn't know, didn't know existed. She offered a silent prayer of gratitude for the two men and opened the cabinet containing the coffee beans. She was a coffee aficionado. A good cup of coffee could improve her disposition as quickly as a bad cup could ruin it. She studied the array of beans before her, chose the Sumatra, and performed the familiar and comforting ritual of grinding and measuring and adding water and inserting the filter and waiting for the sound that preceded the first aroma by just a hair of a second, followed by the first drop of the brew into the pot.

She'd had a cat once, a huge, lazy, gentle, black and white named Patch, who loved the coffee-making ritual as much as she. Every morning he'd race her to the kitchen, leap onto the counter, and watch as she ground and measured. Then he'd hunker down, tail flicking back and forth, and wait for that first drop to fall, knowing it would, but being happy and surprised anyway. Al was allergic to cats, but she'd had Patch first and Al insisted he could adjust. And he had. So well that when, at twelve, the fat cat succumbed to the kidney ailment that frequently challenges older male cats, it was Al who wept like a baby in the vet's office. And for three weeks, every morning, it was Al who watched for the first drop of coffee to fall into the pot.

Carole Ann stood watching and remembering and wondering how many forgotten things about Al would surge to the surface of her memory. Then she wondered what she would do with herself for the remainder of the day, for she would be alone today. Cleo had a new job to prepare for. Her mother was back home in Los Angeles. And judging from their schedule, it would be dinnertime before Mitch and Dave returned. Which meant she was alone. Totally and completely alone. She poured herself a cup of coffee and considered her options. Everything she thought of doing—going to a movie, going shopping, going hiking or biking or antiquing—was something she did with Al. And perhaps one day she'd do these things alone. But not today. Or tomorrow.

She poked around in cabinets and drawers and discovered Cleo had anticipated the return of her appetite. With coffee, apple juice, and a bagel smeared with strawberry preserves, she settled herself in front of the television and switched on CNN. She recognized almost instantly that she didn't care what was happening in the world. She punched the remote control, stopping to watch the next thing that caught her interest, music videos on BET. After the third one, she concluded she didn't like the performers or their music or the jerky camera movements, so she cruised the channels again, stopping this time to watch an exercise program. Muscular young women and men were flexing glutes and abs and obliques on a sandy beach, the ocean shimmering blue in the background. Carole Ann decided she'd spend the afternoon at the karate studio, and then have a massage, a facial, and a manicure, and then come home and cook dinner for Mitch and Dave.

* * *

THEY arrived at six-thirty looking simultaneously grave and happy and told her it was time for a serious talk. She told them it was time for dinner and refused to listen to whatever they had to say until they'd eaten. Preparing the meal—chicken kebabs with spicy peanut sauce cooked on the gas grill on the balcony, saffron rice, salad, and a very sinful, very Southern peach cobbler—had made her feel good. Earlier telephone conversations with Cleo and her mother had soothed and relaxed her. Had made her feel almost happy. Now, both exhausted and relaxed from the karate workout and the massage, and comforted by the act of cooking and by the love she felt from Cleo and her mother, she felt quite content. The obvious enjoyment of these two men, always special to her but now crucial, was as important as it was gratifying.

Finally, settled in the living room with coffee and music and the warm, moist breeze from the river circulating, compliments of the open balcony doors, Carole Ann opened herself to listen to them, to hear and receive their advice.

"You're a very wealthy woman, Carole Ann," her brother began, delivering the news as if it were a jury verdict, and using her name as if it were a title.

Carole Ann shrugged. "I know, Mitch. Al told me we were well-off the day before he . . ." She stopped herself. She didn't want to say the word. It would shatter this peaceful place she'd found for the day. "He told me we didn't really need to work." She shrugged again. How long ago it seemed. And how unimportant.

"Not well off, Carole Ann," Dave said, clearing his throat. "Wealthy."

"Not Hollywood wealthy, Al said, but comfortable," Carole Ann said smiling, remembering. And like a five-year-old, beginning to fidget, as if she'd sat still for as long as could be expected.

"Hollywood, hell!" Dave snorted. "Half the Hollywood high rollers would trade their careers for your solvency. As of this moment, you're worth—"

"Wait, Dave!" Mitch grabbed the older man's arm, genuine alarm in his voice. "She hates money. Really and truly. Don't tell her the numbers." He turned to her: "Sis, you've got a lot of money. A lot. More than you can imagine. More than well-off. More than you want to know about. Am I making myself clear?"

She shook her head at him, numbed by the possibility of what he was saying, and aware of a creeping annoyance. Al wouldn't have lied to her, any more than her brother would. So what was he saying? Carole Ann kept shaking her head as something ugly and uncomfortable began nudging the good feeling she'd worked so hard to achieve. She didn't need this. Dave and Mitch were supposed to come and file the will and notify the insurance company and pay the funeral home and balance the checkbook. And she planned to ask Mitch if he'd take over bookkeeping and other money matters for her. She'd pay him, of course. She'd never take advantage of him like that. Sure, he was her brother, but he was also an accountant who got paid for his services, just like she did.

"You need to know, Carole Ann, so you can tell us what you want to do." Dave spoke slowly, enunciating carefully, as if addressing a small child or a person for whom English was a new language experience. "We have a meeting scheduled with your broker tomorrow and we need to be able to tell him something."

"I don't have a broker," Carole Ann said, snappishness creeping into her tone of voice. "And I don't want one. And I don't want you overreacting like this about some money. Just leave it in the bank account and let it collect interest." She crossed her arms protectively in front of her breasts and looked away from them, looked out the balcony doors into the night.

"You don't leave several million dollars in a bank account to collect interest," Mitch snapped, out of patience with her uncomprehending response. Then he collected himself and leaned forward, across Dave, and took both her hands in his large, square ones, forcing her to look at him instead of at the darkness. "You own a three-thousand-acre working farm in Nebraska and half interest in a five-thousand-acre cattle ranch in Texas and another thousand acres of forest preserve in New Mexico, and you hold majority interest in resorts in Texas, California, and Florida, all of which turn handsome annual profits. Except the forest preserve, which merely increases in value each year. In addition, you now own, outright, this apartment and two others in this building, and an eight-unit building on Capitol Hill, all of which pay you rent every month. The insurance company is waiting to give you a check for two million dollars. But you have to go get it, Sis. They won't give it to us. And Sis? This is just the big-ticket stuff."

"Is any of it worth living for, Mitch?" She withdrew her hands from his and rubbed them together, as if they were cold. "Can I cash it all in and buy Al back? What am I supposed to do with it?" She looked from one to the other, truly expecting an answer. "Tell me!" She slammed her palm down on the table. "You two talk and act like I'm supposed to care about some stupid money." She jumped to her feet and, arms wrapped around herself, began to pace. "Well, what good is it to me now? Tell me!"

"You can take some time off, Sis—"

"I've got all the time in the world, Mitch! I quit my job

the day Al died! We both did. We were going to . . . I don't know what we were going to do . . ."

She was halted by a sound Dave made in his throat, a sound like choking or gasping. She looked at him and was about to ask what was wrong and then the realization hit home: Nobody but Cleo and her mother knew what she and Al had done on that last day of his life.

"Al quit? And he told them, didn't he?" Dave's eyes were open wide and his voice was tight and hoarse.

"Told who what, Dave?" She was as confused by his demeanor as by the question, so confused she almost calmed down and almost relaxed. She stood beside him.

"Those idiots he worked for. Did he tell them he quit?"

"Of course. We both submitted formal letters of—"

"Did he tell them why?" Dave sat perched on the edge of his chair, tension coursing through him like electricity.

Carole Ann considered the question and its meaning, considered Dave's entire response. It was not news to him that Al planned to quit, merely that he'd already done so. But it clearly was important to Dave whether Al had given a reason. And Carole Ann didn't know the answer to that. They'd discussed at lunch that last day how explicit their reasons needed to be, and whether Al needed to restate his already on-the-record concerns about Parish Petroleum. Had he articulated those concerns in his resignation letter? She didn't know, and she told Dave as much, told him what they'd discussed and how they'd returned to their respective offices to write their individual letters.

Then she remembered the message on the answering machine and the three of them rushed down the hall to the den. Carole Ann punched the rewind button, and found the message tape already at the beginning. She punched the play button and heard silence. Her heart ached to hear Al's voice but there was nothing but the silence of the empty tape. After almost a month and a half and several dozen phone calls, it wasn't surprising, and yet she was surprised—at herself for not having the presence of mind to retrieve the tape, and at her mother and Cleo for not thinking . . . but then how would either of them have known? And now the sound of his voice, the sound of his last words to her, was lost to her forever . . . Beside the answering machine, shoved almost beneath it, there was a cassette. She grabbed it up, opened the top of the machine, removed the existing message tape, inserted the newly discovered one, and pressed the play button.

"Hey, babe. The cowboys have circled the wagons and I think I'm the native in the woodpile. I've been in meetings since I got back from lunch, and there's no end in sight. The head honchos are livid, accusing me of breach of contract, among other evils. Larry has been screaming—and I do mean screaming—for the past three hours that I'm wrong about Parish Petroleum. And to tell you the truth, he's making me a little nervous. I've never seen him this out of control. Anyway, we're having dinner with the boys from Louisiana at eight at Pierre's. I should be home before midnight if I eat fast and walk home even faster. Think you can stay awake? I'd be most grateful. Love you. 'Bye."

She again exchanged cassettes, hugging the one with Al's message to her breast and silently thanking Cleo—certain it had to be Cleo who'd preserved Al's final words to her—and wondered how many times she'd play it, just to hear his voice. She placed Al's voice in the top desk drawer, and stopped suddenly, hearing him say, *To tell you the truth, he's making me a little nervous.* And that made her nervous, surfacing the queasy feelings she'd had about Larry Devereaux's two visits and had since buried.

She followed the men down the hall back to the living room, Mitch looking like the last kid picked for the team with his shoulders hunched and squared and his bottom lip protruding, demanding to know why he'd been left in the dark. And she told him—about herself and Tommy Griffin, then about Al and Tennessee and Parish Petroleum. Then she went silent because she needed to wonder about Al's apparent fear of his own boss, for she had heard fear in his voice in the message cassette. Then she returned to the moment, to Mitch and Dave.

The one, a stranger really, yet so familiar. She'd always liked Dave, but they saw him only once or twice a year, usually in the summer. Al's parents had divorced when he was nine, and Dave left New York and started a new family and a new life with an Atlanta law firm. Father and son had communicated superficially but hadn't bonded until Al decided to go to law school. The two men liked and respected each other and, Carole Ann believed, were beginning to love each other. Not the required kind of love fathers and sons expect of each other, but the earned kind.

Then there was her big brother. That they loved each other was unquestionable. They'd been bound by the kind of love only loss can forge. But Mitch was a different kind of man than Al and Dave. Mitch held his emotions and feelings tightly. Too tightly, Carole Ann thought. She wouldn't have wanted to be married to a man like her brother, and her brother's wife wouldn't have anybody but Mitch. As a brother, he was perfect: All her life he'd been there for her and he always would be. That she was sure of. And because of that, she opened the door she'd slammed shut earlier.

"What do you want me to do about the money, Mitch?"

"Will you tell me first whether you'll consider trying to get your job back?"

"Goddammit, Mitch, am I rich or not?"

"You are." His jaw worked as he struggled to contain and control his anger.

"Then what do I need with a job?" Carole Ann was weary in body, mind, and spirit.

Mitch sighed in resignation, acceptance. "I suppose you don't need it, not for the money. But it'll give you something to do, something to take your mind off . . . so you don't just sit around moping."

"I've a right to mope, Mitch. I've earned it. And anyway, the job wouldn't help. I was sick of it before . . . I'd already quit, remember? So going back there won't do anything for my morale."

Mitch raised his hands, palms up, and shrugged. He slid his already loosened tie out of its knot and freed it from his shirt collar. He rubbed his eyes and then stretched and settled back into the armchair, met Carole Ann's eyes, and waited for her to talk to him. She knew he would say no more of his own volition. She looked at Dave, who was staring at some nonexistent thing on the ceiling.

"When did Al tell you he was planning to quit?" she asked Dave. It still rankled that her husband had held this knowledge, this plan, for a long time before he discussed it with her. That he'd discussed it with anyone first hurt deeply.

Dave sighed and, like Mitch, rubbed his eyes before facing her. "He never told me he was planning to quit. What he told me was that he couldn't, in good conscience, continue to work for an outfit that condoned illegal activity."

She thought about his reaction a few moments earlier: he was panicked at the thought that Al had given a reason for his decision. "And you disagreed with him?" She couldn't conceal the surprise she felt. Would Dave actually have counseled Al to engage in activity he knew to be criminal?

"I agreed that he should get out as soon as possible. But without divulging the reason." Dave was sitting erect now, and watching her, like a lawyer.

"Why shouldn't he give a reason?"

"I shouldn't have to tell you that, C.A. You, of all people." There was a slight derision in his tone and Carole Ann bristled. But before she could voice her objection, he continued: "You, of all people, should know that crooks don't like to be called crooks."

She emitted a burst of laughter that came off as a snort. She was about to tell him she hadn't met a single criminal who objected to being called what he was—murderer, drug dealer, rapist—until the image of Patrick Delaney flashed before her eyes. Delaney and the others like him—the fat cats, the suits, the front-office criminals—to a man, denied the moniker "criminal." They were always the victims of circumstance. The hard-asses, the street criminals, shrugged off their predicament with some degree of understanding that if you broke the rules often enough, long enough, you eventually got caught. She was about to explain all this, but something about the way they were looking at her changed her mind. She could imagine that in their minds, her explanation would come off sounding like a defense of killers and drug dealers, and she didn't feel the need to justify herself at the moment. Besides, she couldn't expect that an accountant and a tax attorney would or should understand the finer points of the criminal psyche.

"I don't know exactly what reasons Al gave for resigning, but I'm pretty certain he didn't point fingers . . ." And the memory of Larry Devereaux's two fact-finding missions flashed red warning signals in her brain. Cold,

calculating Larry Devereaux. Al had called him a nasty
bastard, and he was that. Nasty and suspicious . . .

"Al didn't keep anything from you, C.A. He didn't
have secrets from you. You must know that." Dave's
words came out in a rush, as if his sudden understanding
of the reason for Carole Ann's discomfort, and his denial
of it, could eradicate it. Concern creased his face and his
resemblance to Al in that moment was startling. Carole
Ann looked at him and knew what her husband would
have looked like had he lived long enough.

"I know, Dave, and it's all right. Really. Now, let's
decide what to do about all this money." She suddenly
was weak with fatigue. Keeping her eyes open took pure
force of will. "Or more accurately," she said, standing,
"you two decide what to do and do it. I trust you both.
And I trust you to do what Al would do, to make wise
choices and decisions. I don't need or want you to consult
me. Draw up a power of attorney and I'll sign it."

She was talking too fast, and moving away from them,
toward the hall and the bedroom. She knew they didn't
want her to leave, not yet, but she would not be drawn
into further discussion. She had managed to get through
the day without once being overcome and debilitated by a
sense of loss and loneliness. The only way to continue
was to obliterate reality. To sleep. She waved off whatever it was they were saying to her and hurried down the
hallway. She closed the door and, without bothering to
undress, fell horizontally across the bed. She didn't turn
back the covers and put her head on the pillows because
that would feel too familiar, and these days, familiarity
birthed pain. Memory birthed pain. Today, so far, she'd
managed to steer clear of thoughts and memories and
pain. Until now—and the ones she now was having were
not about Al.

Some feeling she couldn't name, and which she certainly didn't like, was elbowing itself into the space with all the other thoughts and feelings. This one felt like an alarm, like a warning. But she'd already given herself over to the notion of escape—from all feeling and thought and certainly from pain. With that, her final conscious claim for the day, she slept. Deep, dark, and dreamless.

4

DEEP AND DREAMLESS SLEEP IS A BLESSING WHEN ITS
purpose is to obliterate consciousness and awareness. For
Carole Ann, every night had brought blessed oblivion for
the past week. Such sleep, however much of a blessing it
can be, also has a downside: it is practically impossible to
achieve sudden, abrupt wakefulness from such a state. So
Carole Ann was oblivious to the first two rings of the
phone. The third ring penetrated her consciousness, and
the fourth awakened that inherent human instinct that signals danger when the phone rings in the middle of the
night. On the fifth ring she struggled to sit up and reach
for the phone, and in the instant before the ring ended and
the automated messaging system would have picked up,
she snatched it up and held it to her ear. She did not speak
because her mouth and brain were not yet in sync enough
for her to form words. So she listened to a vaguely familiar voice call her name: "Miss Gibson." Three times he
said it before she replied.

"Who is this?" she whispered.

"It's Fish, Miss Gibson. I'm sorry to wake you up, but
you didn't return my calls and this is urgent, OK?"

Who, what, when, where, why. Her brain would not

process. Everything about the voice and the urgency it contained was familiar, but the details weren't registering.

"Are you there, Miss Gibson? C.A.?" The voice was hesitant and shy on the "C.A." and she knew instantly who it was and that knowledge woke her completely.

"Is there a problem?" she asked almost briskly.

"Yes, ma'am, a big one," he said, and she heard the hint of a smile in his voice. "I mean C.A. And don't call me anything but Fish. This line may not be secure."

"What the hell are you talking about?" Carole Ann was fully and rationally awake now, awake enough to process not only what he'd said but to begin imagining potential reasons for it. "I'm assuming this is no game you're playing." It was not a question and the tone of his response was as grave as her own.

"No, ma'am. No game. I need you to meet me later today. At your favorite place—at one o'clock your favorite time. Do you understand?"

She shuddered at the words. She'd never heard him speak with such authority or with such fear. "Yes."

"And make sure you're not followed. This is not a game."

"I understand. But at least tell me—" She wanted some hint of a reason for what was happening, but he cut her off.

"I'm very sorry about what happened to your husband, but it was not an accident. Do you understand?"

He must have realized the futility of waiting for a reply because the line buzzed as he disconnected, and still she held the instrument until the loud, computerized warning *beep-beep* sounded, startling her into hanging up. She sat on the side of the bed and looked at the telephone. Marveled, really, at the fact of her presence in this room, the guest room, where she'd slept since Mitch and Dave's departure. Al, with his Buddhist sensibilities, would not have found it worth marveling about, her presence in this room and her proximity to the phone; he would have accepted that she was in the right place at the right time and that's the way things were and should be. However, Carole Ann thought it worth noting. Suppose she'd still been sleeping in their room—hers and Al's. She would not have heard the phone because there was no phone in their room. But she was in the guest room, where there was a telephone.

For the first time she noticed the clock. Almost six-thirty. She'd felt as if it were the middle of the night, and here it was almost time to get up. Fish—Tommy—must already be at work, she thought. He liked working early. She hated it. Hated getting up in the morning. No matter that she'd spent most of her career rising at or before six—a necessary evil since most criminal courts convened at nine and there frequently were chambers conferences and other work to do before court, not to mention the fact that she required coffee and food before beginning her day. Rising early had been a necessity, but she'd never liked it and had never adjusted to it. And in the week since Dave and Mitch left, she had slipped easily into the habit of staying awake reading or watching videos until two or three in the morning, and then sleeping until nine or ten.

She was wide awake now, though. Every nerve ending was pulsating and the blood was pounding in her head. She rushed into the kitchen and, without thought, ground beans and measured coffee and water and pressed the button to begin the brewing. She rushed into the bathroom, stripped off the tee shirt and sweatpants that had become her sleepwear, and stepped into the shower before the water was ready, alternately freezing and scalding herself. Still rushing, she threw on clean shorts and tee shirt and charged into the kitchen, anxious for the now ready coffee. Only when she'd had her first hot, satisfying sip did she permit her brain to take hold, to take over, and direct her actions.

Carole Ann took her coffee to the bedroom—the bedroom she'd shared with Al—and settled herself in his fat, comfortable armchair. She recalled every syllable of Tommy's phone call. Heard again his voice, how serious and concerned—frightened—he sounded. How he'd said Al's death was no accident. How that could mean only one thing. And for her, that simply was not possible, not a rational or logical construct. But Tommy was vehement in his insistence that Al had not been the arbitrary victim of a street mugger, as she'd been told. And she believed Tommy; she just did not believe his words. But why would Tommy lie? Or invent? Or permit himself to be manipulated? Or violate the bond of their trust? He wouldn't. Nor would he make light of her "favorite place" and "favorite time."

Carole Ann encircled the hot coffee mug with her hands, absorbing the warmth, and remembered her first meeting with Tommy Griffin. She'd scheduled it for one forty-five on a Thursday afternoon at a Chinatown restaurant, the Yangtze River. Tommy's first question to her as they seated themselves had been, "What kinda time is one forty-five? What's wrong with regular time, like one-thirty or two o'clock? I never heard of anybody setting a meet for something forty-five!" He'd been truly perplexed, so much so that she'd laughed with real enjoyment. Then she'd explained the legal billing system, how the smallest increment was the quarter hour, and that even though as a pro bono client, he wasn't being billed for their meeting, scheduling in billable increments was a habit. Then it had been his turn to laugh. He said he'd never heard of anything so money-grubbing and greedy and it must be true what they said about lawyers. Then, before she could respond, he'd told her he hated Chinese food—this as he was picking up and opening the menu. Then he laughed again. The entire menu was written in Chinese. "Yep," he'd said with a slow, sad shake of his head, grin still wide. "It must be true what they say about lawyers."

Her ire had evaporated as quickly as it had materialized in the face of his genuinely good-natured and good-spirited jibes at her profession. He was, she'd decided in that moment, a nice guy. She liked him, especially as she'd watched his face open and relax as she'd explained that she loved Chinese food and came here because this restaurant, alone among the dozens of similar ones in Chinatown, was a favorite of the Chinese themselves, which suggested to her that the food must be authentically Chinese. The menu certainly was. So, when she came here, she entrusted her palate to the people who ran the place: she ate what they brought her, as long as the fare didn't include duck toes or chicken beaks or any of the more esoteric cultural delicacies. Tommy, still grinning and shaking his head, had agreed to experiment, and had been vociferous in his pleasure. He had allowed that what he'd eaten on the run from neighborhood carryouts must not have been true Chinese food. Thus, the Yangtze had become special to them during the year of their association. And she'd always arranged it so their meetings occurred at something forty-five. He would not tread lightly on the sanctity of that place or that time.

Carole Ann would meet Tommy in Chinatown this afternoon at one forty-five. But what in hell would she do with herself until then? She certainly could not—would not—sit here thinking about Al being murdered for the next six or seven hours. And she knew better than to turn on the television. Remembering that Mitch, news junkie that he was, had had the paper started, she padded down the hall to the front door and punched the security pad to deactivate the alarm. Instead of the red blinking light turning to green as she expected, a second red light blinked in staccato fashion, not the steady blinking of the armed signal. She frowned and, cursing, reentered the security code. The damn thing would malfunction now that Al wasn't here not only to witness its failure, but to correct it. Dammit! Surely she hadn't forgotten the code. Not overnight, for she'd set it before going to bed last night. She punched in the code a third time and the green light winked at her warmly.

She flung open the door with a great show of irritation and scooped up three papers with an uncharitable whispered comment on Mitch's addiction, which she revised when she realized that in addition to the *Washington Post,* there were the *New York Times* and the *Los Angeles Times.* Suspicious at the latter's arrival given the time difference between the coasts, she looked closely and saw it was Sunday's paper. No matter. It was still her hometown rag and she'd look forward to reading it. It would, she knew, make her feel close to her mother. She tucked the papers under her arm, closed the door, and turned to study the alarm keypad. She entered her code and the light switched from green to blinking red. The system was armed. She entered the code again and was rewarded with a gentle green glare. No second, fast-flashing red light.

She shrugged and trudged down the hall with her bounty of newspapers. She spread them out on the dining room table and, still standing, read the front-page headlines from each of them. She didn't know whether to laugh or cry, but she did know she couldn't sit down and read this amalgamation of misery and mayhem over a cup of coffee like some insufficiently occupied Georgetown matron and then make wry comments on the vagaries of human nature or the sorry state of societal and governmental affairs. So, what would she do with herself until it was time to meet Tommy? She closed and folded the papers and began to pace as if she were in the courtroom. She strode back up the hall toward the front door and studied the alarm keypad. Then she turned and charged down the hallway, through the living room, and flung open the balcony doors. The sun, fully up and already hot, meant she need not overdress for her meeting with Tommy. She crossed into the kitchen and poured herself another cup of coffee, which she took with her to the den.

She was about to plop down on the sofa when she spied the neat folders left on the desk by Mitch and Dave. Despite their pleas, Carole Ann had not read their account of what they'd done and what they needed her to do. They'd left a full week ago, and she'd intentionally ignored the pile of folders. She pulled out the chair and sat at the desk. She put the coffee cup down and opened the top folder. On top was a three-page, single-spaced letter signed by both Mitch and Dave. She scanned it quickly. They outlined in detail everything they'd done and planned to do regarding her finances. She ignored most of the detail, focusing on what she considered to be the salient points. There were now two checking accounts into which funds from several different sources would be deposited regularly. She didn't want to know about those sources, though they were explained in great detail. She read enough to understand that Mitch and Dave controlled one account, from which they would pay all of her bills, including her taxes and credit card charges. All these bills now went to Mitch, who would send an itemized listing of payments to Dave, who would write the checks and then send them to Mitch for signature. Carole Ann's eyes misted at the lengths to which they'd gone to insure that not even the smallest hint of impropriety could exist. She saw that the second account, into which twenty-five hundred dollars would be deposited each month, was hers to do with as she pleased. If she needed more, they'd see to it. If she needed more? What the hell would she do with twenty-five hundred dollars a month if her bills were already paid? Through the tears now spilling from her eyes, she saw she would soon be receiving an ATM card that would allow her to access her new account, along with her new checks. The ones that would have just her name on them. Not her name and Al's.

Carole Ann pushed the chair back from the desk and let the tears flow unchecked. She hadn't cried hard and long for quite a few days, and she got a splitting headache almost immediately. So she stopped crying, wiped her face on her tee shirt, and finished reading Mitch and Dave's letter. They'd suggested several investments and would, they said, make additional recommendations after they'd done more research. They outlined their procedures for making certain that they couldn't cheat her and steal her money and she almost cried again. Then they explained that everything they'd done was in a file in the notebook computer in the desk drawer, along with Al's notes about their existing investments and some of his plans for future investments. Also in the computer was a locked file that Mitch and Dave didn't think pertained to their finances, but that Carole Ann should access, if she knew the password, and let them know.

She didn't want to read any more, to know any more. And she sure as hell didn't want to fool around with the computer, trying to unlock some file. How was she supposed to intuit Al's secret password? That's why it was secret. Anyway, whatever was locked inside the secret file couldn't have any significant impact on the work already done by Mitch and Dave. She counted the folders stacked neatly on the desk: Eleven of them. Investments.

Things she owned. Sources of income. She stacked them neatly and put them in a drawer, on top of the laptop, with a halfhearted promise to review them in detail and attempt to unlock the mystery file sometime soon. But not now. Not when she was so tense and agitated. Not when all she wanted was to talk to Tommy. But it was barely nine o'clock. She had to do something for the next three hours.

With a sigh, Carole Ann opened the desk drawer and retrieved the eleven folders and the laptop, which she connected to the cables that snaked up from the bottom of the desk and switched on. Then, beginning with the top folder, she read every word on every sheet of paper in each of the eleven. Then she pulled up each of Al's files in the computer and read through them. She was surprised by and grateful for the nearness she experienced reading his thoughts and plans. Then she switched to the directory, found the locked file, and tried to open it. Silly endeavor, but it never ceased to amaze her how much time one could waste playing with a computer. She was not a hacker. Computers were useful, efficient, timesaving tools—unless one spent hours playing games or living out absurd fantasies with strangers in chat rooms. Al had locked the file for a reason. He wasn't here to explain that reason. It must mean it was none of her business. She switched off the machine, unplugged the cables, and returned computer and folders to the drawer. Then she went to get dressed for her meeting with Tommy.

A plan for leaving her building undetected had formulated itself in the recesses of her consciousness. Tommy had said to make certain she wasn't followed, and while the admonition had both unnerved and annoyed her, she didn't take it lightly. So, instead of riding the subway— the fastest, easiest, and most convenient mode of travel— she would drive. Almost nobody knew they had a car, a

ten-year-old black Saab convertible that lived covered in
the underground garage of their apartment building and
which they took out for a drive one weekend a month. Al,
like many native New Yorkers, had never learned to drive.
Carole Ann, like every native Angeleno, had learned to
walk and drive at roughly the same time, and she loved
driving. Ergo, the convertible. Had the choice been hers,
they'd have lived in the suburbs, somewhere on a river,
and commuted to work, top down, breeze blowing. But
Al not only didn't drive, he didn't like automobiles.
Didn't like being in them. He liked subways and buses
and trains. So they lived downtown, close to work. And
one weekend a month, they drove. To go camping or
antiquing or hiking or discovering some new and beautiful place. All weekend they would be in the car, on the
road, not returning home until late Sunday night.

Carole Ann, dressed in a filmy white blouse and skirt
and wide, floppy straw hat, chastised herself for her
wardrobe choice as she prepared to slip the dust cover off
the Saab. She hadn't driven the car in almost two months,
and the cover would be filthy. Then she remembered
Mitch and Dave had driven one night to Baltimore, to an
Orioles game, and they would have shaken the cover. She
was relieved to be proved correct. The car started
instantly; she allowed a minute of warm-up time, then
backed out of the space and toward the exit. She inserted
the coded key card that opened the door, and while she
waited, put on a pair of large black sunglasses. She pulled
out of the garage into the afternoon sun and sat there until
the door closed, making certain no car exited on her tail.
She sat there for a moment longer to make sure the door
didn't open immediately, then drove off.

The garage exit was at the rear of the building and
invisible from the front entrance, so anyone looking for

her there would not see her exit. And anyone watching for her exit from the garage would be visible to her because there was no place of concealment at the building's underground rear exit. She made a hard turn into an alley behind the dry cleaners and then made an illegal right turn into K Street. She gunned the engine, shifted into third, ran a yellow light, and ignored the yield sign at the entrance to the Rock Creek Parkway. She headed uptown, wishing she could remove the hat and glasses and let down the top and feel the hot air burn her face and scalp, the way it would in Los Angeles. But she settled for the sheer joy of driving—too fast—in the beauty of the park that ran the length of D.C., from the Potomac River in Virginia, to Maryland.

She left the Parkway at Piney Branch Road and angled over to Georgia Avenue, which she took north out of D.C., across the line and into Silver Spring, Maryland. She prayed to be able to find a parking space in the huge lot at the Silver Spring Metro station, and after driving around for almost fifteen minutes, she whipped a U-turn and beat a Volvo to a just-vacated space. The guy driving the Volvo gave her the finger. Grinning, she dropped three dollars' worth of quarters into the parking meter and trotted toward the station. She was parked at the far end of the lot and her blouse was quite damp by the time she inserted her farecard in the turnstile. The air-conditioned train car would feel good.

She rode the Metro from Maryland south back into D.C., the six stops to Gallery Place–Chinatown seeming to take only a few minutes; it seemed to take longer to walk the three blocks to the restaurant. It was exactly one forty-five when she entered the aromatic dimness that was the Yangtze River. She was greeted with a formal politeness by the owner, a woman whom she had been instructed to call Mrs. Chang, though that, Carole Ann knew, was not her name.

"Hello. Nice to see you again," the woman said with a slight bow. Then she surprised Carole Ann by saying, "So sorry about husband. Please to follow me." And she turned toward the back room that was the special haven of preferred customers.

Carole Ann stood in place, too stunned to follow immediately. How could this woman know to express sympathy to her? She shook off her surprise and quickly caught up with her hostess. "Mrs. Chang," she said, and the woman stopped, turned and faced her with a calmly expectant expression. "I'm meeting someone," Carole Ann began.

"Yes, yes. Police officer already here. Please to follow me," Mrs. Chang repeated, as she repeated the slight bow and her forward motion. This time Carole Ann followed.

Tommy indeed was already there, was already eating. He stopped when he saw her, quickly wiped his hands and mouth on a napkin, and stood. When she got closer he took a step to meet her, then stopped. He opened his arms, then extended his hand, then blushed, reminding her again how young and vulnerable he was. She opened her arms to receive his embrace, grateful for it. She hadn't seen him since the day of his return to work.

"I'd say you haven't been doing such a red-hot job of taking care of yourself," Tommy said, his hands on her shoulders and holding her at arm's length.

"And why would you say that?" she growled, stepping away from him and conscious of trying to reinstitute the control she had exercised in their lawyer-client relationship. She sat down, put a napkin in her lap, and poured herself a glass of water.

"You've lost too much weight and you look like you're running on about three hours of sleep."

"I'll gain it back and it was four, thanks to you. And what the hell do you mean, Al's death wasn't an accident?" She held him by the eyes and he didn't flinch or waver or blink.

"I'm sorry, Miss Gibson. C.A. Truly sorry. But you need to know. I thought you'd want to know—"

"Know what, exactly?" She cut him off, her words a sharp blade.

"Valerie got the call that night. You remember Valerie?" He asked the question to cover his embarrassment for referring to the police response to Al's murder—if it was murder—in jargon. Valerie was Tommy's girlfriend and a patrol officer in the First District, which included Foggy Bottom, the area of town where they lived . . . where Al had been killed. "Anyway, she called me the next morning, early, to tell me about it, and about . . . about who the dude was . . . I mean, that the vic . . . that Mr. Crandall was your husband." They both took long swallows of their water and collected their emotions. "By the way, thanks a lot for the card and the note."

She was about to ask him what he was talking about when it occurred to her, suddenly and correctly, that Cleo would have acknowledged a message of sympathy from Tommy with a personal note. God bless Cleo! "You're welcome. Then what?"

"I asked Valerie to keep an ear on it. To let me know how the case was working. You know they made it a high priority." He paused and rubbed his hands together. "They pulled a lot of guys in off the street. Homeless dudes, mostly. Whipped up on a few of 'em. This went on for a couple of weeks, till the ACLU got pissed off and started talking class action suit. So they sprung all the homeless dudes and nothing happened for another couple o' weeks. Then this homicide dick, fella by the name of Graham, starts making weird noises—"

Carole Ann made a sound, then covered by pretending to cough. She drank some more water. "I know Graham. He's one of the ones who came to tell me that night . . . and I'd met him before. Started making weird noises like what?"

"Like the pieces didn't fit, he said. Like the times didn't jive, when the lawyer dudes said they left the restaurant with the victim and when the dishwasher saw him in the alley. Like the crime scene had been tampered with. Like your hus— Mr. Crandall's briefcase had been planted at the scene. Like Mr. Crandall himself had been planted there."

Carole Ann's head pounded and she felt hot enough to explode. Her blouse clung to her and perspiration trickled down between her breasts. Tommy reached across the table and took her hands and squeezed and wouldn't let go. "First the dishwasher disappeared, the one who saw your husband in the alley. Then Graham took a bullet in the back. Then the Feds took the case away from us . . ."

Carole Ann snapped out of her grief, snatched her hands from Tommy's grip, and sat back in the booth. "How could the Feds take the case from you?" she asked in almost a whisper.

"Some high-up muckety-muck allowed as how Graham was right after all, the body had been planted. The crime really had occurred in Lafayette Park and the body moved to Pennsylvania Avenue. The park is federal property and the jurisdiction of the U.S. Park Police. So, we gave it to 'em. Everything. The case and the case files. In the spirit of cooperation, you understand. And nobody's heard nothin' about it since then." Tommy finished his story, the anger and disgust curling his mouth like he wanted to spit out something poisonous.

"How do you get murder out of that, Tommy?" Carole

Ann asked so quietly and with so much forced control it hurt her to speak.

"'Cause that's what Graham called it. Didn't I say that? Graham said it was premeditated and planned. Valerie said he was making a lot of noise about it, about how he was pissed off he'd wasted so much time looking for a robber or a mugger or some damn homeless dude. Said he oughta have been looking for a hit man. Valerie said that's what the man said: he shoulda been looking for a hit man. Then he took a bullet in the back that'll keep him in a wheelchair for the rest of his life. A bullet in the back, just like your husband. And the dishwasher who could back up his theory disappeared. Vanished."

Carole Ann felt as if she'd been sitting at the table listening to Tommy for years. Mrs. Chang's arrival with a cartload of steaming and aromatic plates was proof it had been but minutes. Without speaking, she placed three dishes in the center of the table. The aroma was both delicate and pungent and unlike anything Carole Ann had ever experienced.

"This is food for hope," Mrs. Chang said to her. "Food to know husband on safe journey." Then she bowed to their table and rolled the cart away.

Carole Ann could not speak for a long moment. The combination of Tommy's information and the unexpected kindness of the Chinese woman whose name she didn't even know stirred her emotions like a tornado. Tommy watched her for a while, then began to eat with a gusto that was enjoyable to behold. Out of courtesy, Carole Ann picked up her chopsticks to sample Mrs. Chang's "food for hope," thinking she'd ask to take it home with her rather than leave it in a display of bad manners and ingratitude. But once she began eating she could not stop. She didn't know what exactly she was eating—she'd never been able to discern what the herbs and spices were, and Mrs. Chang's command of English diminished in proportion to the intensity of Carole Ann's questions about the ingredients.

They ate in silence, savoring the magnificence of the food and the generosity of spirit that provided it. Carole Ann broke the silence once to ask Tommy how Mrs. Chang knew he was a cop. Grinning, he explained how he'd brought Valerie here one night, both of them in uniform and just in time to evict a party of drunken tourists who refused to accept that there existed no menu in English and no Chinese person who spoke English well enough to take their order for pork fried rice and Mongolian beef with broccoli. Since then, they'd been regulars, separately and together, and whenever they arrived Mrs. Chang immediately brought them "good luck" food, which is what he had been eating when Carole Ann arrived. Then Tommy predicted that at the rate she was going, Carole Ann would have regained her grief-lost pounds by the end of the meal. They laughed together, grateful for the lessening of the tension that would allow them to continue the conversation they both knew was far from over.

Carole Ann asked so many questions that she was surprised Tommy didn't object. She appreciated his patience, and told him so, but she couldn't not ask. And as she asked, it became clear that had Al Crandall been anybody's husband but her own, she would have smelled the rottenness of the police investigation a month ago. If it had been anybody's husband but her own, she'd have demanded to know why there'd been no follow-up contact from the law. But it had been her husband and she had been wallowing in her grief and had not wanted to talk to the police, had not wanted to know the whereabouts of Al's briefcase and the clothes he was wearing and the condition of the body and the placement of the wounds. She hadn't even asked—and hadn't hired an attorney to ask—for the return of the victim's personal effects. She'd demanded of Detective Graham that night the return of the ring that had been her father's, and had made no mention of it since. She had, in short, behaved like a grieving widow and not like a criminal attorney. And because of that, her husband's murder was seven weeks cold. The evidence was seven weeks cold. The investigation was more than cold, was perhaps dead and buried and decomposing. Like . . . like . . .

One final question, Carole Ann begged. And although so weary from going over the same material from so many angles that he said he could understand how innocent people broke and confessed under intense interrogation, Tommy acquiesced with a sigh. Why, she wanted to know, did he believe her home telephone might not be secure and her home under surveillance? Did he believe she was a target? And if so, why? And Tommy began to squirm visibly.

"Fish," she said, lowering her voice and drawing the tiny word out across several syllables and making it a question, a demand, an accusation, and a chastisement. It was a tactic employed to great effect by her mother to elicit information from a recalcitrant child. It now worked on Tommy.

"Well," he said, still squirming, "I've been doing some checking on my own—"

"What kind of checking?" she snapped at him.

"I went to see Graham. And I tried to get a line on the missing dishwasher. Talked to Immigration, to see if they had him. He was an undocumented from El Salvador or one of those Spanish-speaking places. But INS don't know jack about him. That dude is just plain gone. Disappeared into thin air." He was shaking his head and pouring tea so he missed the look on Carole Ann's face as she recalled Al's fear that the disappearance of people in Louisiana after contact with him was somehow related to his investigation of Parish Petroleum.

"What did Graham say?" she asked him.

"He said whoever took out Crand—your husband— also took out the dishwasher, and that same somebody put a bullet in his back. I told him he was being paranoid and he told me if I started sniffing around this case I better be paranoid, too. He told me he tried getting a line on some outfit called Parish Petroleum and that's when his troubles started. He said your husband must have pissed them off real bad—whoever 'they' are, 'cause Graham said he can't find out who they are. And he said if I insisted on filling you in, I also better tell you to watch your back."

Tommy sat back and drank some of his tea and watched the effect of his words. He seemed not to mind that he had shown her his fear. And perhaps had she not been so angry with herself, she'd have reciprocated, because she, in truth, felt the vague stirrings of something resembling fear. But the anger was in charge, and that is what she displayed. Anger at herself for succumbing so completely to her pain and loss that she'd forgotten who and what she was. Even as her anger raged, a small voice inside her cried out that it was too late to do anything but accept things as they were. Tommy watched until she took a couple of deep breaths and calmed herself.

"You said Graham would spend the rest of his life in a wheelchair. Was that hyperbole?"

"Was that what?" He scrunched up his face at her.

"An exaggeration, Tommy," she said, not concealing her exasperation.

"Hell, no!" he said quickly and seriously. "The dude has nothing from the waist down."

Carole Ann closed her eyes and leaned back into the

padded cushion of the booth. She found she could easily picture Detective Graham as he had been the night he brought her news of Al's murder . . . found she could not picture the intense, wiry man confined to a wheelchair . . . found she felt pain and sorrow for someone other than herself and her Al.

"Can I ask you something?" Tommy's voice was low, hesitant.

"Of course you can. What is it?"

"Why didn't you return my phone calls?"

"I never got your messages, Tommy." She put up a hand to stop the words ready to rush from his mouth. "I never got them because I don't listen to the message system. Until this morning, when you called, I hadn't answered the phone since the day Al . . . was murdered."

She explained to him about the two phone lines, how the private line was hooked up to an answering machine and the other line, the number published in the telephone directory, was answered by the phone company messaging center. That's the number he, Tommy, had dialed. Since she never used that line, she wouldn't have heard the tone that indicated the existence of messages. She used the private line to call Cleo and her mother and the few friends whose calls she'd bothered to return because their messages were on the answering machine with the light that flashed and flashed until it got the attention it demanded. "I apologize," she said, and digging into her purse for a pen, she wrote the private number on a napkin and slid it across the table to him.

"Are you sure you answer this phone?" he asked with a furrowed brow and a deep skepticism as he folded the napkin and slipped it into his pocket.

"Always," she said solemnly, raising her right hand as if taking the oath. "My mom calls this number."

On the brief walk from the restaurant to the Metro

stop, Carole Ann focused outward, noticing the different energy between the tourists and conventioneers and the office workers pressed to eat and get back to the job: the difference between a merry-go-round and a roller coaster. On the subway ride uptown to the Silver Spring Metro station, and on the drive downtown, back through Rock Creek Park, Carole Ann turned inward and tuned into the shifts and changes taking place within herself. She felt the new knowledge of the truth of Al's death assume its rightful place, displacing the feelings that so recently had taken up residence: grief, longing, loss, heavy sadness. She felt the familiar stirrings of restlessness and competitiveness. And anger. She felt her energy slowing down to a speed that encouraged contemplation and decisiveness. She felt the widow's veil slip away, revealing the lawyer who was one of the best in the business.

Today was June 1 and Carole Ann had something worth living for.

5

FOR CAROLE ANN, THE NEXT TWO WEEKS WERE AN ice-water immersion into the patterns and rhythms of her previous way of life. Not that she'd forgotten how to be a criminal defense lawyer. She couldn't forget that any more than she could forget how to be a Black woman. But she was appalled at how far away from herself she'd stepped once she finally returned. Appalled at how much she didn't know about what had happened to her husband; appalled at how many alarm signals she'd allowed to go unheeded. Why hadn't she been more alarmed about the nature of Larry Devereaux's visits? Why hadn't she wondered at the lack of a follow-up visit from the police? Why hadn't she wondered about the location and disposition of Al's personal belongings? Why hadn't she wondered about the evidence at the crime scene? Why hadn't she wondered about the existence of suspects? And Goddammit! Why hadn't she understood the meaning of the flashing red lights on the alarm system keypad! So clearly did the meaning present itself to her in the present instant that she actually caught and held her breath.

She suddenly and clearly remembered Al explaining a salient feature of the then-new alarm system. It was, he'd proudly proclaimed, one of the most advanced on the market—and one of the simplest to operate. The system "understood" that human operators made errors. So, Al had said, it was OK if she forgot her code. She could, in fact, forget it three times. The system would simply flash a second red light, indicating the error. Then the entry of the correct code three consecutive times would cancel the error. However, a fourth incorrect attempt would activate the alarm—the system "thinking" illegal activity was in progress, and the security company automatically notifying the police.

How could she have been so unaware, so unconscious? Grief was one thing; stupidity was another, and she'd behaved stupidly.

She asked Tommy to arrange for her to meet with Homicide Detective Jacob Graham. He refused to meet her face to face, though he did agree to a telephone conversation, during which he told her everything he recalled about his investigation into Alain Langston Crandall's murder, including the fact that in his expert opinion, "Mr. Crandall was not the victim of a random street crime." She called him on the private line—in homage to Tommy's admitted paranoia—and recorded the conversation, with Graham's griping, grudging permission. Then, armed with Graham's information, she paid a visit to Park Police headquarters, where she received a polite but chilly dismissal and the recommendation that she wait for the investigating officer to contact her. She paid two visits to Pierre's, where Al had dined that night: once for lunch and once for dinner, with Tommy and Valerie.

"You're buying, right?" Tommy had asked quickly when she'd invited them. In the interim, she'd visited the crime scene twice as well. Again, once during the day and once at night, at the time of Al's murder. She made a third trip the night of dinner with Tommy and Valerie, the

three of them walking the route Graham speculated Al
had taken. The following day she returned to Park Police
headquarters, determined to see an investigator. She
waited for three hours, after which time she was informed
that her status as the wife of a victim did not entitle her to
investigative officers or their reports, whether or not she
was a lawyer.

Furious, exhausted, humiliated, and more powerless
than she'd ever been in her life, Carole Ann walked home
via the route Al would have walked the last night of his
life and was in tears when she arrived. For some reason,
that night, the victim was not the victim but her husband.
She envisioned her lanky, lean, wonderful man hurting
and bleeding and, life slipping away, perhaps calling for
her. And she'd been asleep on the couch. She drank an
entire bottle of chardonnay and cried herself to sleep that
night. The following day, a Saturday, she spent convert-
ing the den/office into an office/office.

With silent apologies to Al, she moved the television,
the VCR, and the private line telephone and answering
machine into the bedroom. She left the couch, but moved
it to the other side of the room, to the wall adjacent to the
desk. She brought the two file cabinets out of the closet
and placed them where the sofa had been. Then she
cleaned out the drawers, forcing herself to take the time
to sift through the contents. Most of what the drawers
contained could be disposed of, she concluded. Dave and
Mitch had already taken with them the relevant financial
and business documents.

Next she retrieved the laptop from the desk drawer and
plugged in the cables. "There's a printer and a fax
machine around here somewhere," she muttered to herself as she searched the closet. Sure enough, neatly boxed
on the top shelf, she found them. She hauled in the stool
from the kitchen, remembering the day she and Al had

decided they spent enough time at their respective offices, and they didn't want to work at home or have home resemble work. The small computer was a convenience for Al—he didn't care to have his personal finances and other information on his office computer. Work was work. Personal was personal. And never the twain did meet. She unboxed the fax machine and printer and placed one on top of each of the file cabinets. Then she realized she'd have to return the couch to its original position on the back wall, beneath the window, so the fax machine and printer could be nearer to the desk, which was a built-in. She was sweating by the time all was arranged to her satisfaction, but the fax was connected to the telephone line and the printer was connected to the computer and Carole Ann was ready for work.

This was her new office. She tried on the feeling and was surprised to find it more intimidating than she'd expected. When she quit her job, she'd expected she and Al would, together, do . . . something. Whatever it was, it wouldn't involve the practice of law. And whatever it was, she wouldn't be doing it alone. "What a difference a day makes," she hummed to herself, then laughed, imagining Al saying to her, "Don't quit your day job." Well, she had quit her day job. And now she had it back. After a fashion. She had no assistance, no support, and no backup. She also had no rules and regulations to follow, no executive committee to answer to, no quota of billable hours to maintain. She also had no client. Unless she herself was her own client. She let that notion roll around inside for a while, feeling the vibrations. It was not a comfortable feeling. Not a correct feeling. But she needed a client to work a case. Who was her client? Of course. Al. She was working for him. She would find out for him what had happened and why . . . unless, of course, he already knew.

* * *

TOMMY'S fingers flew over the computer keyboard with the gentle but certain agility and authority of a concert pianist. Carole Ann watched, amazed that the large, square digits consistently found their mark on the compact space of the keyboard, impressed with his obviously extensive knowledge of computer software programs. Why hadn't she known that he was, in common parlance, a hacker?

"You never asked me," he retorted, his eyes never leaving the screen, his fingers never slowing their rhythmic tap-tap-tapping. Tommy was trying to unlock Al's secret file. There was a way to do it, he said. There was always a way to access a file. It just required time and patience. And the proper motivation. And Tommy was motivated by the fact that the locked file could contain clues to the mystery of Al's murder. They tried all the obvious keys: the names of family members and closest friends; Al's fraternity; her sorority; their birthdates and the date of their marriage; the time and place of their births. Then Tommy tried breaking and entering—the questionable if not outright illegal methods. Then he tried the patently illegal stuff. He got close a couple of times, close enough to call a technical support service number once and, lying through his teeth, extract enough information that he should have been able to unlock the file.

"This is really giving me a pain in my ass," he muttered to himself, and Carole Ann giggled in spite of herself. Then she stopped because she felt him stiffen, felt his energy shift. He was tapping in a series of apparently repetitive commands and responses. He'd moved to the edge of the chair, his eyes boring into the tiny computer screen. "Gotcha, you son of a bitch!" he exclaimed as the file opened on the screen.

Carole Ann leaned in closer and, peering over his shoulder at the screen, she read the words *Louisiana Contacts,* and below, a series of names, addresses, and telephone numbers. She read through rapidly, looking for something familiar. There was nothing. Were any of these, she wondered, people who had disappeared after contact with Al? She read the names again, more slowly. Still no hint of recognition.

Tommy scrolled down the screen and pointed to an entry at midpage. "What's that mean?" he asked, pointing to a paragraph that contained a mishmash of what appeared to be aeronautical terms, Spanish, French, and what Carole Ann would have sworn was pig latin.

"I have no idea, Tommy. How much is there?" she asked, and he scrolled down further. Beneath the mishmash paragraph was a description of what Al labeled "a swamp village" and of an elderly woman he called "the conjure woman" with a notation to himself not to attempt again to speak with her without "the proper introduction." Then, in parentheses, he'd typed: *But WHO??* Beneath that, there was another paragraph describing the smell that hung over an entire town, which emanated from the Chicken Shit River. Carole Ann read the sentence again, to make sure she'd read it correctly. "Chicken Shit River? Can that be a real name?"

"From what I hear about Louisiana, anything can be real. Or unreal, if you get my meaning."

But Carole Ann wasn't listening to Tommy. She was reading the next paragraph, a description of people— apparently a family—half of whom were white and half of whom were Black and nobody knew who was what but the family members themselves because they all looked white. There were tales, Al had written, about several of these family members—all from the Black side—who'd escaped the swamp and gone to the city to be educated and who'd never returned. One of them—a girl—had been gang-raped when her true identity was discovered on the all-white campus where she'd been elected homecoming queen. She'd lost her mind and had been committed to a mental institution somewhere near New Orleans. Another was a big shot somewhere, still alive and well and passing for white.

Carole Ann felt a chill run through her. What in the name of God could any of this have to do with Al, with the case he'd been working on, with his murder? The feeling of disquiet settled over her like a shroud. Who were these people? She looked at the screen again, searching for a name. "Is that all of it, Tommy?"

He scrolled down further, to the next page, which was, in its entirety, descriptions of toxic waste dumps and dead and dying bodies of water; descriptions of shriveled, diseased people; descriptions of towns and factories no longer in existence. *What could be worse than this,* Al had written at the bottom of the page. *What could be more than dead?*

"What could be more than dead," Carole Ann whispered, still covered by the shroud of disquiet that had not lifted. "What was Al doing?"

"This has a bad smell to it, C.A.," Tommy muttered, "and I'm not just talking about swamp water. You want me to lock this file back up?"

She nodded at him. "But can you make it easier to access next time? I'll never be able to do what you did."

"No problem," he said, fingers flying once again across the keys. "OK. Now type in a password. Nothing too simple, though."

Carole Ann typed in a word and Tommy closed the file. "Don't forget your word, OK?" Tommy said.

"If I forget, you'll remember," Carole Ann said.

"No, I won't," he said, alarmed. "I wasn't watching what you typed in. My eyes were closed."

"Oh God, Fish," she groaned. "Nobody's as honest as that."

"Just don't you forget that word," he commanded, standing and stretching. "You need to get yourself on-line," he added, an afterthought.

"Don't trust it," Carole Ann replied.

"That's silly," Tommy scoffed. "It's perfectly safe. Millions log on every day—"

"And every day some software company invents a new program to thwart unauthorized access paths invented by the genius who believes, as does a certain unnamed police officer, that there's always a way to access a file." She mimicked him with these last words and he had the good sense to blush.

"There's a lot of useful stuff on-line," he argued.

"I know," she agreed. "I just don't want to expose what's important to me to prying eyes. Besides, I like paper. Anybody wants to send me a message can send a fax. And if I need some on-line information, I'll go to the library."

"Suppose you need it at three in the morning?"

She shot him a look. "Then I'll call you and ask you to look it up for me."

"Then Valerie won't think you're so walk-on-water wonderful if you wake her up at that time of the morning." He was still grinning when she pounced.

"Oho and aha! Our living arrangements have changed, have they? In a domestic partnership, are we?" She laughed at his blushing discomfort and was preparing to really lay it on when the phone rang. "Carole Ann Gibson," she said into the instrument, then frowned when there was no response. "Hello?" Still no response, and then she was listening to a dial tone. She stared at the instrument buzzing in her hand, acutely conscious of each of the emotions that swept through her, the most salient being fear that someone was checking to determine whether or not she was home, followed by helpless rage that quickly turned into pure rage. She cursed and slammed the phone down.

"What?" Tommy asked, eyes narrowed, shoulders squared, hands balled into fists at his sides.

"Phantom of the penthouse," she snarled in response.

"You had many of those?" Tommy asked, a frown creasing his brow.

"Yeah, and it's starting to bug me." Carole Ann frowned, recalling at least three other such calls, though she didn't recall the exact dates. Just that there'd been occasions recently when she'd answered the phone and, after a pause, had found herself listening to a dial tone.

"I don't like this shit at all," Tommy muttered, clenching and unclenching his fists. "You know this is different from what you're used to," he said, sounding like a Jake Graham clone.

"And what am I used to?" she asked dryly.

"Chilled-out crooks," he replied, equally dryly. He then explained that she encountered her "bad guys" after they'd been arrested and charged. "They know they're not on their own turf where they can be bad-asses. They know they have to chill out for you. But these dudes we're dealing with now? They can be as bad as they want to. Who's gonna stop 'em? We don't even know who they are."

Carole Ann studied him closely. She had thought she knew him, knew how his mind functioned. A new and different facet of Tommy Griffin was on display, and it was a revealing performance. Not only was he a real cop, she saw, but he had a real feel for the mean and ugly side of crime and criminals. This was no kid playing cops and robbers. She accepted the accuracy of his assessment of her criminal contact. "Point made, point taken," she said.

Her husband had been murdered. Someone had tried to break into her home. And who the hell had let a stranger up to the penthouse anyway? Where was the doorman when somebody was playing with the code on her keypad?! Perhaps her telephone was tapped and perhaps she was being followed. For the first time she felt real fear.

6

JAKE GRAHAM OPENED THE DOOR TO HER AND THEN turned his back on her, rolling himself through the immaculate living and dining rooms and toward what appeared to be a screened-in porch. Carole Ann closed the front door and followed him, assuming that his leaving the door open was an invitation to enter. She had begged—almost forced—him to see her, so she couldn't, in reality, expect a gracious welcome. When she reached the porch he was already in his place—in the corner nearest the table where the remote controls to the television and VCR and stereo system sat, near the water cooler, near the telephone—and locking the wheels into place. He turned hostile eyes on her.

"What do you want?"

"Somebody tried to break into my apartment—" she began, but he cut her off with a snarl.

"You already told me that. What else do you want?"

"I want to ask you some questions—"

"I already answered 'em," he cut her off again.

"I want to pick your brain," she returned quickly, accurately predicting his response: his eyes narrowed and in them she saw just a hint of interest.

"And what is it you lookin' to find in my brain?"

"Answers, perhaps. More than likely, more questions," she said with a casual shrug; too casual, because she saw that he caught on.

"Give me one good reason I oughta tell you anything," he hissed at her.

"Because you can't help it," she hissed back, meeting and holding his hostile glare. And she knew she was right. Good homicide detectives were puzzle addicts. The satisfaction, for them, was in putting the pieces together. If a crime got solved and a perp brought to justice, fine. But it was the gathering and sifting and assessing of those little bits and pieces of nothing that became evidence that satiated the good homicide detective. And Jacob Graham was reputed to be the best the Metropolitan Police Department had to offer.

He was a wiry little man—if he could have stood, he'd have been about five-eight, shorter than she by an inch—a fact she hadn't remembered from their last encounter. He was dark brown with sparse hair and a skinny mustache, and she guessed him to be in his late forties, perhaps early fifties. He was not exactly handsome, but he had wonderfully expressive eyes, and a very sensous mouth beneath the sinister little mustache. The mouth twitched and the eyes narrowed again, but he did not speak. And she didn't push him to do so. She knew he understood now just how threatened and frightened by the break-in attempt she was. She knew he also knew she wanted information about Al's murder . . . if it *was* murder. So she sat and waited for him to decide what he would do. What he did was flip off the wheelchair locks and propel himself past her and into the dining room.

She sat there for a long moment, actually enjoying the view from the porch. The backyard was as immaculately groomed as the interior of the house, with every imaginable color of flower in full bloom. Carole Ann couldn't identify by name anything but roses and sunflowers and, from her native Los Angeles, birds-of-paradise, none of which blossomed in Detective Graham's backyard. She wondered briefly if the yard and garden had been his pleasure or were his wife's. Then she realized her pleasure in the yard was due to her proximity to it. Her own home was twelve stories in the air, so when she sat on her balcony, her eye-level pleasure was sky. She found she very much liked sitting on a porch and looking at grass and flowers. Bright, green grass and purple, yellow, red, orange, white flowers. But it wasn't her porch and they weren't her flowers and she was an intruder in the home of the man to whom these pleasures belonged. A man who didn't want her here, perhaps because he blamed her for his predicament. She stood quickly and retraced her steps to the front door. Her hand was on the knob when she heard Jake Graham's voice.

"Where·the hell you goin'?" His rough growl challenged her to turn and face him. He gestured with his head to follow him back to the porch. Which she did, reclaiming her place on the wicker couch as he reclaimed his in the corner.

Carole Ann watched a long, lean black and white cat skulk across the yard and smiled as she imagined Patch enjoying such a playground. Then she turned to face Graham. Before she could speak he tossed a stuffed manila envelope at her, which she barely caught. Since he hadn't spoken, she didn't either. Instead she opened the envelope. It didn't take long to understand the nature and significance of the contents. She still didn't speak, but asked her question with a lift of her eyebrows.

"You like cats?" he asked instead of replying.

"Love 'em," she answered, giving him the freedom to take his time.

"That one's the Duke of Earl. I'll have to shoot his ass in about fifteen seconds." Then he laughed out loud at the look on her face. Real, mirthful laughter that transformed his face and made him a handsome man. Still laughing, he reached into the corner beside him and extracted what appeared to be an AK-47. Carole Ann willed herself not to flinch. "The Cadillac of water weapons," he said proudly, raising the thing and aiming it. She looked where it was pointed and saw the Duke of Earl hunched and, butt twitching, ready to spring. She raised her sights and immediately spied some kind of little bird chirping happily on the branch of some kind of flowering shrub. The oldest game in nature about to be played out. Except that Detective Jacob Graham was set to save the victim before it became the victim. He punched the trigger and a forceful stream of water exploded from the gun, nailing the Duke right on his twitching butt. He disappeared into the shrubbery with a howl of anger and indignation, and Carole Ann laughed with Graham. The bird kept chirping, oblivious to the human interference with natural law.

"I made a backup file," Graham said, returning the too-real-looking water weapon to its position on the floor. "What you have is exactly what was turned over to my esteemed colleagues at the United States Park Police," he said with a sneer. "Along with some stuff they don't have," he added with his crooked grin.

Carole Ann held the envelope in her hands, not trusting herself to speak; again, she embraced silence. Part of her knew it was the correct behavior for Graham, though, in truth, had she known what to say, she would have said something. But Graham liked it that she didn't speak. So they watched the yard for a few moments. The birds and squirrels and wasps and the vegetation—and a sneaky flash of black and white. Until, finally, Carole Ann felt ready.

"What prompted you to make this file, Detective?"

"Instinct, Miss Gibson. My turn," he said quickly. "What's prompting you to make your own investigation?"

"I'm angry," Carole Ann said flatly.

"Can you work from the other side?" His question was genuine. She felt no hostility from him, so she was unprepared when he continued. "I mean, you earn big bucks workin' for the bad guys. Hell, if it wasn't your husband in the dirt, you'd probably be tryin' to save this perp's ass. Am I right?"

She felt like the Duke of Earl must have: blindsided. Except the blow was to her gut, delivered by a weight much heavier than water. She literally had no breath with which to speak. "No, Detective," she finally managed. "You are not right." And she explained to him the error of his ways. And it was his turn to sit in silence. He stroked and squeezed his thighs, as if the motion could return life to them. Then he balled up his fists and pounded them. Five times. Then he looked at her.

"Then get even, Miss Gibson."

"Excuse me?" she said.

"Don't get mad, lady. Get even."

FOR three days and half the nights of those days, Carole Ann reviewed Jake Graham's secret file. Read and re-read every word, searched and understood every space between every line, plumbed the depths of every nuance. She made notes, walking and talking herself through the information so she was as familiar with it as if it were her own creation. She made maps and diagrams and peopled them with stick figures whom she moved up and down sidewalks and alleys. She made time and distance charts and graphs by hand and on the computer. She concluded her husband had, indeed, been murdered. But after that point, he was not her husband. He was the victim. He was her client.

According to Graham's reconstruction of events on the night of April 18, Al Crandall had dinner at Le Bistro Pierre on Pennsylvania Avenue between Nineteenth and Twentieth streets, with five other men: Larry Devereaux and Charles Majeskiew from his law firm, and three clients whom Devereaux and Majeskiew both refused to name, citing privilege. (*Bullshit!* Graham had written in the margin, followed by *Put the screws to these guys.*) According to Philipe Marcuse, Pierre's maitre d', the six men had arrived almost simultaneously at eight o'clock, Majeskiew and the three unidentified men perhaps two minutes before Devereaux and Crandall. Graham speculated—and confirmed—they'd taken taxis: Devereaux and Crandall riding together, Majeskiew and the three clients together. The men had been seated immediately at a corner banquette in the second dining room, which Carole Ann knew to be the more exclusive and private of the restaurant's three dining rooms.

Albert, the table's waiter, reported that none of the men had overindulged in alcohol (five of the six had one predinner highball each, and all six had wine with dinner), and that none had overindulged in food (three Maryland crabcake entrees, two roasted chicken entrees, and one blackened swordfish entree, salad and green beans all around). All six men had coffee after dinner, and three of them had dessert: two kiwi tortes and one flan. There was not much talk, Albert observed, for a party of six businessmen. It was the waiter's experience that apparently successful professional men at the end of the business day were gregarious, if not, as was often the case, loud and obnoxious, even in as haute an establishment as Pierre's.

According to Albert, Larry Devereaux had done most of the talking and "the Black man" had done most of the listening, though when he talked, all of the men paid close attention. One of the men, said Albert, became angry at one point, and it was he (identified by Graham as Majeskiew) who left first. The remaining five men talked until shortly after ten o'clock, when Larry Devereaux paid the almost three-hundred-dollar bill with a company credit card (copy attached to report).

After being pressed, and pressed hard, by Graham, Albert offered that he'd heard the words "Parish Petroleum" numerous times—in fact, every time he approached the table; and, he said, one of the unidentified men spoke to him in French. Not good French, Albert said; not real French. But understandable French, as if he'd learned it somewhere other than France. (*Like Louisiana?* Graham had written in one of his many marginal notes.) The five men left the table together, Albert said, and he assumed they left the restaurant at that time.

Maitre d' Marcuse confirmed that assumption: the five men walked out onto Pennsylvania Avenue, which was crowed with joggers, strollers, outdoor café patrons, window-shoppers, ice-cream eaters, and whoever else found enjoyment on that prestigious avenue at twenty minutes after ten on a soft spring night. The men stood together and talked for several moments, Marcuse said, then Mr. Crandall walked away quickly, as if angry. Walked west on Pennsylvania Avenue, toward George Washington University. Toward home. The other four men stood talking for a moment, and then one of the unidentified men ran to catch up with Mr. Crandall. They spoke together for several moments, and then that gentleman rejoined the others. Marcuse did not observe Mr. Crandall further, but assumed he continued to walk west on Pennsylvania. Mr. Devereaux stepped out into the avenue, directly in front of the restaurant, and tried to hail a taxi. He did not succeed immediately, and Marcuse was required to return his attention to his business inside the restaurant, as parties for the post-theatre supper would soon begin arriving.

According to Graham's records, there existed no proof that Devereaux and the other three men actually got into a taxi in front of Pierre's at approximately ten-thirty on the night of April 18 and returned to Devereaux's office, as Devereaux claimed. There was proof that Charles Majeskiew had returned to his office approximately one hour earlier: the security guard, three members of the cleaning crew, and two associates remembered him and would swear to it. None of those people remembered Devereaux and the unnamed Parish Petroleum clients returning, even though the security guard said they could have entered through the garage, bypassing the lobby security checkpoint. By that time, the cleaning people were working on another floor and the associates had all gone home.

At approximately that same time, Esteban Colon, a dishwasher at the Espirit de Mexico restaurant on Twenty-second Street, Northwest, was taking a cigarette and beer break in the alley behind his place of employment. The alley ran east-west between Pennsylvania Avenue and H Street, providing a brief view of both. Colon was sitting atop a large garbage Dumpster at the intersection of the alley and H Street, appreciating the rare lull in the restaurant's patronage that had permitted his moment of freedom. Then he heard running feet, followed by shouts. A tall Black man wearing a suit ran past the alley entrance, followed a few seconds later by two almost-as-tall white men. Yes, Mr. Colon was certain he saw what he said he saw. He noted it because usually it was the Black men who chased the white men. And he noted it because the Black man ran so well—quickly and easily despite the fact that he was carrying a briefcase. No, Mr. Colon did not understand the shouted words because he neither spoke nor understood English. (Colon, interviewed by Graham through an MPD interpreter, had since disappeared. Neither his employer nor his roominghouse landlady had seen him since the middle of May, when Graham turned his files over to the Feds.)

Al Crandall was found facedown in an alley behind H Street, between Twenty-third and Twenty-fourth streets—four blocks in the opposite direction than Colon saw him running. An anonymous caller reported the body. (Graham had scrawled, *BULLSHIT!*) His shoes were scuffed on both heel and toe, as if he'd been dragged. His suit trousers and jacket were ripped and quite dirty—again, consistent with dragging. There were contusions and abrasions on his face and hands, and on his knees and shins. He'd been shot once in the right upper back, from a distance, and once in the chest, at close range. The bullet to the chest punctured the aorta, thus resulting in death. Subject's wallet and jewelry were missing. Subject's briefcase was found three feet from the body, open, and the contents—a newspaper, a black leather appointment book, an electronic calculator, two white cotton handkerchiefs, a silk tie, and thirty-seven pages of legal documents—scattered nearby. (*Ask wife what's missing?* Graham had written.)

None of the detective's handwritten marginal notes were included in the file now in the possession of the U.S. Park Police. Also not included was the testimony Jake Graham had from two eyewitnesses to the murder. Not the reliable kind of witnesses, the kind you can put on the stand, ask to take an oath, and trust that the sworn testimony will be accepted and believed by all who hear. Not that kind. But one just as good to the street cop: the kind of witnesses who, indeed, saw what they say they saw and, for the right price, will tell the right person what they saw. Jake Graham had paid the price and received this information: Al Crandall had indeed run through the alley behind the Espirit de Mexico; had indeed outrun his pursuer, just like Esteban Colon said, exiting the alley on Twenty-second Street. He ran north, his pursuer a full block behind him. Heavy traffic and a red light forced him to stop at the corner of Twenty-third and H. Suddenly a taxi screeched to a halt and as two men jumped out, Crandall began running west on H Street, pursued by the two men. He was running slower by now, and the two men were closing in. Crandall jumped the low fence and entered Lafayette Park. He turned and threw his briefcase behind him, catching one of the men squarely in the face. The man yelled, cursed, and quit the chase. The other man sped up, took a gun from his pocket, and fired once. Crandall fell. Graham's first witness, a homeless man who'd been lying in the grass in the park, gently and quietly rolled himself over and over until he was hidden in the dense shrubbery and flower beds.

The second eyewitness, a Pennsylvania Avenue hustler, viewed the chase and murder from a different vantage point: He was standing up. He'd been engaged in the sale of a laptop computer he'd stolen from a briefcase on the subway earlier that evening. The hustler and a George Washington University student were in the alley beside a caterer's delivery van when Al Crandall and his pursuer dashed through the alley. The student snatched the laptop, dropped the cash, and ran the other way. The hustler grabbed his money and followed the chase. He saw everything, including the people who ducked into doorways to avoid what obviously was a threatening situation. The hustler ceased his pursuit at the entrance to Lafayette

Park. He had no desire to attract the attention of the Park Police, to whom he was well known.

Those were the broad facts. Carole Ann accepted them as such. Combined with Al's description of the Parish Petroleum officials he'd deposed, she concluded they were, at the very least, knowledgeable about the circumstances of Al's murder, if not directly responsible for it. She didn't know who those men were. But Larry Devereaux thought she did. That's why he'd come to visit after Al's murder. Not to console or sympathize or commiserate, but to ascertain how much she knew. She remembered his questions and now understood their intent. Could she reopen that door now? Could she throw a line to Larry Devereaux and reel in her husband's killer?

TOMMY opined she was trying to commit suicide. Jake Graham said it couldn't happen to a more deserving idiot. Neither of them could believe she'd consider an open confrontation with Devereaux, and both strongly advised against it.

"One of his buddies killed your husband, lady. You stay the hell away from the scummy bastard," was Graham's response.

"You're the one who told me to get even," she snarled at him. "I can't very well accomplish that sitting at home baking cookies and darning socks." She snapped her mouth shut around the words and ground her teeth to keep the anger trapped within. He must have realized the depth of her anger because he glared at her but didn't offer a retort.

"And what makes you think he'd tell you those dudes' names, anyway, when he wouldn't tell the police?" Tommy asked, using a tone of voice the condescending reserved for the mentally challenged.

"He's the logical place to start," Carole Ann replied defensively, beginning to regret the lunch date with Tommy and Jake. She wanted more of Mrs. Chang's food for hope and she didn't want it ruined by their carping criticisms. "And because of this," she said, withdrawing from her purse a tape recorder and the answering machine cassette containing Al's final message. She performed the requisite technical tasks and watched them while they listened.

"Not exactly a smoking gun," Jake drawled, looking with interest at the cart Mrs. Chang had just rolled to their table and ignoring Carole Ann.

"Are you saying this gives us nothing?" Carole Ann did not attempt to conceal or control the anger rising within her.

Jake met and held her glare. "What does it give you?"

"The belief that Larry Devereaux has done something worth going to jail for."

"Hell," Jake said with a snort, "most every lawyer in this town has done something worth going to jail for."

Carole Ann looked at him evilly from beneath her eyelids. "Do you really believe that, or are you just solidifying your hard-earned reputation as the granddaddy of hard-asses?"

Graham rewarded her with the laugh that transformed his face into a thing of beauty. Even Mrs. Chang seemed impressed. She bestowed upon him a rare smile, and with a bow for the table, she departed, rolling her now-empty cart before her. Graham looked at his food, then at Carole Ann. "I think Devereaux is dirty, too. And I also think, Miss Gibson, that if there is such a thing as an honest lawyer, maybe you're it."

"Don't patronize me, Graham," she sighed wearily. "And you'd do well to remember all that good advice I'm sure your mother passed on to you. If you had a mother.

Like, it ain't cool for the pot to cast aspersions on the kettle. Or for people who live in glass houses to throw stones."

"I had—still have—a mother. So, what the hell are you talking about?" Graham challenged while chewing and not apologizing for the rudeness.

"You, a D.C. cop, have the nerve to point the crooked finger at my profession? And you should have known my husband."

"Touché, Miss Gibson. And you're right about another thing: this is the best Chinese food in the world. And I've eaten Chinese food in China. And I wish I'd known your husband."

They ate in silence, the three of them, for a long while, speaking only to request water or condiments or to comment on the pleasure being given by the meal. It was Tommy who broke the silence.

"These people really are mean and dangerous, C.A."

"Yes," Carole Ann agreed.

"So, what are you going to do?" Tommy asked.

Carole Ann looked at him hard. She knew he thought she was contemplating an answer. In truth, she was deciding whether to tell him her answer. She decided to tell them both. "I think a change of venue is in order," she said calmly.

"What's that mean?" Tommy asked.

"It means I'm leaving town for a while," she answered.

"Good idea." Graham almost smiled. "Where you goin'?"

"To Louisiana," Carole Ann responded. Watching his face change, she listened with true appreciation as the veteran homicide detective cursed for a solid minute with a proficiency she'd only heard stories about. Then she listened for another hour and received from the two of them lessons in criminal behavior and psychology no classroom or textbook or courtroom could ever approximate. *Cut and color your hair. Change your walk. Change your style of dress. Assume you're being followed. Don't talk to strangers unless you're asking the questions. A stranger is anybody you don't trust. Don't trust anybody.* Prior to Jake and Tommy's seminar, Carole Ann had believed herself to be an astute observer of the criminal mind. She came to understand how little she knew, and was shaken by the experience.

"You're asking me—telling me—to alter my thinking, my behavior, my very approach to life and living," Carole Ann said.

"Damn straight," Graham replied solemnly. "You're out there on your own now, lady, so you better be prepared."

"And that means behaving like a criminal?" Carole Ann asked defensively.

"No, dammit! It means thinking like one! How many times do I have to tell you that?" Graham was not a patient man even on a good day. Explaining the nature of the criminal to a criminal lawyer was not his idea of a good time.

"All it means, C.A., is that you gotta out-think 'em," Tommy offered in a conciliatory tone. "You gotta be prepared for whatever might happen. After all, you're going to be in unfamiliar territory without backup. Just like Jake said. So you gotta protect yourself on the front end."

So Carole Ann prepared herself according to their advice and instructions, as well as accepting their one imposed condition: That she not ask the why of anything. That she merely follow their advice, and then, later, think about it and learn the whys for herself. First she purchased a new wardrobe of "regular people's clothes." Jake Graham was of the opinion that her notion of casual clothes would not only be offensive to the folks who lived in the vicinity of the Chicken Shit River, but that they would call attention—and loudly—to her presence, which already would be noticed because she was an outsider. She purchased two money belts and loaded them with cash. And she purchased two round-trip plane tickets, placing one return ticket in each of the money belts. She had her hair cut shorter than it had been since her Peace Corps days, and lightened: altering one's appearance is the first step into the criminal psyche. She bought a cellular phone—the smallest and most expensive on the market—and rid herself of her aversion to the thing by using it until it felt natural, by which time she was certain she had a phone bill the size of the national debt. She ceased the habit of weekly manicures and pedicures and waxing and massages and all the other trappings of prestige and privilege—the habits and behaviors that make one noticeable and memorable to others.

By the time Carole Ann was ready to depart for Louisiana, she didn't feel like the self whose husband had been murdered three months earlier. That event felt like the memory of a nightmare: terrifying but not necessarily real. The part of that event that remained real to her was the knowledge that someone close to Al Crandall was his murderer, and that knowledge angered her, and that anger smoldered within her, was the fuel that drove her. The murderer was in Louisiana, and she was on her way to find him.

7

JAKE'S FINAL PIECE OF ADVICE TO HER WAS THAT SHE
fly into Atlanta, buy a secondhand car, and drive to
Louisiana. Tommy, by now so in awe of the veteran detective he was occasionally taking notes, pulled up short at
this one and actually disagreed. Carole Ann was impressed
by his temerity, but put off by his reasoning, which was
that if something happened to her—if she disappeared, for
instance—they would need to be able to prove she'd been
in Louisiana in the first place. Jake's reasoning was that if
nobody knew she was in Louisiana, she might be able to
ferret out some useful information. By keeping a low profile and blending into the scenery, Jake thought she might
be able to see and hear enough to develop some leads. A
serviceable and interesting but not ostentatious car with
Georgia license plates would permit that much more effec-
tively than would a shiny, new rental car, he argued. There
was nothing unusual in somebody from Louisiana having a
relative or friend visiting from Georgia. Carole Ann found
she agreed. Tommy held firm to his position.

In Atlanta, Carole Ann bought a six-year-old Chrysler
LeBaron convertible, white with red interior. Actually,
Dave bought it for her with her money, and he had to be

bullied into it. He was adamantly opposed to her going to Louisiana for anything, and most certainly to dig around in the muck and mire that was whatever Parish Petroleum was. Their argument was so acrimonious that when Carole Ann left, they were not on speaking terms. Before he stopped talking to her, however, he gave her the name of a legal services lawyer in New Orleans who also taught at Xavier University, a man whom he knew only slightly but respected greatly. Warren Forchette was his name and he was, according to Dave, well connected in Louisiana legal and political circles.

Almost five hundred miles separated Atlanta and New Orleans. Five hundred of the most beautiful miles Carole Ann had ever seen. She could have made the trip in one day of sustained driving, but she was fascinated by the gentle, rolling hills that were nothing like the craggy, wild mountains she was familiar with in the West. And all of it feeling so close and immediate. She was accustomed to the vastness of California, of Arizona, of New Mexico—places that extended into forever. If she drove all day in California or New Mexico or Montana, she'd still be in California or New Mexico or Montana. If she drove all day here, she'd traverse four states. Just like driving from D.C. to New York: four hours and five states.

She took Interstate 85 south out of Atlanta and into Alabama, toward Montgomery, then began meandering and wandering and alternating between the swift-moving, congested interstate and the snail's-pace two-lane blacktops that crisscrossed Georgia and Alabama and Mississippi, leading, eventually, to Louisiana. On previous trips to Atlanta and New Orleans, Carole Ann had arrived at airports and seen only what there was to see between airports and downtown hotels. On this journey, she saw how the South looked to a Southerner. And felt it, too, because she was hotter than she'd ever been in her life. And that included summers growing up in Los Angeles and three years of Peace Corps field duty in West Africa. And the more she felt it, the closer this heat felt to the African heat than to the California heat.

Georgia and Alabama and Mississippi and Louisiana were hot in the way that the Caribbean Islands are hot: endlessly and inexorably. Carole Ann understood instinctively it was not the kind of heat that could be dealt with intellectually, with some kind of mind-over-matter approach. This heat had to be accepted on its own terms. So she turned off the air conditioner and let down the top and welcomed it. The hot breath of the blowing wind alternately burned and caressed, and she knew that by the end of the day, she'd be toasted carob bronze. She looked forward to the feeling . . . and to the sight of herself browner than she'd been in years. With her new haircut, she'd barely resemble the old Carole Ann Gibson.

At about four-thirty she angled back to Interstate 65 in search of a motel with a pool, preferably located on a thriving commercial strip where she could also find a gas station, a car wash, a grocery store, and a family-style restaurant—her best bet for a decent meal on the road. Prior to her marriage to Al, she'd been an incorrigible roadrunner, and it was only his distaste for automobiles that had curbed her indulgence. She hadn't realized how much she missed the open road.

Carole Ann exited I-65 at a place called Bay Minette, not more than thirty miles from Mobile and the Parish of Mexico, after following a series of billboard advertisements for a Roadway Inn and a Western Sizzler Steakhouse. Sunset would not occur for at least another four hours, but she was tired, hungry, and anxious to delve into the box of files and documents she'd picked up from Ernestine on her way out of town. A box that had belonged to Al. Al's background research notes on the racism of environmental pollution, was how Ernestine had described it, totally baffling Carole Ann, as well as embarrassing her.

Carole Ann had called Ernestine to ask whether she knew the exact name of the town Al had visited on his last trip to Louisiana back in January. She'd fashioned her question so that if Ernestine asked, she could say truthfully that she wished to visit her husband's last work site, without divulging the deeper truth: that she was going in search of a murderer. But Ernestine had asked no questions. She had merely released a pent-up rush of emotion, the end result of which was that Carole Ann now had a box full of information, some of it Al's hand-written notes, on the war being waged by grassroots citizens' groups nationwide against environmental polluters. And somewhere in that box was part of a name: Eldon Somebody—Ernestine couldn't remember his last name—who was Al's off-the-record contact person. Carole Ann had refused herself permission to contemplate the box or its contents all day, focusing instead on enjoying the scenery and the freedom of the road. She could put it off no longer.

Following her good-habits-of-the-road routine, she first got the car washed—to remove the dead bugs baked into the car's finish by the heat—then checked the oil and filled the tank with gasoline so she'd be prepared for an early departure. She ate a better-than-expected dinner of barbecued chicken, grilled potatoes, and salad at the almost-empty restaurant. She bought a six-pack of beer and a bag of popcorn. Then she checked into the Roadway Inn, where she requested and received a corner room on the top floor overlooking the swimming pool. By six o'clock, when the average driver was just coming off the road, Carole Ann was ensconced in a chaise by the pool, beer in a plastic cup at hand, engrossed in the history of the crusade against environmental racism. And feeling a deep sadness settle over her. For clearly this was an issue of extreme concern to her murdered husband, and she had known nothing of it. Had known nothing of Al's realization that the next great civil rights issue was that the neighborhoods of the poor and people of color were being turned into the toxic waste and garbage dumps of the nation.

In Chicago and St. Louis and Houston and Dallas and Memphis and Nashville and New Orleans—and in tiny towns and villages with names familiar only to the few hundred souls who lived and worked in them—government and private industry conspired to bury and burn and ignore waste products in the parts of town inhabited by Blacks and Hispanics and poor people of all colors. And those people were dying because of it. Al had known this. Could have proven it. Except for one small problem: It had been his job to do just the opposite. To use the law to break the law. It had been his job to protect the polluters. They had paid him a lot of money to protect their right to dispose of industrial by-products and waste in the most expedient and economical ways possible—which often were the ways most devastating to the plant, animal, and human life in the vicinity. The more she read, the angrier she became at the callous and unconscionable disregard for life in the name of profit.

Carole Ann reminded herself she'd promised to follow to the letter the advice given by Jake and Tommy, and one of Jake's favorite admonitions was, "Don't get mad, get even." "Focus on the problem at hand" was a Tommy-ism.

She began shifting and sorting through the stacks of files, keeping out only those relating to Louisiana, returning the others to the box. And then she found the name. Eldon Warmsley. He lived in New Iberia. Al had written down his address and telephone number and the notation to call only between seven and nine in the evening. She didn't know where New Iberia was and the map was in the car. No matter. She was beginning to feel the effects of the sun and the beer and a day that had begun shortly after sunup. She dove into the pool, swam a lazy four laps in bathtub-warm water, collected her belongings, and went to her room.

Despite the temperature, she took a hot shower and then climbed naked into bed, relishing the crisp coolness of the sheets. She fully expected to lie there eating popcorn, drinking beer, and watching cable movies until sleep came. She therefore was caught completely off guard when the sadness she'd felt earlier at the pool overwhelmed her, leaving her feeling alone and cut off, not a part of anything or anyone. No longer comforted by the urgency of her purpose. No longer certain of its rightness. What the hell was she doing looking for a murderer? Murderers came to her. And what would she do with him when she found him? Assuming she found him, for, in truth, she had no reason to believe she could penetrate the mysterious and historical veil of secrecy and silence that was Louisiana. Not even with the help of Warren Forchette and Eldon Warmsley. And there was no guarantee they would help; they didn't even know her. The tears rose up and spilled over before she could stop them. Hot, burning tears she didn't want, didn't need. She choked them back, snatched up the remote control, and aimed it across the room at the television. Images appeared almost instantly, cartoon figures running. She punched the buttons and the images shifted, none capturing her attention. She drifted off to sleep.

The loneliness was still as heavy as the humidity when she awoke the next morning. Unable to shake it, she decided to try and outrun it. She loaded the car, returned her room key to the motel office, where she poured herself a cup of muddy-looking coffee, and got directly on the interstate and didn't slow down until I-65 merged with I-10 just south of Mobile. She was on the Mississippi state line, low-riding I-10 along the Gulf of Mexico, when the thought struck: Stay on I-10 straight through to Los Angeles. Go home. Screw New Orleans and Parish Petroleum and environmental racism and murderers. It would be a straight shot to L.A. and home. That thought sustained her all the way through Pascagoula and Biloxi and Gulfport—wonderfully gothic, peculiarly Southern names. Places she'd have had to see firsthand any other time. Hell, yesterday she'd have had to leave the hustle and bustle of the interstate and take the back roads into these places, ignoring the historical response of Mississippi to people who looked like her.

What did Main Street look like in some place named Pascagoula? And could she find out before she was lynched? Did they still lynch Black people in Mississippi? She knew what they did to Rodney Kings in her hometown, and it didn't get much worse than that. She also knew that untold thousands of Black Louisianans and Mississippians had flocked to California two generations ago seeking . . . something. Her parents' parents had been part of that exodus. So was this, perhaps, a homecoming of sorts, negating the need to follow I-10 to its asphalt conclusion? Because she would go to L.A. and do what—bore her mother silly? And live forever with the knowledge that someone had murdered her husband and she'd done nothing to discover the who or the why?

Such was the state of the traffic on her emotional and mental byways when the green sign overhanging the road read NEW ORLEANS 20 MILES. Carole Ann followed directions from that point on. Those of the road signs directing her to the legendary heart of the Crescent City, the French

Quarter, and those of Jake Graham directing her to the Embassy Suites in the French Quarter. Another of Jake's lessons: As a stranger, seek to blend in during the day. As a stranger, seek the safety of bright lights and crowds at night. "You go to a big-name hotel and act like a big name when you get there," he'd told her. "Wear your fancy New York and L.A. clothes in the hotel at night and when you go out to dinner, and use your gold cards," he'd said. "Act like you're a three-hundred-dollar-an-hour lawyer. That way, hotel security will know to keep a protective eye on you."

Carole Ann's top-floor corner suite delivered exactly what was promised to the business traveler: an office away from home. Ignoring her clothes, she unpacked and plugged in her laptop and stacked her notes and Al's files neatly on the desk. She located Warren Forchette's telephone number and called him, listening to Scott Joplin on the line while she was holding and waiting to be connected, and thinking she liked the New Orleans brand of canned music. When Forchette came on the line, she heard her first authentic Louisiana accent. It was different from the Southern accents with which she was familiar in a way she could not define, but which she recognized as distinct. In a low, easy, warm voice, he directed her to his office, and he had her read back to him those directions, with an apology and the explanation that his office was not located in the most convenient part of town. Any time she arrived would be acceptable, he said. And Carole Ann quickly showered, changed into a comfortable skirt and blouse, applied lipstick as her only makeup, and hurried out of the air-conditioned chill of the room into the early afternoon sauna of New Orleans summer.

ORLEANS Parish Legal Service Center was located in the kind of place that lends itself to stereotypically excessive descriptives. But Carole Ann couldn't help herself. It was in a ghetto. A dark, ugly, filthy, loud ghetto. Where the streets were unpaved. Where the sidewalks were narrow wedges of chipped brick and rock and dirt that would be muddy mire in the rain. Where children ran wild and women sat hunched over on broken chairs drinking and smoking and casting evil glances at life. Where every visible structure listed and leaned so dangerously that Carole Ann could not imagine they provided adequate shelter. Where all the people were Black. And where the heat was a despairing, oppressive presence that felt as if it had been trapped and held in these narrow little streets for a century—somebody's Voudoun curse realized.

Few of the buildings, whether commercial or residential, had numbers, so Carole Ann was creeping along, peering first at the buildings on one side of the rutted street, then across at those on the other, muttering to herself that Warren Forchette must be a master of understatement to consider this location merely inconvenient. And as she scrutinized the neighborhood, a vague pattern began to reveal itself to her: In front of the single-story commercial structures—the tiny grocery and liquor stores, the candle shops, the pool hall, even the churches—crowds of people stood talking, smoking, drinking, listening to music. In front of the two- and three-story residential structures people—usually women—sat, usually alone.

The Orleans Parish Legal Service Center was recognizable because embedded in its grassy front yard was a neatly lettered sign suspended from cast-iron chains attached to a post arm, like a real estate For Sale sign. Carole Ann parked, got out of the car, and took in the full effect of the legal center's presence. The three-story structure had obviously once been a family home like its neighbors. Now, it was painted a pristine white and adorned by shiny black shutters at the windows, from which protruded loudly whining air conditioners on each of the three floors. Severely clipped deep green grass was bordered by the kinds of flowery things Carole Ann remembered seeing in Jake Graham's yard—bright and colorful and plentiful. The walkway was of obviously ancient brick, perfectly spaced and aligned, worn smooth by years and feet. The front yard, like those of its neighbors, was deep, and on the journey to the front door, Carole Ann looked around, taking stock. The houses on either side of the center, perhaps shamed into it, were considerably better cared for than the other houses in the area. Both had been painted in the relatively recent past—one white, like its imposing neighbor, the other pale yellow. The yards of both were planted and reasonably well cared for.

The loud whirring of the air conditioners ceased to be irritating the moment Carole Ann opened the front door and felt the soothing cool of the office. She looked around at an interior that provided an extreme contrast to the outside. In here all was basic functionality. Multicolored metal folding chairs lined the walls of the rectangular waiting room that was the entrance, and bodies occupied each of the two dozen or so chairs. The floor was highly polished but well-worn oak, and bare. The receptionist's desk was heavy, wooden, and old-fashioned, as was the armless swivel chair that held her. She, the telephone, and the computer at which she worked swiftly and efficiently, even as she constantly answered and forwarded calls, were the most modern aspects of the office.

Carole Ann approached the desk and waited for the young woman's attention. Given the incessant ringing of the phone and the speed with which her fingers danced across the keyboard, getting it could take a while. She looked around, beyond what she presumed to be the center's caseload seated quietly and calmly in the hard folding chairs, toward a staircase in the center of a hallway that ran left and right from the stairs. A constant procession of foot-traffic up and down the stairs, back and forth in both directions on the hallway, created the feeling that there should be lots of noise. It was, however, strangely peaceful. Then Carole Ann became aware of the music in the background, a gentle, jazzy sound; and with that recognition, as if her more sensitive side were awakened, she became aware that the walls were a collector's paradise. Virtually every space on the gallery-white walls was home to some treasure: paintings, sketches, photographs, mounted sculptures. Her fascinated scrutiny was cut short by a voice behind her.

"Thank you for your patience, miss. Can I help you?"

Carole Ann turned to face the young receptionist, smiled, gave her name. "I'm here to see Warren Forchette. He's expecting me."

"Yes, ma'am, he is," the young woman responded with polite efficiency, and directed her up the stairs and left, to the end of the hall. Carole Ann's thanks went unheeded as the young woman returned her attention immediately to the computer screen and the ringing phone.

Whatever Carole Ann had expected, Warren Forchette wasn't it. He was about six feet tall and possessed a weight lifter's physique and attire. He wore blue jeans and a navy blue tee shirt with XAVIER UNIVERSITY stenciled in white letters across the front. The shirt was designed to display the massive muscle structure that bulged and rippled beneath it, and the tight, faded jeans suggested an equally impressive lower body development. He was completely bald, and wore rimless wire spectacles, the silver of which glinted against his dark

brown skin. He stood and extended his hand when Carole
Ann entered, but remained behind his desk and offered
her a choice of seats—the armchair adjacent to his desk,
or the sofa against the wall. His voice was as warm and
gentle as on the telephone, but there was no warmth or
gentleness in his eyes or in his manner. He was polite but
not gracious, accommodating but not effusive. He
seemed a reflection of the center itself. More likely, the
center was his reflection: a pleasing and impressive exterior; a coolly functional interior.

Carole Ann took the chair nearest the desk. "Is the
crowd in your reception area par for the course?" she
asked without preamble, guessing, correctly she noted,
that he was not the kind of man who appreciated ceremo-
nial chatter.

"Day in and day out. Though not all of them are
clients. About half are witnesses, and as you might imagine, they are not at ease with the workings of the criminal
justice system. We prep them for trial here."

"Then you must be very well respected in this community, Mr. Forchette," Carole Ann observed with true
admiration.

He leaned back in his desk chair and calmly scruti-
nized her without embarrassment for a long moment.
"We are, Miss Gibson. Thank you for understanding that.
Now. What do you need from me?"

"Help finding an outfit called Parish Petroleum. Help
finding Eldon Warmsley from New Iberia. Help finding
the Chicken Shit River, which is not on my map. Help
finding someone who will go with me to talk to an old
conjure woman who lives near the Chicken Shit River.
And a crash course in how to do all this without insulting
anybody's feelings or customs." Now she leaned back in
her chair and watched him watch her. She was certain
something had happened in his eyes when she mentioned

Eldon Warmsley, and again when she mentioned respect for customs. Still, he gave nothing away. Indeed, he solidified his control over the situation by his response, which caught her completely off guard.

"You ever heard of Lillian Gailliard and the United Parish Tenants' Organization?" he asked, and when she shook her head, continued: "Lil blows the horn and carries the flag and generally leads the charge in the local fight against polluters. She knew your husband. Here's her address," he said, writing on a yellow legal pad but keeping his eyes welded to hers. "She's expecting you."

IF Warren Forchette looked like he could bench-press the Grand Canyon, Lil Gailliard looked like she could bench-press Warren Forchette. With one hand. She was a very large woman. Not fat, but bulky, and not the kind of bulk that suggested softness or weakness or laziness. She was as tall as Warren—taller than Carole Ann herself—and firm and solid and mighty. A fortress of a woman. When Carole Ann entered her office, Lil got up, crossed the room to greet her, and enveloped her in a powerful hug.

"I'm so sorry 'bout your husband, dahlin'. And I'm so glad you came to see me. Sit down, *cher,* Rest yourself." Lil released Carole Ann and waved her in the direction of an armchair that held a cardboard box stuffed with papers. Lil waved her arm again and Carole Ann lifted the box and put it on the floor, grateful to have something to do, some way to cover the sensation that her name was Dorothy and she was all of a sudden living in the middle of a tornado. In that moment, she understood fully the concept of an out-of-body experience. Al would be proud, she thought.

"How long did you know Al? How well did you know him?" Carole Ann heard herself ask as she sank into the chair.

"Long enough and well enough to 'like him. Long enough and well enough to trust him," Lil replied with a smile that conveyed the comfort of the hug she'd bestowed moments earlier.

"This all comes as such a surprise to me . . ." Carole Ann said, unable to harness her out-of-control thoughts and feelings. "I'm not sure what to say to you . . . what to ask you . . ."

"I know, *cher*," Lil answered soothingly. "How 'bout I talk for a while and you listen?" Lil Gailliard was a hell of a talker.

The twenty-five-year-old United Parish Tenants' Organization had originally been founded to be a voice for the rights of public housing and other poor and ill-educated tenants, of which there were many thousands in New Orleans and surrounding parishes. In the early days, the focus was on the basics: demanding indoor toilets and sinks, electricity, screen doors and windows in public housing projects. Demanding regular trash pickups and street cleanings. Demanding streetlights and police protection. In short, the UPTO fought to put forth the notice that poor people were regular people, and that fight kept the group busy, for the resistance was formidable in a place that not only wore well the Southern mantle of racism, but which also carried the added burden of intraracial racism. Skin color among Blacks in Louisiana was a crucial and defining factor; more important, even, than money or education. That people in need would accept assistance only from people of a certain skin color made the work daunting at times.

Lillian Gailliard had come to the UPTO for help in the winter of 1976. She was then a twenty-six-year-old mother of two whose husband and children were dying of cancers the doctors could not explain. Lil was convinced that the company-owned compound where her family lived caused their illnesses, and she set about working to convince the UPTO that she was right. She began by documenting the fact that most of her neighbors and practically all of the men who worked with her husband were dying of the same inexplicable cancers. The first year of her fight, Lil's youngest child—a two-year-old boy—died.

The second year, her husband died, and the UPTO created the Anti-Pollution Task Force and hired Lillian Gailliard to run it. It was the first paying job she'd ever held. The third year of her fight, in the month of July, Lil began to hemorrhage while sitting at her desk talking to an UPTO caseworker. She almost bled to death before the ambulance could transport her to the hospital, where during seven hours of emergency surgery it was discovered her uterus was overgrown with massive and strange tumors. The tumors were determined not to be cancerous, but they were poisonous: they emitted a foul odor and an ugly bile that was eating away at Lil's internal organs and had they not been removed, Lil would have been. From the earth. The doctors could not explain the nature or the origin of the tumors. Lil knew exactly what they were and what had caused them: the emissions from the plant where her husband had worked and beside which they had lived for eight years. During the six months she was in bed recovering, the UPTO hired an attorney to handle the legal work of the Anti-Pollution Task Force that Lil, unschooled and untrained, had handled up until that point.

The fourth year, Lil's eldest child died on what would have been her seventh birthday. The following week, the UPTO filed a class action lawsuit against Parish Petroleum on behalf of Lillian Gailliard *et al.* Better than half of the *et al* by that time were deceased, a fact that pricked the attention of the legal reporter at the newspaper, but only because he found it amusing that a lawsuit could be filed by a bunch of dead Colored people. That story, in turn, pricked the attention of a wire service reporter, who included the story in a regional news wrap. And that story pricked the attention of a reporter in Chicago who called Lil Gailliard. Seems that the Chicago reporter was working on a story about a similar lawsuit there, and he'd heard about another case in Houston, Texas. All of the plaintiffs in both cities, said the reporter, were Black, and a good number of them were dead. That's when Lil Gailliard realized what she'd taken on was bigger than her neighborhood. So, while she was waiting for the lawsuit that bore her name to wind its way through the legal system, Lil began poking about in other New Orleans neighborhoods, looking for people dying from strange cancers and poisonous tumors. Twenty years later, she was still finding them.

It was beginning to be too much. First, here were these people who'd known her husband, and who were so casual about that knowledge. Then this woman—this stranger—had let drop from her lips the words "Parish Petroleum" without the slightest understanding of their impact on Carole Ann. Or perhaps she did understand. *Who the hell was Lillian Gailliard anyway?!* Several times during Lil's recitation, she had stopped to answer telephone calls or to wave someone into the office who had a matter to discuss that couldn't wait, always begging Carole Ann's forgiveness for the interruption. Carole Ann learned during these digressions that Lil called everyone "dahlin'" or "*cher.*" She learned Lil was the driving force behind the UPTO's Anti-Pollution Project, which had its own staff and budget and life force, in the person of Lillian Gailliard. She learned to read the gentle cadences of Lil's sweet voice: the softer the voice, the more dangerous the message.

It clearly was unwise to trifle with Lil Gailliard, Carole Ann learned. As Lil juggled her visitors, her calls, and her conversation with Carole Ann, what she heard convinced her Lil probably knew enough law to pass the bar in several states and the District of Columbia. Carole Ann also concluded Lil was personally and intimately acquainted with every neighborhood within a hundred-mile radius of New Orleans, and that she possessed the same level of knowledge about every factory, plant, landfill, dump, oil well, and natural gas pit.

And now she also knew this woman was connected to her murdered husband and to Parish Petroleum. *What did he tell you!* Carole Ann wanted to scream. Instead, she asked what she hoped sounded like a simple question: "So, Al came to see you because of your work with the UPTO?"

Lil's hesitation before answering was so slight as to defy notice, but Carole Ann was an astute student of nuance and she noticed and girded herself for what she intuited would be a hard-to-handle response.

"Al contacted me because I'm an expert witness on environmental pollution. I've testified in dozens of trials all over the country, as well as before Congressional hearings and committees. In fact, I first met Al in Washington when I challenged his testimony before a hearing on somebody's environmental impact statement. Told him he was woefully ignorant on the subject, as I recall." Lil chuckled at her private memory of that moment, then grew serious again. "He called me about a month later to prove he'd smartened himself up. By the time he called me about this Parish Petroleum mess last year, he knew almost as much as I did and was ready to switch sides."

The tears Carole Ann had been holding back spilled out and she sat quietly weeping for a moment. Lil offered a box of tissues across the desk and Carole Ann wiped and blew and took a few deep breaths.

"I didn't know anything about that part of his life. And I don't know why he didn't tell me. Do you know, Lil, why he didn't tell me?"

"I think, *cher*, because somebody stole his time away from him."

"I hope that's the reason," Carole Ann said softly, and then she talked for a while, telling Lil everything about the events that had led her to be in New Orleans. Carole Ann opened herself and let everything out because she had not yet done that and she needed to. No other person knew everything that had transpired within and to her since the Tommy Griffin trial. Her mother and brother and Al's father and Cleo and Jake Graham and Tommy knew parts and pieces. Al had known the most. But Al was dead. Lillian Gailliard, on the other hand, was the most alive person Carole Ann had ever encountered and therefore the perfect repository for her released self.

Lil received everything Carole Ann gave. She nodded and smiled. She grimaced and shook her head. Her eyes narrowed and her lips tightened and she muttered curses in French. Or, more precisely, Carole Ann thought, Creole. Once, she wrote very rapidly on a small notepad of pale pink paper, quickly filling up three of the small pages, and when Carole Ann hesitated, Lil waved her on with her other hand, signaling she should continue talking. When she finally ran out of words, Lil heaved herself up and walked around the desk to stand beside Carole Ann. She stood there for a moment, patting her shoulder. Then she left the office, left Carole Ann sitting there, free to sit and think and feel, or to roam and browse about the office that reflected the woman who called it home.

It was a large space—perhaps thirty feet square—and it clearly doubled as office and home-away-from-home, as witnessed by the blanket and pillow on the floor beside the sofa and the pink satin slippers peeking from beneath the sofa. There were two distinct work areas in the office: the formal desk area, which was relatively neat and orderly, and a long worktable surrounded by chairs on either side and piled high with documents that a brief perusal informed Carole Ann were depositions, pleadings, filings, motions. More of the same overflowing boxes were lined up and stacked against one wall. Two floor-to-ceiling bookcases occupied one wall, and the adjacent wall was covered with photographs. But not like the photographic art that adorned the walls in Warren Forchette's legal center. These images were of the point-the-camera-and-shoot variety. These were photographs of poisoned land and poisoned people—and yet, within them was captured a sad beauty: land and rivers made barren by buried toxins still receive setting and rising suns; men and women made barren by the same evils can still display battered but unbroken spirits.

Carole Ann walked along the wall and the images changed. Now they depicted meetings and protest demonstrations, most of them featuring Lil prominently: waving a picket sign; being arrested and resisting arrest; speaking at a podium, fist raised defiantly; shaking hands and hugging and kissing. And then, in one photograph, there was Al and he was talking to Warren Forchette. Both were seated in folding chairs at a meeting of some kind, and they were leaning toward each other, heads bent forward and angled toward each other, faces grim, arms folded across their chests, legs crossed. Mirror images of each other, the corporate lawyer and the activist lawyer. They who should have been on opposite sides of some fence—of some toxic waste dump or landfill—were seated side by side, together, sharing something grave and serious. And Warren Forchette had never indicated he'd known Al Crandall.

Lil reentered the office to find Carole Ann still holding, still staring at the photograph she hadn't realized she'd lifted from its hook on the wall. Whatever Lil was about to say when she entered the room was quickly forgotten as she registered an understanding of the look on Carole Ann's face and the object in her hands.

"Good Lord! I forgot I had that picture of Al. I'm so sorry, Carole Ann. I hope it wasn't too much of a shock." Lil's face now was puckered with concern.

"I continue to be shocked, Lil, by how little I knew about an obviously important part of my husband's life. Every time I think I can't be shocked further, I'm proven wrong." Carole Ann was not able to disguise the bitterness and disgust that crept into those last few words.

Lil opened her mouth to speak, then closed it, biting off whatever she was about to say. She patted Carole Ann on the shoulder again and crossed to her chair behind the desk and sank down with a grunt, confirming Carole Ann's earlier suspicion that the woman was in physical pain, and causing her to wonder whether it was related to the mysterious tumors of twenty years ago.

"Warren wants you to meet him tomorrow at the center at two o'clock. Y'all been invited to dinner out to Eldon Warmsley's place. Eldon, bless his bones, is a swamp baby, and he believes in two things—cookin' and eatin'—so take your biggest appetite with you. And wear some clothes you don't mind gettin' dirty."

Carole Ann was about to reply that Warren Forchette could go skinny-dipping in an alligator bayou—who the hell was he to tell her where to go and when!—but the words were choked off by the change in Lil, whose eyes and mouth and body were taking on a glinting hardness

that was totally transforming. Here was the Lillian Gailliard who'd created a civil rights movement by sheer
force of will, the Lillian Gailliard determined to make
good on her promise to take better care of Al Crandall's
wife than had been taken of Al Crandall. She raised her
right hand and pointed a beautifully manicured, tanger-
ine-colored fingernail at Carole Ann.

"Learn your way around. Learn one good route to and
from every place you go, and stick to that route. Don't get
lost. And don't go explorin' or sight-seein' unless you go
with one of those tour groups. And don't go nowhere or
do nothin' at night alone. You understand what I'm tellin'
you?" No more dahlin's and *cher*'s, no more gentle
bayou humor.

"You're telling me I'm in danger." Again, Carole Ann
experienced the sensation of mind and body separating
and lost the struggle to control it.

"Everything your police friends told you is the truth.
And if you didn't believe them, then believe me. Three
people are dead 'cause they talked to your husband, and
another one is missing . . ."

"Al said . . . Al's notes said . . . five people were dead
or missing . . ."

"Eldon Warmsley is number five. And he is still missing for all you know." Lil pronounced these words hard
and slow and Carole Ann had to work to keep her spine
straight.

"I thought I wanted to die after Al was killed. But I've
since changed my mind. I promise not to do anything to
jeopardize myself or anyone else. Enough people are
dead."

Lil nodded her head once. "You're lucky to have
friends like your two cops. There ain't a cop in this town
I'd trust as far as I can spit. Let your friends help you. Let
'em help us. We need the help. That's why we were so

glad to see your Al ready to work for our side, and then we made the mistake of not warnin' him, of not takin' right care of him. We'll do better by you. And while I'm thinkin' about it, you better give me the number of that cellular phone."

Carole Ann left the UPTO surprised it was late enough that the sun was well into its westward journey, and grateful it was still light enough to see clearly. She'd never have been able to retrace her route to the legal center at night and at the same time pay close enough attention to her surroundings to ensure she wasn't being followed. Warren Forchette had given her "the quickest route, not the most direct route," to Lil Gailliard, and that meant a series of turns at landmarks instead of at street signs in areas Carole Ann could see did not have streetlights. At least the streets were paved in this neighborhood . . .

She struggled to fathom unpaved streets in a major city in America in the last half of the last decade of the twentieth century. She'd never before witnessed such a phenomenon and would not have believed it possible. Perhaps in some tiny, backwoods hamlet in Maine or West Virginia or Oregon. Or in the Louisiana of swamps and bayous. But not in a city with an international reputation. Didn't Lil just tell her that the UPTO had been established to correct this kind of injustice? If the city's power brokers didn't care about the well-being of their own citizens, didn't they at least care how the rest of the world viewed their city? People from all over the world toured New Orleans. She looked around and answered her own question. The tourists were living the life in the French Quarter or on the *Mississippi River Queen,* where they belonged, and the locals didn't appear to be the voting kind. She forced herself to concentrate on driving, on not getting lost, on not being followed.

8

CAROLE ANN DRESSED FOR HER ASSIGNATION WITH
Warren Forchette as he'd been dressed at their initial
meeting yesterday, in a white tee shirt, her favorite and
most well-worn jeans, and her running shoes. Around her
waist she wore a nylon pouch that contained her driver's
license, some cash, a credit card, and her tiny telephone.
She wore a white Atlanta Braves cap with a long bill to
help her sunglasses shade her eyes. And when she drove
up to the legal center promptly at two o'clock and spied
her escort waiting on the steps for her, she alternated
between feelings of chagrin and amusement. His Braves
cap was blue and the only difference in their wardrobes.
He lifted a hand in greeting when he saw her drive up.
She acknowledged the gesture with a similar one and
backed into a space while he walked to a dusty red, 1960s
vintage Chevy pickup parked at the curb.

"You like baseball?" he asked in greeting when she
reached the truck, as he opened the pickup's passenger
door.

"I'm learning to," she replied, grabbing the inside door
frame to help boost herself up into the truck.

"You surprised at how difficult it is?" he asked as he seated himself, slammed his door, and started the ignition.

"Overwhelmed," she said with a dry chuckle, noting that the powerful purr of the truck's engine belied its ancient appearance, and wondering if everything about the man had separate exterior and interior realities.

"Which were you—a basketball or a football junkie before you discovered the subtle joys of baseball?"

"Both," she answered grinning, "though it's infinitely easier in D.C. to be a Redskins fan than a Bullets fan. But if you forced a truly honest response from me, I'd have to claim a preference for basketball because the season lasts longer and because there are more games. That way, if I get heavily involved in a case—which I often do—and miss three or four games, I don't feel like I've missed the season."

He gave her a sideways grin in return but didn't speak, concentrating on maneuvering and manipulating the big truck through the heaviest traffic Carole Ann so far had seen in New Orleans. She knew they were headed west—they were on I-10 and west was the only possible direction unless he intended to go to Mississippi—and she expected him to head south once out of town, to connect with the state highway that would take them the 160 miles or so to New Iberia, where Eldon Warmsley lived. But once out of town, Warren kept driving west on I-10. He spoke only once, to ask if she wanted him to turn on the air-conditioning, and he grunted what she interpreted to be approval at her negative reply; she spoke not at all, not wishing to give him the satisfaction of questioning their destination. She wanted to know where they were going if not to Eldon Warmsley's, but Warren Forchette clearly was a man unaccustomed to having to explain himself and she was equally unaccustomed to having to ask. So she observed in relaxed silence.

He was a good driver and handled the truck easily and expertly. But he didn't like driving, didn't enjoy it the way she did. She could tell by the tension that hunched his shoulders up toward his ears and the tightness of his grip on the steering wheel. The external scenery was less interesting. The area around New Orleans was not attractive by the wildest stretch of even the most fertile imagination, and traffic bunched and tangled itself in the approaches to I-310 and I-55. Hot, bored, and more than a little annoyed at Warren, Carole Ann settled herself in the wide seat and closed her eyes. She had slept very little the night before, plagued by the guilt she felt over her ignorance of Al's interests and concerns, and excited by the growing belief she could actually learn what had happened to him and why. The combination of heat, fatigue, and a taciturn companion conspired to lull her to sleep.

She awakened, according to the dashboard clock and the radio disc jockey, at four-fourteen, surrounded by the ugliest terrain she'd ever seen, in Louisiana or anywhere else. They were no longer on the interstate, but on a narrow, raggedy strip that had once been a two-lane blacktop, on one side of which lay swampy, marshy, muddy land, and on the other hard, cracked dirt from which sprouted, in ugly patches here and there, wilted knee-high weeds and the occasional stunted, barren tree. In the distance, near and far, she could discern the outlines of weathered shacks. The horizon was flat and endless.

Carole Ann was about to apologize for having fallen asleep and demand to know where they were, when Warren downshifted and almost brought the truck to a halt. He inched along in low gear, then braked and turned into a rutted road that Carole Ann never would have noticed. The big truck was a pinball in a game machine, bouncing up and down, back and forth. She was thrown right and left, up and down. She looked at Warren, but he was looking for something in the distance and seemed oblivious to the motion of the truck. Suddenly he grunted and pointed and Carole Ann looked and was rendered speechless. There, literally in the middle of nowhere, was a ghost town, comprised of four or five long, one-story, rectangular, brick-and-mortar structures that were now broken and crumbled. Beyond the buildings, laid out in grids, were rows and rows of what had once been one-story houses.

Warren drove into the town, down what had once been a paved road, toward the first—and largest—of the buildings. He turned right, drove along beside it, and then turned left, behind it, and Carole Ann could see she'd been mistaken about the number of the low-slung brick and concrete structures that had once existed here: there were almost a dozen of them, identical in size and shape, except for the larger one in the front. Warren drove, following the road as if it were a maze, weaving in and out of and up and down the broken streets. Carole Ann could see there had once been signs on the streets and on the buildings, but none were legible now. No windows or doors remained intact in any of the buildings, and few had roofs remaining. Neither were there contents of any kind. Everything had been removed.

The same was true of the houses that fanned out from the buildings like fingers on a hand, five perfectly symmetrical rows of identical one-story houses. Warren drove slowly down one of the streets and Carole Ann counted the houses: thirty-two of them. All broken and falling down. No windows and doors remaining. Hard, broken, gray dirt in front and behind and between the houses, with patches of ugly weeds growing here and there. At the end of the street, Warren turned onto a curved road that served as the end of all the streets and stopped. Fanning out from this curved road was an open field. Or it should have been a field. It was an acre of dead earth. Carole Ann recognized the remnants of playground equipment—swings and slides and jungle gyms, rusted and rotting and collapsed. Warren drove on, turning into another of the streets. When he stopped again, he turned off the motor, opened the door, and got out of the truck. Carole Ann followed.

"This is where Lil lived," he said, facing one of the same-looking empty houses. "Back there is where her kids played. Where all the kids played," he said, pointing toward but not looking back at the dead field. He was still staring at the little dead house, eyes far away in memory. Then he turned and looked toward the buildings. "They worked three shifts, seven days a week. That's why they provided housing. You see how far this is from the city. Imagine how removed and isolated this all was thirty years ago. Also imagine how green it was. And how pretty. And how easy it was for people to believe in the gift of a good-paying job and nice place to live." His voice was as flat and lifeless as the landscape.

"When was it abandoned?"

"A year after the lawsuit was filed. By that time, so many of the workers were dead or dying they couldn't operate at capacity. The suit was costing them money and they weren't making their production quotas. And they couldn't convince any new workers to sign on. Not even for free housing. So they emptied all the buildings and walked away, leaving behind permanent proof that they lied when they said they'd done nothing wrong here. Does this look like nothing's wrong?" He turned suddenly and strode toward the truck, leaving her standing there. But she couldn't move. She stood there looking at the little house where Lillian Gailliard had once lived with her husband and young children. She closed her eyes and tried to imagine Lil young and happy, her little children running on the playground. She wondered what Lil had looked like then, unworried and certain her babies were safe and protected.

Carole Ann returned to the truck. Warren was sitting sideways in the driver's seat, his door open, looking at nothing in the distance. She climbed in and slammed her door. He turned and looked at her and changed his mind about whatever it was he had opened his mouth to say. Instead, he, too, slammed his door and turned the key in the ignition. Carole Ann leaned back in the seat, then shot forward, eliciting a crooked grin from Warren.

"My shirt's as soaked as yours," he said. "If you sit forward, it'll be dry by the time we meet up with Eldon."

"Where are we?" she asked. "I'm sorry I fell asleep on you," she added before he could respond.

"Apology accepted but not necessary," he said. "This heat is a butt-kicker. Besides, I'd much rather have a partner who slept through the heat than one who complained about it." And he gave her another of his sideways grins as he hit a rut in the road that bounced the truck like a ball, causing Carole Ann to bump her head on the roof. "Goddamn!" He braked and slowed to a crawl, still cursing and muttering under his breath and Carole Ann could have sworn she heard the same Creole she'd heard Lil use yesterday.

"I take it nobody comes out here." It was a question, but she made it a statement, the answer already obvious. What she really wanted to know was how it was possible that somebody—some company—was permitted to kill the land and then abandon it.

"Nobody in their right mind," Warren said under his breath. Then added, "Every couple of years or so, geologists come out and check the soil and issue a report. The result is always the same. I could give them the same results for free. All you have to do is look around. If it ever happens that green leaves appear on the trees, or the weeds grow taller than six or eight inches, or the birds and squirrels and grasshoppers and snakes return . . ." He left the sentence hanging up there on that high, hopeful note. "You may have noticed Lillian Gailliard is an optimistic human being. That land just might revive itself because she wants it to."

"What's Lil got to do with it now?"

Warren turned to look at her. "It's hers," he said, unable to keep the surprise from his voice. "She didn't tell you about the lawsuit?"

"She didn't tell me the outcome of the suit." Carole Ann turned sideways in the seat so she could watch Warren as he told her how Parish Petroleum had thrown in the towel early in the fight once it was revealed the company's owners had been skimming the considerable profits from the top for years, leaving it unable to withstand the rigors of expensive litigation. By the time the final settlement agreement was worked out—which included a cash award of ten thousand dollars to each plaintiff, and the plant itself—all but ten of the original plaintiffs were dead. Eight others succumbed in the intervening years, leaving Lil and the son of one of the workers the sole owners of the ghost town that had once been Parish Petroleum. Warren's mouth worked as if he'd been chewing—popcorn, perhaps—and had kernels caught in his teeth. Carole Ann continued her observation of him. She wasn't waiting for him to say more; she knew he had no more to say. She was looking for a way to see inside him, to see who he really was, because she knew she didn't know. Here she was in the middle of nowhere—literally—with a man she'd met for the first time little more than twenty-four hours ago, and about whom, if pressed, she could say precious little. She didn't like the feeling.

Once they had left the ghost town and were back on the two-lane blacktop, he turned to watch her watch him and she did not lower her eyes or alter her position. *Who are you,* she asked his eyes. *And can I trust you?* There was no flicker of a response, though he allowed her to hold his gaze until he was required to return his attention to his driving. She saw him notice something in the distance, saw him ease his foot off the gas pedal and drop his left hand to the turn signal and raise his left foot to the clutch to prepare to downshift. She looked to see what he saw. A general store–cum–gas station. Old. Ancient. From another millennium, it seemed. Gas pumps short and round-shouldered and reading ESSO. Clapboard building squat, square, and so weathered no sign of paint remained. But the building was in good repair and looked solid, and the front porch was new, and a new, slatted wooded bench held forth on one side of the screen door, while an almost new, almost shiny, red and white Coca-Cola dispenser—the chest variety, not the upright—occupied the space on the other side.

"Would you like something to drink?" Warren asked.

"The coldest beer they've got," Carole Ann responded, already tasting it.

He halted his exit motion, one foot on the ground, and looked at her as if she'd dropped into his space like a spider from a web. "You like beer?" he asked.

"Goddammit!" Carole Ann jerked open the passenger door and hopped out of the truck, forgetting its height and almost falling on her face. She strode around the front of the vehicle, meeting Warren there and glaring at him. "You," she said through clenched teeth, "are getting on my nerves. Why do you think I asked for a beer?" She brushed past him, heading for the store, when he grabbed her arm. She swung around to face him, fully furious. "What?!"

"I just . . . it's not . . . most women don't like beer," he managed with an apologetic shrug.

"I'm not most women," she snapped and felt moisture dripping down the side of her face.

"No shit," he mumbled under his breath and stamped away from her and into the store, leaving her standing in the heat berating herself for her outburst, using her arm to wipe away the sweat, and wondering what the hell she was doing in whatever part of Louisiana she was in. That she didn't know where she was or where she was going was only part of the source of her irritation. The greatest part was her inability to figure out how to deal with Warren Forchette. He responded to none of her arsenal of tactics: he would not be bullied, cajoled, convinced, or berated. He would not even respond to direct, open inquisition. He gave absolutely no information; even more infuriating, he asked for none. They were so evenly matched she knew full well they could spend days together, riding around Louisiana, with neither of them giving an inch. Perhaps that was why, within moments after their first meeting, he'd sent her off to Lil Gailliard.

She sprawled on the shaded bench in front of the store, trying to ward off the disappointment of discovering it was no cooler there than out in the full sun of the dusty parking lot. She could hear voices coming from inside the store, but could discern no words; could not distinguish Warren's voice from any other, could only be certain there were several men within. Then the door opened, squeaking on rusty hinges, a perfectly exquisite sound effect from a 1940s film, and a wiry, reddened man emerged. He looked into the western sun without shading his eyes, then looked down at her.

"Evenin'," he said and touched the bill of his cap.

"Hello," Carole Ann replied, looking up at him and then away. He walked to the corner of the porch and stood looking into the distance before he turned back toward her. He studied her without apology or embarrassment, so she studied him: His skin was burnished red and leathery, clearly that of a man who spent most of his time out in the open. He was tall and lean and probably in his fifties, though the weathering of his face and hands and arms made it difficult to judge. Longish, dark brown hair curled beneath the edges of his cap. He wore threadbare overalls and a faded tee shirt beneath, and scuffed workshoes. His clothes were old but they were clean.

"You not from 'round here," he said, and waited for a response though he had not asked a question, and all of Carole Ann's instincts went on full alert.

"No, I'm not," she said lightly and crossed her legs.

"Where you from?"

"Atlanta," she responded, the lie coming as quickly and easily as her understanding of the need for it.

"You don't sound like you from Atlanta," he said in a voice gone flat. "Don't look like it, neither." And he waited again for her to explain herself and her presence. She looked up at him and was about to ask what people from Atlanta looked and sounded like when Warren appeared with two beer bottles dripping ice chips and water, and a huge bag of popcorn. Her irritation with him diminished, even as it increased with the man who was standing over her, challenging her presence. Warren let the screen door slam behind him and stepped closer to Carole Ann, placing himself between her and the other man, forcing him to backpedal. Then Warren turned to face him. He nodded a greeting but did not speak. The other man returned the greeting in kind, stepped down off the low porch, and walked around the side of the store.

They listened to his feet crunch on the gravel, listened to a car door open and slam shut, listened to tires spinning gravel.

"Got yourself a dinner date?" Warren said dryly as he lowered himself onto the bench and handed Carole Ann one of the beers.

"Would have, if it weren't for you," Carole Ann answered in an even drier tone.

"What did I do?" he said with such exaggerated innocence that Carole Ann had to work to retain her chastising composure.

"Since I neither know where I am, where I'm going, or when I might be returned to where I came from, I couldn't very well tell him when to pick me up," Carole Ann retorted with a sniff and a toss of her head, and Warren laughed out loud. A full, healthy, hearty laugh that was infectious. Carole Ann could not suppress the giggle that began, so she drowned it in a gulp of ice cold beer.

"Ooh! What is this?" She struggled to catch her breath and suppress a burp while she scrutinized the lable on the beer bottle.

"You like it?" Warren asked, wiping his mouth and trying to stifle a burp of his own.

"It's wonderful," Carole Ann said, once again looking for something recognizable on the bottle's lable.

"An indigenous brew," he said, opening the popcorn and offering it to her. "We got lots of good beer in Louisiana."

She took a fistful and sat chewing and drinking beer and no longer minding that the sweat was pouring off her as if she were running a marathon. Warren propped the popcorn bag against her and went into the store. He emerged again in seconds with a map of Louisiana that he spread out on their laps. It was a very detailed map, and he pointed out to her the route they'd taken away from New Orleans while she slept; the ghost town that on the map was called Parishville; their present position at the intersection of two tiny country roads; and their eventual destination, Eldon Warmsley's place, twelve miles deeper into the woods.

"We're not expected till six, and it won't take but a few minutes to get there. You've even got time for another brew," he said. "But I'd go easy on the popcorn. Eldon invited us to dinner, and he's a serious man when it comes to food."

"I'm pretty serious myself, in that regard." Carole Ann chewed and swallowed and studied the map, confusion wrinkling her brow. "Why did we come such a round-about way?" she asked, running her finger along the route they'd taken. "Why not the most direct route?" She felt him stiffen even before she completed her question.

"People are dead, Miss Gibson. I shouldn't think you'd need to be reminded of that fact." He sighed deeply and drank the last of his beer, touching her knee and shaking his head in a silent apology. Then he told her about Eldon Warmsley, who owned the general store where they currently were sitting and another one on the water, and who had owned and managed a similar facility twenty-five years ago within the Parish Petroleum compound.

Close to three hundred people had lived in the compound in its heyday, including Eldon Warmsley, who slept on a cot in a small room adjacent to the store four nights a week, and who went home to his wife on Thursday nights and returned on Sunday. But for the others, Parish Petroleum literally was a way of life. In addition to the general store, there was a cafeteria that served breakfast, lunch, and dinner to workers on shift at those times. The workers and their families could get their hair done at a combination barbershop/beauty salon that operated three days a week, get their souls saved or their spirits lifted at a meeting hall that also served as church, movie theatre, and indoor recreation center. For the sick, there was a clinic with a full-time nurse and a part-time doctor. For the young, a nursery school. School-age children were bused to a public school six miles away. Although he was never employed by Parish Petroleum, Eldon, by virtue of his status as shopkeeper, was considered part of the management team. Which meant he was privy to secrets and information not available to the general population—a circumstance that was both blessing and curse since Eldon was the only Colored person who enjoyed such status. All the Parish Petroleum workers and their families were Black; all the plant managers and other officials were white, except the barber, the beautician, the cooks, and the nurse.

Eldon and the plant doctor, who spent Tuesdays and Thursdays at the plant, became friends, in large part because Eldon kept for the doctor his own private supply of roasted, salted peanuts. Such a popular item very often sold out by the middle of the week, so that by Thursday, the good doctor would have had to munch on pork rinds or potato chips, like everybody else, had not Eldon kindly put aside a couple of bags of the nuts for him. That small courtesy, along with keeping a couple of Coca-Colas near the fan so they'd be extra cold, endeared Eldon to the doctor, until the doctor began to think of the shopkeeper as a friend. And began to confide in him. Began to tell him of his puzzlement and concern over the number of workers having trouble breathing, having trouble keeping their food down, having trouble with loose bowels. Then there were the stillborn babies, and the babies whose mothers the doctor had told were stillborn because they'd been born so hideously deformed the good doctor could not, in good conscience, have allowed them to live. Then there was the strange anemia becoming almost epidemic among the toddlers, something weakening the blood, causing once strong, healthy children to succumb to a slow, deathly lethargy.

Unknown to the doctor, Eldon himself had been a witness to the strange sicknesses in an equally clinical manner, for it was Eldon who sold the ancient African and Indian remedies to the already dying when the white man's medicine failed them. It was Eldon who led the spirit doctors and conjure women on their nocturnal visits to cure those whom the white doctor had failed. It was Eldon who sent or, more often than he cared to, personally delivered the message to the relatives of a Parish Petroleum worker hovering at death's door that it was time to make arrangements. And it was Eldon whom the doctor told, in a choking whisper, that the plant manager had destroyed all the doctor's files and records and then fired him on the spot, taking his key to the clinic and locking him out.

Parish Petroleum gave the plant nurse a fifty-dollar-a-week raise and put her in charge of the clinic, where she took temperatures and blood pressures, dispensed antacid and aspirin, and where she collapsed and died one night after being bitten by a rattlesnake that had curled itself up to rest in the drawer where the cottonballs were kept. Health-care services were not provided by Parish Petroleum after that. Unwell workers would need to drive twenty miles to the nearest town to see a doctor, an expensive and time-consuming journey, one not made by many workers.

Eldon Warmsley closed his store on the day Parish Petroleum closed the plant, opening his current establishment on that same day. And he never mentioned what he knew about the strange sicknesses of Parish Petroleum until asked all those years later by Al Crandall. Eldon had never before told anybody what he knew because nobody had ever before asked him. But Eldon also told Al Crandall quite a bit more—not because Al asked, but because Eldon liked him. Now Eldon had literally been sickened by the fact that what he told Al Crandall had gotten him killed. Al and at least three other people—maybe even four, since nobody had seen the good doctor since Al paid him a visit back in February.

"Now Eldon wants to see you, Miss Gibson—which is why I drove fifty miles out of the way to get you here. And I'll tell you up front that he hopes to convince you to give up the notion of looking for your husband's murderer and to go home. But his main reason for wanting to see you is to apologize for what happened. That old man really liked Al Crandall."

"And what did you think of him, Mr. Forchette?" she asked coldly. He looked hard at her and she saw part of him retreat and close down. She didn't care because her annoyance had returned. Why the hell hadn't he told her he'd known Al?

"He was a courageous and honorable man and it shames me to face you knowing I hold some responsibility for his death. I almost passed out when Dave Crandall called to ask me to meet with you. I'd met Dave exactly twice, and liked him. But I never once connected him with Al Crandall."

"What makes you think you own some responsibility for Al's murder?" Like Warren, Carole Ann had retreated and was now cold and distant. Warren Forchette did not respond well to the change.

"I'll let Eldon tell you," he said, standing. He folded the map and returned it and the empty beer bottles to the store. She closed and folded the popcorn bag, brushed the crumbs from her hands and pants, and went to wait for him in the truck. Neither spoke on the short ride on the barely visible path to Eldon Warmsley's place deep in the woods.

* * *

ESTATE would have been more like it, though Carole Ann had to admit she'd have found the term presumptuous prior to seeing it. But Eldon Warmsley had himself an estate, no doubt about it. The three-story sparkling brick and wood structure sat atop a gentle rise of lush, manicured green edged on all sides by orderly rows of blooming things. Ancient, towering trees—magnolias?—surrounded the house at a respectful distance. The house was a flawless jewel in a perfect setting, each worthy of the other. The contrast between this paradise and the wasteland that had once been Parishville defied understanding. She wanted to say something to Warren, wanted him to say something to her that would help make it make sense. She wanted that assurance at the same time as she understood that she was on her own now, and if sense were to be made of the things she was learning and feeling, she'd have to make it herself.

Warren parked in the circular drive in front of the house and they exited the truck simultaneously. Carole Ann suddenly felt too dirty and sweaty to be joining strangers for dinner, but that feeling, like so many others lately, wound up on the back burner as the front door opened and Eldon Warmsley came out to greet them. He looked like a Gene Hackman–Clint Eastwood merger—attractive and appealing and clearly a man to be taken on his own terms. He wore a white cotton shirt with the sleeves cut out to reveal lean, sinewy biceps, khaki slacks, and nothing on his feet. Carole Ann had opened her mouth to greet him when she realized she'd been expecting to meet a Black man. The only person of color in what was considered a management position at Parish Petroleum, Warren had said. But this was not a Black man, and that was not the kind of thing people made mistakes about. Not in America. One did not call a white man Black by mistake. Yet Carole Ann was standing as close as good manners permitted to Eldon Warmsley and what she saw was a white man. He took her hands and held both of them in both of his.

"I can't tell you how bad I feel about what happened to your husband, Miz Crandall." Lil Gailliard's reference to cooking and eating notwithstanding, Eldon Warmsley proved himself to be a swamp baby by the sound of the words that came from his mouth. Creole or Cajun, Carole Ann didn't know, but she did know this was pure Louisiana and it was fascinating and beautiful to hear. The meaning of the words also came to her in some form of delayed transmission: She saw his mouth move, heard him speak. The sound traveled to her ears, and sometime later, the meaning registered. It seemed considerable time had elapsed when she responded.

"I wish you wouldn't feel badly at all, Mr. Warmsley. I believe you were a friend to Al, and that you will be to me, and I'm very grateful."

He smiled at her. A warm, generous smile that crinkled his hazel eyes and revealed a set of strong, white teeth. "You and your husband are two halves of the same nut, Miz Crandall. I like you as quick as I liked him. And I'd like the chance to get to know you a lot better, which means we got to do a better job keepin' you healthy. Ain't that right, boy?" He kept Carole Ann's two hands enclosed in his left one, and reached around her with his right hand to clap Warren on the shoulder. But he was still looking at Carole Ann. "I known this boy since before he knew hisself. They don't come no better." And with that, Eldon Warmsley released them both and reentered his house. "We gon' eat in the kitchen. Merle got everything ready. Y'all come on." And he led them through four rooms of such simple, understated elegance Carole Ann had to resist the urge to pinch herself.

The kitchen was made for cooking and eating. There were three ovens along one wall, an indoor barbecue pit, a six-burner range, a three-bowl sink, and a refrigerator the size of Texas. The table, of worn, highly polished pine, was nestled in a bay window that looked out over a broad expanse of yard. But Carole Ann's attention was on Merle Warmsley, who was taking a loaf of freshly baked bread from the oven. She was almost as tall as her husband, and as brown as he was not. Her hair was softly, purely white, and when she turned, she greeted them with eyes the color of the Caribbean Sea—blue and/or green, depending on the position of the light. She wiped her hands on her jeans and came quickly to Carole Ann and, like Lil, wrapped her in a warm embrace. She whispered condolences in her ear, then released her and held her at arm's length.

"You look to be holdin' up real well, dahlin'," Merle Warmsley said in an Eartha Kitt voice.

"I'm fine as long I keep busy, keep my mind busy," Carole Ann replied, grateful for the woman's open, direct manner. So many people did not know what to do with death and those death left behind.

"Then you come to the right place at the right time," Merle said with a dry chuckle, and indicated that Carole Ann should seat herself at the table, where Warren, who had not spoken since their arrival, already was sitting. Merle and Eldon spent the next few moments bringing food to the table, and the four of them spent the next hour and a half eating, talking, laughing, in such relaxed joy Carole Ann could not believe they were strangers to her. She was more comfortable than she'd been in a very long time.

During coffee and dessert, Eldon casually, easily, turned the discussion to her presence, and Carole Ann told them exactly what she'd told Lillian: everything.

Then Eldon talked, adding significant details to what Warren had told her. Like the fact that the snake in the nurse's cottonball drawer had been placed there deliberately. Like the fact that several of the white plant managers had become become ill, too, and Parish Petroleum had paid a quarter of a million dollars each for their silence. Like the fact that the ghost town Carole Ann had just visited was not the only Parish Petroleum site.

"I have three questions," Carole Ann said. "Who are the other three people killed because of all this? What is the former plant physician's name, what are the circumstances under which he disappeared, and why is it no one is certain about his fate? And how much of all this did Al know?" She leaned back in her chair to await the answers, then shot forward again. "Make that four," she said. "What did Parish Petroleum produce or make or develop? What the hell *is* Parish Petroleum?"

Nobody said anything for what seemed to Carole Ann like a very long time. Warren Forchette broke the silence. "You can't count worth a good goddamn. How you get four outa that is a mystery to me." He put to his mouth a coffee cup that had been empty for half an hour. He frowned at its emptiness and put it down, still frowning at its transgression, thereby missing Carole Ann's bewildered look at him, for Warren had sounded so much like Eldon, she'd have sworn it was the swamp baby instead of the lawyer who'd spoken.

"Should we start answerin' from the top or the bottom of that list?" Eldon said, head tossed back in thought.

"You know, that's the first time anybody has asked about those poor boys," Merle said, blue-green eyes flashing. "I don't know their names, do y'all?"

Then they all began to talk at once, first slowly and softly, and then loudly and so rapidly that Carole Ann did not understand any of the conversation. She held up her hands, right palm flat and perpendicular to the fingers on the left hand, and the talk automatically ceased. Eldon grinned sheepishly.

"I 'pologize for that. Guess we got a little carried away. Aw'right. Here we go." And he began answering her questions, beginning with the last question first. She listened without interruption—or significant interest— while he explained in great detail how Parish Petroleum made a component for plastic bottles from the by-products of an oil refinery owned by another division of the same company, operating under another name but technically still Parish Petroleum. She felt a stab when Eldon said, without preamble or discourse, that Al had known everything there was to know. Her heart pounded so hard it hurt when Eldon identified the physician as Lafayette Devereaux and explained that his status was unclear because his brother was Congressman Leland Devereaux, and it was well known that the best way to get along with Leland Devereaux was to stay well out of his way. Asking about Lafayette would just make Leland mad.

Each time Eldon said the name, Carole Ann's heart thudded in her chest, a slow, hard thud she could hear, and wondered if the others could. The thudding sound was so loud she only heard part of what Eldon said about the three dead boys: that all three had drowned in what everyone considered peculiar circumstances, since all three boys were swamp babies—born and raised and lived all their lives on the water. Swamp babies don't just drown, Eldon said, and by the time Carole Ann could make herself understand both his words and their meaning, she was so tired she wanted just to lay her head down and sleep. Right there at the table.

"Just one more question, please," she said instead, not attempting to cover the fatigue. "Why do people think you're missing, Eldon, when you're sitting here, king of the hill, for the whole world to see?"

Again there was the silence, but not so deep as before, and not for nearly as long, for Eldon broke it with a laugh that sounded just exactly like a goose honking.

"Don' many people know 'bout this place," he said with the shrug that was becoming as familiar as a "*cher*" or a "dahlin'." "I lived my whole life on the water. But Miss Merle here is a land crab. She grew up in this house, and after her ma passed on, we fixed it up, bit by bit, still livin' mostly on the water, but comin' up here more and more in the winter and durin' the storm season. But since . . . well, since all the trouble started, we been stayin' here. Ain't but one way in and one way out, so it's safe enough. But goddamn, I'm bored!"

Then Warren and Merle explained further that people who'd known Eldon all his life would know where to find him if they really needed to, and that people who didn't know him—outsiders—would never know where to find him if he wasn't at his house on the water; insiders would never give outsiders any information other than the fact that Eldon was no longer living there. And Carole Ann could see the shrug of the shoulders, the pursing of the lips, and the dismissal of the outsider who'd had the temerity to ask the whereabouts of a swamp baby. So the outsider—Al Crandall—would surmise Eldon Warmsley was missing, just as the three boatmen were missing, and later found drowned; just as the former plant doctor was missing and presumed dead. The doctor whose name was Devereaux. With the congressman brother whose name was Devereaux. Leland. Lafayette. And Larry. Devereaux.

Fifteen minutes later they were in the truck, on their way back to New Orleans. Carole Ann's insides pounded

on the seemingly endless drive, even though she knew the
return trip would be shorter by at least an hour. She apologized in advance for falling asleep—then remained
wide awake, marveling at the completeness and the com-
plexity of the darkness that surrounded them.

"What did Eldon say that got to you?" Warren asked so
suddenly it made her jump.

"What do you mean?"

"You know good and goddamn well what I mean," he
snapped. "Eldon Warmsley said something that scared
you, worried you, or made you mad. My guess is it has
something to do with the infamous Congressman Devereaux. Am I right?"

She was too tired to try to hide the truth from him.
"You are. Al's boss's name is—was—Larry Devereaux."
She could have sworn she heard an intake of breath from
him, but it could easily have been the sound of the wind,
or of something in the night.

"What do you plan to do?" he asked after a while.

"I plan to find out everything I can about Larry Devereaux," she said with a shrug that made her feel like
Louisiana.

"What do you want me to do?" he asked, his voice
totally devoid of emotion or expression.

"You have more than enough to do," she said, recalling
the crowd in the legal center's reception area. "You don't
need to add this to your list. Besides, it may turn out that
Larry Devereaux is from Boston or Terre Haute or Seat-
tle." *And I don't think I trust you worth shit.*

"Do you really believe that?"

"No," she said, and leaned back and closed her eyes
and tried to hurry the distance between wherever they
were and her hotel room in the French Quarter.

She walked into her room at eleven-fifteen and picked

up the telephone. She barely noticed that Billy was so surprised to hear her voice that he stumbled over his greeting to her.

"Cleo, I need you to listen very carefully to me, and to understand exactly what I'm telling you. OK?"

"What's wrong with you? Terminal case of heatstroke or something?" Cleo snapped at her, sounding mean and nasty.

"Listen to me, Cleo, please. I need all the information and background you can dig up on Ernie's boss once removed. Do you understand me?"

"Who the hell is Ernie and do you know what time it is, C.A.?"

Carole Ann had never heard Cleo angry and for a moment it threw her. This woman was her employee. This woman did what Carole Ann told her to do. She did not display anger to Carole Ann. Then reality slapped her. Hard. She took a deep breath and gripped the phone so hard her hand hurt. "I apologize for waking you, Cleo, but I need your help. Please listen carefully. Please. Ernie. Unemployed Ernie, the erstwhile social engineer." She waited for Cleo's response for what seemed like an hour, and hearing absolutely no sound on the other end of the phone, almost panicked. "Cleo? Are you still there?"

"I'm here. You did say Ernie's boss once removed?"

"That's what I said."

"Such a lovely dream I was having." Cleo pronounced the words "lovely" and "dream" separately and distinctly and emphatically and Carole Ann breathed an audible sigh of relief and gratitude.

"I am very sorry to have disturbed you, Cleo. I didn't think about the time difference. And . . . and . . . I . . . um . . . guess I forgot that things were different . . . and I just got in and wanted to call you right away." Carole Ann worked hard to disguise the relief she felt and to convey, instead, remorse and to seek forgiveness.

"It's not the middle of the afternoon, you know?" Cleo, now awake and fully caught up in the drama of the charade, was enjoying herself. "I do have a few other things to do," she said archly.

"I understand," Carole Ann replied meekly. "By the way," she said, quickly changing her tone, "how's Billy's back these days? You-all able to engage in kinky sex once again?"

Cleo let go a throaty burst of laughter tinged just slightly with lewdness. "How did you guess?"

"Billy sounded quite mellow when he answered the phone. And as you know, I always wish the best for you, Cleo. And I won't forget my place again."

"I know, C.A. And I appreciate it. I'll fax the info to you tomorrow before five." And with that, Cleo severed the connection, leaving Carole Ann missing, for the first time, her other life. The one in which she had had nothing to fear. How long ago that time seemed—so long ago it felt more like dream than memory. But the fear she felt was real. She truly was afraid to think her husband's murderer was his law partner and boss. But it was that thought—that Larry Devereaux had murdered Al Crandall—accompanied by the fear it generated, that stomped around her insides all that night and the following morning until she fled the hotel and joined a tour group for an afternoon riverboat cruise on the Mississippi. It was late afternoon when she returned to her room to retrieve the respectable pile of faxed pages waiting for her.

Thirsty and hungry and still too jittery to endure the confines of the hotel room, she scooped up the info sent by Cleo and strolled around the corner to an establishment that couldn't decide whether it wanted to be a down-and-dirty café or an upscale restaurant. It boasted of serving the best po'boy sandwiches in the state of Louisiana and had a wine list to rival K-Paul's. Carole Ann asked to be seated on the patio and was early enough to secure an umbrella-covered table in the rear corner of what was a surprisingly lush garden, which gave her not only a view of the entrance to the patio, but of the glass-enclosed interior dining room as well. She removed her hat and sunglasses, retrieved her reading glasses from the bottom of her purse, and waited for the nineteenth-century-clad hostess to take her order. Then she settled down to work, focusing first on Larry Devereaux's entry in the D.C. Bar Directory. It could easily have been the bio of any man of similar age:

Lawrence W. Devereaux, born November 1, 1940, in Baton Rouge, Louisiana. Enlisted in the United States Marines June 1959; honorably discharged July 1963, recipient of a Bronze Star and a Purple Heart. B.A. cum laude in political science, University of Pennsylvania, J.D. cum laude from George Washington University in Washington, D.C., 1971. Admitted to the D.C. Bar November 1971; admitted to the Maryland Bar 1973; admitted to the Virginia Bar 1974. Member Trial Lawyers Association of America. Married Angelina Carro of San Francisco, California, in August 1971. No children.

Carole Ann got out her map, wondering idly what Larry had done to earn medals, and realized with a jolt that he would have been in the Army at approximately the same time as her father, who'd been killed in action. She sloughed off that thought and returned her focus to the map. Baton Rouge, the state capital, was less than two hours away. It had been many years since she'd done a records search, but she found herself looking forward to it. The search would help her organize her thoughts, which at the moment were behaving like a roomful of unruly teenagers.

She pulled a pen from her purse and began jotting down some of those thoughts, corraling them, taming them. First and foremost, there was the Devereaux connection: Leland, Lafayette, and Larry. Then there was the Parish Petroleum situation to unravel. How could it be that Parish Petroleum had perished in the early 1970s, brought down by a class action lawsuit, and yet was still alive enough to hire an attorney to represent it before the regulatory authorities? Two different sites, Eldon had said . . .

She wrote down information she'd need from both Warren and Lil before launching her search and, feeling a bit more in control, finished her iced tea, gathered up her belongings, and walked back to her hotel, deciding along the way to treat herself to a real Louisiana dinner.

Carole Ann hadn't eaten dinner alone in a restaurant in fifteen years. Not a formal, elegant dinner in a world-famous, world-class restaurant, wearing clingy peach silk that dramatized her newly acquired bronze hue and short haircut. She'd followed Jake Graham's instructions to the letter, choosing to dine at Dooky Chase's, a short taxi ride away from the French Quarter and her hotel, because she knew that despite her discomfort with the notion of dining alone, she was hungry enough to appreciate and enjoy the meal. She was not disappointed. She ordered what sounded interesting—shrimp Clemenceau and fried catfish and sweet potatoes and for desert a bread pudding that brought a sincerely sensual joy. She was gratified to catch a glimpse of the legendary, regal Leah Chase across the dining room chatting with a table of celebratory customers—birthday or anniversary, Carole Ann couldn't discern. And rather than allow the sadness that was creeping up in her to take hold and spoil her magnificent meal, she declined a second cup of coffee and went out to join the cast of characters in the French Quarter.

She was acutely aware that the crowd swirling about her did nothing to ameloriate her feelings of loneliness and isolation, but she allowed herself to be carried along Bourbon Street, and turned with it at Chartres Street, ambling slowly because the sidewalk was too packed for the swift stride she'd have preferred. She stopped to watch a group of drunken men watch a strip show from an open doorway. Inside were more drunken men like the ones outside, who were fumbling in their pockets for the price of admission to the club. Carole Ann peered over their heads again and into the darkness where the almost-nude female forms were backlit in shades of pink and purple. The noise, masquerading as music, was as garish as the scene it kept time for.

Carole Ann walked on, stopping here and there to peer inside the open doorways. Sounds and smells and sights mingled to create the kind of sensory overload she'd imagined the French Quarter would supply. Yet she didn't recall this experience from the one time she'd been here before, with Al. Hadn't they walked about the Quarter? Certainly they'd eaten . . . but not at Dooky Chase's, and she didn't remember where. Nor did she recall the name of the jazz club where they'd heard Ellis Marsalis, or the blues club where they'd heard Aaron Neville, or the honky-tonk where they'd heard Dr. John. How could she have forgotten? These were moments she'd shared with Al, who would never again be any more than a memory. How could she have forgotten? The sorrow enveloped her, wrapped around her like a straitjacket, tight and confining. And so was the growing crowd, bumping and jostling.

Then she understood that the pressure she felt on her

back and on her arm was not the idle jostling of someone in a crowd but a deliberate attack on her person. Reacting instinctively, she reached across herself and grabbed the heavy hand on her left arm, quickly found the pressure point, and squeezed. Then she pushed back on the thumb and quickly stepped away from the man who screamed and dropped to the ground. She did not look around, but continued to propel herself forward through the crowd. As she walked, she checked her pockets and her purse to make certain she hadn't been robbed, and berated herself once again for losing herself in her misery. Not only was it counterproductive, it was dangerous. She was a woman, alone. Displaying her sadness openly like that made her all the more vulnerable, and that was a luxury she could not afford.

IT was a lesson she took with her to Baton Rouge the next day, though she gave up early on worrying about being followed. There were too many cars on the road— in front of her, behind her, and in the lanes beside her—to make herself paranoid that one of them was stalking her. Carole Ann did watch her back at the state office building, and in the federal court building. And while she was careful not to place herself in any position that invited trouble, she could not have sworn she did not encounter one man more than once during the long, exhausting day. She also could not have sworn to the contrary. Men were beginning to resemble each other, especially tall, lean, reddish-hued men with pale eyes and dark brown, curly hair. Men like the one at Eldon's general store who doubted she was from Atlanta; men like Eldon Warmsley himself; men like Larry Devereaux . . .

LAWRENCE W. Devereaux had not been born in Baton Rouge on the first of November 1940. Or if he was, the

State of Louisiana did not have a record of it. Lafayette and Leland were duly recorded, the former in May 1937 and the latter in February 1935, both in Assumption Parish. Carole Ann looked it up and found it to be south of Baton Rouge and west of New Orleans. While she was at it, she'd looked up Warren Forchette and Eldon Warmsley. Forchette, like Devereaux, was as common a surname in Louisiana as Smith or Johnson or Jones elsewhere in America, and it took some looking, but she found Warren—or who she thought was Warren, if he'd been born in 1955 in New Orleans. And she found Eldon Warmsley, born in Assumption Parish in August of 1939. And she found the original filing of the articles of incorporation of the Parish Petroleum Company, and the charter licensing it to do business in the parishes of Assumption, St. Martin, St. James, and St. Mary. Four sites, not two or three.

Carole Ann left Baton Rouge with a headache, and not just from eye strain and the heat. Assumption damn Parish! Surely to God it was not mere coincidence that Assumption Parish kept popping up like the jackrabbit in the shooting gallery. Where had Warren taken her yesterday? Had she been in Assumption Parish? Where "on the water" was Eldon from? He'd made it sound far away, or perhaps that's merely how she'd interpreted his comments because she'd applied her own reference points to his words. She'd learned enough of the topography of New Orleans and its environs to know water was everywhere. In fact, New Orleans rode so low that portions of it were actually below sea level. Swamps and bayous and watery pathways to the Gulf of Mexico were everywhere. The place was so wet that people couldn't be buried underground, because there was no underground. There was only swamp. So. Wherever Assumption Parish was, it was nearby. Wherever "on the water" Eldon Warmsley was from, it was nearby. And it was the same place that was home to the Devereaux brothers. Including Larry, she was certain . . .

She looked into the rearview mirror and jumped when she saw the big pickup so close. She flipped on her signal light and moved quickly from the center lane into the far right lane. The truck moved with her, on her tail. She took her foot off the gas pedal and her car slowed suddenly. The truck slowed with her. She returned her foot to the gas pedal with increasing pressure, causing her car to accelerate with increasing speed. The truck stayed with her. Without signaling, she swerved into the left lane, causing the red Jeep she cut off to give her a loud, angry blast of its horn. She accelerated and moved left again and sped past three cars before returning to the center lane. A check of her mirror showed the white pickup in the far left lane and gaining speed quickly. Carole Ann looked ahead, checking to see if there was an exit, and quickly abandoned that notion. She'd get off the interstate and go where? She forced the rising fear back down her throat. Fear wouldn't save her life. But her phone could!

She reached into her purse, retrieved the little phone, and flipped it open. Steering the car with her left hand, she activated the phone with her right and punched in the emergency number.

"Operator, this is an emergency," she said in what she prayed was a calm voice. "I am being chased by a vehicle," and then she gave the operator her exact location, the description of the truck following her, and a description of her own car. She'd been watching the big truck in her rearview mirror the entire time and it was only the density of the traffic that prevented his being directly behind her. Then she saw the flashing lights on the approaching overpass and saw the police car swerve on the ramp leading to the expressway. A Louisiana state trooper. She sped up, quickly cut in front of an eighteen-wheeler, and slid on to the shoulder. She slammed on her brakes, threw the car into reverse, and spewed gravel as she backed up to where the trooper was entering the flow of traffic.

She stopped, shifted into park, and cut her engine. Shaking and sweating, she took several deep breaths, then opened the car door.

"Get back in the car, miss, and put your hands on the steerin' wheel where I can see 'em." The hollow, loud-speaker voice shook Carole Ann in a way she wouldn't have believed possible, but she did as she was told, awash in fear, anger, and irony. As she climbed back behind the wheel, the big, white truck sped past in the right lane. She leaned her head into the steering wheel, understanding the helplessness Black people everywhere feel when confronted by the law. She might have led a sheltered existence, but she wasn't ignorant of the realities of being Black in America.

"Is something wrong, miss?" She heard his voice so close she jumped, sat up too quickly, and made herself dizzy—heat and fear obviously a dangerous combination.

"Someone . . . I was being followed, chased," she managed, and looked up into the face of the trooper and saw her own reflection in his mirrored sunglasses.

"Can you give me a description?" He was serious to the point of gravity. He took out a notepad and pen and waited for her to speak.

"A white pickup. A new one. And big. A Chevy. It just passed us. I couldn't see the driver . . . couldn't see his face. I know it was a man . . ."

"Color?" asked the trooper, and it took Carole Ann a moment to understand he was asking the driver's race. She grinned wryly and shrugged, Louisiana-style.

"I hope you won't take offense, Officer, when I say I haven't spent enough time in Louisiana to be able to tell sometimes."

The trooper relaxed his face and his posture. "No offense, ma'am. And I take your meanin'. But what do you think he was?"

"I think he was a swamp baby," Carole Ann said, surprising herself as much as the trooper with that response. But she knew it was true, and that knowledge, somehow, reduced her fear and brought both clarity and comfort. For someone to openly threaten her must mean she was getting too close to whatever the truth was. Just as Al had. Only Al hadn't known enough of the truth to know that what he knew was dangerous. Carole Ann did know. And she also knew it was time to seek some protection. But from whom? She didn't think she could trust anyone: not Warren, not Eldon, not Merle. Lillian? Jake! Jake and Tommy.

"Could I see your license and registration, miss?" She resisted the urge to remind him that it was she who'd asked for help, that it was she who was the potential victim, and gave him what he asked for; then she explained her presence in Louisiana when he read her out-of-state identification: to research a book on precedent-setting cases in Louisiana and Georgia. She explained she'd spent the day in the archives at the federal court in Baton Rouge, and she showed him her D.C. identification, as well. He was particularly impressed to learn she was admitted to practice before the Supreme Court of the United States. He suggested the business with the pickup was an isolated incident. "Some of these ol' boys get carried away now and again. Too much heat and beer, and here you come—pretty Black lady with Georgia tags— and the stupid overtakes 'em. If it'd make you rest easier, I'll tail you back to your hotel . . ."

"There's no need for that, Officer. You're probably right, and I feel much calmer now." Especially since all the while she was talking to him, she was imagining herself talking to Tommy and Jake. She accepted the return of her license and registration and the trooper's wishes for a safe and pleasant stay in Louisiana. She started the car and inched along the shoulder until she found enough of a break in the traffic flow to enter the interstate. She saw no further evidence of a white Chevy pickup and the trooper tailed her until she exited the expressway.

9

JAKE GRAHAM WAS WORRIED ABOUT CAROLE ANN
Gibson. She'd been gone almost a week and he'd heard
nothing from her. He hadn't really expected her to check
in every day as he'd asked. He knew she was too independent and too stubborn for that. Still, he had expected
to hear from her by now, and it was only the habitual cau-
tion honed by long years of detective work that prevented
him from calling her, for he had the number to her cellular phone. He didn't want to call her and risk having the
ringing of a secret telephone interrupt—or worse—whatever she was doing. The phone was her protection, her
secret weapon. She was out there on her own and that
phone was her only backup. And that's what worried him.
No detective worked alone. Nobody seeking information
probed and pried without backup close at hand, especially in foreign, hostile territory. And whether she'd
admit it or not, Carole Ann Gibson was in over her head,
in hostile territory, in danger. With no backup. He
pounded his useless legs and cursed and worried.

Not that he doubted the woman's ability to take care of
herself. Jake Graham harbored no illusions about the
capabilities of strong Black women. He'd been sur-

rounded by them all his life: his grandmothers, his mother, his sisters, his wife. All of them tough and smart and resourceful and hardheaded. But Jake Graham also had observed these women closely enough over a long period of time to have better sense than to equate strength of purpose and character with invincibility. Carole Ann Gibson was vulnerable. On several fronts. And he had withheld information from her, information that perhaps she could fashion into armor, if not a weapon; information that could hurt her if she confronted it and didn't understand what it was.

Technically, what was floating around in Jake's head, trying to take shape, was not information as much as it was speculation and extrapolation. Hunches, to the uninitiated. Puzzle pieces that fit no as yet discernible pattern. But they would fit, in time; this he knew. For instance, he knew it was significant that the man who'd shot Al Crandall in the back had first cursed him in a foreign language before he shot him. That's what his informant had told him. He'd heard the man clearly, and he'd concluded it was a curse by the tone of the man's voice. "I know when a son of a bitch calls another son of a bitch a motherfucker and it don't matter what language it's in," was how the informant had explained himself, and that was good enough for Jake Graham.

He'd also accepted his informant's belief that the man who shot Al Crandall was a Southern white man. If you'd been born in the South, as Jake's homeless informant had been, you recognized and understood that all white people did not look alike, any more than all Black people looked alike, and the man who'd shot Al Crandall was a Southern white man. "Even though he cussed him foreign, it was still from down home. They look a certain way and they sound a certain way. You know what I'm sayin'?" And Jake had known. Had known that what the homeless man saw and heard was relevant and crucial. He just didn't know what to do with it. Didn't know how to use it to help. In fact, he couldn't do anything to help, and his frustration over that fact was increasing every hour of every day. He'd become such a pain in the ass that his wife threatened to go visit her sister down in Virginia and leave him home alone. Of course he'd told her to go ahead, terrified she would. Finally, he gave up trying to contain his worry about Carole Ann Gibson and told his wife the whole story. The first time he'd ever told her the intimate details of a case. And then they both worried about Carole Ann Gibson.

So it was with a smile and a kiss that she brought him the phone in the middle of his dinner—and the middle of an Orioles game—and the information that it was Carole Ann Gibson on the line.

"Are you OK?" he asked without preamble.

It was not, she knew, a yes-or-no question, so she didn't respond to it in that manner. Instead, she told him everything that had transpired since she arrived in Louisiana, without embellishment, leaving him to his own assessment and interpretations. He said nothing until she was finished, and then he told her about his eyewitness's description of the man who'd shot Al Crandall, and it was her turn for silence. She stretched it out for a while before asking, "So it could have been Leland who killed Al and not Larry? Why? And what's the connection between Leland and Larry?"

"You gotta believe they're blood-related," Jake mused.

"Why would Larry lie in his bar entry?"

"People do it all the time." The shrug in Jake's voice carried long-distance. "And nobody checks unless or until there's a problem."

"That bar listing's not new," Carole Ann said, thought wrinkling her brow. "And if Larry wanted to conceal his connection to Leland, why not change his name instead of his place of birth? Unless he figured Devereaux was so common a name it didn't matter . . ."

"That might have been a part of it, but I don't think it was all of it."

"I don't, either. I think it's got to do with whatever Parish Petroleum is. That's what worried Al: he said he couldn't unravel the pieces."

"Yeah. But if Parish Petroleum is dealing dirty, how come they brought Crandall into it? Why didn't Devereaux just handle it himself if they were cooking up something crooked?"

"I don't know. Doesn't make sense to me, either. And here's another interesting question: if Larry's doing the legal dirty work, what's Leland got to do with it? Remember Eldon said nobody would go looking for Lafayette for fear of pissing off Leland?" And something began to take shape and form in Carole Ann's mind. "How bored are you, Jake?"

"I'm so bored it ain't even fun anymore killing the Duke of Earl."

"Then consider yourself rescued," Carole Ann said, laughing at the memory of Jake "killing" his cat. And she outlined an investigative venture that would keep him occupied for several days unless he could enlist Tommy and his computer skills.

"Good thinking," he growled, sounding less like the concerned father and more like Jake Graham. "Glad that heat down there isn't having negative effects on your brain."

"Like D.C. is any cooler," she growled right back, and smiled to herself when she heard him chuckle.

"So, what are you gonna be doing?" he asked.

"Finding out who Larry Devereaux is, where he's from, and why he's working so hard to hide the truth," she said. And after she promised to check in with Jake in seventy-two hours—sooner in an emergency—she hung up the phone and took stock.

The fear she'd experienced earlier was gone. Her mind and emotions were clear. She felt calm and focused and ready to work. More importantly, she understood clearly what her mission was, and she was buoyed by the knowledge that Jake could and would help. As she assessed her feelings, Carole Ann realized that the largest single source of her discomfort and anxiety had been her sense of aloneness. Even though they were in D.C., Cleo's response yesterday and Jake's response today provided some comfort. She was not alone. And as she thought about it, she realized Jake had actually paid her a compliment. "Good thinking," he'd growled at her.

Carole Ann sat down at the desk with her notes and turned on her computer. She entered the password and opened Al's no-longer-secret file. Rereading the list of names, she was now able to understand many of the entries. The list of names that had meant nothing to her before she now saw included the names of the three boys who had drowned under mysterious circumstances; Lil Gailliard's name and number; and Parish Legal Services. She had purchased three maps, and now spread them all out on the floor. With her notes in one hand and a magnifying glass in the other, she got down on her knees and searched for something in the maps that would connect with something in Al's notes or in her own. Searched the areas of Assumption Parish, of St. James Parish, of St. Martin Parish, of St. Mary Parish. Searched until she found, in Assumption, the bayou where three swamp babies had drowned after having talked with Al Crandall; until she found, in St. Martin, a tiny tributary of some larger water called the Poule Creek. The Chicken Creek. Chicken Shit Creek? She scrambled on her knees to the table and grabbed at the pile of tourist material. Something was playing around at the edges of consciousness and it was more than the low-down strains of "St. James Infirmary Blues." It was . . . the St. Mary Parish Museum.

CAROLE Ann took Highway 90 south out of New Orleans. She left before dawn—making certain she wasn't followed—and didn't stop until she reached Houma, an hour away. She felt as if she were driving into the bottom of the sea. She knew, from having studied the map the night before, that she could, quite literally, drive directly into the Gulf of Mexico. She just hadn't imagined how that would feel. She'd grown up on the ocean. Water was not a new experience. Yet there was something about this water . . . something about this land . . . that felt enveloping and enclosing. In California, the ocean was "out there." Even when one was in it, surfing or swimming, or on it, boating and fishing, it felt distant and cold. This water, these swamps and bayous that were not yet the Gulf, felt immediate and intimate.

Comfortable she hadn't been followed, she left the main road and followed the tourist signs to a likely place for coffee and breakfast. Since Houma was home to renowned antebellum plantations and overbooked tours of the magnificent, mysterious swamps, she didn't expect to have trouble finding food. She was not disappointed. She drove up to and parked in front of a place called Sadie's just as a young woman was turning around the red and white sign from CLOSED to OPEN and unlocking the front door. She was the palest person Carole Ann had seen since arriving in Louisiana—light blond hair and almost translucent skin. Carole Ann sat watching until the young woman noticed her and, with a smile and nod of her head, beckoned her to enter.

The dining room was empty when Carole Ann entered,

so she took a seat in the front window providing a panoramic view of the street. She heard movement and turned to see not the pale girl, but a gingerbread brown woman who was so old as to defy speculation about her age. She was dressed as if from another time: red-and-white-checked bandana tied around her head and white apron covering a dress of the same checked material as the head-wrap. She wore no shoes and walked with a regal majesty awesome to behold. She was not very tall—certainly not as tall as Carole Ann—and reed thin. While Carole Ann observed her, the woman loaded a woven straw tray with a cup and saucer, napkin-wrapped silver, a goblet of water, a pot of coffee, a pitcher of cream, and a bowl of sugar. Then, as if by virtue of magic, a basket of some kind of steaming hot bread appeared in the window behind the counter and the old woman picked up both tray and basket and crossed briskly to Carole Ann's table.

"Mornin', *cher*," the old woman said in a young girl's lilting voice, and bestowed upon her a smile that felt to Carole Ann very much like a blessing.

"Good morning," Carole Ann replied, and struggled to think of something to say, some way to open conversation with this woman she wasn't even certain was real on some level she didn't fully understand.

"You sight-seein' today?" the old woman asked as she transferred the items from her tray to the table, relieving Carole Ann of some of her anxiety.

"Yes, ma'am," Carole Ann replied, surprised at the Southernism that eased from her mouth as if she'd been born to it. "And I must say, I'm already overwhelmed and the sun's barely up."

The old woman nodded, the smile gone, and poured coffee. "This place'll take you if you ain't careful. This a powerful place, you know."

"I know," Carole Ann said quietly. "I can feel it." And she could, though she hadn't known what she was feeling until the old woman spoke the words. "But I can't tell what kind of power it is."

"What you mean, *cher?*" the old woman asked after a beat.

"There are many kinds of power. Good and bad power. Power that helps and power that wounds and destroys. All of it is strong and I feel it here, but I don't know what kind it is."

"Eat your beignet, *cher.* They just come from th' oven. I be back with a menu for you." And she departed, head high, spine erect, arms straight at her sides, bare feet making no sound on the worn-smooth wooden floor. And Carole Ann wondered who she was as she took a sip of the best coffee she'd ever tasted. The thing called "been-yay" was so sinfully rich and delicious she was prepared to accept any explanation for the mysterious old woman and the incredible food, natural or supernatural—Voudoun included—for anything she encountered here in Houma, and for the rest of the day, for that matter. She took her map from her purse, along with the tourist brochure, and was so engrossed she wasn't aware at what point the old woman returned and began studying the map over her shoulder.

"I'm going to St. Mary Parish," Carole Ann told her. "To the museum. Do you know it?"

"Oh, yes, *cher.* I know everything 'bout here. St. Mary Parish. Terrebonne Parish. Lafourche Parish." She looked down at the map again. Then she looked directly at Carole Ann. "St. Martin and Assumption, too. I know everything. What it is you want to know?" she asked in her quiet voice, as she offered Carole Ann the menu.

Carole Ann studied the hand-lettered page, aware of the nearness of the old woman who stood silently beside her, aware of the futility of closing the map with its highlighted orange areas. "Do you know about Chicken Shit Creek? Do you know about some people named Devereaux? Do you know about plants and factories that make people so sick they die?"

"I think you like the seafood omelette, *cher.*" The old woman took the menu from her hand and walked away, graceful and stately. But it was the young blond girl who refilled her coffee cup and served the omelette to her and brought her a basket of fresh beignets and wrote out her check and collected her money. The old woman was invisible until Carole Ann made her way through to the rear of the now-full café in search of the ladies' room. When she opened the door, she came face to face with her.

"You go to the St. Mary Museum, *cher.* And when you come back this way, make sure to visit the Terrebonne Museum. At two o'clock this afternoon."

Carole Ann drove the forty miles from Houma to Franklin tangled in her own emotions, buffeted by conflicting messages and signals from her brain. Never before in her life had she entrusted herself to so many strangers. Never before in her life had such trust been necessary. But as she was constantly reminded by Tommy and Jake, she was on her own now. She was operating without backup. And her fear told her she didn't know how to do that. Nor did she know how to trust. To say nothing of trusting strangers. Yet, that's all she'd done since arriving in Louisiana: She had trusted Warren Forchette and Lillian Gailliard and Eldon and Merle Warmsley. And now, here she was, poised to trust an old woman who resembled a runaway slave, for she would certainly be at the Terrebonne Museum at two o'clock, as instructed.

But didn't that mean, she asked herself in the ongoing dialogue, that she was, in fact, trusting herself? Trusting her own good judgment? And in reality, didn't she have, backup? After all, she'd called Jake, she'd called Cleo, and they'd responded. And because they had, she now had two potential suspects in Al's murder . . . if that was to be considered positive. *But what you have isn't really information,* her skeptic self warned. *What you have is speculation and pieces that don't fit any puzzle, and a headful of hunches.* Sure, she could awaken Cleo in the middle of the night and play clue games. But the reality was that Cleo was however many miles away Washington was, living another life that had nothing to do with this one. Cleo was in another world. And so was Carole Ann.

In another world and time; in a time and place that, had she been born then and there, she'd have been a slave. And here she was behaving like a tourist, gaping at plantation manors and rice fields in which her ancestors might have toiled, planning to meet an old woman—a stranger whose name she didn't even know—an old woman dressed as a slave. She laughed out loud at a sign announcing the annual Catfish and Petroleum Festival, giving meaning to the phrase, "If you can't beat 'em, join 'em." Then she saw the road sign indicating that New Iberia was but twenty miles ahead. New Iberia where, according to Al's notes, Eldon Warmsley lived . . .

CAROLE Ann toured the St. Mary Parish Museum and took a walking tour and an open-bus tour and hired a taxi to drive her around and found no evidence of death and destruction caused by Parish Petroleum or any other source. She questioned everyone she met: the taxi driver, a sixty-year-old native of the town; the tour guides; the shopkeepers along the main street; people fishing along the bayou banks; a police officer; and a postal employee. Of course environmental pollution was something they knew about. After all, they lived in Louisiana. And occasionally oily air and water and dead fish were part of the price paid for successful industry: successful industry was what put paychecks in pockets; environmental pollution was what put people on the unemployment line. And sure they'd heard of Parish Petroleum. You live in Louisiana long enough you hear about all the big oil companies. But anything specific? Anything negative? Nope.

Carole Ann returned to Houma, now confused as well as skeptical, and becoming something close to angry. She pulled into the parking lot of the Terrebonne Museum at exactly two o'clock, got out of the car, slamming the door much harder than necessary, and was looking for the building's entrance when she spied the old woman, wearing not a slave costume but a simple and pretty flowered cotton dress and a wide-brimmed straw hat. Her feet were encased in blue canvas espadrilles. A straw purse dangled from the crook of her left arm. She looked like anybody's grandmother. She raised her right hand in greeting, raised it like a person taking the oath, and everything that had been brewing inside Carole Ann dissipated. She felt all the heaviness drain away as she crossed the parking lot. And the closer she got to the old woman, the more relaxed she felt.

"Good afternoon," Carole Ann said.

"You keep good time, *cher,*" the old woman said, and took her arm and guided her around the side of the building, where Carole Ann saw a boardwalk leading to a dock. "My grandson is waiting for us at the boat," she said, walking that brisk walk again, a stride that belied her age.

Oh shit, Carole Ann thought. *Grandson. Boat. Water. I still don't know this woman's name or who she is and I'm getting into a boat with her and her grandson.* "Where are we going?" She tried to conceal the fear and anger and skepticism and helplessness that suddenly reclaimed her. She stopped walking when the old woman tightened the grip on her arm.

"You want to go to Poule Creek, no?"

Carole Ann was about to say "No!" when some instinct took control of her mouth. Poule Creek . . . Chicken Shit Creek . . . "Yes," Carole Ann said, and resigned herself to accepting whatever was ahead. Whatever it was would certainly be different than anything she'd seen thus far. And, she hoped, more informative.

The grandson was a man Carole Ann's own age—perhaps older—who'd apparently inherited his grandmother's preference for verbal conciseness, along with other genetic traits. He was less than six feet tall and brown-sugar brown and reed thin and wiry and erect. A lot like Jake Graham, she thought, though where Jake almost quivered with pent-up energy and emotion, this man was as calm as the swamp waters. He helped his grandmother into the flat-bottomed boat and into one of two chairs. Then he reached for Carole Ann, helping her to the other chair. Then he turned from them and started first one, then the other of the boat's two engines, and powered the boat out into the water. In a matter of seconds the dock and the museum were specks on the horizon and Carole Ann was thinking perhaps they were cruising in the Gulf of Mexico. Then the grasses appeared. Tall and wavy and green-brown. And there was nothing else to see. Except . . . egrets and herons and turtles—huge ones, not the tiny pet store variety. And oh dear Christ, water moccasins and alligators. Or were they crocodiles . . . ? Alligators, she told herself. Crocodiles lived in Africa and South America. Didn't they? She watched the horny, ancient beast . . . watched its snout and eyes . . . and pondered the majesty of creation.

They were now further inland, or perhaps they had

been all along and Carole Ann had not noticed. But now she noticed because the alligator cruised in for a landing, causing quite a commotion on the bank as several varieties of fish, fowl, and mammal vacated the reptile's space. The overhanging trees and the moss that dangled from them created a mottled shade that neither cooled nor protected from the sun, which played and danced on the water like nothing she'd ever seen. This truly was another world. Another way of life and living.

The grandson cut the engines with one hand and, without seeming to look, grabbed for a long-handled net behind him with the other. A smile creased the old woman's face and she raised her hand to silence Carole Ann even before the thought to speak reached her brain. So she watched instead as the grandson held the net, watching the water . . . watching . . . and swoosh! In a single motion, the net swooped into the water and returned, full of a huge, wiggling, glistening fish. The old woman clapped her hands like a delighted child and watched the man dump the fish into an ice chest. He turned to face his grandmother, no longer a grown man, but a boy proud of having pleased his grandmother. He grinned, blushed, ducked his head, and restarted the boat's engines. And soon they were skimming along the water again, creating a momentary path in the reeds and grasses that sprung back into place and obliterated their intrusive presence forever.

"I'm called Sadie Cord," the old woman said, leaning toward Carole Ann but not speaking any louder than before. And she smiled her powerful smile at Carole Ann's reaction and explained that her family had owned the restaurant in Houma for two generations but always assumed a subservient public role because that was what the white tourists wanted and expected from antebellum Louisiana. So Sadie dressed as a slave and cooked and occasionally served the food, all the while owning the most prosperous eating establishment in a town comprised of and sustained by tourist attractions. She shrugged eloquently. "They were so happy back then," Sadie said gently, and Carole Ann almost missed the flash of steely irony. She patted Carole Ann on the knee and pointed to the rear of the boat. "He is my firstborn grand. Named Hervé, after my husband, who died long before that boy was born. He's my favorite." She shrugged again. "The first is always special, *cher.* Don't mean the others are less. I now have thirty-two of them. Grand and great-grand and great-great-grand. And they all are special. But he"—and she pointed over her shoulder—"is the favorite special."

Carole Ann was about to comment when she suddenly was assaulted by a powerful and disgusting odor. She raised her head to the wind to determine the direction of the smell, and as she did so, Hervé turned the boat toward it, into it, and Carole Ann almost retched. She tried to take a deep breath but could not. She felt faint and dizzy and nauseous and lurched to the side of the boat and leaned over. What she saw choked the sickness back. The water had changed. There no longer were green-brown wavy swamp grasses. There no longer was vegetation of any kind, or fowl or reptiles or mossy trees. The swamp was ugly and heavy . . . it no longer even looked like water. Hervé cut one of the engines and slowed the boat and crept through the rank, oily sludge. Carole Ann's guts settled and she pulled her eyes away from what should have been water to study the coastline. As if rising from the sea, it appeared: first the dock and then the boats and then the village itself. Al's "swamp village." The Chicken Shit River. And the "conjure woman." Who was seated behind her in this boat.

Carole Ann was buffeted by emotion more powerful

than any she'd felt since the night Jake Graham told her Al was dead, and it was not only because Al had been to this place, but also because of what this place was and had been. It was ancient and Carole Ann could feel its antiquity. As strongly as she could smell the destruction devouring it. Looking at Sadie and Hervé was like looking at images in a history book, except that bound version of the past was flat and dead and Sadie and Hervé were life itself. Past life and present, Carole Ann mused, recalling Sadie's slave masquerade. And Al had been here. Had seen it all. Had known and understood and had died because of it.

"The man who came here, Mrs. Cord. I don't know how he found you, but he was my husband. Al Crandall was his name and they've murdered him. And I've come to find out who and why." Carole Ann was shaking and boiling inside. She closed her eyes as Hervé eased the boat to the dock, and put out a hand to steady herself. Her hand was caught in a firm, gnarly grip, and she held on. Suddenly, it all felt like too much. Last night's clarity and security evaporated on a whiff of death and destruction.

"I can tell you the 'why,' *cher*," Sadie whispered in her ear. "And I will help you find the 'who.' "

Hervé helped them out of the boat and onto the dock— his grandmother first, and then Carole Ann. He secured the skiff, then hopped back into it, straightening and ordering what must have been the neatest craft on the bayou. Then he hoisted the cooler and stepped from the boat onto the dock as if from a carriage to a red carpet. He bowed from the waist to his grandmother and ducked his head to Carole Ann and, without a word, lifted the cooler to his shoulder and walked off down the road.

"Then please tell me why, Mrs. Cord. Perhaps if I can understand the 'why,' the 'who' won't matter quite so much."

"I think perhaps it will matter more, *cher*," Sadie Cord said quietly, and taking her hand again, began to walk and talk.

Pointe Afrique—the town had been called that by the people who founded it and whose descendants had lived in it for more than one hundred years—was the only entity in that part of St. Martin Parish not owned by Parish Petroleum. But it turned out not to matter, since Bay Afrique and everything in it and near it and around it had been poisoned by the sludge Parish Petroleum had been dumping into the Poule River for twenty years. For twenty secret years, for this is where the company had moved its operation after the lawsuit that closed its Assumption Parish operation back in 1976. Pointe Afrique inhabitants had supported themselves fishing and harvesting rice until about 1985, when the land and the people first began to display the effects of Parish Petroleum's poisonous activities. Because they were familiar with the events in Assumption Parish, most of the younger residents fled, taking their children. Most of the older residents and a handful of single men remained behind to preserve and protect Pointe Afrique, and to prepare for the day when it would be safe for the refugees to return. It seemed as if that day finally would arrive when word filtered through the surrounding towns that Parish Petroleum was shutting down. And indeed, surreptitious surveillance of the place confirmed the rumor.

Sadie stopped talking and took a deep breath, giving Carole Ann a welcome and much needed opportunity to ponder all she'd seen on her walking tour of Pointe Afrique before settling down in the old woman's living room to drink strong, sweet gingerroot tea and listen to her talk; what she'd seen had astounded, excited, and angered her. Pointe Afrique was indeed a village, a very old one comprised of weathered wooden buildings on stilts, sturdy and in good repair. The commercial district was comprised of a general store, a smaller version of Eldon Warmsley's; a church with a cemetery; a barbershop; a carpenter's shop that doubled as a shoemaker's; and an establishment that could best be described as a juke joint, though it seemed its liveliest days and nights might have been in the past. Still, the place contained a dozen round tables and assorted chairs, an ancient jukebox, and a stocked bar.

The hard-packed dirt roads of the village were swept smooth and clean and hugged by bright green borders, which Carole Ann realized were some form of artificial turf. Colorful plastic flowers bloomed in urns in the cemetery, and a profusion of greenery and flowering shrubs lived and thrived in planters in front of every structure, residential and commercial. So desperate were these good and simple people for some semblance of real life that they'd laid down fake grass and planted plastic flowers. Carole Ann ached at the thought of it.

"It wasn't till he came that we understood we weren't safe. That we weren't never gon' be safe," Sadie said, the sadness that settled over her making her look like the old woman she was. "Your man is the one who told us the truth, told us what that Parish Petroleum really was up to."

And what that was, Carole Ann learned, was an expansion of operations, not a cessation. Production had been halted at the St. Martin plant only until surveyors and engineers could complete an assessment of the long-dormant property in St. Mary Parish: land area more than double that of the St. Martin property and extremely valuable now because of its popularity as a tourist retreat. Parish Petroleum officials were in the process of deciding whether to build a new plant in St. Mary or sell that land and use the proceeds to expand the St. Martin operation.

"But it's not their land to sell," Carole Ann blurted out,

so angry that she wasn't thinking rationally, and instantly realized the error, for the old woman had gone still and silent. Had closed up her eyes and her expressions and her movements. Had locked Carole Ann on the outside. So, for the third time in almost as many days, Carole Ann found herself telling her story, leaving out many of the details, but including what Warren Forchette had told her about the judgment awarding Parish Petroleum's assets to the plaintiffs, and her discovery of the original Parish Petroleum filing in the state archives. The more she talked, the more the old woman relaxed. Until finally she was ready to speak again.

"Nobody knows that but you, *cher*. They thought your man knew and that's why they killed him. He was trying to find the proof for us when his boss sent for him to come home . . ."

"When was that?" Carole Ann stiffened.

"Last time he was here. Back in January. He told his boss Parish Petroleum didn't own that St. Mary Parish land so they couldn't sell it and his boss told him to drop everything and come on home. He was sittin' right over there, talkin' on that phone you see there." Sadie Cord turned and looked at the old-fashioned black rotary telephone perched in the center of the white lace doily in the center of the three-legged table in the corner of the room. Carole Ann followed her gaze, easily imagining Al's long, lanky body perched on the edge of the chair that would have been too small, legs splayed out in front of him. Could imagine his anger at being ordered to return home . . .

"Did he say anything to you then, Mrs. Cord?"

"He said he would get us the proof that Parish Petroleum cain't sell that land. And he said he'd make 'em pay to clean up our little place here and our river."

"Now I'll do it, Mrs. Cord. And hang Larry Devereaux out to dry in the process."

"Who?" The old woman snapped to attention, her eyes flashing and her hands trembling. "Who you say you gon' dry?"

Carole Ann smiled at the malapropism. "Al's boss. The one who made him come home. Larry Devereaux is his name . . ."

The old woman emitted a heavy sigh and slumped back into her chair and into herself. Her eyes no longer flashed but dimmed as they looked far into some other place. "So that's what happened to Lawrence," she said, more to herself than to Carole Ann, to whom she said, looking directly at her now, "Well, *cher.* That's your 'who.' "

"Who is?" Carole Ann was now confused, unable to follow the old woman's ramblings.

"That Larry Devereaux. If he's who I think he is, his true name is Lawrence Warmsley . . ."

Carole Ann lost control and gave full rein to all the feelings and emotions that had been gathering force inside her all day. She cursed and wept and cursed again and, finally spent, listened to Sadie Cord tell her the story of a woman—a white woman named Ella Mae Scarborough—who lived on an Assumption Parish bayou and who had the same two lovers all her life: a Cajun named Leland Devereaux and a mulatto named Lawrence Warmsley. Ella Mae had given birth to seven children: Lafayette, Leland, and Jeanette Devereaux; and Lawrence, Eldon, Ella Mae, and Earlene Warmsley. Eldon Warmsley, Sadie said, would be the older brother of Larry Devereaux, who had joined the Marines after his high school graduation and had not been heard from since. Everyone had assumed he was somewhere passing, and no one had attempted to locate him, to violate his privacy or threaten his secret life.

Carole Ann shook her head and laughed out loud. It was all too ludicrous. Had Al known this? Had he suspected? This alone would be reason enough for Larry Devereaux to have killed him. Maybe Al's death had nothing to do with Parish Petroleum after all. She stopped laughing when she remembered she'd told Warren Forchette about Larry Devereaux. Would he have told Eldon Warmsley?

"Of course, *cher!*" Old Sadie exclaimed, looking at Carole Ann as if she were a strange new species. And after she finished explaining why, she went into the kitchen and got Carole Ann a beer. The same kind of beer Warren Forchette had given her on the porch of Eldon Warmsley's store. The same night they'd had dinner at Eldon Warmsley's house. At his Uncle Eldon's house.

It was all too much to imagine, to believe, to process, to understand, to fit into a familiar framework, to build a murder around. It was her experience that crime was usually simple—even stupid. Vicious, violent, evil—of course. But it rarely was complicated. Even the white-collar criminals—the embezzlers, the racketeers—ultimately were easy to figure out: They were motivated by greed or money or power. Or all those things. Even when they attempted to construct elaborate schemes, first to effect and then to conceal their avarice, their crime eventually unraveled and deconstructed into a simple formula—they wanted more and they did whatever it took to take it.

But this mess! Her husband had been murdered by a Black man who'd been passing for white . . . a lawyer who faced certain disbarment for his part in whatever the Parish Petroleum business would turn out to be . . . whose white brother just happened to be a member of the United States House of Representatives. Any one of which sufficed as a motive for murder. Not to mention the Parish Petroleum money. And she, Carole Ann, had entrusted her mission to the white-looking Black brother and nephew of the murderer, either or both of whom might already have warned him he was under suspicion. Louisiana was swampy, murky, in more ways than she cared to consider . . . the familial ties as intricate and unfathomable as the rivers and tributaries and bayous and swamps that all connected, that all sprung from the same source and led to the same eventual destination. She felt nauseated, and it had nothing to do with the odor emanating from the Chicken Shit River, which she'd almost ceased to notice.

"You are safe, *cher,*" Sadie Cord said softly, and Carole Ann shook her head. There no longer was such a thing as safe. And if there was, Carole Ann no longer believed in it.

"I'd like to go back . . . to my car, please."

"Hervé cooked the big fish for you," Sadie said, again softly. She said "feesh," so it took Carole Ann a moment to understand, and when she did, she knew enough about being Southern to know that to refuse would be an unforgivable breach of etiquette. So she nodded and tried to smile and finished her beer and followed the old woman through the three rooms of her tiny house out the back door and onto an enclosed porch that was also an outdoor kitchen. Hervé was there, with the big fish and a dozen big shrimp on a grill and a huge glass bowl of chopped vegetables resting in a tub of ice, surrounded by bottles of beer. He removed two, opened them, and placed them on a pine table. He nodded at the two women, and they both sat.

As they ate, Sadie and a reluctant Hervé explained how the remaining few men of Pointe Afrique had to venture further and further away from their village to catch edible fish, meaning that they were away from home most of the time. That's why the town seemed so empty. Hervé himself worked the waters every day, returning home on Fridays and bringing his wife and children, who lived during the week with her sister in Houma. Sadie herself slept most nights in a room above the restaurant. Since few people knew of the existence of their village, and fewer still knew how to find it, it was safe enough. But they all feared that if the poisoning weren't stopped soon, Pointe Afrique would die. Just like the land and water around it.

They all were silent on the boat trip back to the dock and the parking lot of the Terrebonne Museum, where Carole Ann's car was the only one remaining in the lot, now chained and locked. In a matter of moments, Hervé located a surly guard whose disposition improved quickly and dramatically when Carole Ann offered him twenty dollars to unlock the chains and release her car. She shook hands with a still silent Hervé, who bowed slightly at her thanks for the truly fine meal. And she accepted and returned the embrace of Sadie Cord, who whispered in her ear before releasing her. Those whispered words reverberated in her brain on the way back to New Orleans and her hotel room:

"Just as Eldon Warmsley is uncle to Lillian and Warren Forchette, I am aunt to Eldon Warmsley. Just as Eldon is brother to Ella Mae—Lillian and Warren's mama—I am sister to Eldon's papa, Lawrence Warmsley."

THAT night, Carole Ann dreamt of hybrid people—Black on one half of their bodies and white on the other half—and all of them had masks for faces. Dreamt of people who merged and blended together until they were all the same person, all identical to each other. Dreamt of angry swamps that bubbled and boiled and erupted, spewing poison and cleansing themselves of their sickness.

Dreamt of fish and alligators and long-legged birds walking on the surface of water that did not ripple and flow. Dreamt of Al, running over dry, dead earth, gathering children into his arms and running with them.

Despite feeling drugged and sluggish from the dreams, she spent the following morning in the library, reading about the history of Louisiana, reading about the differences between Creoles and Cajuns and the many varieties of Colored and non-Colored people, differences that had blurred over time but that still had deeply significant meaning in Louisiana. And while she was at it, she looked up the music—Creole and Cajun and Zydeco—noting the differences as defined, and understanding that only someone born to the culture that was Louisiana could truly understand it. She spent the afternoon touring historical sites, ending up at the home of Marie Leveau, and noting that the dry history, the words on a page, offered her no real feel for the New Orleans of Marie I, Marie II, and the Creoles of their day.

Feeling hungry, she wandered in and out of half a dozen restaurants in dissatisfaction until she understood that what she wanted was food prepared by Merle Warmsley and Hervé Cord. And that wasn't possible. So she returned to her hotel, changed clothes, retrieved her car from the underground parking lot, and went in search of a track. She remembered having seen a large park on the way to Warren Forchette's legal center.

It felt good to run, though she didn't like running on a track or under the sun. Technically, it was sundown. But this was Louisiana, and though it was well after eight o'clock at night, it was still fully light, and still hot. She ran hard and fast and welcomed the perspiration that soaked her shorts and tee shirt before she'd completed the first lap. The *crunch-crunch-crunch* of the gravel as her feet pounded was a soothing, rhythmic sound, and she gave up counting laps and distance and trusted her body to tell her when she'd run her four miles. Because there were no sights to see, she took in the geography of the park. At the north end of the track were the tennis courts, four of them, all filled. They were too far away for Carole Ann to judge the quality of the play, but she could see the towering banks of lights and knew that play would go long into the night.

The swimming pool lay east. Already closed for the day, the water shimmered blue in the distance. She imagined she could still hear the screeches and squeals of youngsters carried on the moist air. Adjacent to the main pool, Carole Ann noticed, was the smaller, toddlers' pool. And as she took the curve, she noticed the standard playground equipment: swings and slides and those convoluted metal things children loved to climb and swing from and fall from. Both of her nieces had suffered a broken arm from falling from one. Jungle gym. What, she wondered, was the origin of that? Probably the originator of the thing had convinced his own children they were exploring the wilds of Africa . . .

South and west lay the fields: a baseball diamond where a game was in progress under the lights, a soccer field where it appeared that several games were in progress, and a patch staked out by volleyball aficionados. Having seen all there was to see, Carole Ann turned inward and ran, feeling her body relax for the first time in days. She slowed her pace and lengthened her stride. The heat was taking its toll. Perhaps she'd only run three miles. Christ! It was hotter and more humid here than in D.C. and that was not a complimentary observation.

She noted with gratitude that dusk was descending, without any real expectation that it would be any cooler. Though perhaps it was necessary to hold out hope, she mused, noting the arrival of two men at the far north end of the track. She thought it odd that neither man stretched before stepping onto the track; and even at so great a distance, it was obvious neither had a runner's body. New to the game, she thought. She also thought it rude that they were running toward her. Track etiquette dictated that newcomers follow the established direction. As they drew closer, Carole Ann noted that neither seemed properly dressed. It was far too hot to be running in long pants. Then she noticed they weren't running exactly . . . in fact, they were chugging right toward her, flat-footed and slope-shouldered.

A thousand warning sirens went off in her brain. "Goddammit!" She whispered the curse through clenched teeth, her eyes darting from the two men closing in on her toward the street where her car was parked. She could easily outrun them, she concluded, at the same time as the taller of the two men reached into the waistband of his pants. "Goddammit!" she said again, close enough to them to discern with clarity that he held a gun. Anger surged through her like increased electrical voltage. She kept watching the gun and increased her speed. She was close enough now to see their facial expressions, and what she saw was confusion. She continued to run toward them, instead of away, and their confusion slowed them, caused them to falter. Carole Ann let go a shriek that caused them to stop in their tracks. By the time the one with the gun raised his arm, Carole Ann was close enough.

She turned her body, spun, and kicked. The gun was still sailing when she kicked again, higher this time, slamming the side of her foot into his face. Blood gushed from his nose and mouth. She dropped into a crouch, rolled around behind him, regained her feet, and angled a kick at the knees of the second man. He howled like a kid pushed from the top of the jungle gym as his kneecap shattered, and he dropped to the ground, supporting himself on his good knee. Carole Ann slashed at him, the side of her hand connecting with the side of his neck, and he went all the way down. Still in motion, she changed direction and cut across the track, angling toward the gently sloping grassy knoll to the street where she'd left her car, aware of her heart thudding against her chest, of her brain pounding against her cranium, of her blood rushing hot and fast through her veins. Until this moment, her years of martial arts training had been nothing but study, nothing but contrived and controlled mental and physical routines demonstrated with partners in mirrored rooms with mats on the floor. As was usually the case with real life, her real-life fighting had borne little resemblance to the theoretical. True, her masters would be proud: she'd perfectly executed the moves she'd learned. But she'd never wanted to kill her instructors or her partners. She'd very much wanted to kill her two attackers. All the while imagining they were Larry Devereaux.

THE muscular man in the tight jeans and tighter tee shirt had started down the hill at a jog that increased in speed to a run when he saw the two men step onto the track. But he stopped and backpedaled when he saw the woman could take care of herself. "Well, I'll be a son of a bitch," he muttered under his breath as she landed the final chop and jogged off up the hill, looking smugly self-satisfied. He sauntered toward the two broken men, wondering how long it would take them to recover their senses. He'd wait, however long it took. Warren Forchette wanted to get the license number of their car, wanted to know who they were, so he could find out who'd sent them. Because whoever it was had a big payroll. In addition to the two sprawled on the track, two watchers were still parked in front of the Embassy Suites hotel, and two others were parked across from the entrance to the underground garage, waiting for the emergence of a white Chrysler LeBaron convertible with a red interior. And it would be a long wait, for Carole Ann Gibson Crandall was now driving a rented blue Pontiac Firebird.

CAROLE Ann had a hot shower and ordered from room service. She tried to order the beer she liked—the one Warren had bought from Eldon's general store and Sadie Cord had served her at Pointe Afrique. But she didn't remember the name of it, and the room service waiter said there were many good beers in Louisiana, so she ordered a bottle of chardonnay instead, and fried catfish and a salad. She'd finished the food and was almost halfway through the chardonnay when the knock sounded. She jumped, sloshing wine all over herself and the table and onto the floor. Paralyzed with fear, she sat holding the glass and looking at the door. There came a second series of knocks, followed by a voice. Carole Ann forced herself to cross to the door, making no sound with her bare feet in the plush carpet. She reached the door just as there came a third set of stacatto knocks and the insistent calling of her name. She looked through the peephole. Lillian Gailliard. Carole Ann opened the door.

"I been worried about you, *cher*," Lil said, something strongly resembling worry creasing her brow and tightening her voice.

"Thanks but no thanks," Carole Ann said tersely and moved to close the door.

"*Cher!*" Lil blocked the door with her strong hand, and stopped Carole Ann with the power of her voice. "We are not your enemies."

"Perhaps," Carole Ann said with a shrug. "But since I

don't know what you are, I'll feel better keeping you at a distance."

"Please let me talk to you," Lil insisted.

"And what will you leave out this time? Maybe you're really the Queen of Sheba and your brother, Warren, is the King of Siam?" Carole Ann was not in a conciliatory frame of mind, and she had not yet picked up enough Southern that a display of good manners overrode anger, fear, and confusion. "I don't want to hear anything you have to say, Lil. I'm tired and I'm going to bed." She tried again to close the door and again Lil blocked the effort.

"You don't know what it's like to be from here," she said into the space between them, the narrow space between the door being open and the door being closed.

"So now you're the victim," Carole Ann snapped.

"No. Yes," Lil replied decisively. "How many people do you think I could tell I have a white grandmother?" There was so much pain in the words that Carole Ann stepped away from the door, allowing it to open and Lil to enter. "Warren and I had classmates at Howard who didn't believe we were related, to say nothing of believing we were brother and sister. You have trouble believing it yourself," Lil said softly, closing the door and stepping closer to Carole Ann.

"That's not true!" Carole Ann rushed to defend herself in the face of the truth, while at the same time seething in anger that the woman had just revealed another secret— that she'd lived in D.C. and had never mentioned that fact during their previous meeting.

"Sure it is," Lil said. "Just like you have trouble believing Eldon is our uncle. That Miss Sadie is his aunt. You look at us and think about your own family and the families of your friends and you think how everybody is the same color: white people's relatives are white and Black people's relatives are brown and nobody is confused. Well, here in Louisiana, we've lived with the confusion for so long we don't think about it or worry about it. We also don't talk about it."

"And what does color have to do with the fact that until this moment you failed to mention that you attended Howard? You know I'm from D.C. and it doesn't occur to you to say, 'How's life on Georgia Avenue?' Cut the crap, Lil, and say whatever it is you came to say and then leave me alone." Carole Ann slouched over to the table and poured herself another glass of wine, pointedly not offering the bottle to Lil, who had dropped onto the sofa and removed her shoes. She settled her back into the corner and raised her legs, sighing with relief. And Carole Ann again was impressed with the notion that the woman lived with constant pain.

"Warren is the third-born, though he acts like the big brother because he's the one who took care of me when I was so sad and sick that time."

That time. Carole Ann needed several long seconds to interpret "that time," and when she understood that Lil was referring to the time when the strange cancers claimed her husband and children, when the poisonous tumors almost claimed her life, she instantly regretted her open display of hostility. She sloughed off her anger and listened as Lil told how her baby brother, Warren, had left his junior year at Grambling University, where he was the star quarterback on that school's renowned football team, and assumed responsibility for his big sister's life and her affairs and her effort to make somebody accountable for her undeserved misery. That was when and how and why nineteen-year-old Warren Forchette had decided to become a lawyer instead of a professional football player. With her Parish Petroleum settlement money, Lil had taken them both to D.C. and to Howard University . . . a respite from the pain of Louisiana and loss.

"We believed we'd stay. I never wanted to see Louisiana again, and Warren was afraid to leave me alone for longer than five minutes at a time." Lil closed her eyes and faded back into her memory. Carole Ann poured her some wine in a water glass and took it to her. The relief on her face spoke her gratitude. "We were there for six years. Warren finished his undergrad degree and went to law school, and I got a bachelor's and a master's in political science. And neither of us made a single friend. Not even among the kids from Louisiana, because they didn't want to be reminded of the peculiar color thing. But they wouldn't let us forget. So we came back home."

She took a sip of her wine and shifted position on the sofa, placing a pillow in the middle of her back. She wasn't looking at Carole Ann, and seemed not even to be talking to her. "The UPTO welcomed me back with open arms, and Warren hung up his shingle in the shittiest part of town and immediately built a solid practice. He won a wrongful-death suit against the police department and his fee from the settlement with the city allowed him to open that legal center and hire a second lawyer. Then he won a major medical-malpractice suit, collected another big fee from the county hospital, and expanded the legal center . . ."

Carole Ann swallowed the remainder of her wine in a big gulp, jumped to her feet, and began pacing. Lil stopped talking and sipped her wine and watched and waited. As a woman once consumed by grief and anger, Lil knew what she was seeing when she watched Carole Ann pace and prowl—a woman forcing an emotional storm to die down.

The effort was more of a struggle than Carole Ann would have admitted to anyone. Grief and anger she could control. Fear was a new challenge. So was confusion. A couple of hours ago, two men had tried to kill her and the fear was still with her. Twenty-four hours ago, a white man had become a Black man and she remained confused. She decided it was easier to be angry with Lil and everybody in New Orleans than to control the fear or sort through the confusion.

"That's all very interesting," she said dryly, standing near Lil but not looking at her. "Moving, even. But none of it explains why Warren couldn't have said to me the day I met him, 'My sister, Lil, knows more about environmental racism than anybody in town.' None of it explains why, when I said I needed to find Eldon Warmsley, you couldn't have said to me, 'He's my uncle. I know exactly where he is.' None of it explains why, when I mentioned Larry Devereaux, Warren didn't say, 'Holy shit! We now have a motive for your husband's murder!' God only knows how long it would have taken for me to learn all this if I hadn't stumbled into Sadie Cord and if she'd hadn't, for whatever reason, taken me into her confidence." Carole Ann was pacing again, covering the length of the room in long strides, slashing the air with her hands as if reliving the earlier attack. "I think all this color shit is really fascinating, but I quite frankly don't care if your grandmother is white or sky blue and pink with purple polka dots! I want to find out who murdered my husband, and why!"

"And we want to help you," Lil said, sitting up and swinging her feet around to the floor.

"Oh, yeah. Right," Carole Ann snorted rudely. "When the most likely suspect is your Black uncle Larry Warmsley, also known as white Larry Devereaux?" And she took momentary satisfaction in the fact that Lil blanched slightly at that. "By the way," Carole Ann said quickly, taking full advantage of her upper hand, "whatever happened to Earlene?"

Lil looked hard at Carole Ann for a long moment before she shrugged and shook her head in a gesture that was both sorrow and something like disbelief. "She came to a bad end. Took herself up north to Shreveport, to LSU and came to a bad end."

Lil slipped her feet back into her shoes and stood up. The effort caused her to flush with pain but she covered it with a wry grin. "The blood is important, *cher,* I won't deny that. But the land means more when it is a question of survival."

Lil closed the door softly but definitely and was gone. Carole Ann was left to ponder too many large things that held consequences too important for her to risk misunderstanding or misinterpretation. Never before had she experienced such confusion—confusion so intense it felt like despair. Not even the fear was this debilitating. People she wanted very much to like—people she needed desperately to trust—were blood-bound to her husband's murderer. Would Lil and Warren and Eldon and Sadie help her avenge Al if it meant exposing one of their own as a murderer? Would they expose one of their own as a murderer to preserve their land?

Carole Ann knew the answers were not in her head. So, once again, she gathered every scrap of information she had so far collected and spread it out on the floor in orderly piles. Then, sifting through each of the piles, she wrote down the questions that remained unanswered. And when she was finished, there were five of them, and the conviction that when she found the answers, she would have found both murderer and motive. Then she thought of a sixth question, and remembered Warren Forchette's comment that she couldn't "count worth a good goddamn." She smiled at the memory. Briefly. And the smile and the memory wafted away on a wave of sadness, and leaving the mess in the middle of the floor, she double-locked the door, extinguished the lights, climbed into bed, and dreamt of running from something she could not see or hear but which smelled like something ugly and awful burning. Then she was no longer running but dancing, her feet trying desperately to keep up with too fast music, and the burning smell was no longer ugly and acrid but that of food—many gigantic fish cooking on a grill.

10

CAROLE ANN SPENT THE NEXT THREE DAYS DEVISING new and ingenious means of disguising herself and escaping from the hotel undetected in order to find the answers to her six questions. She purchased two wigs—a brassy orange shoulder-length one and a cap of pseudo-dreadlocks—and an assortment of secondhand clothing from a thrift store in the neighborhood of Warren's legal center. One day she exited the hotel from the service entrance wearing the orange wig and a white uniformlike dress, hoping she'd be dismissed as hotel staff. That day she rode the Amtrak train from New Orleans to Baton Rouge, changing clothes in the foul-smelling, minuscule compartment mislabeled as a toilet. She spent hours immersed in filings and pleadings and court orders covering the last thirty years of environmental litigation in Louisiana. She did not find the document she was looking for but she did find several others that contained the information she sought. She also did not find evidence that Parish Petroleum currently had a legal license to do business anywhere in Louisiana. No license fee, no filing fee, and no taxes had been paid to the state in the company's name in the last twenty-four months. Carole Ann also knew that in a place like Louisiana, where the business of oil took precedence over most matters, such an oversight would not be considered serious, and she had no doubt that whoever served as Parish Petroleum's legal counsel could make the case that such failures were nothing more than oversight.

And then she had a thought that sent her burrowing back into the dusty files she'd just reassembled and stacked: she did not recall seeing the name of an attorney of record on any of the documents. There had to be a local attorney of record. And yet there was not. She closed the files again, returned them to the clerk, and trudged across the square in the blistering heat to the state office building. The clerk in the licensing office recognized her, quickly processed her request, and then told her how to get to the Louisiana state bar association headquarters.

Her visit to the historian's office in the statehouse was brief and productive, if not entirely pleasant. The elderly clerk apparently had not quite adjusted himself to the notion of Black female lawyers, and he needed prodding into late-twentieth-century reality. Carole Ann was of the perfect mindset to prod, and she left the statehouse not believing the old clerk's insistence that copies were fifty cents each, but gladly paying the charge to get what she wanted. Her return trip to the Department of Vital Records was brief and productive, and she told herself she deserved to sleep on the train ride back to New Orleans.

On the day she would drive to Shreveport, home of Louisiana State University, Carole Ann, head covered with dozens of mock dreadlocks and body draped in too-big shirt, jeans, and shoes, first attached herself to a large group on a walking tour of the French Quarter. As the group snaked its way down Royal Street, she ducked into the Historic New Orleans Collection museum, double-timed her way across the lobby, quickly exited from a side door, and hurried across St. Louis Street into the Omni Hotel, where she'd arranged through the concierge to have a rental car waiting. She changed clothes in the hotel bathroom—a much more pleasant experience than that afforded by Amtrak. Then she spent the drive alternating between self-congratulations and self-pity, for she knew that no matter how clever and resourceful she imagined herself, she could not escape the reality that someone had sent two thugs with guns to kill her. Just because she'd so far succeeded in avoiding them didn't mean they'd changed their minds about finding her or they'd admitted defeat and retreated. What she was doing was dangerous and she knew it, and the fear that generated was becoming more and more difficult to keep at bay. Not even the anger that also increased with every new discovery was sufficient to quell the fear.

"I don't mean any disrespect, ma'am, but this campus wasn't integrated in 1960." The young woman's brow was wrinkled and she held her hands palms up as if preparing to ward off a blow while she awaited Carole Ann's response, which was a while in coming because it took a while for her to understand the girl's meaning. And when she did, another few seconds were required to formulate a response that indicated that she, in fact, had not been offended, while at the same time covering the ignorance she did feel.

"I appreciate your observation," Carole Ann said with a warm smile and more than a little embarrassment. "I do understand about LSU's enrollment policies in 1960. But the young woman I'm inquiring about would have been enrolled as a white student."

Then it was the young woman's turn to process information. "Oh! You mean she was passing," the girl said, her voice all but becoming a squeak on that innocuous word that conveyed so much. Then her brow rewrinkled itself as her thoughts took shape. "But . . ." she began, and then leaned forward to meet Carole Ann in the middle of the counter.

"They found out about her," Carole Ann stage-whispered, then leaned back into her own space on her own side of the counter, leaving the girl angled there alone for several seconds. Then she, too, returned to her own space, her face reflecting the workings of her mind—first horror, then pity, then deep sadness. This very brown girl, this student working her way through the university Blacks had only been allowed to attend for less than a generation, coming at once to understand and sympathize with a young girl very much like herself who, in another time, chose a dangerously self-destructive path in search of what she believed would be a better life for herself.

"If you don't mind waiting a few minutes . . ."

"I don't mind at all," Carole Ann said gratefully, and sank down into a green Naugahyde armchair and picked up an outdated copy of *Southern Living* magazine to help her pass the time. Which turned out to be relatively short. The young woman emerged from the office with the name and on-campus address of a retired librarian who served part-time as a university archivist and who, fortuitously, was working today. That lady, a dead ringer for the Southern belle stereotype of two generations past, greeted Carole Ann with genteel courtesy, apologized for the disheveled state of her workroom, and listened as Carole Ann again repeated her request. The lady blushed deeply and her breath seemed to catch in her throat, but she nodded politely, pointed to the only chair in the cluttered filing room, and hurried away deep into the rooms of open-shelved filing cabinets. Two hours later, Carole Ann left the campus of LSU with a photocopied record of the sad and sorry tale of the matriculation of Earlene Warmsley.

* * *

"You damn well oughta be scared!" Jake Graham yelled at her as if she were a kid in big trouble. "These assholes have killed six people by my count, including their own relatives! There ain't nothin' says you can't be number seven! There ain't nothin' says you *won't* be number seven you keep muckin' around down in those swamps!"

"I'm too close to quit now, Jake." Carole Ann was almost pleading with him to encourage her to continue. She wanted to stop, to turn over her information to the appropriate authorities, to let somebody else bring the Devereauxes to justice. Except she knew that in Louisiana, either there was no such thing as justice, or if there was, it was spelled L-E-L-A-N-D D-E-V-E-R-E-A-U-X.

"Didn't you hear what I just told you about Devereaux? Or didn't you understand what I just told you?"

"I heard you, Jake. And I understand." She understood that Representative Leland Devereaux had been in Congress long enough to hold and wield extensive power— over people and over things. And among the things over which Leland Devereaux exercised power were the Congressional committees with oversight responsibility for the troubled Environmental Protection Agency and the U.S. Park Police. According to Jake, Leland was leading the charge to dismantle the EPA; and while there was growing support in both houses of Congress for EPA's demise, the agency still had significant and powerful supporters, including the President of the United States. But that didn't prevent Leland from behaving like a frontier dentist and pulling the EPA's enforcement teeth with rusty pliers every chance he got. And no, Jake said, Leland had not bothered to note in his official Congressional biography that he owned the majority interest in the Parish Petroleum Company. He listed his occupation as "attorney," but certainly not as attorney of record for the same Parish Petroleum Company.

"And I hear," Jake added, "that the Park Police muck-ety-mucks are as big a bunch of brown-nosers as you'll find anywhere on Capitol Hill. Do big favors, get big budgets. Law of the Hill *numero uno*," he said.

"That's amazing," said Carole Ann.

"What are you talking about? You're the one who told me to check Devereaux's committee assignments. You must have known—"

Carole Ann cut him off, exasperated. "I didn't *know* anything, Jake. I was merely checking every possibil-ity—"

"Yeah," he snarled at her, "and it checks out and now you go all weak on me. What's that about?"

"Dammit, Jake! They're cops! Employed by the U.S. Government!"

"So fuckin' what?" Jake asked with scathing cynicism. "Leland's a lawyer. One of the lawyers—employed, I might add, by the U.S. Government—who writes the laws the rest of us have to obey. Does that mean you believe he ain't likely to break 'em?"

Carole Ann needed to change the subject. "Speaking of which, what's the word on Larry?"

"Nothing."

"What do you mean, nothing?"

"Just that," Jake said, and Carole Ann could picture him scrunching up his face the way he did when he was exasperated with her. He hated it when she questioned him—when anybody questioned him. "Nothing. The guy's a member in good standing of the D.C., Maryland, and Virginia bar associations. He goes to their meetings. All of 'em. He belongs to the downtown YMCA, where he swims and works out every morning at six o'clock except Sunday. That's when he goes to church. Catholic.

He takes his wife out to dinner every Friday and Saturday night. And he goes to work. In the office every morning by eight, out every evening by eight. Been livin' by the same pattern for years, as far as we can tell. Buuuttt . . ." and he dragged the word out aggravatingly.

"Jacob Graham!" she hissed at him. "Don't you dare hold back on me!"

He laughed the laugh that altered his face—she could picture him, transformed in an instant from grim to good-looking—then turned serious to tell her Larry Devereaux had placed nineteen calls to Louisiana in the past eight days, almost half of them—eight—to one number. Carole Ann had been in Louisiana for fifteen days, which convinced them both that Larry had a direct connection to somebody Carole Ann had encountered. During those eight days, Larry had also made a dozen calls to his brother—both to his Capitol Hill office and his Fairfax, Virginia, home. "Seriously, C.A., it's time for you to take cover and turn this mess over to somebody who can expose the bastards without being killed."

"You know as well as I do I've got nothing any state's attorney or district attorney or U.S. Attorney could take into any grand jury and ask for a murder indictment! Dammit, Jake, the only thing we can probably prove is that Larry Devereaux isn't white. And while that may be pathetic and dumb, it ain't illegal."

They both were quiet for a while. Then Jake said, "Yeah, that's probably true. But spread out everything you've got on the front page of the *Washington Post* and nobody'll give a good goddamn about a grand jury indictment. The blood-lusters in this town'll hang the Devereaux boys by their nuts from the pointy top of the Washington Monument and light a bonfire at the bottom."

Carole Ann considered the nature of the insatiable beast that was Washington and understood the correctness of Jake's pronouncement; shivered at the thought of it. "I don't talk to reporters," she said.

"I do," he snapped back at her. "It's called logrollin' or backscratchin' or some such, and it's a tried-and-true Washington tradition. Closely related to good ol' quid pro quo. You know him, don't you?" His sarcasm bit hard.

Carole Ann had the good sense not to try to dig herself out of that trap. She calmly asked for and wrote down the Louisiana telephone numbers that Larry had called. Then she said, "I want two things, Jake. I want Al's murderer in jail. And I want Parish Petroleum or somebody to pay the people whose lives and homes have been destroyed. That's what I want, Jake. I don't mind hanging Leland and Larry out to dry. But I want them wearing big *M*'s, for *Murderer.* I don't want them to get away with being thought of as your garden-variety crooked politician and lawyer." She thought she heard Jake snicker; she was certain she heard him sigh deeply.

"Will you talk to me at least once every twenty-four hours until you leave there?" he asked quietly.

"I will, Jake, and that's a promise," she said, and hung up the telephone. Then she programmed his telephone number and Tommy's into her cellular phone. And as an afterthought, she added Dave Crandall's and Lil Gailliard's and Warren Forchette's. She tried not to think about why she was doing what she was doing, then told herself that's exactly what she needed to do: to think long and hard about the fact that her life was in danger and that she was taking steps to protect herself. The truth presented itself to her, but she damped it back down. The truth was that Jake's advice, as usual, was the best advice. Leaving Louisiana was the best protection she could give herself. But she could not and would not leave now. Not yet. Not until she was certain she could have the two things she'd told Jake she wanted.

So, instead of leaving town, she decided to change hotels, even if she was followed. Her current location had become too familiar, and she'd exhausted all means of undetected escape from it. She considered and weighed the advantages and merits of large hotels like the Embassy Suites where she was currently registered, against the smaller, European-style establishments, and after studying Fodor's and Frommer's, opted for the middle course: the five-hundred-room Le Meridien, a block away on Canal Street. Not only did it possess all of the necessary amenities, it was expensive enough that she could expect the kind of personal attention Jake recommended. She rode the elevator down to the lounge and called Le Meridien from a pay phone and made a reservation for a late arrival. She left the Sheraton at midnight and checked into Le Meridien five minutes later, relinquishing her car and keys to a uniformed valet, and wondering—worrying—whether such service was beneficial and protective, or would prove to be dangerous. And wondering whether this kind of dissection of the facets of every thought and action would become—had become— a permanent part of her existence.

She remained within the luxurious confines of the hotel for the next forty-eight hours, taking full advantage of the establishment's restaurant, health club, heated swimming pool, business center, and concierge, who made it his business to find for her the beer she craved. She dressed in her finest silk and gold and donned her four-hundred-dollar-an-hour-lawyer attitude and pressed upon the concierge that under no circumstance was anyone on the hotel staff to acknowledge the fact of her presence to anyone who did not ask for her by name and room number. Then she pressed a hundred-dollar bill into his hand to make her point. She slept and she worked . . . worked out all of the details of her case . . . and she made two telephone calls, in addition to the promised daily check-in with Jake, who heartily approved of her change of venue.

On her third day in Le Meridien, her cellular telephone rang while she was running on the treadmill in the health club. She barely slowed to answer it, because she didn't intend to talk. She listened briefly, then said, "Call me at exactly five o'clock and I'll tell you where to meet me," and she severed the connection and resumed her pace. The pounding of her heart had nothing to do with the speed at which she was running.

At exactly five o'clock she was standing in front of the Doubletree Hotel. The phone rang. She answered it, spoke four words, terminated the call, and entered the hotel. Fifteen minutes later, she watched him enter the sunlit mezzanine lounge, watched him look around for her, watched him walk toward her. She studied Larry Devereaux and saw a white man. She did not move or speak when he approached the table and sat down across from her. She continued to watch him, to study him, searching for a clue to an opening to him, and receiving nothing. He sat still and silent, looking everywhere but at her, appearing more bored than interested or concerned. And perhaps that was the way to open . . .

"I don't mean to bore you, Mr. Devereaux—"

He whipped around to face her, blue-green eyes icy and mean and matching the words that cut her off mid-sentence. "Well, you do bore me, Miss Gibson. Or Mrs. Crandall. Or whatever you're calling yourself these days. I didn't stop my work to fly down here to play mind games with you. You said you had vital information for me. Either you have something to say or you don't. If you do, get on with it. If you don't, cut the crap and let me get on with my life."

The muscles in her jaw worked as she fought for control. "I really want you to go to prison for murder, but I'll settle for having you disbarred. I've got enough proof—"

"Oh, fuck you, lady!" He exploded but the sound wasn't loud. The words were hissed through jaws and teeth clenched tighter than her own. "You got nothing, and certainly nothing that matters to me!"

"You fuck yourself, Devereaux, you lying, low-life piece of garbage." Carole Ann was out of control, knew it, and didn't care. She leaned across the table, into his face. "You stopped your work and flew down here specifically because you know good and goddamn well that I've got something and you want to know how much I've got. You didn't make nineteen telephone calls to Louisiana in the last week to check on your poor, sick mother. The one you haven't seen since 1959—"

He reached across the table and grabbed her shoulder and dug his fingers in and pulled her in even closer, close enough that she could see the contact lenses on his eyeballs. "You better have nothing more to say about my mother." Spittle collected in the corners of his mouth.

"Why not? You don't give a good goddamn about her. Or about any of the rest of your family. Except Leland, your brother in crime and deception. And everybody knows you'd do anything for Leland, including murder your law partner. Isn't that right, Larry?" She made her voice as light and as matter-of-fact as if she were asking if he'd tell her the time of day.

He blinked once. "You're crazy," he said, just as quietly, the slight widening of his eyes the single signal that his calm exterior was about to fracture.

"You're right. I am," she said, digging her fingernails into his hand, forcing him to release his grip on her shoulder. "That's really why I wanted you down here. I wanted to ask you, and see your face when you told me, why you murdered my husband. That's how crazy I am. Did you kill Al to protect Leland? Or to protect yourself? Since you've been passing for white since you left Assumption Parish and joined the Marines." She watched his face change and knew that whatever he expected her to say, this wasn't it. First he flushed deep red; then all the color drained from his face, leaving just a bright red splotch on each cheekbone. His breath came in short, shallow puffs, and he closed his eyes tightly, squeezed them shut like a little kid about to throw a tantrum. No other part of him moved. Then he opened his eyes and tried to speak. His mouth opened and closed and his Adam's apple was an elevator in his throat, but no words came. Then he sighed and slumped back in his chair.

"Did Al know about . . . my background?"

"You mean, did he know that you're passing for white? Yes, he knew." Carole Ann enjoyed the cruelty even as she felt the guilt it brought.

"He could have exposed me. He could have ruined me," Larry said, his voice gaining strength. "Why didn't he?"

"You worked with Al for more than ten years. To hell with you if you think that's the kind of man he was." She spat the words at him, the anger fully returned and obliterating the guilt. "You're a first-class bastard, Larry Devereaux. Or Warmsley, as the case may be. Which is the only rationale I need to understand how you could think my husband capable of that kind of cruel insensitivity. You could walk away from your entire family and never look back. What could be more cruel than that? And how you could prefer a bastard like Leland to the others—"

"What are you talking about, lady? Who the hell do you think you are!" He raised his voice in exasperation. "You can actually sit here and discuss me and my family as if you know us? You don't know me. You don't know Leland. And you don't know 'the others,' as you call them—"

"You don't know what I know. So I'll enlighten you. I know that Leland is a murderer—"

"That's a goddamn lie! Leland is a good man and a good friend."

"But he's dog shit as a brother. And if you don't believe me, why don't you ask good ol' Leland where Lafayette is? And while you're at it, why don't you ask him what happened to Earlene?"

"Earlene?"

"Your baby sister, Larry. I know it's been a long time, but even you must remember you had a younger sister whose name was Earlene. She followed in your footsteps, Larry. Left home after high school graduation and enrolled at LSU's Shreveport campus. As a white student, of course. And excelled. Won all kinds of academic and social honors. Including homecoming queen, Larry. Imagine that! And then there was the biggest prize of all: engagement to a first-year medical student, a member of Chi Alpha-something fraternity. She must have been delirious with joy—and fear, don't you think? That it could all unravel? Or perhaps she viewed all of her accomplishments as confirmation that she'd made the correct choice. In any case, she couldn't know her fiance's fraternity would announce their engagement in its newsletter, or that said newsletter was received by all its members, including State Senator Leland Devereaux. And Earlene most certainly could not know—could not have imagined—that Leland, her own brother, would feel a deeper kinship to his fraternity brother, who, after all, was white—"

Larry was shaking his head back and forth, funny, choking sounds coming from his throat. "No. No. No—"

"Oh, I think so, Larry. From what I've been able to piece together, it certainly seems Leland told his white fraternity brother that his betrothed was really a Colored girl from the wrong side of an Assumption Parish bayou. Old newspaper clips about the story, which was a very big deal at the time, make oblique references to a Chi Alpha-whatever brother now living in another state who supplied information about the girl's family. So the angered and embarrassed groom-to-be gathered together all his brothers and they gang-raped Earlene. For three days."

Larry Devereaux could not prevent the escape of the anguish that rose from his throat because it was propelled by the power of thirty-five years of remorse and sorrow and fear and pain and self-hatred. He neither noticed nor cared that the handful of happy-hour imbibers in the massive lounge all turned to stare at him, to be embarrassed for him at his unmanly loss of control. He merely felt something akin to gratitude that some of what he'd kept corraled within for so long had finally been released. He grabbed the glass of ice water before him and drank it down in a long gulp. Then he drank Carole Ann's water, wiped his face on a napkin, and looked up at her.

"She was fifteen when I left." He blew his nose on the napkin, crumpled it, stuffed it in his pocket, and looked around, as if surprised to find himself in a lounge of the Doubletree Hotel in New Orleans. A waiter appeared as if delivered by a genie and Larry ordered a double vodka on the rocks. Carole Ann asked for more water.

"Big brother Leland is garbage, Larry, and I'm going to see to it that he joins you in prison. For killing Al. Perhaps for killing Lafayette. God knows I'd like to nail him for what he did to Earlene. If that happened today, he'd be just as guilty as the rapists. Not a one of whom was punished, by the way. After all, she was just a nigger, passing for white. Got what she deser—"

"Fuck you!" Larry hissed at her. "How dare you judge me! You don't know what it was like . . . you could never know."

"That's what Lil said. Do you remember Lillian, Larry? She's your niece. Your sister Ella Mae's daughter. She'd have been just a little kid when you ran away from home—"

"God damn you! So fucking pious. So self-righteous. Just like your saintly husband. So sure you're right."

"No, I'm not, Larry. I'm not sure I'm right. But I am sure you're wrong—"

"How could you be? You can't possibly know what it was like to look at three of your siblings and know that life for them could be whatever they wanted it to be, knowing at the same time that no matter what *you* wanted, your life would be hell. Because you were Colored. You looked white, but everybody knew that *your* Daddy had some Black and Indian blood in him. He looked white, too, but he wasn't and everybody knew it. So you and your brother and two sisters who had this Colored man for a Daddy were Colored. And everybody treated you like you were Colored. Everybody knew your mama was white, and that you had white brothers and sisters. But *you* were Colored. And you had that one very definitely brown sister . . . Ella Mae. Prettiest girl I ever saw. But she was definitely not white. And you know what? Ella Mae was the only happy one. She knew what she was. She despised Leland and Lafayette and Jeanette because they were white. But she never saw . . . I don't really know how she saw Eldon and Earlene and me. I just know she loved us. She was our big sister and she took care of us and she loved us."

Carole Ann tried to feel it. Tried to put herself in that place that Larry had just described. She knew very well how it felt to be Black. Every child born Black in Amer-

ica knew what that felt like and what it meant. She tried
to imagine what it would feel like if her Aunt Gladys or
Uncle Buddy or Uncle Gary just vanished, and could not.
Could not imagine being born into Larry Devereaux's
world, though she was beginning to understand how and
why Lillian and Warren and Eldon did not readily or easily divulge the secrets of their family connections.
"You're right. I don't know, and I owe you an apology,"
she said to Larry.

"And you know what's really sad?" He spoke as if she
hadn't, as if from an only partially awakened state. "I
could have stopped it. I wanted to stop it. As soon as I
saw how things were changing for . . . for Black people.
As soon as I saw that as bad as things were, it was worse
being Colored in Louisiana in a lot of ways than it was in
the rest of America. I could have been Black and gone to
the Army. I could have been Black and gone to the University of Pennsylvania and to law school at GW. But I
didn't know those things. I've met people who looked
like me—men and women—who identified as Black and
who never dreamed of passing as white as a way to sur-
vive or succeed." He picked up the drink he hadn't
noticed the waiter deliver and drank half of it in one deep
swallow, welcoming the pain of the liquor burning his
throat. For a brief moment, it gave him something else to
think about.

Carole Ann, well-seasoned in the art of emotional
manipulation, recognized his need to harness his
thoughts and feelings, and did not begrudge him sufficient time. She sipped at her water and let her eyes wan-
der around the room, returning them at intervals to assess
Larry's restorative process, and to try to see him as Al
had seen him. This man had been her husband's colleague for more than ten years, and his boss for half that
time, and she knew practically nothing about him. Par-

tially because Al hadn't liked him, partially because of their practice of not intertwining their professional lives, and partially, she was surmising, because of what must be Devereaux's need to distance himself from Blacks. Did he fear the astute observer would discover his secret? Carole Ann thought it unlikely. How many Black people walk around looking at white people and wondering how many of them are really passing? Absurd, she thought.

"I know the Parish Petroleum history, Larry. All of it. And I know what you and Leland are trying to do. And I intend to stop you. I plan to turn my proof over to the appropriate authorities in Washington."

"Then why did you call me, why did you have me come down here?" he asked wearily, drained of his anger and his fight and his belligerence. "What do you want from me?"

"I told you, Larry. I want to know why you killed Al."

He shook his head and covered his face with both his hands and rubbed, hard, as if wanting to obliterate something there; when he removed them, his eyes were sad and vacant. "I didn't kill Al. I've done some stupid things but I haven't killed anybody. I helped Leland with the Parish Petroleum business because he helped me. He got me my first job in Washington. While I was still in law school. I was waiting tables at the Palm and he came in for dinner one night with a group of congressmen. I tried to avoid him but he saw me. Jumped up from his table and rushed over and grabbed me and hugged me. Wanted to know what I was doing all the way up in D.C. And when I told him, he laughed. A big, hard laugh. Said he didn't know I had it in me. Then he asked me if I was married. Strange question, I thought at the time, though now I think I understand why. He wanted to know if I'd married a white woman. But my wife is from the Philippines, though she grew up in California, so I guess that was alright with him. Anyway, he made me write down my telephone number and the next day he called and told me I had an interview at a high-powered K Street law firm, and I've been on K Street ever since."

"And you've been killing people ever since, Larry." She held up her hand to halt his protest. "Parish Petroleum has been killing people for as long as it's been in operation. Parish Petroleum and all those other companies that dump and bury and burn poisons that have never and will never be compatible with the earth and the air and the water. That's why Al was getting out. It wasn't personal. It had nothing to do with you, except to the extent that you represented all that was wrong with how he earned his living." Carole Ann stood up and backed away from the table. "And if you didn't kill Al, then Leland did—"

"It was a mugger, for crying out loud! The cops told you that! What is your problem, lady?"

"Leland. If it's not you, then Leland is my problem," she said slowly, the possibility planting itself in reality. "If you didn't kill Al, then Leland did."

He looked at her, shaking his head as if at some hopeless case. "Why do you keep saying that?"

She told him why. Told him about about Jake Graham's witness in the park and what he saw and heard— the tall white man with the Southern accent who chased and caught and shot Al Crandall in the back. Told him about the bullet in Graham's back that halted his investigation of the case. Told him about the transfer of the case from D.C. police to the U.S. Park Police. "You are familiar with Leland's committee assignments, aren't you, Larry? You do understand the power he has over the Park Police and the EPA?" And she walked away from him just as his face was registering the impact of the implication. Her face already wore the look of one registering the notion of a member of the United States Congress as a murderer.

Carole Ann walked the three blocks back to her hotel in double time and was dripping perspiration when she arrived. Her heart was thudding and she was light-headed and her mouth was as dry as the California desert. She rushed into her room, stripped off her clothes, and collapsed onto the bed. Tears burned her eyes and she swiped at them, angry at their intrusion. She'd invested so much in hating Larry Devereaux and in constructing his downfall and it wasn't he who had killed Al! She believed his denial just as she believed the look of betrayal on his face when she'd confronted him with Leland's history of evil. It was Leland Devereaux who had murdered her husband. A man she didn't even know. Didn't know what he looked like or sounded like. But it didn't matter. She knew what kind of man he was. Southern white man who shot her husband in the back after cursing him in a foreign language. The language of the bayou. The language of swamp babies.

SHE awoke to the simultaneous ringing of the telephone and an insistent pounding on her door. She answered the phone first and was walking with it to the door when she realized she was not dressed. "Hello?" she said into the phone and heard a click and a dial tone. She slammed the phone down, cursed under her breath, and stepping into her jeans, crossed to the door. "Who is it?" she asked, peering through the peephole. The fish-eye lens provided an oblong view of an empty hallway. She hurriedly zipped and fastened her jeans, pulled a tee shirt over her head, and slipped her feet into her sneakers. It was dark and she was disoriented. She'd obviously been asleep for several hours, and she was recalling why when the knocking resumed at the door. This time it was a waiter with a tray resting in the palm of his hand. Instead of asking anything, she said, "You've got the wrong room. I didn't order anything."

"Compliments of Mr. Sevier, Miss Gibson," he said, hoisting the tray higher above his shoulder. Randy Sevier was the concierge and he'd taken it upon himself to keep her supplied with her favorite beer. She opened the door and closed it quickly behind him, standing well away while he uncovered three bottles of beer and arranged them in a silver ice bucket. While she was watching him the warning sirens in her brain exploded. He'd called her "Miss Gibson." She was registered as "Mrs. Crandall." He was no waiter. Keeping him in view, she backed up to the door, reaching behind herself for the handle. She lifted the handle and the door swung in with a powerful force, knocking her forward. The waiter grabbed her, twisting her arm behind her back at an upward angle, completely immobilizing her. She knew if she attempted any defensive action, the bones in her arm would be shattered at the elbow and the shoulder. She marveled at her own stupidity and was about to curse herself when Leland Devereaux oozed around the corner and into the room. She cursed him instead.

He slapped her hard across the face and she cursed him again. He hit her again, across the mouth this time, and harder, and she tasted blood with the pain. He turned away from her as if she didn't exist and strolled around her room. A third man followed him in, followed him around the room, picking up the things Leland touched: her computer, her legal pads and all of her notes, and the cardboard box of Al's files. Devereaux hadn't been in the room a full thirty seconds when he strode out, followed by the man carrying her belongings. She and the waiter followed, keeping pace, Carole Ann grateful for the pain in her arm that diverted her nervous system's attention from her face and mouth, which were burning and swelling. Instead of turning right and taking the hall leading to the passenger elevators, they turned left and marched down a long hallway unfamiliar to her. At the end of it, a freight elevator stood open and waiting. They entered and Leland started it with a key, and Carole Ann understood with a clarity that weakened her the full extent of the power wielded by men like Leland Devereaux, and the great lengths they would go to protect it.

11

"**I KNOW SOMETHING IS WRONG AND I KNOW WHAT** that something is and if you'll kindly give me the opportunity, I'll tell you all about it."

"Who the fuck do you think you're talkin' to, you snotty son of a bitch!"

"Gentlemen, please!" Even on a telephone conference call, Dave Crandall was the kind of man other men listened to and heeded. Even men of the temperament of Warren Forchette and Jacob Graham.

"You just better not let anything happen to her," Jake snarled in what for him was a chastened attitude.

"Or you'll do what?" Warren returned acidly, the fact that he still was connected to the call proof of his acquiescence.

"Warren, do you really know where she is?" The older man controlled his exasperation and his fear, both of which had joined forces to harness the anger that had been fueling him ever since he'd received confirmation that his son had, in fact, been murdered.

"I know that Leland Devereaux and two of his boys have her and that they drove her to Houma, where they boarded a boat—"

"And they coulda tied rocks to her feet and dropped her in the fuckin' swamp by now." Jake was talking through clenched teeth and pounding his helpless thighs with his fists.

"Detective Graham, please," Dave Crandall said. "If either of us really believed that, there'd be no reason for this conversation. Would there?" And he accepted Jake's grunt as nonverbal confirmation of the logic of the statement. "What else, Warren?"

"My cousin Hervé and your man Griffin are following as best they can, without knowing exactly where they're headed; Leland owns land all over the place. My uncle, my aunt, my sister, and myself are positioned in different places along the bayou, and thanks to you, Detective Graham, we're all connected."

"What's that mean?" Jake was too curious to growl.

"Means everybody's got a cellular phone. That was damn good advice you gave Miss Gibson," Warren said, and Jake grunted. Maybe this boy had some sense after all, he thought.

"Is everybody armed?" he asked.

"Yeah," Warren answered. "And Hervé has a high-powered rifle with a night-vision scope—"

"Armed?!" Dave croaked in alarm and waited in vain for Warren to explain. "Are you saying everyone has a weapon? Including your aunt and your sister?" And still he waited for more than the silence Warren offered.

"Mr. Crandall," Jake said, clearing his throat and unclenching his teeth, "Leland Devereaux has killed six or seven or maybe even eight people, including your son. He now has possession of your son's wife and he intends to kill her, too. Our sole purpose in havin' Forchette and half his family, not to mention Tommy Griffin, runnin' around in a fuckin' swamp in the middle of the night is to keep that from happenin'. And if it means blowin' his ass to kingdom come, then so be it!" Jake's voice was getting louder and louder so he was shouting by the time he finished. Only he wasn't finished. "Tommy Griffin's job is on the line, man. He got no damn business huntin' criminals down in Louisiana!" He said "Loo-see-anna." "D.C. finds out about it and they'll fire his ass! But he'll risk that in order to save Miss Gibson. In fact, he'll also shoot Leland fuckin' Devereaux and feed his slimy ass to the crocodiles before he lets harm come to her."

"Alligators," Warren said quietly. When Jake failed in his attempt to suppress a giggle, Warren began to think maybe this cop wasn't such a jerk after all.

"Where are you right now, Forchette? And where is that location relative to where Tommy and your cousin are, and relative to where you think Devereaux is headed with C.A.?" Jake asked.

"I'm at Pointe Afrique," Warren said, straddling the cane-backed chair in Sadie Cord's tiny living room, "and everybody is headed in this direction. Devereaux could stop somewhere before he gets here, or bypass us and head out into the Gulf, or he could head inland, though I don't know why he would. The plan was that Hervé would follow as closely as he thought safe. But he can't run behind him with engines. They have to paddle, him and your man Griffin. So, by now, they've probably dropped pretty far behind . . ." He didn't want to say more. Didn't want to think more. Didn't want to think about how easy it was to get lost in a bayou. Didn't want to think how easy it was to hide in the tall swamp grasses in the daytime, to say nothing of at night . . .

"Forchette?" Jake spoke the name almost softly, something in his voice both foreign and familiar.

"Yes?" Warren responded, the single word both question and answer, in the same dual tone in which it had been asked.

"Are there really alligators in the water down there? Near where people are? Near where you are? Near where C.A. and Tommy are?"

Nobody breathed in the hour-long seconds before the answer came. And when it came, there was nothing more to say: "Yes, sir. There really are alligators in the water here. Very near."

JAKE Graham hung up his telephone and rolled himself into the dining room, where every light was blazing bright in defiance of his wife's preference for moody dimness. But Jake needed light to see the table where he had laid out, in very orderly fashion, Carole Ann Gibson's equally orderly case against Leland and Larry Devereaux and the Parish Petroleum Company. She had sent him by Federal Express, three days ago, her complete notes, including a copy of every document she'd unearthed during her searches, along with a copy of Al's notes and files. Her notes were detailed and thorough and more than sufficient to hang the brothers Devereaux from the top boughs of a very high tree; more than enough to keep his reporter friends occupied for several days. He had followed her train of thought—the tracks being the documented evidence—and earned a new if grudging respect for criminal lawyers, especially those who worked with this degree of proficiency. He had also come to agree with her conclusion about who killed Al Crandall, and his suspicion was confirmed when Leland Devereaux, after receiving a telephone call from Larry, hired a private jet and set off for New Orleans. Carole Ann's call to Larry had had the desired effect: he'd left Washington for New Orleans within twenty-four hours. But Leland had beat him out of the gate by half a day. That's when Jake had called Tommy, who flew south on the same plane with Larry, though not in first class.

Jake had tried to talk Carole Ann out of baiting Larry, but she was too tired and too hurt and too scared to listen to his reason. She was also too damn stubborn to do it his way.

Jake wanted media justice. He wanted to leak the file to the press and let the reporters nibble Leland and Larry to death with their piranha teeth. But not only did Carole Ann hate the press, she hated Larry Devereaux and wanted to confront him face to face, not nibble him to death. But she did agree to send Jake the information for him to do with as he pleased, and of course it pleased Jake to share it with two reporters with whom he had traded information and favors for a decade. But he knew the reporters could do nothing until they checked and double-checked the facts themselves, and by that time, Carole Ann herself could be nibbled to death—by the goddamn alligators! That's why he'd called Dave Crandall . . .

DAVE Crandall leaned back in his desk chair and put his feet up on the desk and noticed he had the beginnings of a hole at the big toe of his left sock. His wife was always after him to cut his toenails on a regular basis so he wouldn't ruin his socks, and he was sorry he didn't pay more heed to her requests. Just as he was sorry he hadn't paid more heed to his only son's requests that they spend more time together. And now his son was dead. Murdered by his own law partner. And his son's wife, whom he'd had to learn to like, had taken it upon herself to avenge that murder. And it seemed she would succeed if she could avoid becoming a victim herself. Victim number seven or eight or nine, depending upon how one counted.

Dave and Adrienne Crandall had divorced when Al was a very young boy, and he had had very little contact with his son until he entered law school. Then Al, believing they must be connected in other important ways since he had chosen the profession of his father without paternal inspiration, advice, or example, had pursued a relationship with his father and the two had come to like and respect each other. Al and Carole Ann had visited once or twice a year, and as Dave observed them—observed her—he began to change his impression of her. He'd originally thought she had edges, and he didn't like women with edges. Then he'd had to admit that what he objected to was what he had perceived, erroneously, to be Carole Ann's competition with Al. Not only did she not compete with her husband, they so seldom discussed their work that the casual observer would never have known they shared a profession. What Dave observed was that Carole Ann was as good a wife as she was a lawyer; that his son was as good a husband as he was a lawyer; that the two of them were as perfect a couple as he'd ever encountered.

And now this son who had become his friend and confidant was dead. And the woman who had become his daughter-in-law was in danger. And a foul-mouthed cop from Washington, D.C., had had the nerve to tell Dave Crandall it was his responsibility to help save her life! Dave Crandall the tax attorney. Dave Crandall the sixty-seven-year-old tax attorney who abhorred violence in any form, including details of it in the courtroom. Yet he supposed there was a certain rightness to it. After all, he had put Carole Ann in touch with Warren Forchette, even though he'd believed at the time he was doing nothing more than being polite . . .

WARREN Forchette had not wanted to meet Carole Ann Gibson Crandall but he'd had no choice, for two reasons: First, he'd known the woman's husband and should have been able to predict the man was in danger, so he felt guilty in her presence and he didn't like feeling guilty.

For any reason. Second, he'd been asked by a colleague to extend a professional courtesy to another colleague, and to refuse would be bad form for a lawyer, and bad manners for a Southerner. So, though he agreed to see her, he'd made the decision to limit his contact with her even before he met her, though he later could not explain or define his reasoning. His Tante Sadie sucked her teeth and rolled her eyes at him; his big sister Lillian called him a horse's ass; his Uncle Eldon called him uncharitable; and his Auntie Merle opined he'd been bitten by the love bug. Even Hervé, who did not and had never liked anybody not related to him, felt something different and special for this woman from D.C. And still Warren did not want to forge a connection. And still he had no choice, for the deeper she dug in search of the reasons for her husband's murder, the muddier she made the soil that supported Warren and his family and his way of life.

So Warren had driven to Atlanta for a heart-to-heart talk with Dave Crandall the day after he'd witnessed Carole Ann demolish the two thugs on the track. And when they finished talking to each other, he was committed to doing whatever he needed to do to help her. But he would keep his distance, and that turned out not to be a difficult proposition, owing largely to her distrust of him which, perversely, he found annoyed him. How dare she mistrust him! She was the stranger, the interloper, the bigfoot clouding the water in the bottom of the pond. But put off as he was, Warren acknowledged a healthy respect for the reputation of Carole Ann Gibson the criminal lawyer. He'd thought his paralegal was joking when she dumped the two-inch-thick file in the middle of his desk, and he'd laughed out loud when he finished reading about Carole Ann Gibson—her courtroom successes and her out-of-court skirmishes with the media. He'd laughed, but nothing was funny. This woman was the kind of lawyer he'd dreamt of being. And she'd relinquished her hold on the brass ring because she'd found it was tarnished and her hands were being stained.

He walked outside and his senses began their automatic adjustment to the night. Since he was a very young boy, Warren had always felt like a nocturnal being when he prowled Pointe Afrique in the dark: believed he saw with cats' eyes and walked with their careful, padded feet; believed he heard with owl ears, and his nose received scents with wolflike clarity. These things Warren had felt all his life and felt them without ever needing to claim awareness of them. But tonight was different. Tonight there was danger. The Jake Grahams of the world no doubt would consider the presence of water moccasins and alligators a danger, but those born on the bayou learned early how to share life with every other being born on the bayou, and danger existed only when one being—usually it was the two-legged human variety— forgot how to live and let live. And indeed, as always, it was the human variety responsible for the danger this night.

He felt a moment of heavy sadness for the misery human beings caused each other and so many other species. Then he tried to feel what one particular human being was feeling at this very moment, and in doing so, resolved he would not allow Carole Ann Gibson to be prey for any vulture this night.

12

THERE IS NO LIGHT. OR SOUND. OR ANYTHING. AND *no feeling. Especially no feeling. There are no feet or hands. And if there is no light, what is flashing behind my face? And if there is no feeling, what in God's name is this pain? Where is it? Everywhere or nowhere? It feels total, but that can't be because there is no feeling.*

Carole Ann would not have moved even if she could have, and she could not, though she wasn't certain why. She was bound, hand and foot, that she knew, but she was not certain that that situation alone accounted for her inability to move. Had she not been bound, she could not have moved her hands and feet because she could not feel their presence, though she could feel extreme pain in the places where hands and feet belonged. Most of her body she could not feel. Specific places on her body she could feel as intensely as if every nerve ending were being probed: her right shoulder and the left side of her face, from the eyeball to the corner of her mouth, and the exact center of the top of her head. These specific places pulsated with pain so excruciating Carole Ann didn't have the energy to fight the nausea that ebbed and flowed with her consciousness. Some part of herself, until this moment unknown to her, seemed to be commanding her responses, for she certainly could not claim credit for controlling the nausea, yet it was controlled, and mercifully so, for since there was something foul in her mouth she would surely suffocate on her own vomit and die. For she could not move, and would not if she could. It would have been better, she believed, to have remained unaware and unconscious.

The awareness that she was alone was only marginally comforting. She was bound and gagged and lying in the bottom of a boat and absolutely unable to help herself. The darkness was as complete as anything she could have imagined, and the night sounds were painfully loud. She must not be, she thought, anywhere near Pointe Afrique because everything in that bayou was dead. So much seemed to be alive here, even the water, which lapped and tapped gently against the side of the boat. She found the rhythm and the gentle rocking of the boat soothing. Perhaps she could sleep . . . or die. She'd like to die before Leland returned. She very much would like to thwart his plans by dying before he could kill her. She'd already witnessed his childish displays of rage when confronted with adversity. His rage at finding every file had been deleted from the computer and that every one of her legal pads contained blank yellow pages had been almost comic. And the realization that every file she'd copied had been sent to Jake Graham and Dave Crandall—though she hadn't given him those names—had left him so angry he was almost speechless.

He'd done his questioning of her in a house somewhere outside New Orleans, though not too far from the city. They'd driven about half an hour before stopping in an area that was sparsely populated, though not really rural, as she could see lights from other houses. She hadn't been blindfolded, though she had been forced to lie down in the back well of some kind of four-wheel-drive sport vehicle—a Jeep or an Explorer or similar vehicle—so she'd seen where she was, though she did not know where she was and could not have provided directions. Just that it was a modest house with a well-tended yard and twenty-year-old, inexpensive furniture. The place was in total darkness when they arrived and only the lights in the kitchen and bathroom had been turned on. Leland sat at the white Formica kitchen table with rounded, fat silver corners and sorted through her things and threw his first tantrum by turning over the table and then smashing her computer. And he'd hit her again, this time with his fist squarely on the right shoulder she thought was dislocated. She'd fallen and was yanked to her feet by the waiter. She still thought of him as the waiter; how else could he have known about the concierge and the beer?

By the time Leland accepted the reality that he would find no clue as to how much Carole Ann knew, his rage was a tornado, touching down here and there, shattering whatever objects and people happened to be in the path of destruction: he broke two lamps and a chair; he hit the waiter in the chest with a windup cuckoo clock; and he hit her twice more and kicked her once, on the shin of her right leg—perhaps that was why she couldn't move that limb? That's when she'd gone down and decided to stay down; that's when she was still thinking about what she was doing, still thinking she had choices about her life. So when she crumpled to the floor, she remained there, eyes closed, breath held. He kicked her again, on top of the head, and the choice to remain down was no longer hers.

When she awoke they were riding again, she in her position in the back of the vehicle next to the spare tire, the rubber smell new and oily. This time, her hands were tied behind her back. She wriggled her fingers and pain ran up her right arm and lodged in her shoulder socket and became bright colors that danced behind her eyes. The drive this time was much longer and reminded Carole Ann of the drive she'd taken to Houma . . . of the drive to the Gulf. They were heading to the water. She could feel it. Could smell it. Only this time the smell wasn't full and heavy and soft and wet. It was more like the shape of an alligator—all sharp points and rough ridges. She recalled instances of senses merging, of something tasting like the smell of another thing, of describing the feel of an object as being like the taste of a food. That's how she experienced scent at that moment: In a tactile fashion. Hard and sharp and dangerous.

She must have fallen asleep—or something—because when she became aware of herself again the vehicle was still and empty. She attempted to sit up and was glad she was alone because the pain caused her to groan. So far, she had managed not to cry or cry out at Leland's brutality, though she did not know how much longer she could manage such macho self-control. She was contemplating another attempt at sitting up when she heard voices. Then the back door of the truck opened, but she could not see because she was lying on her side with her back to the door and she did not move. A voice told her to get out— she thought it was the waiter—but she still did not move. Then her legs were grabbed and she was yanked out of the truck. Gravity and instinct took over and Carole Ann struggled not to lose her footing. She stood up straight and looked directly into the face of the waiter. She did not see Leland or the third man. The waiter, perhaps beginning to realize his mistake, took a step backward. Carole Ann kicked him in the groin so hard he could make no sound. He doubled in half and she kneed him in the face, breaking his nose and propelling him upright.

She turned and kicked him a third time, shattering most of the bones in his face. Then she ran. Screaming.

They were on a wooden dock, like the one at the Terrebonne Museum where Hervé had docked his boat. There was a building at this dock, too, and several parked cars. She ran toward them, screaming. The third man gave chase, cursing and almost begging her to stop. The door to the building opened and she ran faster, toward it. And then stopped. It was Leland who emerged. She stopped running and screaming and turned to face the man who'd never have caught her had she had somewhere to run. Somewhere to hide.

Leland beat her badly this time, punching her with his fist in her stomach and side and shoulder. When he was finished beating her, he bound her feet and tore off a strip from the bottom of his shirt and stuffed it in her mouth and tied it in place with another piece of the shirt. Then they carried her down the dock to the edge—Leland had her feet and the other man her shoulders—and tossed her into a flat-bottomed boat. The kind of boat Hervé had. Except Hervé's boat had been clean and orderly, all his tools neatly organized and his ice and fish chests clean. This boat was filthy and crammed with junk and it stank of dead fish and old oil and spilled beer and unwashed bodies. They threw her into the bottom of the boat and walked back up the dock and that's when she knew she would die. As she was fading to black, into sleep or a darker form of darkness, she understood clearly that wherever the boat was going, she wouldn't be on it when it returned.

Some segment of her awareness heard them return, felt them clamber aboard the boat, heard the engine being coaxed into a choking existence (Hervé's engines had purred smoothly), and felt the boat moving through the thick water and the tall grasses. She didn't try to open her eyes or try to move, even when Leland nudged her with his foot and asked the other man to look and see if she was awake. She didn't feel awake, and she most certainly did not want to be awake. So she drifted, on the water, in her mind. She told herself she appreciated being able to see the man who had killed her husband, and she was surprised to find that Leland and Larry Devereaux looked nothing alike. Leland very much resembled Eldon Warmsley, much more so than did Larry, who was his full brother; and interestingly enough, there were aspects of Warren in Leland . . . or of Leland in Warren . . . pieces and places of resemblance, though the wide streak of evil that resided within Leland like oil beneath the bayou floor differentiated him from the other three, especially from Eldon, whom he most resembled.

Leland was tall and athletically trim, though he had more of a weight lifter's bulky build than a runner's lean one, and no one would guess he was sixty-two years old. His hair was light brown with well-placed streaks of silver, and thick and luxurious, like Eldon's. And his eyes were hazel, like Eldon's. But Eldon's mouth was generous and sensuous and Leland's mouth was a stingy slit— he barely had lips—and the slit curved downward in an arc of permanent distaste. She exercised her mind by remembering the dates that Ella Mae Scarborough's seven children had been born. Ella Mae was the firstborn, and Leland was second. The firstborn boy and the firstborn white child. Was that the reason for his domineering nature? Eldon and Larry were the middle children, separated in age by a year. Lafayette was the middle Devereaux, older than both Eldon and Larry. Was he a good big brother to them? She recalled the story of the "friendship" that had developed between the Parish Petroleum doctor and the shopkeeper—between Dr. Lafayette Dev-

ereaux and Eldon Warmsley. Of course they were friends.
They were brothers . . . Did Eldon know where Lafayette
was? Did Eldon know Lafayette was dead? Had that just
been more subterfuge, his telling her it wasn't wise to
interfere with Leland Devereaux?

THEY'D now left her bound and gagged in the dirty boat
for . . . she didn't know how long. She had lost all concept of time, drifting as she did in and out of states of
darkness. She didn't call it sleep. Sleep was rest and she
was not at rest. But she was oddly at peace. She had
redeemed herself for her lack of awareness of Al's concerns in the final months of his life. And she had avenged
his death. Though she would not live to see it, Leland and
Larry would be punished. And not merely punished for a
murder—or for several murders—but humiliated for
deeds more heinous than murder, for what Leland had
done to Earlene was worse than if he'd killed her. And
what Larry had done to himself was worse than death.
And he knew it. And soon millions of people would know
it. Jake would see to that . . . Jake! She hadn't called him
tonight. He'd be worried, now, and very angry.

And suddenly her acceptance of her impending death
evaporated, perhaps due to the thought that her final
memory of Jacob Graham would be his anger with her.
Or the hurt she knew Tommy would feel. He cared deeply
for her, and she very much appreciated that. Her mother
would be devastated, as would Mitch, and she didn't
want them to suffer that kind of pain. They didn't deserve
that. They deserved more and better than her giving in
and giving up.

For the first time since being snatched from her hotel
room however many hours ago, she wept. And not
because of the pain in her body or from fear of death, but
because she was helpless and had willingly embraced her

helplessness. Then the anger kicked in, as it always did when she was feeling sorry for herself. She welcomed it, her old familiar friend, and as she wondered why the hell it had taken so long to arrive, she used it to work herself into a sitting position. She imitated Jake Graham and cursed Leland for all she was worth and rolled herself around in the bottom of the boat, rocking and wiggling against the ice and fish chests, trying to inch upright. Every motion, every breath, was agonizing, but she told herself nothing could be more painful than death by acquiescence. Sweat was pouring off her now, stinging and burning what felt like millions of lacerations. God! How many forms of pain were there?

She finally managed to sit up, her back resting against one of the metal chests, and she was rewarded by the sight of a fat full moon that provided enough light for her to study her immediate surroundings. The boat that was her prison was tied to an old wooden dock between two other craft—a raggedy cabin cruiser with huge, new twin motors, and another flat-bottomed boat full of junk. She looked over the side and into the water and thought it was probably not as dead as that at Pointe Afrique. The moonlight swayed and danced in the ripples of this water, and the marsh grasses grew tall and thick. She looked inland from the dock but could see nothing. There was no dockside building, and no light visible in any direction.

Where the hell were Leland and his stooge? She wanted them to return. She wanted to confront him now. She had so far refused to speak to him, a tactic that had enraged him. Leland was not accustomed to having people ignore him, and Carole Ann had ignored him. Had refused to look at him or speak to him or acknowledge his presence or his power. And that had infuriated him. Now she wanted to change her tactics. She wanted to talk to him and she was afraid he wouldn't return; that he'd left her here and gone inland, to a waiting vehicle, denying her full vengeance.

The panic rose swiftly and the gag did not permit her to hyperventilate, so she forced herself to calm, and to take slow, deep breaths, inhaling through her nose. She counted as she inhaled and counted as she exhaled. Slowly, deeply. She wriggled her fingers and toes and kept herself breathing through the pain that galloped back and forth, up and down her arms and legs. She closed her eyes and continued counting and breathing and thought she was imagining the sound of voices. But they were real. She opened her eyes and looked inland down the dock and soon two figures appeared, at first too distant to determine their identities. As they came nearer she saw it was Leland and the other man and that they were hurrying; though they were all but running, their feet made only a muffled sound on the rotting wood of the dock.

"What have you done to me?" Leland shouted at her as he jumped down into the boat, almost capsizing it, and leaning down over her, his face not six inches from her own. She made sounds in her throat and it seemed to take a moment for him to understand that she could not speak because of the binding about her mouth.

"Take that off," he snapped at the other man with a flick of his wrist at her face, and the other man reached into his pocket and withdrew an ancient Swiss Army knife, which he hastily opened and just as hastily used to slit the material covering her mouth. As soon as the cut was made, Leland reached out and snatched the binding away, taking with it skin attached to the blood that had dried on her cracked and split lips, forcing from her throat a sound that startled and surprised her, so inhuman was it.

"What have you done to me?" Leland demanded again, his face in close to hers.

She tried to open and close her mouth, tried to make sound come out of her mouth, tried to swallow, but could not; her tongue and lips were parched and swollen and her face ached from Leland's abuse. She tried to lick her lips and could not; tried again to make sound and could not. So she merely shook her head, then dropped her chin on her chest. Leland reached around her and opened one of the coolers. He brought out a beer that hadn't been cold in several days and unscrewed the top. He slapped her lightly, then forced up her chin and put the bottle to her mouth. She ignored the discomfort of the stinging and burning—and the awfulness of the beer—and welcomed the wetness on her lips and in her mouth and down her throat. She gulped in relief until the bottle was empty.

"Answer me now." Leland tossed the bottle into the water and squatted down next to her.

"I . . . I . . ?" She felt as if speaking were new, something she was doing for the first time, and the sound she emitted was hoarse and strange. ". . . Discovered the truth about who you are and what you've done," she croaked.

"What truth?"

"That you own Parish Petroleum," she said in a voice just barely louder than a whisper. "That you've concealed that ownership for more than twenty-five years. That you murdered my husband," she managed in an almost normal voice, which caused excruciating pain in her throat.

"Who did you tell?" Leland hissed the question at her, blowing hot, sour breath in her face.

"A lawyer friend and cop friend." Her voice felt and sounded normal.

"Who else?" he snapped at her. "And don't lie to me!"

"By now, a couple of reporters," she said, hoping she sounded offhand, "thanks to my cop friend. Whom I think you know, Leland," she said in her best social-whirl tone of voice. "A former homicide detective named Graham. I don't know if you met him formally before you put a bullet in his back—"

Leland slapped the words out of her mouth, then stumbled backwards as if he'd been punched himself at the harsh and bitter force of the laughter she barked at him.

"Stop being such a fucking coward," she snarled at him, ignoring the blood running from the side of her mouth. "Aren't you tired of that by now? Or have you been a coward so long it's part of your nature?"

"I am going to kill you," he said.

"You're going to jail, so I don't mind dying." She was almost shouting now, forcing her voice to have at least volume if not its usual power. "But before you go to jail, Leland, the whole world will know who you are and what you've done. Including what you did to Earlene."

He looked like a confused dog. First his head tilted to one side, then to the other, and his mouth opened and closed like an aquarium fish at feeding time.

"Oh yes, Leland, I know about Earlene. Didn't Larry tell you?" And his reaction told her the answer. "I'd take that as a not-so-good sign if I were you, Leland. You know, every basically decent human being has a breaking point, and what you did to Earlene may be Larry's." She worked hard to keep her tone off-the-cuff conversational, which was difficult when speech itself was an effort. "I'm sure the U.S. Attorney would be happy to cut a deal with Larry—"

Leland pushed her into the side of the boat and she lost her balance and fell over, hitting her head on the side of the chest. She didn't have the energy to try to sit up again so she lay there wondering if her head would erupt from the pounding. Then she felt herself being jerked up to a standing position. Dizziness and nausea rushed up to meet her and she swayed and slumped and drifted back to the blankness that had become so familiar.

HELLO. *Hello? Hello! Who is it? Answer the phone. Somebody answer the phone. The telephone is ringing. No, not that one. Not the big one. The little one. The cellular phone. The new one. The one Jake made me buy. Where is it? It's not here. Leland didn't bring it. Because he didn't see it. It was under the pillow. That's right. I put it there so I would hear it in case someone called while I was asleep. It's not here. Somebody answer the phone.*

She hit the ground hard, and groaned. They'd thrown her on the ground! They'd been carrying her and had thrown her on the ground when the phone rang. She landed on her back, and thanks to the full moon, she could see the panic on their faces. Even Leland appeared more panicked than mean and angry, which took her mind off the pain of having hit the ground so hard. Something was happening . . . something serious enough to frighten Leland.

"What the hell was that?" he whispered.

"Sounded like a telephone," the other man said, pulling a gun from his pocket and peering into the darkness. "One of them little portable kinds." He turned around and around, still looking into the darkness, fear pouring out of him with the sweat. "Who out there?" he shouted to the darkness.

"Shut up, you idiot!" Leland hissed, and slapped him on the back of the head. "Get her and let's go," and he bent over and reached for Carole Ann's feet. But the other man didn't move. He was frozen in place, his eyes closed, his head cocked in a listening mode.

"Somebody out there," he whispered, the fear rendering his Cajun accent almost unintelligible to Carole Ann, who heard nothing but the usual night noises. In fact, so attuned to them had she become she wasn't aware of hearing them until she listened. The bayou was a loud place at night, as loud as the city with its horns and sirens and music. Then the other man raised his arm, leveled his pistol, and fired toward the dock and the water. The sound ricocheted off the deep night and silenced the night creatures for an instant. Then they all screamed back at whatever the foreign sound was that had destroyed the cadence of their night songs.

"Help me pick her up so we can go!" Once again Leland bent over and grabbed Carole Ann's feet, and again received no assistance. He straightened up and was about to speak when his face changed. There was movement. Even Carole Ann felt it, like a shifting in the direction of the wind. Somebody was out there in the darkness.

"I'm gon' outa here," the other man said, backing away, his head swiveling from side to side.

"Shoot her first!" Leland screamed at him.

He threw the gun at Leland's feet. "Shoot her yourself," he whispered, and ran off down the dock.

Leland cursed and reached for the gun, but dropped it when he heard the unmistakable sound of running feet . . . feet running toward them, not away from them. He grabbed for the gun again, fumbled with it, cursing and sweating all the while. He finally got a grip on it and stood up.

"Drop the gun, ass-wipe." The voice was cold and mean and very near and extremely familiar.

But Leland did not drop the gun. He waved it at the darkness. Then there was a shot and Leland and all the night creatures screamed and Leland fell down, his left hand grabbing for the right shoulder covered with blood and bone fragments. Leland looked at his left hand, dripping blood and tissue and bone chips, rolled over, curled himself into a fetal ball, and cried like a baby. The spoiled brat deprived for the first time of having his way.

Carole Ann, still lying on her back, looked up, and instead of seeing sky and moon, looked into the face of Tommy Griffin, who was shaking his head at her.

"You can't take care of yourself worth shit, can you?" He stooped down and scooped her up in his arms and began working to untie the ropes that bound her arms.

"What are you doing here, Fish?" she croaked at him.

"Jake sent me," he said with a shrug and a grin.

"But how did you get *here?*" she asked, and looked behind him when he gestured over his right shoulder with his head. And there was Hervé, stepping out of the darkness. He had a rifle slung over his right shoulder and a very long, shiny knife in his left hand. She looked up at him and tried to smile but couldn't. He nodded his head at her, knelt down, and cut the ropes from her feet with a single swipe of the knife. "Will you cook me a big fish, Hervé?" she asked. She said it "feesh," and he nodded again. And almost smiled.

13

"He always was mean and he always was a hitter."
Ella Mae Warmsley Forchette looked far into the past to
explain the present, the soft cadence of her voice an equal
mixture of anger and sadness. Though she'd had no personal contact with Leland Devereaux for almost forty
years, he was still her baby brother and, as the big sister,
she still felt responsibility for him. During Carole Ann's
recuperation from her twelve-hour ordeal as Leland's
hostage, the Warmsley family had assumed Carol Ann as
their joint responsibility. It was Sadie who had nursed her
for two weeks, ignoring and abandoning from the first the
medication prescribed by the hospital and relying on her
own mixture and concoction of herbs and teas and vita-
mins and minerals; it was Eldon and Merle who had
offered their home as sanctuary; and it was Lillian who
had brought her books and ice-cold beer and fresh
popped popcorn. But it was Ella Mae, Lillian and Warren's mother and Leland's big sister, who had explained
and apologized for the pain her brothers had caused Carole Ann.

"He used to beat on poor Lafayette and Lawrence all
the time. Jeanette and Earlene, he was just mean to them.

Pulled their hair and dismembered their dolls and smashed their little dollhouses. Mean, petty stuff like that. Me and Eldon he pretty much left alone after we showed him what would happen if he messed with us. Eldon went upside his head once with a two-by-four and knocked him out cold." She smiled wryly at the memory and patted Carole Ann's hand. "We sure are sorry, all of us, about what happened to you. And to your husband. We knew Leland was mean, but we didn't any of us know he had become a monster."

Carole Ann had gratefully accepted the hospitality of the Warmsley family, and pleaded with them to believe she did not hold any of them responsible for what had happened to her or to Al. She worked hard to convince them that it was only with their help she had been able to expose both Leland and Larry, for they all—including Warren—expressed the belief that she single-handedly had effected Leland's fall from grace and power. Even when she reminded them of Jake and Tommy's input.

"But it was you who began it all, *cher,*" Lillian insisted. "It was you who muddied up the waters down on the bottom and made the big fish swim to the surface. It was you who made Larry turn Leland—"

Carole Ann protested, "I did not make Larry do any-thing—"

"You told him about Earlene," Eldon said, explaining that none of them ever spoke of Earlene, just as they never spoke of Lawrence. They had found a way, individ-ually and collectively, to accept their siblings' long absence as permanent. And now they had been returned to present memory, the long-lost brother and sister, and those left behind struggled to deal with the pain. Espe-cially Eldon, who had been close to Larry when they were boys. "Larry always was crazy 'bout Earlene. Looked after her like Ella Mae looked after me. Anything that hurt or bothered Earlene, hurt or bothered him. Even after all this time she still was his soft spot, his weak spot."

"And what happened to her?" Carole Ann asked and then wished she hadn't as she watched pain spread like a blush across Eldon's face. He squeezed his eyes shut and rubbed them with his fists. Then he took a deep breath that looked as if it hurt his lungs and told how, after the rape, Earlene had completely lost touch with reality and had to be hospitalized, an experience that proved even more destructive since, back then, state facilities were segregated and Earlene was convinced she was white.

"After three years in the state asylum for crazy Coloreds there was nothing left of the Earlene we knew," Eldon whispered, tears falling freely. "Mama went and got her out. Swore she was white, that it was all a mistake saying she was Colored. We haven't seen her since then. We send her money—through the Western Union 'cause she won't come near us . . ."

Carole Ann regretted having asked, regretted having used Earlene as a weapon against Larry.

And Larry had vanished, though not before revealing the one secret about Parish Petroleum that had not yet been uncovered, the reason for Leland's bizarre and brutal campaign to establish the legal existence of the company and return it to his control: oil had been discovered on the St. Mary Parish property, which technically and legally belonged to Lillian Forchette and any remaining survivors of the earlier lawsuit against the company. He had returned to Washington immediately after his anguished rendezvous with Carole Ann in the Doubletree Hotel lounge, collected his case file on Parish Petroleum, and had it Federal Expressed to Carole Ann in care of Lillian at the UPTO. Included was documented proof of Leland's efforts to conceal his ownership of Parish Petroleum and the illegal activities of the company under Leland's direction for the last twenty years, along with a sworn affidavit of Larry's own involvement as legal counsel. And Larry had informed them his wife had always known he was Black. He'd thought it necessary to explain to her why he didn't want children.

"But why did he involve Al?" Carole Ann asked Warren, who having combined Larry's documentation with Carole Ann's had finally unraveled the truth about Parish Petroleum's history.

"Because he couldn't—wouldn't—risk returning home," Warren replied. "He was convinced somebody would recognize him, and he was right. Somebody certainly would have had he gone tromping around St. Martin or St. Mary. That's why Leland did that part of the dirty work. Nothing unusual about him sloshing around the bayous."

"And it was Leland who did all the dirty work? All the murders were Leland's doing?" she asked.

He nodded and laid out the history of Parish Petroleum: From its inception, he said, the company operated illegally, even before the Environmental Protection Agency imposed standards and guidelines for the operation of chemical plants and the disposal of waste and by-products. Parish Petroleum was the parent of three distinct entities, all of them petrochemical companies and all of them producers of highly toxic wastes. "Parish always dumped, buried, or burned what it couldn't use. That's why the ground at the Assumption compound is forever poisoned," Warren said. "That's why the people who worked there are forever poisoned. Lil will never be healthy," he said bitterly. "The fucking poison is in her, is a part of her now."

"And the Assumption Parish operation was independent of the other two operations?" Carole Ann asked quickly, to shift Warren's focus from the pain she saw rise in him when he spoke of Lil's pain.

"Not at all," he replied, just as quickly, grateful to her for the return to the subject at hand. "In fact, the chemical being produced at Assumption, where Lil's husband worked, was derived from a by-product of the St. Martin operation. *But,* and it's a very big but," he emphasized, "the *workers* never knew of the connection. Only the owners knew. And it was set up that way by Leland to conceal his thievery." And he explained how Leland and the other two owners habitually skimmed the profits off the top of each of the three producing entities, leaving the legal entity, Parish Petroleum, barely functional . . . at least on paper. "That's why, when Lil filed her lawsuit, they folded so quickly. Gave up and gave in. They didn't want a probe of the operation. So they declared bankruptcy, and because there was no record of any profits, they gave the company to the plaintiffs. A useless, dying patch of land."

"While the other part of Parish Petroleum continued to operate?"

Warren nodded his head. "Kept operating, kept making money, and kept killing people and land."

"But how is it possible that no one knew?" Carole Ann was both bewildered and dismayed, for it seemed the only answer was that lawyers like Al had made it possible for Parish Petroleum to evade, avoid, and ignore the law.

"Leland Devereaux is a powerful public figure. His partners are powerful private figures. Extremely wealthy men, all of them. They own people as well as property and the means of production. Even anyone inclined to suspect anything odd wouldn't be foolish enough to confront Leland. Everybody's always known what a mean bastard he is. That's why we help get him reelected. So he'll stay away."

Surprise creased Carole Ann's face. "Have you always known that Leland owned Parish Petroleum?"

Warren smiled an honest, true smile, and said without the slightest hint of derision, "Of course, *cher.* You can't do anything around here without your family knowing about it." And Warren continued his narration, explaining that Parish Petroleum's clandestine operation had continued for more than fifteen years until, suddenly and without warning, the St. Martin operation was shut down. And Carole Ann recalled the afternoon spent with Sadie Cord.

"Mrs. Cord said everybody took that to be a hopeful sign."

"Shows you how stupid we were," Warren said, the bitterness back full force in his voice. "The old folks, like Tante Sadie, believing it was possible because they naturally believe in good; the rest of us believing it was possible because we believed in nothing, and having something to hope for was a relief. But we should have known better. People like Leland don't do things without reasons, and the reasons usually involve money, and Leland's reasons usually involve some violation of the law."

"Which returns me to my original question," Carole Ann said. "Why, then, did Leland involve Al? Or was that Larry's doing?" And she realized that she didn't know if Al had known Leland and for a moment the thought so disturbed her she could think of nothing else, could not complete her thought or her question to Warren, which, in turn, disturbed him.

"Are you alright?" he asked, jumping to his feet, concern clouding his eyes behind their silver rims as he squatted down beside the brightly colored overstuffed chair that had become her favorite resting place.

She told him what she'd thought and was overcome by a massive wave of sadness when Warren explained that he, Jake, and Tommy had concluded Leland had been one of the Parish Petroleum men Al had dined with the night of his murder. Leland had dined with Al and then murdered him. He held her hands tightly, helping her traverse the moment, then returned to the adjacent recliner and put his feet up.

"Al had all of it figured out. Everything but the reason for the sudden push to get Parish Petroleum right with the EPA. I also think he ceased to care about the reason, C.A. Because by that time, he was so involved with the people and their lives that his mission had totally shifted," Warren said quietly. "He was no longer the company lawyer. He'd switched sides."

"And what was that reason, Warren? Why did Leland kill him if he didn't know the final piece to the puzzle?"

"Oil. On the St. Mary property. And Leland believed Al knew because Al had gone there and taken a boat trip with the three St. Vincent boys, who just happened to be on Leland's rigging crew. But Al didn't know that. He hired them because they knew the bayou."

"So Al died for nothing." Carole Ann spat out the words.

"Oh, no. Not for nothing. At least not from Leland's perspective. Don't forget Al knew Parish Petroleum had not been in compliance with EPA regs for years—"

"So what?" Carole Ann's interest in Parish Petroleum was waning.

"So Leland couldn't drill for oil unless Parish Petroleum was right with the EPA, and without Al's cooperation, the EPA would never certify Parish Petroleum, and Al wasn't about to cooperate," Warren said smugly, aware that Carole Ann didn't have the full picture.

She sighed and looked at Warren, who was sitting patiently, waiting for her to regain her equilibrium and to ask him to fill in the missing blank. "Alright, already.

What is it I don't know?" She didn't succeed in fully covering her irritation with him, and she noted he smirked.

"It would cost a fortune and take a lifetime for a new company to obtain EPA permission to drill for oil. An old, established company, however, would have a much easier time of it. So Leland paid off a bunch of clerks and regulatory functionaries to backdate documents showing Parish Petroleum had paid taxes and filed emission and waste disposal reports in a timely fashion . . ."

Carole Ann was no longer listening to Warren, but instead, hearing Al's voice tell her that Parish Petroleum seemed not to exist except on paper . . . that there were records of bribes and payoffs to officials . . . that the men of Parish Petroleum had dead eyes. She remembered the feeling of his fear and his pain and ached to think he'd known so much and shared so little with her. Somewhere deep within, she believed he would have told her everything once he'd quit and was free to discuss the case. But she knew she would always carry this sadness with her: her husband had undergone a transformation of spirit and had not thought it safe to share that with her. She would never forgive herself for being whoever it was Al hadn't believed it safe to confide in. And she would never forgive him for not telling her she had failed him in so fundamental a way.

LELAND had been arrested and charged with kidnapping, assault, felonious assault, aggravated battery, assault with deadly force, and half a dozen other felonies and misdemeanors in a brilliantly conceived and drafted complaint filed by Warren Forchette, Esq., on behalf of his client, Carole Ann Gibson Crandall. Leland had also been released on his own recognizance—he was, after all, a member of the United States House of Representatives—

and had enjoyed exactly thirty-six hours of freedom before he was again arrested and charged with negligent homicide (among other things) in the deaths of three fishermen who had drowned mysteriously in Assumption Bayou earlier in the year. He was being held without bond due to the presence of a corroborating witness—the same witness who had agreed to testify against him in exchange for dismissal of the charges against that witness for participating in the kidnapping and battery of Carole Ann Gibson.

DURING her more than two weeks of recuperation, Carole Ann spent long hours assessing her feelings. About everything and everyone. Her life had changed so dramatically that the most important people in it were people who'd either been strangers to her a month earlier or whose presence in her life had been peripheral, at best: Jake Graham and Tommy Griffin and Hervé Cord and Warren Forchette quite literally had saved her life, and she had come to rely on them and trust them in ways she had never before trusted men. Ella Mae Warmsley and Lillian Gailliard now were emotional anchors more crucial to her well-being than her closest friends, and her closest friends would never know the depth of the pain and fear and horror and shame she had spilled out to the two Warmsley women. Even her mother would never know those things. Eldon Warmsley and Dave Crandall loomed large and powerful in her eyes—not as father figures, for not only didn't they seek to nurture her, she did not seek nurturing from them; rather, they were prophets and teachers to be studied and heeded. And Sadie Cord was something so ancient as to defy nomenclature and definition; something fundamental and essential and elemental. She did not understand the reasons for it, but Carole Ann did understand that to be held in the old woman's embrace and to receive her ministrations eased the pain, both in her body and in her spirit.

Carole Ann drank Sadie's teas and the broths she made and bathed in the mixtures she concocted and did not wonder that the fever and the pain dissipated. Carole Ann slept as Sadie rubbed salves into the battered places of her body, and did not wonder that the bruises lightened and faded and disappeared. Carole Ann listened as the old woman spoke of the paths of forgiveness and harmony and beauty and joy, and felt the healing of her mind and emotions and spirit.

On Carole Ann's final evening in New Orleans, Eldon and Merle had a big party for her. A come-back-soon party, they called it, refusing to call it a going-away party. Dave and his wife drove over from Atlanta and would drive her back since he didn't trust her to drive back alone, and Tommy and Valerie flew in from D.C. They had plenty of time on their hands, both of them having been suspended without pay from the police department for "gross misconduct," which was the polite way of expressing dissatisfaction with the fact that they had involved themselves in criminal matters outside their own jurisdiction. And when Merle learned they were newly engaged, the fete became an engagement party as well.

Eldon hired a band and constructed a dance tent in his backyard and roasted a whole pig and half a cow. Hervé grilled a dozen big "feesh" and Warren brought four different kinds of beer for her to sample. Merle and Lillian and Ella Mae and Sadie made gumbos and stews and salads and cakes and pies, and everybody who attended brought a casserole or a loaf or a bowl or a dish.

Carole Ann, who loved to dance, could not; she was

still too stiff and sore for more than the most basic movements, like walking, sitting, standing, and she wondered what shape she'd be in had Sadie not cared for her. But there was nothing wrong with her appetite, and she ate until she thought she'd burst, and she learned that night to love a new kind of music.

She also learned that night that she had more than just a new and good friend in Lillian Forchette Gailliard. For the first week of her recuperation, Lillian had read to her and Carole Ann had found herself fascinated by the other woman's eclectic tastes: she'd read the poetry of Lucille Clifton and Audre Lorde, June Jordan and Rumi; the social and political theory of Angela Davis and bell hooks and Cornell West; the science fiction of Octavia Butler and Samuel Delaney. Then she'd brought books for Carole Ann to read herself—Eastern philosophy and religion and the history of Voudoun in Louisiana and in the Caribbean. And they'd discussed everything, including Lil's belief that all Black people should return to the South—the source of their roots in America. Comfortably reclined in chaise lounges on the gentle hill behind Merle and Eldon's house, looking down on the party, Lil again proffered that theory.

"But what if they're not from the South? I'm not from the South," Carole Ann said, not wanting to be argumentative but not wanting to accede to what she perceived as a fallacy.

"You got South in you, *cher*. I can tell. I can always tell," Lil said with an aggravating smugness that, for some reason, irritated Carole Ann.

"That's ridiculous," she said, displaying her irritation.

"Where's your mama from?" Lil asked lightly.

"Los Angeles," Carole Ann replied smugly. "My father, too."

Lil nodded wisely. "Uh-huh. And what part of Mississippi or Louisiana or Arkansas did your grandparents come from?" And she chuckled at the disbelief spreading on Carole Ann's face. "Only one part of the great Southern migration led to New York and Chicago and Detroit, *cher*. Black folks from this part of the South went west. To California . . ."

Carole Ann raised her hands palms up in a gesture of defeat. "They were from Mississippi. Near Hattiesburg, I'm told, but all my information is secondhand. I never knew my grandparents and my mother was a bit sketchy on the details." And Carole Ann grinned and told Lil how her mother's parents had refused to permit their overprotected daughter more than one date with any of the young men she brought home. Her father's only conversation with Grayce's suitors had been to inquire about the boys' parents' birthplace. Three times, Grayce told Carole Ann, the answer had been Los Angeles; once, Mexico; and once Arkansas. That boy she'd been allowed to go out with twice. Then the increasingly frustrated Grayce had brought home Mitchell Gibson, whose parents were from Biloxi, Mississippi. Her father had grinned, clapped the young man on the back, and invited him to dinner. The rest, as they say, is history.

"You get your mama to tell you everything she remembers about what her folks told her," Lil said, turning serious. "You hear me, *cher?* Those stories will tell you more about who you are than any amount of education or money. Those stories are why you're sittin' out here in the middle of the Louisiana countryside surrounded by people who now consider you family and who will forever defend and protect you."

Carole Ann looked out at the crowd that filled Merle and Eldon's yard. Old people and young, and those in the middle. Black people and people she once would have assumed were white but whom she now easily and readily accepted could be—and probably were—relatives. Prosperous-looking city people dressed in silk and linen, and swamp babies she knew to be prosperous—Eldon and Merle and Ella Mae and Warren and Lil—dressed in blue jeans and overalls and walking barefoot. Most of them had greeted her at some point, shaking her hand or hugging her or smiling and thanking her for righting old wrongs. Stories. Yes, stories definitely were why she was sitting out in the Louisiana countryside.

Lil sat back and took a long swallow of her beer. The ice had melted and now was running down the side of the bottle and dripping onto her pink blouse, creating a polka-dot pattern. She had a faraway look in her eyes for a moment, then she forged ahead. "You know, Hattiesburg's not that far from here. We could be related. I got plenty Mississippi kin. Let's see now. Do I know any Hattiesburg Gibsons . . ." Lil made an elaborate show of tilting her head back and pursing her lips and squeezing her eyes shut, working to conjure up some knowledge of Gibsons from Hattiesburg.

"My mother was an Asher . . ." Carole Ann was smiling, playing along with Lil, enjoying the exercise, when the other woman snapped to attention.

"Asher!" Lil exclaimed, pronouncing it "As-shay." "My Daddy was first cousins to some Ashers from up around Hattiesburg. Melvin and Leotha and . . . and . . . Clarence? Clyde! That's it." And Lil sat there, the smug, self-satisfied look easing gently into the creases of her face as she read the disbelief in Carole Ann's. "What? WHAT? Tell me what!" Lil screeched, dancing her feet up and down on the ground and wiggling in her chair. "You know Clyde Asher, don't you?"

"My grandfather's name was Clyde Asher. My mother's father . . ."

Now Lil actually did jump up from her chair and do a

little dance. "Mama! Tante Sadie! Where y'all?" Her eyes roamed the crowd. She waved her hand at a man in overalls carrying a fiddle. "Uncle Bo, you see my Mama and Tante Sadie over by the table? Ask 'em to come here quick, please." And she turned back to Carole Ann and laughed and then scooped her up in a big hug and danced around with her and Carole Ann forgot she was in pain. Within the hour, every person at the party knew of the blood relationship between Carole Ann and the late Warren Forchette, Senior, and though it was so distant a connection as to have questionable legal authority, it didn't matter. Carole Ann had already been gathered into the Warmsley clan and was considered family. So were Dave and Jean Crandall, Tommy and Valerie, and, in absentia, Jake Graham. A legitimate blood tie, no matter how tenuous, was serious business on the bayou. Carole Ann learned how serious when a humble, somber Warren Forchette led her to the dance tent and, after leading her gently and slowly through a two-step, led her to the edge of the makeshift dance floor and presented her to the crowd:

"This is my cousin, Carole Ann." And with one voice, they yelled her name back to her for a long, long time, and she was reminded of something Lil had read to her about the family one chooses being as crucial as the family into which one is born. Carole Ann opened her arms in a wide embrace and accepted her family.

"**You** some kin to me. You understand what that means? What that means to us in this part of the world?" In an instant Lil had lost her erudite, citified way of speaking and now sounded so much like Eldon Warmsley it was eerie. Carole Ann almost didn't understand her. Lil had said "woild" instead of "world"; "unnestan" instead of "understand." Startled as she was, however, Carole Ann did understand.

"It means nobody better fuck with you or I'll kick their ass," she said to her cousin. Lil was still laughing when Carole Ann got in the car with Dave and Jean Crandall to make the drive back to Atlanta.

14

DAVE READ AND REREAD THE DOCUMENT CAROLE Ann placed in the center of his desk. Then he studied it, scrutinized it, dissected it. Then he took a pen from his pocket and a yellow legal pad from one of the desk drawers and began writing, and he wrote for what felt to Carole Ann a very long time. When he finished, he looked up at her with a wry, sheepish smile.

"Dave, I only wanted you to tell me how to go about implementing this plan. I didn't need you to restructure it." She worked at not sounding peevish, but almost the entire time she'd been in Atlanta, she and Dave had argued about money. Her money. And she was weary of the battle. The only reason she hadn't left two days ago was because dealing with Mitch would be worse than dealing with Dave, and because having to manage the money herself would be worse than death.

"Your intentions are admirable, C.A., but your proposal is lacking. I've reworked it in what I believe to be a way that both adheres to your principles while at the same time providing for your own welfare and well-being." He spoke calmly and deliberately and without the slightest trace of emotion in his voice. Carole Ann did not respond in kind.

"Goddammit, Dave!" she erupted. "If you can't do what I've asked you to do, I'll hire someone who can and will! I'm tired of justifying and explaining myself to you."

"And I'm tired of your self-righteous bullshit!" It was Dave's turn to erupt, and he did a masterful job, first pounding the desk in anger, then jumping to his feet and beginning to pace the floor. Carole Ann was as impressed as she was surprised as he revealed a side of himself she'd never seen and a response to her that was totally out of character. "You walk around wrapped in your full-length, I-hate-money fur coat, without ever understanding or acknowledging that it is precisely because you have as much money as you do that you can afford your snotty little attitude. If you were broke, Carole Ann, and had to work for a living, you could not have afforded to indulge your ego in the dangerous game of catching your husband's murderer. You were able to go to Louisiana and play cops and robbers precisely because you're rich. You were able to sue that crooked law firm and the crooked congressman because you're rich. And now you're even richer because of it. So, why can't you reach way down inside yourself and find the button marked 'gratitude' and punch it!" He was shouting at her, and sounding like Jake Graham.

"Why can't you accept that I'm not comfortable with having all that money and help me dispose of it in ways that help other people? Why can't you understand that in my view, that is the only real advantage to having money you don't need: you get to help people who do need it." She held her hands out, palms up, willing his acquiescence.

"And that proves my point exactly," he exclaimed, crossing to her and placing a hand on her shoulder. "Only the wealthy can afford to be altruistic about money, Carole Ann. The poor are too busy trying to make ends meet."

She responded bitterly, "Do you call that a slap in the face, Dave, or a kick in the ass?" She walked away from him.

"Do you have any idea how much money you spent in Louisiana?"

"It doesn't matter," Carole Ann responded wearily.

"It would if you hadn't had it to spend," Dave snapped at her. "And since you neither know nor care to know, I'll tell you: more than many people earn in a year. People feed and clothe and educate children and pay rent and utility bills on what you spent in less than a month in Louisiana. And you've got the gall to say it doesn't matter! Climb down off your high horse, Carole Ann, before it bucks and throws you on your ass."

Dave was visibly tired after his tirade, and Carole Ann was too shocked to speak. So they stood there looking at each other across the room until Dave returned his body to his desk and his attention to the yellow legal pad. He scribbled out a few more lines, ripped off the page, and extended it to Carole Ann. It could have been five feet of venomous cobra for her reaction to it. But Dave did not withdraw it, so she accepted it. And finally read it, as he talked her through it.

"You will see that your plan to endow college trust funds for your nieces remains intact. I eliminated a similar trust for the UPTO because Lil Gailliard is richer than you are, owing to the fact that she now owns a plastics factory and a few oil wells—"

"But they're not going to drill them, Dave," she wailed

in renewed exasperation. "Don't you understand? And they've already closed that awful, poisonous plant."

Dave was shaking his head. "Only until it can be be brought into compliance with EPA guidelines, C.A. Lil didn't want any part of putting two hundred people out of work. And all the drilling will take place off-shore . . ."

Carole Ann's mood shifted suddenly and dramatically. "How do you know so much about it?" she snapped at him.

"'Cause I'm the new tax attorney for the new corporation," he said with a shrug and a grin, and Carole Ann could only give in graciously. She bowed to him from the waist, sat down, crossed her legs, and gestured for him to continue. "I left in your money for Orleans Parish Legal Services, but structured it so the gift will become self-sustaining. All you need do is stipulate that the money be used only for hiring lawyers, paralegals, researchers, and their support staff, and the fund can receive in-kind, tax-deductible contributions and perhaps live on forever. The plan I propose for Jake Graham is a little different because his needs are different, but the objective of having him financially secure for the rest of his life is met. My ultimate objective, you will note, is to reserve a healthy chunk of the proceeds for you. Which we will invest in such a way that you can spend the rest of your life chasing murderers if you like, and still have money left to give away."

Carole Ann folded the yellow paper and returned it to Dave. She slumped into the chair nearest his desk and buried her head in her hands. She didn't like the feeling of having profited financially from Al's death a second time. She'd listened reluctantly to Warren and Dave when they urged her to sue Al's former law firm and its partners. As a senior managing partner, Larry Devereaux had acted as an officer of the firm every time he engaged in an illegal activity—he'd acknowledged as much in sworn depositions. Ergo, reasoned Warren and Dave, the firm was liable for Al's death. The same reasoning made Leland Devereaux's assets vulnerable to a civil suit. Because both the firm and Leland were extremely prosperous, she now was wealthier by several million dollars. Money she felt she neither deserved nor wanted.

She raised her head and looked at Dave across the desk. Looked at Dave and heard his angry words to her: "Find the button marked 'gratitude' and punch it." Looked at Dave and saw Al and recalled his plans—their plans—to spend the balance of their lives doing the things that made them happy. How joyful she'd been those few, precious hours when she and Al had known they were free. And Dave was correct: the money had bought and paid for the freedom. So, she would keep it and her freedom. And pray for a return, someday, of the joy.

"I guess I'd better go get dressed," she said, standing. Warren and Lil were driving over from New Orleans and they were all going to a parade and a football game. Then they were going to the city's Christmas tree lighting ceremony, then to dinner, and finally to a new jazz club on the west side of town that also served what was reputed to be the best sweet potato pie in town. Carole Ann tried to smile at Dave, but the effort broke on her face and he rushed from behind his desk to hold her. He didn't speak because there was nothing to say, and she was glad he didn't try. The last thing she wanted was for another person to tell her everything would be alright. It was Thanksgiving and her husband had been dead for almost eight months and there was nothing right about that. But there were things for which she was thankful. There was the money. But the money didn't fill every one of her waking moments, making certain she wasn't alone and brooding. People did that. Friends. Family. And for them, she was thankful.

15

CAROLE ANN'S BAGS WERE PACKED. THE LIMOUSINE was scheduled to arrive in exactly one hour to take her to Dulles Airport. She was ready to leave. To go to Denver, ostensibly to spend the holidays with her brother and his family and her mother, who was flying in from Los Angeles. But she and everyone else knew she'd spent as little time in Washington as possible since Al's death, and that she certainly would not spend Christmas here, alone. Could not welcome a new year that would not contain her husband. That would, instead, contain memories of a year that would haunt her dreams for years to come.

She stood at the balcony door looking out at the velvety black and bitterly cold December night. The sky was almost white with glittering stars—usually a sign of the severity of the cold. Tommy would be arriving at any moment. With a surprise, he'd said. She'd made him promise he wasn't bringing her a Christmas present. She didn't want any presents. She wanted only to leave as soon as possible. But he'd insisted on seeing her before her departure, since she could not say when she planned to return. So he and Valerie were coming to say good-bye. Coming with a surprise . . .

The ringing of the phone broke her reverie. Tommy, no doubt. She crossed quickly to the wall phone in the kitchen and answered, listened, and told the doorman to send them up. Tommy and Valerie. Wonderful young people who'd become her friends. Closer: her family. They cared about her and for her and she would miss them, for she didn't know when she would return to D.C. from Denver; had no specific plans to return.

The doorbell chimed and she hurried down the hallway to admit them, the smile ready on her face. The smile that turned to astonishment when she saw, standing between Tommy and Valerie, Jacob Graham. Standing. A metal crutch under each arm for support, but standing. She knew her mouth was hanging open in speechless amazement, but she couldn't help herself. And she readily accepted the good-humored laughter at her expense.

"So, you gonna invite us in, or what?" Tommy finally said, and she stepped away, holding the door open for their entry. Valerie entered first, followed by Graham, slowly propelling himself, step by step, down the hall. Tommy stood with her as she watched him. She closed and locked the door and set the alarm: old habits die hard. Then she followed them into the living room in time to watch Graham lay his crutches aside and lower himself into the armchair. The grin on his face was a priceless treasure. Still she did not speak. Could not speak. Tommy, as usual, found words.

"So, how do you like your surprise?" he asked innocently.

"It's . . . I'm . . . what . . ." she stuttered and sputtered to the amusement of the other three until finally Tommy rescued her again.

"I'm glad you saved me from the firing squad before you caught this hoof-and-mouth disease," he said uncharitably. "Who ever heard of a lawyer who couldn't talk?"

"Jake, what happened?" she finally managed, shooting Tommy an evil look under hooded eyelids.

"I took the money you got for me from the crooked law firm and took a chance that the Good Lord didn't mean for me to spend the rest of my life in a wheelchair," Jake Graham said with a satisfied grunt, and explained that he'd flown to Havana, Cuba, for the operation that no American physician would perform. "I'd heard and read about this Cuban guy. Pioneer in spinal cord injuries. Heard he had lots of successes, and more than a few failures. It was the failures that people kept throwing in my face, and it was the successes that I kept seeing in my mind. Suppose I could be one of those successes? My wife agreed with me. She was so sick of me moanin' and groanin' about bein' tied to that damn chair that she said she'd rather both of us took Doc Malina's offer."

"And what was that?" Carole Ann asked.

"That I'd either be walking or be dead," Graham said without a hint of emotion. "My wife said either way I'd be dead 'cause she was gonna kill me if I didn't stop complainin'." Graham laughed his growly laugh. "And here I am," he said, arms extended in a wide embrace of the world, kicking his legs like a toddler learning to swim. "He sliced open my back and stole that bullet that was layin' on my spinal cord. I knew soon as I woke up from the anesthesia that I could walk because my legs were tingling. You know how it feels when the circulation comes back after you've sat in one position too long? That's what I felt in my legs and I hadn't felt anything in my legs in months. I knew I wasn't dead and I knew I was gonna walk."

Carole Ann sat there soaking up Jake Graham's joy, grateful he'd wanted to share it with her. She'd known he partly blamed her for the bullet he took, though only partly. She also knew he knew that taking bullets was what cops did. Still, she relished sharing his happiness. And that's what she was thinking and feeling when she realized he had pushed himself up to a standing position and, using one of the crutches for balance, had reached into his pocket and extracted an envelope, which he offered to her. She quickly took it from him and looked at him and then at the envelope.

"What's this?" she asked.

"Your fee," Jake said.

"What fee? What are you talking about?" Carole Ann's hackles were up as she ripped open the envelope: a check, made out to her, for . . . "What is the meaning of this?" She was angry and didn't mind letting him know it.

Jake Graham had been a homicide cop too long to let anger directed at him affect him. He answered calmly, "If it hadn't been for you, C.A., I'd still be chained to that damn wheelchair. Or be dead, 'cause my wife really was gonna kill me. You didn't have to make those bastards pay me. But you did. And I'm grateful. Even if the operation hadn't worked, I'd be grateful. But it did work. And I owe you. More than money. But, again, thanks to you, money is all I got. So, you just pretend that I hired you to right a wrong and now I'm paying my bill." And with that he leaned down and retrieved his other crutch. They were the metal kind with cuffs. He fit his arms into the supportive circles and grasped the padded hand bars. Then, stepping slowly but surely, he crossed to the couch where Valerie and Tommy sat and reached for the brightly wrapped package Valerie held. He took it and both hands and extended it to Carole Ann. "This is from my wife. Grace is her name. You'll have to meet her sometime. She's a hell of a woman. She asked me to give you this. She painted it herself."

Carole Ann stripped away the paper to reveal an eight-by-ten stretched and unframed canvas. On it, in brilliant oils, a sunset and water and trees and a path leading into the trees. Tears sprang to her eyes and Carole Ann did not attempt to wipe them away. "Tell her . . ." she began and was stopped by emotion. The stark, simple beauty of the little sketch released all the emotion she'd been holding. She allowed the tears to spill up and out, down her cheeks. "Tell your wife my mother's name is Grayce," Carole Ann said, and hugged the picture to her heart.

Here is an excerpt from
Where to Choose,
Penny Mickelbury's new exciting
novel featuring Carole Ann Gibson—
now available in hardcover from
Simon & Schuster . . .

SHE FACED HIM ACROSS THE DESK AND THEY TOOK
their time, each taking the measure of the other. Carole
Ann sat erect in the cushioned armchair because that's
how she sat—not because she was tense or nervous. She
was more relaxed than she'd been in months. The beige
linen suit and the white silk and linen skinny tee shirt she
wore exhibited barely a hint of a wrinkle. She rested her
arms on the chair's arms and crossed her long legs. She'd
said what she'd come to say and was comfortable waiting, still and silent, for his response.

Jake leaned back in the swivel chair that enveloped him
like a schoolkid who'd sneaked into the principal's chair
and which would have made many men look ridiculous.
His hands were folded on the top of the darkly gleaming
rosewood. Only someone who knew her well—and Jake
Graham knew her better than most—could have seen past
the surface elegance to note that the exquisite suit, tailor
made for her, hung too loosely on the too-lean frame.

She was a striking woman—only three inches shy of
six feet tall and so sure of herself that many who encountered her thought her arrogant. Jake knew better. He
hadn't known her very long—just a year—and didn't pre-

sume to think that he knew all there was to know about her; but he did know that she'd earned the right to be called the best damn trial lawyer in town. And in a town like Washington, D.C., where the criminals sometimes were the people who wrote the laws, that was no mean feat.

"I've been begging you for the last month to help me out on this case," he said, tapping the maroon file folder in the center of his desk. "And for a month you've been telling me to shove it up my ass."

"I have never, ever said those words to you, Jacob Graham, and you know it." She leaned forward, her eyes flashing as she fixed him with a stare that unnerved every human who'd experienced it—except him.

"Intent, Counselor," he said with a small smile, the one that if it grew would transform his compact, dark brown face into a thing of miraculous beauty. "I understand what you mean no matter what you say." He pushed the chair back, stood up, and began to pace the room slowly, deliberately, nothing in his movement giving clue to the fact that four months ago he needed two crutches to walk; that not quite a year ago he was confined to a wheelchair, unable to move his legs, the result of a bullet he'd taken in the back while investigating the murder of Carole Ann's husband.

"You're what made me change my mind, Jake. The fact that you're so often correct about my life. You've been insisting for weeks now that I should help you with this case, and I agree with you. So I come here ready to help, but instead of the welcome mat I get questions and suspicions. So. What am I supposed to do with that?" She shrugged, raised her hands palms up, beseechingly, and looked past him, as if she could see through the charcoal mesh curtain that covered the wall of extra-thick security glass behind his desk.

He strolled back to the desk and lowered himself into the chair and resumed his *tap-tap-tapping* of the folder. Then he looked directly at her. "You wanna tell me what's chewing on your ass so you can stop chewing on mine?" he growled at her.

So she told him about the article she'd read in Sunday's *Washington Post* about a young man arrested for assaulting and robbing a female jogger the previous Friday evening and tossing her into the Tidal Basin, where she'd drowned in just a few feet of water because she couldn't swim. He watched her face as she explained how, five years ago, when she'd been that young man's attorney, she'd pushed and prodded and pleaded and cajoled until the system finally blinked and she was able to get that young man tried and sentenced as a juvenile instead of as an adult, as the prosecutor had intended. And because of her efforts, instead of still being in jail as he would have been had he been tried as an adult, he had served his time and had been released to commit another murder. A woman was dead and it was her fault.

"You're here because you're feeling guilty?" Jake asked.

She nodded. "In part."

"What's the other part?" Unease crept in as he recalled an old adage: Be careful what you ask for because you just might get it. He'd asked for her help and now that she was here, it could prove to be a major mistake.

She sensed his shift. "I felt badly about not helping you," she said, eyeing him warily. "You came to me as a friend. I should have responded as such." She sat back in her chair and folded her hands in her lap. She began turning the heavy gold wedding ring on her finger—a recent habit that she vowed to end.

"Timing is either everything or it ain't shit," he muttered, running his hands through hair he didn't have.

"What does that mean?" His unease had spread to her and she sat even more upright.

He tapped the folder that was almost the same color as the desk with his index finger, then picked it up, studied it as if deciding what he should do with it, and tossed it across the glossy surface of the desk to her. "Does the name Gloria Jenkins ring a bell?" And when she shrugged he added, "How about Ricky "Ricardo" Ball?"

Carole Ann stared at the folder in her hands, then dropped it into her lap, still staring at it as if she could read the words through the cover. Eyes still down, she nodded slowly as the recollection of Gloria Jenkins and Ricky Ball rushed back. *It's not his fault*, she told herself as she recalled another case, a much earlier one, in which she'd defended a young man whom she later came to believe should have been incarcerated.

"He's in prison and she's in the witness protection program, probably thousands of miles from here. So what's the case, Jake?" She struggled to maintain her normal voice.

"He escaped from a halfway house and she's behind that glass," he said, gesturing with a nod of his head over his right shoulder to the security room behind the wall behind his desk.

"Ricky Ball in a halfway house? How is that possible?" He'd been convicted of three counts of premeditated, first-degree murder, as well as rape, aggravated assault, kidnapping, malicious wounding, and a few things she couldn't remember. What she did remember was that he remained one of the most vicious people she'd ever encountered and that she'd had no regrets when her defense of him failed.

She'd been his court-appointed attorney, back in the days when there existed a pool of private defense attorneys from which judges would choose defenders of the indigent. Back in the days when she was just building her reputation as one of the best criminal defense attorneys in town. On the entire East Coast. She'd lost the case but had won considerable attention for her handling of it. That case had put her on the map.

"He served a third of his sentence. He behaved himself in the joint, where he also found Jesus. Or Mohammed. Or some damn kind of savior. He got his high school diploma. And he convinced the parole board that he was a worthy risk. It's all right there in the file," he drawled, pointing to the closed folder in her lap, and she knew that his jaws were clenched so tightly to prevent him from expressing the disdain that most, if not all, cops who've worked homicide have for most, if not all, lawyers who've defended murderers. She also could discern his regret at confronting her with exactly the brand of guilt she'd been battling when she walked in the door.

One man was everything she wanted.
And he was black.
Another was everything she needed.
But he was white.

THE REAL DEAL

MARGARET JOHNSON-HODGE

In the tradition of *The Color of Love*, the fresh, funny voice of Margaret Johnson-Hodge tells a completely contemporary story, rich with wisecracks and wisdom about interracial relationships and about the crisis every woman knows, falling in love...

"Margaret Johnson-Hodge brings a sassy, witty and contemporary edge to a novel that explores the ups and downs of love complicated by an interracial dimension."

—*Romantic Times*

THE REAL DEAL
Margaret Johnson-Hodge
0-312-96488-9_____ $5.99 U.S. _____ $7.99 Can.